Praise for Catherine Bybee

Wife by W...

"A fun and sizzling romance, grea   's like fist punches, and the dream of ...

—Sizzling Hot Book Reviews (5 stars)

"A good holiday, fireside or bedtime story."

—Manic Reviews (4½ stars)

"A great story that I hope is the start of a new series."

—The Romance Studio (4½ hearts)

Married by Monday

"If I hadn't already added Ms. Catherine Bybee to my list of favorite authors, after reading this book I would have been compelled to. This is a book *nobody* should miss, because the magic it contains is awesome."

—Booked Up Reviews (5 stars)

"Ms. Bybee writes authentic situations and expresses the good and the bad in such an equal way . . . Keeps the reader on the edge of her seat."

—Reading Between the Wines (5 stars)

"*Married by Monday* was a refreshing read and one I couldn't possibly put down."

—The Romance Studio (4½ hearts)

FIANCÉ BY FRIDAY

"Bybee knows exactly how to keep readers happy . . . A thrilling pursuit and enough passion to stuff in your back pocket to last for the next few lifetimes . . . The hero and heroine come to life with each flip of the page and will linger long after readers cross the finish line."
—*RT Book Reviews* (4½ stars, top pick [hot])

"A tale full of danger and sexual tension . . . the intriguing characters add emotional depth, ensuring readers will race to the perfectly fitting finish."
—*Publishers Weekly*

"Suspense, survival, and chemistry mix in this scintillating read."
—*Booklist*

"Hot romance, a mystery assassin, British royalty, and an alpha Marine . . . this story has it all!"
—*Harlequin Junkie*

SINGLE BY SATURDAY

"Captures readers' hearts and keeps them glued to the pages until the fascinating finish . . . romance lovers will feel the sparks fly . . . almost instantaneously."
—*RT Book Reviews* (4½ stars, top pick)

"[A] wonderfully exciting plot, lots of desire, and some sassy attitude thrown in for good measure!"
—*Harlequin Junkie*

TAKEN BY TUESDAY

"[Bybee] knows exactly how to get bookworms sucked into the perfect storyline; then she casts her spell upon them so they don't escape until they reach the 'Holy Cow!' ending."

—*RT Book Reviews* (4½ stars, top pick)

SEDUCED BY SUNDAY

"You simply can't miss [this novel]. It contains everything a romance reader loves—clever dialogue, three-dimensional characters, and just the right amount of steam to go with that heartwarming love story."

—Brenda Novak, *New York Times* bestselling author

"Bybee hits the mark . . . providing readers with a smart, sophisticated romance between a spirited heroine and a prim hero . . . Passionate and intelligent characters [are] at the heart of this entertaining read."

—*Publishers Weekly*

TREASURED BY THURSDAY

"The Weekday Brides never disappoint and this final installment is by far Bybee's best work to date."

—*RT Book Reviews* (4½ stars, top pick)

"An exquisitely written and complex story brimming with pride, passion, and pulse-pounding danger . . . Readers will gladly make time to savor this winning finale to a wonderful series."

—*Publishers Weekly* (starred review)

"Bybee concludes her popular Weekday Brides series in a gratifying way with a passionate, troubled couple who may find a happy future if they can just survive and then learn to trust each other. A compelling and entertaining mix of sexy, complicated romance and menacing suspense."

—*Kirkus Reviews*

NOT QUITE DATING

"It's refreshing to read about a man who isn't afraid to fall in love . . . [Jack and Jessie] fit together as a couple and as a family."

—*RT Book Reviews* (3 stars [hot])

"*Not Quite Dating* offers a sweet and satisfying Cinderella fantasy that will keep you smiling long after you've finished reading."

—Kathy Altman, *USA Today*, *Happy Ever After* blog

"The perfect rags to riches romance . . . The dialogue is inventive and witty, the characters are well drawn out. The storyline is superb and really shines . . . I highly recommend this standout romance! Catherine Bybee is an automatic buy for me."

—*Harlequin Junkie* (4½ hearts)

NOT QUITE ENOUGH

"Bybee's gift for creating unforgettable romances cannot be ignored. The third book in the Not Quite series will sweep readers away to a paradise, and they will be intrigued by the thrilling story that accompanies their literary vacation."

—*RT Book Reviews* (4½ stars, top pick)

NOT QUITE FOREVER

"Full of classic Bybee humor, steamy romance, and enough plot twists and turns to keep readers entertained all the way to the very last page."
—Tracy Brogan, bestselling author of the Bell Harbor series

"Magnetic . . . The love scenes are sizzling and the multi-dimensional characters make this a page-turner. Readers will look for earlier installments and eagerly anticipate new ones."
—*Publishers Weekly*

NOT QUITE PERFECT

"This novel flows extremely well and readers will find themselves consuming the witty dialogue and strong imagery in one sitting."
—*RT Book Reviews*

"Don't let the title fool you. *Not Quite Perfect* [is] actually the perfect story to sweep you away and take you on a pleasant adventure. So sit back, relax, maybe pour a glass of wine, and let Catherine Bybee entertain you with Glen and Mary's playful East Coast–West Coast romance. You won't regret it for a moment."
—*Harlequin Junkie* (4½ stars)

NOT QUITE CRAZY

"This fast-paced story features credible characters whose appealing relationship is built upon friendship, mutual respect, and sizzling chemistry."
—*Publishers Weekly*

"The plot is filled with twists and turns, but instead of feeling like a never-ending roller coaster, the story maintains a quiet flow. The slow buildup of a romance allows readers to get to know the main characters as individuals and makes the romantic element more organic."

—*RT Book Reviews*

DOING IT OVER

"The romance between fiercely independent Melanie and charming Wyatt heats up even as outsiders threaten to derail their newfound happiness. This novel will hook readers with its warm, inviting characters and the promise for similar future installments."

—*Publishers Weekly*

"This brand-new trilogy, Most Likely To, based on yearbook superlatives, kicks off with a novel that will encourage you to root for the incredibly likable Melanie. Her friends are hilarious and readers will swoon over Wyatt, who is charming and strong. Even Melanie's daughter, Hope, is a hoot! This romance is jam-packed with animated characters, and Bybee displays her creative writing talent wonderfully."

—*RT Book Reviews* (4 stars)

"With a dialogue full of energy and depth, and a twisting storyline that captured my attention, I would say that *Doing It Over* was a great way to start off a new series. (And look at that gorgeous book cover!) I can't wait to visit River Bend again and see who else gets to find their HEA."

—*Harlequin Junkie* (4½ stars)

STAYING FOR GOOD

"Bybee's skillfully crafted second Most Likely To contemporary (after *Doing It Over*) brings together former sweethearts who have not forgotten each other in the eleven years since high school. A cast of multidimensional characters brings the story to life and promises enticing future installments."

—*Publishers Weekly*

"Romance fans will be sure to cheer on former high school sweethearts Zoe and Luke right away in *Staying For Good*. Just wait until you see what passion, laughter, reconciliations, and mischief (can you say Vegas?) awaits readers this time around. Highly recommended."

—*Harlequin Junkie* (4½ stars)

MAKING IT RIGHT

"Intense suspense heightens the scorching romance at the heart of Bybee's outstanding third Most Likely To contemporary (after *Staying For Good*). Sizzling sensual scenes are coupled with scary suspense in this winning novel."

—*Publishers Weekly* (starred review)

FOOL ME ONCE

"A marvelous portrait of friendship among women who have been bonded by fire."

—*Library Journal* (best of the year 2017)

"Bybee still delivers a story that her die-hard readers will enjoy."

—*Publishers Weekly*

HALF EMPTY

"Wade and Trina here in *Half Empty* just might be one of my favorite couples Catherine Bybee has gifted us fans with so far. Captivating, engaging, lively and dreamy, I simply could not get enough of this book."
—*Harlequin Junkie* (5 stars)

"Part rock star romance, part romantic thriller, I really enjoyed this book."
—*Romance Reader*

FAKING FOREVER

"A charming contemporary with surprising depth . . . Bybee perfectly portrays a woman trying to hold out for Mr. Right despite the pressures of time. A pitch-perfect plot and a cast of sympathetic and lovable supporting characters make this book one to add to the keeper shelf."
—*Publishers Weekly*

"Catherine Bybee can do no wrong as far as I'm concerned . . . Passionate, sultry, and filled with genuine emotions that ran the gamut, *Faking Forever* was a journey of self-discovery and of a love that was truly meant to be. Highly recommended."
—*Harlequin Junkie*

SAY IT AGAIN

"Steamy, fast-paced, and consistently surprising, with a large cast of feisty supporting characters, this suspenseful roller-coaster ride will keep both series fans and new readers on the edge of their seats."
—*Publishers Weekly*

MY WAY TO YOU

"A fascinating novel that aptly balances disastrous circumstances."

—*Kirkus Reviews*

"*My Way to You* is an unforgettable book fueled by Catherine Bybee's own life, along with the dynamic cast she created that will capture your heart."

—*Harlequin Junkie*

HOME TO ME

"Bybee skillfully avoids both melodrama and melancholy by grounding her characters in genuine emotion . . . This is Bybee in top form."

—*Publishers Weekly* (starred review)

EVERYTHING CHANGES

"This sweet, sexy book is just the escapism many people are looking for right now."

—*Kirkus Reviews*

The
Whole
Time

OTHER TITLES BY CATHERINE BYBEE

Contemporary Romance

Weekday Brides Series

Wife by Wednesday
Married by Monday
Fiancé by Friday
Single by Saturday
Taken by Tuesday
Seduced by Sunday
Treasured by Thursday

Not Quite Series

Not Quite Dating
Not Quite Mine
Not Quite Enough
Not Quite Forever
Not Quite Perfect
Not Quite Crazy

Most Likely To Series

Doing It Over
Staying For Good
Making It Right

First Wives Series

Fool Me Once

Half Empty
Chasing Shadows
Faking Forever
Say It Again

Creek Canyon Series

My Way to You
Home to Me
Everything Changes

Richter Series

Changing the Rules
A Thin Disguise
An Unexpected Distraction

The D'Angelos Series

When It Falls Apart
Be Your Everything
Beginning of Forever

Paranormal Romance

MacCoinnich Time Travels

Binding Vows
Silent Vows
Redeeming Vows
Highland Shifter
Highland Protector

The Ritter Werewolves Series

Before the Moon Rises
Embracing the Wolf

Novellas

Soul Mate
Possessive

Erotica

Kilt Worthy
Kilt-A-Licious

The
Whole
Time

CATHERINE
BYBEE

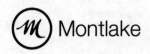 Montlake

Published by Montlake, Seattle

www.apub.com

Amazon, the Amazon logo, and Montlake are trademarks of Amazon.com, Inc., or its affiliates.

ISBN-13: 9781542038638 (paperback)
ISBN-13: 9781542038621 (digital)

Cover design by Caroline Teagle Johnson
Cover image: © Elektrons 08 / plainpicture; © whatapicture / plainpicture

Printed in the United States of America

This is for every strong, independent woman out there willing to take a chance on themselves.

CHAPTER ONE

Salena juggled the cardboard box from one hip to the other as she attempted to open the door to her room. It would have been easier to leave the door open, but that would invite an argument from her parents, who still refused to accept that she was moving out. It didn't matter that her twenty-sixth birthday had passed by six months ago, or that none of her friends still lived with their parents. She was Italian, second generation in America, and the traditions and culture brought over by her grandparents were ones her parents insisted on following today.

Daughters lived with their parents until they were married.

Then and only then did they move away.

Daniella, Salena's older sister, had squeezed some of their parents' hardheadedness out of them at the age of nineteen. She moved out and found herself pregnant within a year. Completely messing up Salena's life from that day forward.

Salena was exhausted by the constant critique of her life and was finally bucking the system.

It was before-the-sun-came-up early, and her parents were still asleep. Most of the time, she was sneaking in at this hour, only now she was tiptoeing out.

Her shoes sat on top of the box in her arms and her purse was slung over her shoulder. This was the last of the six boxes that she could shove in her small car for the short drive to her new place.

With careful precision, one well practiced, she backed out the door and quietly closed it behind her. The WD-40 she'd squeezed into the hinges to avoid the squeak had paid off.

Releasing a soft breath, she turned on her heel and straight into her father's chest.

She squealed so loud, the sound of her voice bounced off the walls in the hallway. Salena's heart rate skyrocketed and her stomach launched to her throat. "Holy shit, Papa!"

Her mother came running from their bedroom, yelling, "What happened?"

Her father glared, his bulky arms crossed over his chest.

"You scared the crap out of me," Salena chided.

Her mother had grabbed the god-awful yellow ball of fuzz she called a bathrobe before storming toward them.

"What do you think you're doing?" her father asked.

She looked at the box in her hands and back at him. "I think that's obvious."

"Sneaking away in the middle of the night." It wasn't a question.

"Technically, it's first thing in the morning."

"Don't get smart with me," her father scolded.

"Yes, Papa." Salena struggled to look at him over the bulk of the box and her dirty tennis shoes that were blocking her view. "I thought this would be easier."

He reached for the box and started to pry it from her arms.

She attempted to hold on.

The struggle resulted in her shoes sliding to the floor, one of which landed on the edge of her toe and made her yelp.

Her father wasn't a tall man, but he outweighed her by a good eighty pounds that he used to push around her.

The door to her bedroom flung open, and he dumped the box in the middle of the doorway.

He lifted his chin and narrowed his eyes as he looked around her room.

Salena knew what he saw. Even though she'd left a smattering of her personal belongings in her dresser and on the walls, most of the things she held dear were either boxed up or already at her new place.

"You've been busy."

She sighed.

It was then her mother joined her father as they inspected the bedroom.

"I've respected your thoughts and beliefs on when is the right time for me to move out. I have—"

"This is how you show your respect?" Her dad was pissed.

"Did it ever occur to you that maybe I won't get married?"

"Don't be ridiculous." Her mother clicked her tongue.

This was an old argument. One Salena had danced around many times with her parents. "It's occurred to me." Especially with everyone in her friend circle in the throes of weddings and the honeymoon phases of their lives, and nothing remotely romantic shining down on her.

"You'll find—"

"And maybe I'm not looking," Salena interrupted her mother. "Maybe I don't want to be somebody's wife."

Her father rolled his eyes, dismissing her words.

"I'm not Daniella. I'm not cut out to be a housewife and move wherever my husband's job takes him." Her sister, ten years her senior, had married the father of her unexpected baby, likely by gunpoint, and relocated to Arizona before Salena had graduated from elementary school.

Salena had been dubbed the "miracle baby," which was code for "oops." As much as her parents had tried to have a dozen kids, Daniella came right about the time they were giving up on the idea at all. Her mother had been in the latter part of her thirties with her first pregnancy, so when Salena came, everyone thought she was going through menopause. The story had been retold so many times she could recite it word for word.

Now her dad was retired. Her mother never had a job outside of the home . . . and they'd both turned their eyes toward relocating closer to Daniella and her family to be near their grandchildren. And even if they denied it, Salena knew it was her keeping them grounded in San Diego.

Her mother turned and started down the hall. "Let's have breakfast and talk this over."

Salena put her hand up and shook her head. "No, Mama. We've talked. *I've* talked. Neither of you want to listen. I'm moving. I'm a grown woman. I've made my decision."

"Just like that," her father flung at her.

Salena raised her voice. "There is no 'just like that.' I've been talking about this for months. I took a management job at D'Angelo's. Giovanni moved out of the upstairs apartment. This makes sense for me."

"It's less than a mile away."

"Which means I'll see you all the time. You'll hardly know I'm gone." Not really what Salena intended, but what Brigida, her mother, needed to hear.

"It's stupid to pay rent when you can live here for free."

The rent Mari D'Angelo was charging her was laughably small. "I want to be on my own, Mama. Not tiptoe past your room when I come in late or offend you when I eat at work and have no more room for what you've cooked."

"We don't mind your late hours."

Salena's eyes moved to her father's. Aldo scolded her with only a glare. "You do. You pretend you don't, but you do."

"Do you think you'll worry your mother *less* when you're not here at all?"

"Maybe not at first, but you'll get used to it."

Her mother huffed.

"Where is Daniella right now?" Salena asked.

"At home with her husband and kids."

"Is she? Are you sure? And what about last night . . . or the night before?"

"She has a husband to take care of her and worry where she is." Aldo crossed his arms over his chest.

The three of them stood in the narrow hall as they argued.

"I'm not waiting for a husband to start living my life. I'm capable of taking care of myself." Salena moved past her mother and stood in front of her father, willing him to move.

"Your sister said the same thing." Her father's words were cold.

"She was nineteen and naive." And thought her parents would find out if she went on birth control pills, so Daniella hadn't bothered. Even after she moved out, she'd depended on condoms. One tequila-filled night, and nine months later . . . "I'm twenty-six . . . and not."

Her father's glare alone made her sweat.

"I'm not asking you to like my decision. But I am asking you to accept it," she finally said.

Salena stood nearly nose to nose with her father. Her stubborn streak she'd gotten from him.

Their standoff lasted for several breaths before Aldo stepped aside.

"Thank you." Salena bent over to retrieve her shoes, this time putting them on her feet since sneaking out of the house was a moot point now.

Behind her, she heard her mother sniffle and walk away.

Guilt seeped in. "It's just down the street."

The door to her parents' bedroom slammed shut. Her mother and all her yellow fluffiness were out of view.

Her father grumbled.

"This is for the best, Papa."

"You keep telling yourself that."

"I won't get pregnant."

The tightness in her father's jaw reaffirmed he was holding back his words.

There was no winning.

The arguing exhausted her.

She repositioned her purse on her shoulder and lifted the box.

"I can pick up the rest later . . . or wait until you're both out if that will make it easier."

Her father didn't say anything, he simply turned and walked away.

Salena cussed under her breath, her parents' Catholic guilt working overtime in her head, and rushed out the door before she could cave.

~

A loud knock on her new apartment door was quickly followed by Chloe's singsong voice calling out her name.

"Saaaleeena!"

"I'm back here."

Her bestie bounded into the bedroom, her smile radiating through the space. "You're here!"

"I know. I can't believe it." She transferred clothes from the suitcase to the dresser.

"Did your parents finally accept your move?"

Salena stopped what she was doing to look up at Chloe. "What do you think?"

"Ugh!" Chloe dropped onto the bed.

"Mama was crying. When my papa stopped yelling, he refused to meet my eyes. Wouldn't talk to me."

"I'm sure they'll get used to it." Chloe tapped her toe against one of the boxes. "How much more do you need to bring over?"

"One more load should do it. It's not like I've accumulated a lot of necessities to live on my own." No dishes, toasters . . . or even bath towels were on her list of personal belongings. The top-floor apartment of the D'Angelos' building was fully furnished, the kitchen had all the basics. For years it was used as guest quarters for family and friends that visited. Then Mari, Chloe's mother, rented the space to Brooke, who ended up marrying the oldest D'Angelo son, Luca. Now they lived on the floor below Salena, and Mari lived on the one below that.

The restaurant itself was on the ground floor and supported the whole operation.

"I'm sure you'll have everything you need already here."

"This place is a stepping stone anyway. I hope to have my own place within a year."

Chloe shrugged. "You'll probably crave a move before then. You know my family . . . they'll poke their head into your life all the time now that you're living here."

"It can't be nearly as bad as living across the hall from my parents," Salena challenged.

"It will be easier than that, but that doesn't mean Mama or Luca would be okay with overnight male company." Chloe's look challenged Salena.

"I have no intention of bringing men over." She waved her hands in the air. "Female energy only."

Chloe lifted an eyebrow and smirked. "Something you're not telling me?"

Salena tossed a rolled-up pair of socks at her friend. "You know what I mean. It's funny, though, when you think about it. I had my first kiss in this apartment."

"Me too. Robbie Corselette. Spin the bottle."

Salena paused before picking up a stack of shirts. "He was the only one here with four girls. How he talked us into playing spin the bottle, I'll never figure out."

"We were young and stupid."

Before the night was over, Robbie had kissed all of them . . . some of them twice.

"Good times," Salena teased. She shifted her attention back to unpacking. "You don't have to worry. There won't be any Corselettes sneaking in." It was one thing to have the reputation of dating a lot of men, it was another thing to prove it.

Salena had always been flirty and self-assured. That confidence attracted plenty of men, but they didn't stick around. Which was fine with her. Only now that her best friend and wingwoman was happily married and only available for the occasional girls' night out, Salena had to fend for herself.

The club scene had lost its appeal.

Or maybe she was growing up.

Either way, the results were the same.

A lot more of her time was spent by herself, giving her a chance to plan her future.

"Luca will be relieved," Chloe said.

"He told you to say something to me, didn't he?" Luca had hinted about male company but hadn't come right out and forbidden her. "Did he ask you to tell me the house rules?"

Salena could see by the look on Chloe's face that she was trying to come up with a clever lie, half truth, or something to gloss over the answer. Except Chloe sucked at that skill. She couldn't keep a secret to save her life, and lying wasn't in her wheelhouse.

"He would have said something himself, but Brooke stopped him."

Salena emptied the suitcase, zipped it up, and put it on the floor. "I'll reassure him the next time I see him."

"Luca trusts you, it's the guys he has issues with." Even though the apartments were separate, they were all attached with a common stairwell. Luca had two kids and a wife to think about . . . not to mention his mother, Mari. Outside of an infant son, Luca was the only man in the building now that Giovanni had moved out.

"Thank you for that. I'll be going to 'their' place if someone comes into the picture. Just be sure and hint to your brother to not ask me questions if I'm not home and it's not my day to work."

Chloe smiled. "I'll pass that on."

They moved out to the living room and sat on the sofa. Salena changed the subject. "Is everything ready for the wedding?"

Chloe nodded. "It's hard to believe it happens in two weeks."

Giovanni, the second son, and Emma lived an hour outside of San Diego in Temecula on a vineyard. They'd vowed to have a small wedding right on the property as soon as harvest was over. Even though Mari had wanted the wedding to happen in the church, she settled with a priest blessing their marriage and a minister performing the ceremony outside. Now that the harvest was behind them and the grapes were fermenting away, the final D'Angelo was getting married.

"Your whole family got married in one year," Salena said.

"Mama couldn't be happier."

"I'm sure a brand-new grandson helps."

"Thank God for Luca and Brooke. They sure took the pressure off me," Chloe said.

"I bet."

"Dante and I want to wait a couple of years."

The wistful look on Chloe's face made Salena think her friend was weighing that timeline and wondering how to shorten it.

Salena, on the other hand, wanted to put a sign on her uterus that said "Out of Order."

"How about ten years?"

Chloe missed the fact that Salena was referring to herself and continued, "I doubt he'd hold off that long. A couple of years should have the businesses where we want them, and hopefully, we'll have our own house. I don't regret growing up in this building, but we want a yard. A neighborhood that isn't filled with tourists year-round."

Yup, her friend had certainly been thinking about all the criteria needed before popping a bun in her oven. "You'll definitely have to get out of Little Italy for that."

"We will."

Salena looked around the room. "I'm good here for a while. Just the thought of sleeping in my own bed without my parents in the next room has me dancing on air."

"I think the 'living with your parents until you're married thing' is archaic."

"Says the woman who did just that," Salena teased.

"Mama's guilt trips are epic. Anytime I hinted about moving away, she'd talk about Papa and how much he wanted our family together. I'm pretty sure she said 'turn over in his grave' a hundred times. Our high school plot of getting an apartment together was nothing but a dream."

"If we'd done that, there would have been trouble."

"We managed to find enough without that." Chloe laughed.

Salena smiled at her best friend. "Right! Just look at Vegas. I hooked up with that stripper, and you ended up eloping."

Chloe squeezed her eyes shut. "That was a rough weekend."

"Those hangovers were well earned."

"Don't remind me."

"I had a great time."

"I bet you did. Whatever happened with that guy?"

Salena shrugged. "He called, said to look him up when I'm in Vegas. But you know . . . stripper. I could *not* do that long-term. Even though he was hot as fuck."

"Wasn't he in med school or something?"

"Chiropractic doctor. Super smart."

"Smart and hot—I'm not sure why you didn't keep that going."

"A stripper and a waitress . . . that makes sense. A doctor and a waitress . . . not so much. Besides, long distance never works."

Chloe nudged her shoulder. "Hey, you're a manager now."

"Who still waits tables." Part of the job was training anyone new and jumping in for anything that was needed. From hostessing to waiting tables . . . to tending bar. The only thing the D'Angelos didn't ask of her was to help in the kitchen or wash dishes. She'd basically taken over the jobs of Chloe and Gio, now that they'd moved out. Management was split between Mari, Luca, and Salena. Mari and Luca treated her like family and never asked her to work harder than them.

But . . . that didn't mean Salena wanted to make a career out of restaurant management. Not that she'd thought long or hard about what came next. She hoped that moving out would give her some insight and motivation to find a path.

"It's not the most glamorous job," Chloe said. "I know."

"It works for now."

Chloe's phone buzzed and she pulled it out of her back pocket to check her message. "It's Dante. We're going to breakfast. Wanna come?"

Salena shook her head. "I'm good. I want to settle in before my shift."

"Are you working tables tonight?"

"Just lunch. Jackie had a dentist appointment she forgot about."

Chloe got to her feet and headed toward the door. "I'll call ya later."

"Ciao."

Once the door closed, Salena leaned her head against the back of the sofa and spread her arms out wide.

And she smiled.

"Freedom. At last."

CHAPTER TWO

"Where do you want these?" Ryan pointed to two small round tables that sat beside the outside wall of the wine cellar. His voice carried over the driveway toward Giovanni, his soon-to-be brother-in-law.

Gio, as he was most often called, looked up and shrugged. "I have no idea . . . Ask the boss."

Ryan chuckled before his eyes roamed the yard for his sister. He spotted her talking to one of the many people running around the winery as everyone helped to set things up for the wedding the next day. He curled his tongue and ripped a high-pitched whistle through the air.

Emma twisted toward him. She was too far away to attempt a question, so instead of yelling, Ryan pointed to the tables before lifting his hands in the air with a shrug.

She raised a hand up, telling him to hold on.

Gio walked over. "It's coming together."

"When you have this many people to help, it's bound to happen fast."

Gio had a close family, and every one of them was there. "My family doesn't idle well."

"I've noticed." The wedding coordinator had brought in a crew, who were busy in the open tent where the reception was going to take place.

Temecula weather during late fall could range from summer-like temperatures to wind events to the occasional rainstorm. But the one thing it nearly always did once the sun went down was get cold.

A massive white tent filled with lights and portable heaters would make everyone happy during the reception.

"I thought you guys said you wanted a small wedding," Ryan said when he noticed yet more chairs being pulled out of the back of a truck for the ceremony.

"This is small," Gio countered. "Immediate family, close friends. There isn't one person flying in from Italy."

Ryan narrowed his eyes. "How many family members do you have there?"

"Not many. Cousins, aunts, uncles. My grandfather was just here for Chloe's wedding, and two of our cousins. We promised to come and visit them soon. I think they were relieved to not have to make the trip again. It gets expensive after a while."

Ryan smiled. "I bet. There's still a lot of tables in that tent."

Gio hedged. "Some of the people who work at the restaurant have been there for years. They would have been offended if we didn't invite them."

"Who's going to run the place if everyone is here?"

Gio shook his head. "We close it down."

"On a Saturday?" Ryan found that hard to believe.

"Over half the staff will be here. Making some stay behind would be an insult. One night isn't going to make or break anything."

Emma jogged over to them, a clipboard in her hand. "This is crazy."

Ryan laughed. "Yeah . . . imagine if you were having a *big* wedding."

She rolled her eyes. "We tried."

"There must be at least a hundred chairs set up over there." Ryan pointed.

Emma looked up, frowned . . . one hand planted firmly on her hip. "What is that? We said no arbor."

Before Ryan could say another word, Emma was walking over to the men setting up chairs.

"What about these tables?" he called after her.

She twisted. "One sits right there in front of the cellar, and the other goes in front of the tent."

And she was off.

"Do you know what they're for?" Ryan asked.

Gio nodded a few times, his eyes fixed on Emma. "Yeah, no . . . I have no idea."

"Said every groom known to mankind," Ryan teased.

Gio's smile split from ear to ear. "Damn, I love that woman."

From the admiration in the man's eyes, Ryan believed him. The joy in that smile was a living thing. "Good. I'll kick your ass if you ever hurt her."

"I'd expect nothing less." Gio took a breath, turned his attention to Ryan. "I'd just as soon cut off my right nut than hurt her."

Ryan pointed a finger in his direction. "I'll give you a nice dull blade if you do."

"Deal."

With the brotherly love noted and expectations voiced, Ryan picked up one of the tables to move it toward the tent.

From a distance, the sound of an unhappy car sputtered its way onto the property.

Ryan glanced over his shoulder. "What is that?"

Both of them watched as the old car limped closer. One that should have been put out of its misery twenty years after it came off the production line. Yet there it was . . . taking its last breath in Emma and Gio's front yard.

Gio started to laugh. "Trouble."

Ryan dropped the table, rather unceremoniously, as the door to the car opened and legs stepped out.

Wrapped in spandex that hugged every inch of her femininity, *Trouble* slapped the top of her car as if it was a bad date who had just insulted her.

"*Who* is that?"

Without knowing it was coming, Ryan felt a hand on his shoulder. "*That* is Salena." A deep sigh left Gio's lips.

"Holy—"

"Yeah . . . she's all that. And more."

Spandex and a sports bra. Long dark hair pulled into a ponytail. Olive skin and attitude.

Yeah, Ryan could sense the attitude a mile away.

He blew out a breath.

"Is she single?" The words escaped Ryan's mouth without permission.

Gio's slow chuckle had Ryan moving his gaze from Trouble.

"Yeah . . . *very* single."

He narrowed his eyes. "What does that mean?"

Gio slung his arm around Ryan's shoulder and started toward the woman kicking the tires of her car. "Not married, not dating anyone . . . that kind of single."

"Why do I feel there is more to that explanation?"

"Because you're a smart man . . ."

And that's all Ryan pulled from Gio before they arrived within the breathing space of Salena and her excuse for an automobile.

"Hey, Salena," Gio called, raising his voice.

"Godforsaken piece of shit!" One last kick to the car.

The arm on Ryan's shoulder disappeared and wrapped around the woman waging war with her vehicle.

"I'm surprised this piece of junk made it," Gio teased.

"Trash-talk her and maybe she'll become your driveway art long-term."

"Please, no."

Salena smiled and turned to Gio and pulled him into a hug. "I can't believe you're getting married tomorrow."

Ryan cleared his throat once the two of them stopped hugging.

Gio stood back. "I don't think you two have met. Salena, this is Ryan . . . my soon-to-be brother-in-law."

Her eyes caught his, an eyebrow lifted, and her eyes did a lazy scan of him.

And she smiled. "Hello."

Holy—

"Oh, boy." Gio sighed.

There was heat in her gaze . . . the kind he would expect at a bar, three drinks in.

"Hello." Ryan let his greeting linger. "Car trouble?"

She shrugged. "It got me here."

"Will it get you home?" Gio asked.

Salena didn't lose eye contact with Ryan. "That's Sunday's problem."

He couldn't help but laugh.

"Salena!"

From the steps of the house, Chloe called Salena's name.

With a sideways glance, Salena walked out of Ryan's orbit and toward the house. Her chemical pull, painfully, departed with her. "Damn."

Just as spectacular walking away as she was beating up her car.

"Fair warning," Gio whispered at his side. "She will chew you up and spit you out."

"Who said I was—"

"Oh, please."

Ryan chuckled. "Might be a risk worth taking."

Gio's hand patted Ryan's back. "We have plenty of wine and beer when you need to have a good cry after it's over."

"Fuck off." How bad could it be?

Gio tossed his head back and laughed. "C'mon. Emma was about to have a meltdown. Let's make sure she's okay."

A few steps toward the vineyard and Ryan asked, "Is she a cousin or something?"

CHAPTER THREE

Salena tossed the keys to the pile of crap she called a car on the kitchen island and took a deep breath. "That was painful."

"Traffic?" Chloe asked as she handed Salena a bottle of cold water from the refrigerator.

"It wasn't so much the traffic as my heart jumping every time my car made a noise. The last thing I wanted was to have to call one of you to fish me off the side of the freeway."

"You should have caught a ride with someone."

"I wanted to make sure everyone on the dinner shift showed up." Salena slid onto a stool and twisted off the cap of the water.

"You could have waited until Sergio or someone else drove here."

"Almost everyone is waiting until tomorrow. You know me. I have a serious case of FOMO."

Chloe laughed. "The only thing you'd miss out on tonight is the work. Well, and dinner."

Salena gulped some water and narrowed her eyes at the empty kitchen. "Where's dinner?"

"Over at Emma's parents' place. It's like ten minutes from here. Super fancy."

Salena wrinkled her nose. "Formal? I only brought one dress for tomorrow."

Chloe shook her head. "No . . . their house is fancy. I'm going dressed like this." She pointed to her simple blouse and jeans. "Brooke,

Franny, Leo, and Mama are at the Rutledges' now. Everyone else is outside setting up."

Salena glanced over her shoulder at the massive window that looked out over the property. Her thoughts turned to the welcoming committee that met her in the driveway. "What do you know about Ryan?"

"Emma's brother?"

"Yeah . . . tall, dark, and tatted." She found her lip caught between her teeth. She'd always been a sucker for tattoos. From the way his T-shirt hugged his torso, the man wasn't a stranger to a gym . . . or hard labor.

"Oh no . . . I recognize that look."

"What?" Salena asked and released her lip.

Chloe waved a finger in the air. "He's Emma's brother."

"So? I mean . . . unless he's married."

Chloe hesitated and then released a breath. "You're right. Just know you'll see him on occasion . . . after."

"I don't make enemies. You have to be committed for that." She exaggerated a shiver.

Her best friend laughed and rolled her eyes. "No. Ryan is not married. And I haven't been introduced to a girlfriend."

"Kids?"

"No."

Salena rubbed her hands together.

"Oh, boy."

~

Ryan stood next to a tree and watched the rehearsal from the nosebleed seats.

They'd set up everything, so all that was left was for the florist to come in the morning and do their thing.

He heard gravel crunching beneath feet and glanced to find Salena walking his way. He felt a smile on his lips and an extra beat in his chest.

"Why aren't you up there?"

Her question came before she stopped at his side.

"You're only obligated to stand in that line one time. And since this is Emma's second round, I opted out."

"Ouch. You make it sound like she has more ahead of her."

Ryan shook his head. "Not at all." Giovanni and Emma were holding hands and smiling into each other's eyes. "This is the real thing. I mean, look at them. Everyone is talking around them, fidgeting . . . and they're focused on one thing."

"Huh." Not a word or a comment . . . just a huff of breath.

Ryan risked a sideways glance at Salena. She was staring at Gio and Emma. Her jaw slack, her eyes laser-focused. "Each other."

"Yeah."

Salena's eyes blinked, twice, and turned to him.

"Have you ever looked at someone like that?" Ryan asked.

She recoiled.

Ryan laughed so hard and loud, several people turned toward them.

"I have two looks when it comes to men."

"Oh yeah?" This he wanted to hear.

Salena cocked her head to the side, slid a smile on her face. "Hungry."

Oh, fuck.

"And?" Why was his mouth suddenly dry?

"Done." Her smile morphed into a smirk.

"Holy shit."

"Too much?" she asked.

"I can't say I've ever met a woman more sure of herself." Which was true.

She dismissed him with a shrug and turned her focus to the bride and groom. "Let me know if you do. My best friend got married and I need someone to hang out with."

Ryan laughed and turned his attention back to the rehearsal. Yeah . . . she was worth the risk. He could do *hungry* and *done*.

The wedding party started to walk their way.

"How are you getting up to my parents' place?" Ryan asked.

"You saw my car." Salena licked her lips. "I'll catch a ride."

So aloof.

So fucking sexy.

"I'll drive you."

She looked him up and down. As if measuring his worth. "Okay," she said.

Their eyes met.

Hunger stared back.

Chloe jogged over. "We're headed for dinner. Are you coming with us?"

"Ryan already offered," Salena told her.

Chloe stopped, straightened her spine . . . looked at them. She waved a finger between them and then laughed. "See you there."

Salena dropped her composure for half a second, shook her head. "Ready?" she asked.

He looked her up and down. Still sporting the spandex she'd arrived in, with a button-up shirt tossed over the sports bra, but open to show the aforementioned bra.

The Rutledge estate wasn't ready for this.

And that made Ryan's smile even brighter. "Do you need to grab a purse or something?"

She looked at him like he was crazy. "I assumed it was an open bar. Aren't your parents wine people?"

Somewhere in the back of Ryan's head, the warning about a woman who didn't bother with a purse rang.

"Let's go."

Everyone around them divided up and piled in cars.

He stopped in front of his Ducati and removed his leather jacket hanging from the handlebars.

Salena paused. "You don't disappoint."

"Have you ever ridden one of these?"

The woman didn't miss a beat. "I'll let you know."

Ryan stumbled with a smile, handed her his jacket. "Damn, woman."

Salena shrugged into the jacket, refused the helmet he handed her. "You're too easy, Rutledge."

"I'll play hard to get."

They both laughed at that.

Ryan swung his leg over the bike and nodded her way.

Her hand touched his waist as she joined him on the bike. Her thighs straddled his hips, one hand rested on his leg as if it had always been there.

When her body molded to his to keep from falling, he caught his breath.

Suddenly, his sister's boring wedding with a bunch of people he either didn't know or didn't like was looking up.

~

The ride to the Rutledge estate was entirely too short, and the driveway up to the house from the road was entirely too long.

She thought Gio and Emma's house was something out of this world.

Rutledge Vineyards was on another planet.

Massive double gates with a tree-lined lane that ended in an enormous circular driveway with a four-tier fountain as a centerpiece. The sun was setting, and the lights on the property were illuminating the house and mature landscape.

It screamed money.

Ryan pulled his bike to a spot beyond the cars and turned off the engine.

Salena sat there for a moment and looked up at the house, her hands still resting on Ryan's hips. "This is crazy."

"Overkill," he agreed.

"You grew up here?"

"Here and the bigger house in Napa."

She leaned to the side and looked him in the eye to see if he was joking. "There are two of them?"

"I'm convinced my parents don't like each other. Mom spends the majority of her time here, and my father stays up north. They're either geniuses when it comes to a happy marriage—by living in separate houses—or this is cheaper than a divorce. I don't really know."

"That's mental."

"You guys coming?" Chloe jumped out of a car and yelled across the driveway.

Salena waved a hand and swung her leg off the bike.

Ryan followed her action and stood tall.

She pushed beside him, smiled, and then used the mirror on the bike to check her appearance. Her cheeks were flushed with color from the brisk ride, her hair was less than perfect. She quickly pulled the tie out of her hair and combed her fingers through it.

That's better.

She straightened her shoulders and smiled.

"Ready?"

"Yeah."

Ryan nodded toward the front of the house as she fell into step beside him.

"Have you met my parents?" he asked.

"I was introduced to your dad tonight for the first time. Your mom was at the bridal shower. She seems nice."

"She is. Dad's an asshole, though."

Salena had heard about him through Gio. "I was told he was coming around."

Ryan laughed. "Old dogs and new tricks. We'll see."

Salena had an unfamiliar urge to know more about the frown and tension that seemed to wash over Ryan the closer they came to the front door.

Much of the D'Angelo family was still gathered in the foyer, chatting, when they made it to them.

"How was the ride?" Chloe asked with a smirk.

"I held on for dear life." Salena chuckled.

Ryan laughed at her side as she shrugged out of his coat. He pulled it from her shoulders.

From nowhere, a woman dressed in black and white appeared and took the coat from Ryan, then walked away without a word.

"Who is she?"

"That's Christy. My mother's help."

Salena met Chloe's eyes. "They have *help*?"

"Strange, right?"

Beth, Ryan's mother, started ushering everyone out of the hall and farther back in the house.

From a grand foyer with a sweeping staircase, they moved into a great room that could have housed Salena's parents' condo times three. A massive table was set for dinner to fit everyone. It rivaled a five-star restaurant setup, with full place settings, candles flickering, and splashes of flowers absolutely everywhere. The elegance was greater than most wedding setups, and this was just the rehearsal dinner.

"No fold-up chairs and card tables, eh?" Salena whispered to Chloe.

"Emma told me her mother rented the table and chairs to accommodate all of us. And hired a professional designer to come in and decorate just for tonight."

Ryan moved past them and over to a bar, out of earshot.

"This is nuts," Salena whispered.

"I know. Beth tried to hire the dinner, but Mama jumped on that. Said since the meal tomorrow is catered, we needed a good Italian meal tonight."

Salena would expect nothing less from a woman who'd worked as a chef most of her life.

A young man dressed in a formal black uniform walked out with a tray filled with glasses of wine. "Waiters?"

"Mama didn't scoff at that."

Salena glanced once again at Ryan, who was in a conversation with a man and a woman she didn't know.

"Who is Ryan talking to?"

"His brother, Richard, and his wife, Kristen."

Richard wore a suit, and his wife was in a cocktail dress. "Either they're overdressed, or I'm entirely underdressed."

"Look around. It doesn't matter. Most of us have been working all day."

Which was true. Almost everyone was wearing what they'd spent the day in. Chloe had tossed on a sweater and brushed her hair. Nicole, Emma's best friend, was also wearing black leggings and an oversize T-shirt and didn't look the least bit uncomfortable talking to Beth, who was in a pantsuit that probably cost more than a month's pay.

The noise in the room started to rise as a few more people arrived.

Salena and Chloe both grabbed a glass of red as the waiter walked by and clinked their glasses together.

Dante scrambled through the crowd and made his way to Chloe's side. "You two whispering can only mean trouble."

"You have trust issues, Dante," Salena teased.

"Ha. I have years of history to support my claim," he countered.

Chloe pushed into Dante's side. "We were just talking about how impressive this place is and the effort Beth has put into tonight's dinner."

"It's nice."

Salena caught Chloe rolling her eyes. "Nice? You're such a guy."

Dante kissed the side of Chloe's head. "Lucky for you."

Franny, the nine-year-old D'Angelo, ran over to them, nearly missing one of the servers in her haste.

"Zia Chloe? Mama wants you in the kitchen."

"And your papa doesn't want you running in the house."

Franny wrinkled her nose.

"There's a lot of fancy things here, Franny. You wouldn't want to break anything," Salena added.

Francesca D'Angelo had only one dial on her speedometer . . . and it was *fast*. It didn't matter how often she was told to slow down, she didn't comply. Willful, strong, and opinionated, Franny was hard not to adore.

"I'll go see what Mama wants."

"And I'll find a bathroom." Not that Salena needed one, she just wanted to explore without being obvious.

"There's one—" Dante pointed behind him.

"No, no . . . don't tell me. I'll find it."

Salena moved in the opposite direction of Chloe and the others to snoop.

She skirted the outside of the people in the room and averted eye contact to avoid being drawn into a conversation.

She colored herself lucky when she found an empty hall and started down it.

Relatively sure a bathroom was right there off the main room, she purposely bypassed it and pushed open another door a little farther down. "Oh no . . . this isn't a bathroom," she somewhat whispered to herself.

It was a picture-perfect bedroom that didn't look lived in. Too small to be the primary, but bigger than the one she had now. A guest room, she concluded, complete with a suitcase at the foot of the bed.

Across the hall, another closed door . . . she knocked twice. "Is this the bathroom?" She glanced behind her in case someone was there and then opened the door.

This guest room was ivory walls and wood tones. Not lived in, and no suitcase.

Salena stepped in and looked around. It was beyond beautiful. Another door in the room, and she found a bathroom . . . again, bigger than the one at her apartment at the D'Angelos'. Walk-in shower, spacious vanity. She glanced at herself in the mirror and tucked a strand of hair behind her ear before turning away.

Her heart jumped, and so did her feet, when she saw Ryan standing in the doorway, his shoulder resting on the frame.

"Shit. You scared me." Good thing the wine was in a tall glass and she hadn't spilled it everywhere.

Ryan pointed his beer her way. "Get lost?"

"No. I, ah . . . was looking for a bathroom."

He grinned, raised an eyebrow. "You found one."

"Right, uhm . . ." She glanced behind her at the commode that she hadn't used. "I wanted to check my hair."

Ryan shook his head, not believing a word. "Sure."

She sighed, let her shoulders go lax. "Fine. I was snooping. I've never been in a house like this and wanted to look around."

He laughed and pushed away from the wall. "Let me give you a tour, then."

She walked past him, out of the bathroom, and toward the door. "Great idea."

In the hall, he took the lead and turned her down a hall that opened into what looked like another living room. Only this one sported a large sectional couch and a TV the size of the wall. "Media room . . . what was once a game room when we were kids."

"I bet you had some great parties in here." She noticed a small kitchen station to one side with a wine fridge, microwave, and sink.

"First time I got laid was in this room."

"Daring of you. Was anyone home?"

"No. But someone figured it out."

Ryan's eyes were skirting around the room as if chasing memories. "Did your parents ask you?"

"No. But within a week, there was a construction crew in here removing the double doors that used to close this space off." He pointed to the large opening to the room. "And girls weren't allowed in our bedrooms, so that ended that."

Salena leaned into the image of young Ryan figuring out the birds and the bees in his childhood home. "I'm sure you had a backup plan."

"Yeah." He sipped his beer. "My car."

"Hard to take the doors off that." She grinned, poked her head into an open door, and found another bathroom. "How many bathrooms are in this house?"

"Seven . . . wait, eight if you count the one at the pool house."

"That's a lot of toilets to clean."

"My mother has people for that." They passed through the room and back into a hall.

"You were never put on toilet duty?"

"I didn't scrub a toilet until I moved out. It's not that hard." They walked out of the room and continued.

"Which bedroom was yours?"

He nodded toward another door, this one open.

Lots of plants, green and white décor. A suitcase was opened on a stand beside the bed.

"It doesn't look like you."

"Not anymore. My old room at the Napa house hasn't changed too much. Mom left things alone for a year after we moved and then boxed whatever we left behind and turned them into guest rooms."

"I almost forgot about the other house."

Ryan shrugged, uninterested.

"What was it like?"

"What was *what* like?"

"Growing up with all this?"

"Annoying."

Salena snapped her gaze his way. "Really?"

"Yeah . . ." They walked out and into what had to be the primary bedroom. "We went to school in Napa. Spent weekends down here . . . summers. Or anytime my mother wanted to get away. It made friendships hard and relationships impossible. After high school, I moved here. Told my parents I was taking classes in San Diego."

Salena walked into the center of the room. A huge bed and massive windows that likely overlooked the vineyard outside, but the sun had set, and all she saw were a few lights in the back of the house illuminating trees. "You *told* your parents . . . which means you weren't taking classes."

"You catch on quick."

She smiled at him, ran a hand on the curtains. Linen . . . they had to be stupid expensive. "What were you doing when you weren't taking classes?"

"Learning about bikes. Drinking in San Diego."

"You don't work with your dad and the vineyards?" Salena tilted her glass his way, took a sip.

He groaned. "No. Wine is not my thing. That's all Emma and Richard."

"What about—"

"Hold up. You've asked me a dozen questions. What's your story?"

Through a door, she found a walk-in closet. "Holy shit." Her jaw dropped. Finished cabinets with glass doors. Purses and shoes . . . so many pairs of shoes. "This is crazy."

"Every girl's dream," he said.

"I don't have enough to fill even a tenth of this space."

"Do you have siblings?" Ryan asked, changing the subject.

Salena felt a bit like she was invading Ryan's parents' privacy by lingering in the closet and backed out. "Older sister. She's married, lives in Arizona."

"But you grew up in San Diego."

"Ah-huh. Little Italy. I grew up in an apartment. Well, condo, but when someone lives above you, below you, and on each side . . . it's an apartment."

"Doesn't sound like you cared for it."

"No. It was fine. All my close friends lived a similar life, so it isn't like I knew any different. Besides, San Diego has plenty of places to escape the sidewalks and tall buildings."

Ryan leaned against a wall as she meandered around. The bathroom was exactly what she expected after the grandness of the rest of the house.

"Do you surf?"

"No." She raised her voice once inside the bathroom since Ryan didn't follow her in. "When I go to the beach, I don't get my hair wet."

"Then what's the point?"

A shower with three heads and a massive glass door. "Boys."

"Of course."

Salena heard Ryan laugh.

"The first time I got laid was on Fiesta Island."

"Ahh, yes. Campfires on the bay."

"Good times."

"I've had a few memories there myself."

Back in the bedroom, Ryan watched her walk his way, his eyes doing a slow dance over her frame.

"I bet you did," she said.

Salena stopped about two inches into his personal space and smiled. "How often do you get to San Diego?"

"All the time."

The man had very kissable lips and kind eyes despite the hardness of his jaw. "Huh."

He raised an eyebrow, glanced at her lips. "Huh," he repeated.

Footsteps in the hall had Salena pulling back.

"There you are. Have you seen Salena?" Chloe's voice came from the hallway.

Salena skirted past Ryan, who took up half the doorway. "I'm right here."

Chloe chuckled. "Why did I get the feeling if I found one of you, I'd find you both?"

"I don't know what you're talking about," Salena pretended. "Ryan was just giving me a tour of the house."

"Whatever. We're about to start dinner."

Salena walked beside Chloe and felt the weight of Ryan's eyes.

A single glance over her shoulder and she caught Ryan looking at her ass with a grin.

CHAPTER FOUR

Ryan didn't idle well.

Unlike the day before, when muscles and men were needed to move all the heavy things, the day of the wedding was a whole lot of waiting around and doing nothing.

He'd slept in his own apartment in town . . . all by himself. Which was a crying-ass shame since Salena had kept him in a simmering state of arousal just by looking at him all night long. He knew, without a doubt, she was just as attracted as he. But her intention was to stay the night at Emma's and then relocate to his mother's house in the morning with the bridal party to get ready. None of those plans involved him getting to know Salena a little better.

Or even a whole lot better.

Giovanni had his brother and best friend to keep him occupied, and Ryan wasn't needed at the venue until an hour before the ceremony.

Under any normal reality, sitting around waiting to shower and dress in a suit to attend a wedding wouldn't provoke any excitement at all. Even for his sister's wedding. As a nonmarried, heterosexual male— very happy with his single life—Ryan held zero fantasies of matrimony, rings, and forever.

Then why the hell was he watching the clock, anxiously awaiting the time he could show up at the venue to be a part of it?

Salena.

In one word . . . or name, as it stood.

She was all kinds of sexy and sass, and Ryan could hardly wait to see how the afternoon and evening progressed.

By noon, Ryan had changed the sheets on his bed and cleaned out the inside of his car, deciding that if Salena needed or, more importantly, wanted a ride to wherever, the car was a better bet than his bike. There was always a chance of her wearing a dress to the wedding. The image of what she might look like wearing a dress danced around in his head for a good fifteen minutes as he stared at the napkins on the floor of said dirty car.

Then, because he still had an hour before he even needed to consider getting ready for the wedding, he ran over to the drugstore to fill his bedside table with necessities.

Twice he texted his mother and asked if he might be needed earlier for any reason, and twice his mother said everything was taken care of.

Even with his morning and early afternoon filled with trivial activities, Ryan arrived at Emma and Gio's home thirty minutes before he was expected.

He noticed Gio, Luca, and Dante, all wearing tuxes and standing under an oak tree, with a photographer directing them.

The florist, a robust man, was collecting empty buckets and baskets and shoving them in the back of a van . . . obviously finished with his job for the day. "Looks like it's going to be a hell of a party," the man said as he saw Ryan watching him.

"I'm sure it will be." Ryan folded his jacket over his arm, not quite ready to put it on as the midday sun reminded him why he lived in Southern California and not New York. "Have you seen the bride and her party?"

"Only on FaceTime. They haven't arrived yet."

"Hey, Ryan!"

He looked up to find Gio calling him over.

The sound of his shoes hitting the cobblestone drive echoed until it turned to the crunch of gravel once he was off the driveway.

The smile on Gio's face and glow in his eyes were evidence of how much this day meant to him.

Ryan extended his hand when he was within range to shake his future brother-in-law's. "This is it."

"I can't believe it."

The handshake quickly turned into a hug. "I'm early," Ryan stated the obvious. "In case there was anything I could do."

A round of handshakes to Luca and Dante commenced.

"I think we're all set. All we need is the bride," Dante said.

"Have you seen her?" Gio asked Ryan.

"No. I'm guessing they're still at my parents' house."

Gio rubbed his hands together. Nerves dangled on the edge of his fingertips.

"Are you guys doing that 'first look' thing?"

"No." Gio shook his head. "My mother thought it was bad luck."

Luca nudged Ryan's side. "This is hard enough on our mother since the ceremony isn't being performed by a priest."

"You'll still be married," Ryan pointed out.

"Tell that to an Italian Catholic mother and she'll have you in church this Sunday and every Sunday for the foreseeable future."

Dante lifted his left hand in the air and flashed his wedding ring. "Mari insisted Chloe and I get married a second time, in the church, after we eloped."

Gio narrowed his gaze at his best friend. "Are we sticking with the elopement story? I seem to remember you and my sister getting drunk in front of a chapel before you even went on a first date."

"Which should have proved my intentions," Dante defended himself.

Luca's hand met Dante's shoulder. "Damn good thing you married her before you—"

"Yeah, yeah . . ." Dante shrugged off Luca's hand with a good-natured grin.

Ryan laughed along with them. All the while, the photographer was snapping pictures during their conversation.

Dante's phone buzzed. He glanced at the screen. "Looks like we need to make you disappear. Chloe said they're driving here now."

Gio's eyes darted toward the drive, excitement dancing in his eyes.

"We have a flask in the winery office. I think now might be a good time to relax," Dante suggested.

The photographer stopped looking at the pictures on his camera and stepped forward. "I'll take a few more pictures of you guys inside and move on to the bride."

Ryan glanced toward the front of the house as the others started walking away.

"You coming?" Luca asked.

"I wouldn't want to interrupt."

"Oh, please." Gio nodded in the direction of the winery.

Thankful for the invitation, Ryan joined his future brother-in-law to partake in the obligatory pre-ceremony shots.

~

Salena sat in the back of a black rented SUV alongside Brooke, Franny, and baby Leo, along with Emma's older brother, Richard, and his wife, Kristen.

Emma, her parents, Mari, Chloe, and Nicole all drove ahead in a limousine.

Franny was bouncing with excitement. She wore an age-appropriate version of the bridesmaids' dresses so she could toss flowers before anyone else walked down the aisle. A job she'd done twice in the last year.

"You know, Franny, the next time you're in a wedding, it will probably be as a bridesmaid or even a bride," Brooke pointed out.

"Boys are gross."

"Yes, we are," Richard said from the front seat.

"See," Franny said as if Richard's opinion on the subject was law.

Richard smiled into the rearview mirror as he drove.

Salena couldn't help but notice every stark contrast there was between this man and his younger brother.

Richard was quiet, reserved, and looked completely in place behind the wheel of an oversize SUV. "Richard . . . do you drive a motorcycle, too?" Salena asked, guessing the answer was no.

"Oh, Lord, no," his wife answered for him.

"I leave that to my brother."

She guessed he didn't have one spot of ink on his body either.

They were both tall and seemed to have their mother's hair color . . . that was where their physical similarities ended. It was only recently revealed that their father wasn't theirs by genetics. A secret Robert Rutledge wanted to keep to the grave. But when one of your children ends up with a genetic disorder, and everyone has to get tested . . . secrets come out.

Salena smiled into the thought. With a family as rich as theirs, she expected something more profound behind the question of "Who's your daddy?" than the need for a fertility doctor.

They'd barely settled into their seats before Richard was pulling into the driveway.

There were a few cars parked to the side, but the guests hadn't started to arrive yet. Salena's eyesore of a car had been pushed to where it rested far away from the house. She had serious concerns about the thing getting her back to San Diego.

Tomorrow's problem.

Richard pulled in behind the limo.

Ahead of them, Chloe had exited the massive car and was walking into the house by herself.

Salena assumed her best friend was checking to make sure the coast was clear.

Franny bounced from the car, and Brooke worked on unbuckling the car seat without waking her son.

Stuck in the back of the SUV, Salena looked down at the youngest D'Angelo with a smile. "He's such a good baby," she whispered.

"I'm biased, but I think so."

Even with Leonardo D'Angelo's good-baby graces . . . staring down at him didn't stir any eggs to start dropping. Salena was perfectly content to be the "kinda aunt" that lived upstairs and watched over him from time to time.

By the time Salena had been freed from the back seat, everyone from the other car was standing in front of the house, with the photographer at Emma's side, pointing out where he wanted Emma to be.

Salena scanned the area but didn't see Ryan's bike, which, strangely, disappointed her.

There were two young guys, likely no more than twenty-one or twenty-two, wearing black and white and offering to park the SUV.

"Valet service?" Salena asked Brooke under her breath.

"Makes sense when you think about the number of cars they're going to have to pack in here."

Salena smoothed the front of her dress as they both made their way inside.

On the porch, Mari looked beyond them to the drive and said, "Oh, good . . . they made it."

Salena followed her gaze, and the smile on her face fell. "Are those my . . ."

"Parents. *Sì.*"

Two people she really did not want to see at this wedding.

"I thought Gio wanted a small guest list."

Mari tilted her head. "Your mother is having a hard time with your move. I thought an invitation might smooth things over."

Or steer the conversation to how easy it is to find a man and settle down. A conversation Salena had heard at both Chloe's and Luca's weddings. At least at Chloe and Dante's formal wedding, Salena was busy playing maid of honor and didn't have time to listen to her parents' disappointment for hours on end. *"That could be you up there"*; *"You need to find a nice Italian boy and settle down"*; *"You never introduce us to the men you date"*; *"How are you supposed to have babies if you don't get married?"* That last comment had been especially nice and pushed Salena to remind her parents that babies came from sex, not wedding cake. A fact they well knew but decidedly ignored. Salena's nephew was born five months after Daniella's marriage, premature, at seven pounds three ounces.

Mari's hand reached Salena's shoulder, and her voice softened. "The sooner they see that moving out isn't a threat to your safety and well-being, the sooner they'll accept your decisions."

"The only way they'll accept anything is if I have a ring on my finger."

Mari's shrug suggested she agreed. But instead of making a comment, she smiled and walked down the steps to greet Salena's parents.

"Brigida . . . Aldo, I'm so glad you made it."

Even from a distance, Salena saw her mother's gaze take in her dress and stamp it with disapproval.

Spaghetti straps attached to a tight-fitting dark blue dress that stopped right above her knees. The dress gave way to two-inch heels that she'd swapped out from the stilettos she preferred when she learned of the cobbled drive and uneven terrain. Salena knew that one of the first things out of her mother's mouth would be a question about a sweater or cover for her shoulders.

Salena cringed at the sight of the black sweater her mother had draped over her arm when she got out of the car. If Salena didn't come up with something quick, that would be on her shoulders before the ceremony even began.

"Someone is in deep thought," Nicole said as she walked to Salena's side.

"Those are my parents."

"I take it that's a bad thing."

"I wasn't expecting them." Salena blinked and moved her gaze to Emma's best friend. "Do you think Emma has anything in her closet that I could use as a cover-up?"

Nicole's eyes widened. "I'm sure she does. But it's warm—you sure you want to?"

"I don't *want* anything. But my mother will pout and make my life miserable until I put on whatever monstrosity she deems appropriate. Likely that blanket she calls a shawl she's holding right now."

Nicole's eyes moved to Salena's mother. "Ewhh."

"Yeah. Welcome to my life."

"C'mon." Nicole nodded toward the house.

"You sure Emma won't mind?"

"Positive. I'll mention it to her when she's not playing supermodel."

They both looked at Emma, who was being posed in front of the house.

"Thank you."

Nicole walked with her into the house and through the main rooms to the bedroom. The walk-in closet opened to reveal a whole bunch of expensive things that Salena wouldn't be able to afford in her lifetime. "Wow."

"Yeah. She has great taste and the money to buy it."

They walked to a section that looked to be dedicated to jackets, cardigans, and cover-ups. Salena filed through the hangers to see her choices as if she were shopping at a department store.

A high-end silk and cashmere department store.

"I think black." Nicole reached for two different styles of light covers.

Nicole held up the smaller one, where the waist stopped just below the breasts. Cap sleeves and tiny gold buttons that weren't meant to be used. The second one was longer, with three-quarter sleeves and fabric that felt like a lover's kiss on the skin.

"Either of these would be perfect," Nicole said.

"Which one do you think is more expensive?" Salena asked.

Nicole looked at the label and shrugged. "This one is Chanel. And this one . . . I don't know the brand. It looks like something she bought on our trip to Italy."

"So, stupid expensive or irreplaceable if I spill something on it." Maybe her mother's shawl wasn't a bad option. Salena shook her head. "You pick."

Nicole shoved the Chanel at her and put the other away.

She put her arms in and turned toward the mirror. "It's like a cloud."

Nicole smiled. "I love raiding Emma's closet."

Salena turned to one side, then the other. "I need richer friends."

They exited the bedroom and found Brooke and Chloe backing out of one of the bedrooms.

Chloe put a finger over her lips. "We put Leo down. Hopefully he won't be cranky during the ceremony."

"I haven't seen him cranky yet," Salena said.

"He has his moments," Brooke informed her as they walked out of the hall and into the living room.

Chloe looked at the cover-up on her shoulders and grinned. "Going for conservative over sexy, are we?"

"My parents are here."

Chloe scowled. "What kind of *Brigida sweater* does she have today?"

"It looked more like a blanket than a piece of clothing," Nicole answered for Salena.

"It can't be that bad," Brooke said.

"It is."

Back outside, they caught sight of Salena's parents walking toward the location of the ceremony, with Mari at their side.

The photographer called Chloe and Nicole over for more pictures, which left Salena and Brooke standing alone. "Where did Franny run off to?"

"To find Luca to show him her dress."

"Oh, yeah. Where are the guys?"

"In the winery. I'm going over there now to drag her back in case the photographer needs her. Wanna join me?"

"Love to, but if I don't greet my parents, I won't hear the end of it."

They both stepped off the porch and headed in different directions.

Salena rolled her shoulders back and lifted her chin as she approached her parents.

"Oh, good," Mari said the moment Salena was in earshot. "I'll leave your parents with you so I can go find my son before everything begins." Mari kissed Brigida's cheek and patted Aldo on his shoulder as she walked away.

"Mama." Salena leaned in to kiss her mother's cheek.

"It's been forever," Brigida complained.

"It's been three days since I visited."

"Don't correct your mama," her father chided.

Complaint number one and snap number one . . . Do we hear a two?

Salena moved to her father and received a cold shoulder, though he did allow her to kiss his cheek.

"I'm glad to see you found something to cover your shoulders. This is a wedding, not a nightclub," her father said.

Snap and complaint number two! All in one statement.

"Can we please leave the nastiness back in Little Italy. Today is about Giovanni and Emma. Not about your disdain for my choices in life."

Her father shifted his eyes to hers. "Are you schooling me on propriety, young lady?"

"No, Papa. I would never be so bold." Yeah, she would. But not at a wedding before it even began.

Her mother looked away, as if uncomfortable. "I see your car made it."

Salena tried to smile. "I'm just as surprised as you."

"If you were living at home instead of paying rent, maybe you could afford a newer one."

Salena took a deep breath and bit her tongue.

Oh, why did Mari have to invite her parents?

CHAPTER FIVE

Ryan was two shots and one beer in before the guests started to arrive.

Gio and Luca stopped at one shot while Dante and Ryan kept up with each other.

He supposed if he were the one getting married, he wouldn't want to be tipsy during the ceremony either. And Luca, well, he was a family man, and Ryan assumed that responsibility for his wife and two kids would keep him from overindulging this early in the day.

"Here." Dante held the flask out to Ryan.

"I'm good for now."

"No, hold on to it. If Chloe catches me with it, she's going to remind me of our wedding day and the green hue on her finger that lasted a week."

"I never saw it," Gio said.

"Me either," Luca added.

"You bought her a fake ring?" Ryan asked.

"We were drinking . . ." Dante pointed the flask at Ryan. "There was this chapel in Vegas."

"Ah!" Ryan reached for the flask and set it aside before putting on his jacket and securing it in an inside pocket. "You know where to find it."

"Okay, well, I'm going to go check on my sister and my parents," Ryan announced as he reached to shake Gio's hand. "I'll see you out there."

"Tell Em I love her."

Ryan smiled. "I will."

He slipped out of the winery and glanced through the crowd that was starting to assemble.

His gaze found his brother and sister-in-law above all the others. They were talking with one of his father's employees that had been invited. Not bothering to join them, he walked to the house, where he knew Emma would be waiting. All the while, he scanned the guests, looking for Salena. With many of the D'Angelo guests being Italian, most had dark hair and olive skin. So only looking for those features wasn't going to work.

He didn't see her.

He passed the reception tent that was buzzing with caterers rushing around, setting up the bar, and preparing for the party.

At the house, he let himself in without knocking and found his mother talking with Brooke, Chloe, and Nicole. Franny sat on the couch with a cell phone in her hands. "Hello, ladies."

"Don't you look handsome," his mother said.

"I can't be completely upstaged by all the beautiful women. You all look fantastic."

"Nothing that three hours of prepping won't accomplish," Nicole teased.

"Where's Emma?"

"In her room talking with your father," Beth said.

"Ouch."

"Oh, stop. I'm sure it's fine," she said.

Ryan glanced at Nicole, who knew the family history better than anyone. While Emma and their father were on better terms, you never did know when their father would turn on the professional asshole switch.

Nicole faked a smile.

"How is it looking out there?" Chloe asked.

"It's filling up."

Heavy footsteps accompanied his father as he walked into the room. "Oh, good. You're here. I was beginning to wonder," Robert said when he noticed Ryan in the room.

"I've been here since before you arrived. Gio and the guys needed my support."

Robert narrowed his eyes. "And whiskey, I assume."

Ryan didn't deny the facts. "They only needed help drinking it."

"Oh no," Chloe huffed.

"Don't worry, I cut them off after five shots."

His mother gasped.

"Joking, Mom." Ryan walked around them. "I have a message to deliver to my sister."

"That boy . . . ," he heard his mother going on as he left the room.

He found Emma standing with her back to the door and staring out the window.

She wore a long fitted silk gown that many women couldn't pull off. Her hair was piled high, with only a spray of flowers sprinkled in against the amber hair that matched her temper.

Ryan cleared his throat to gain her attention.

Emma twisted and instantly smiled.

He caught his breath. "Wow."

She laughed and looked down at herself. "Is it okay?"

"Giovanni is going to lose his shit when he sees you."

"Ahh . . ." She opened her arms, and Ryan pulled her in for a long hug. "I'm so happy."

"I know," he said in her ear. "Dad didn't upset you, did he?"

"No," she said, pulling away. "He really is trying."

"Good."

"I appreciate you looking out for me."

Ryan held both her hands. "Always will, sis. Married or not."

"How is Giovanni?"

"Anxious to see you."

She smiled.

"He wanted me to tell you he loves you."

Emma's eyes instantly swelled with tears, and she blew out a quick breath.

"Don't do that, you'll mess stuff up."

She released his hands and started fanning her face as if that would stop the crying.

Ryan reached into his jacket and handed her a handkerchief.

"Oh my God, you have one of these in your pocket?" She lightly batted her eyes and controlled the waterworks.

"Dad sucked at a lot of dad things, but he taught us some of the basics."

Emma handed him back the handkerchief and hooked her arm through his, and they walked out of the room. "Have you seen Salena?"

"Who says I'm looking for Salena?"

"Oh, please. I might be busy getting married, but I know when my brother is flirting with a woman."

He huffed. "I'm that obvious?"

"Gio says she's a bit wild."

"Oh yeah?"

They approached the living room, and she said softly, "I reminded Gio that so are you."

The wedding coordinator approached them as soon as they entered the living room. "It looks like most of the seats are filled and only a couple of cars waiting to be parked." The woman glanced at her watch and then at the clipboard in her hands. "Right on time."

Twenty minutes later, Ryan eased himself into a seat in between his brother and his aunt and uncle as the music changed and the grandparents were seated to the music.

Ryan took the opportunity of twisting around in his seat to watch the processional to scan for Salena. He found her a row back from his on the other side of the aisle.

Her eyes stared into his and then shifted to the man on her left. Older, a little stocky, and saying something close to the ear of the woman sitting beside him.

Her parents, maybe? Ryan wasn't sure. But she looked about as happy sitting beside them as Ryan usually felt beside his father.

He offered her a smile and a shrug. As he did, he opened his jacket enough that she could see the flask hidden inside.

She glared and mouthed the word *bitch* but then quickly smiled.

Their across-the-aisle attention was quickly diverted to the activity at hand.

Everyone filed in as they normally did at a wedding, and when it came time for the bride, Ryan watched Giovanni's composure when Emma came into sight.

Just as Ryan predicted, the man lost his shit. Like a person who was sucker punched in the chest, Gio let the vision of her blow him over as tears filled his eyes.

Yeah, this man adored his sister.

And Ryan loved him for it.

~

As soon as the ceremony was over and the bride, groom, and wedding party departed for the last formal pictures . . . everyone else headed to the open bar.

Salena abandoned her parents as soon as she could and sought out Ryan and his handy flask instead of getting in line.

He stood outside the reception tent, his eyes locked on hers.

She opened her palm the moment she stopped by his side. "You're a tease," she told him.

Ryan reached into his pocket. "That bad, huh?"

Salena accepted the flask and opened it. "I was not expecting my parents." She sniffed the contents of the container, thankful it wasn't tequila, and drank. The burn down the back of her throat helped soothe the tension.

"Aren't they friends of the family, too?"

"Yeah, but this was supposed to be a small wedding, and my parents hadn't made the cut."

Ryan placed a hand on her waist and encouraged her to move to the side as a couple walked past them into the tent. "Funny how that didn't work out. At least it wasn't as big as Emma's first wedding."

"How many people were there for that ill-fated marriage?"

"At least three hundred."

Salena coughed at the number. "Who knows three hundred people?"

Ryan shrugged. "The wine industry is always trying to one-up the other. And my father had his hands in that pie. The fact that there aren't any wine magazine paparazzi here proves he stayed out of it."

She looked around, recognizing at least half of the faces in the crowd. After another short swig, she handed the flask back to Ryan.

"There you are." A voice behind Salena caught their attention.

Richard stood close, pointing at Ryan. "The photographer is looking for you. They want a family picture."

"Coming."

Richard walked away.

Ryan held open his jacket. "Want to keep ahold of this?"

She shook her head. "I'm good."

Ryan moved to go around her and hesitated. He leaned close and said in a voice only she could hear, "You look incredible." And he was gone.

It wasn't her norm to get too excited about a compliment from the opposite sex, but the way his voice dropped and the feel of his breath on her ear had a shiver singing down her spine.

"Who is that?"

Her mother's voice felt like nails on a chalkboard as the woman caught Salena drooling over Ryan's backside as he walked away.

"Nobody." Her reply was instant. Something she did whenever her mother asked about a guy Salena was seen with.

"Obviously not a nobody. Everyone here is a somebody."

"It's Emma's brother."

"Oh." Her mother turned to look at Ryan, too. "Not Italian."

Thank God, or Salena would be on her mother's matchmaking list all night. "Nope!" She headed into the reception. "I think it's time for a drink."

The afternoon bled into the evening, and the music turned up when the party got started.

Thankfully, with the music filling the space, Salena's parents moved to the outer edges and talked with the people they knew from their neighborhood. As the men stripped their ties from their necks, Salena left Emma's cover-up at the table she sat at and hit the dance floor.

Disappointment shot from her mother's eyes from time to time, but Salena ignored it and took comfort in the sheer number of people that were shedding their jackets and sweaters.

Salena danced with Chloe and let Dante swing her around a time or two. Brooke and Franny jumped around together as baby Leo was passed from family member to family member. It was when Salena was dancing with Luca that Ryan made it onto the dance floor. A crowd favorite was playing, and all the dance moves were fast and entertaining.

"'Bout time you got out here," Salena told Ryan.

"You've been busy," he teased.

"You've been watching."

His eyes did a quick dance up and down her frame. "Not a hardship."

Ryan wasn't out there for a minute before the DJ switched pace and played a slow song.

He reached out a hand and wiggled his fingers. "Much more my style," he told her.

"You're timing is suspicious." Not that it stopped her from stepping into his arms.

"I might have said something to the DJ."

His hand pressed into her spine and pulled her closer.

"You're pretty sure of yourself." Salena gave him the side-eye. Easy to do with his face so close to hers.

"I think we have that in common."

Understatement.

Salena looked over his shoulder at everyone watching the dance floor.

Her father's gaze moved over them dancing, but her mother was in deep conversation with the woman on her right.

Beyond them, Ryan's parents were standing apart from each other, both talking with different groups of people.

"Men have it easy," Salena whispered.

"Oh? Why is that?"

"Your parents couldn't care less you're dancing with someone." She moved so that Ryan could look at her father without being obvious. "My dad is pitching flames from his eyes."

The moment Ryan's eyes found her father, she felt him pull back slightly. "That's a cold stare."

"You would think I was sixteen."

"Some fathers protect their daughters."

"More like smother. It gets old."

"Emma would say it's better than being ignored," Ryan told her.

Another turn and glance her father's way took all the joy of dancing right out of her.

"Do you need some air?" she asked Ryan as she fanned herself with the tips of her fingers. "I need some air."

Ryan stopped dancing. "Let's go."

With a hand on her back, he directed her off the dance floor and outside of the massive tent.

A deep breath pulled cool air into her lungs that instantly soothed the jumping nerves her parents had created.

Several people were outside mingling. Some were snapping pictures, taking advantage of the gorgeous sunset. This was where people went to escape the noise.

After walking away from the reception tent, Salena felt some of the tension her parents put on her shoulders ease. "Today has not gone the way I wanted it to."

"Your parents really rattle you." His eyes found hers.

"Tensions are high right now. My sister got pregnant within a year of moving out. So of course, they believe that is going to happen to me."

His eyes narrowed. "You don't seem like a person who makes someone else's mistakes."

"I'm not. I make plenty of my own. I don't need Daniella's suggestions."

Ryan laughed. "I understand family drama."

"What about Catholic guilt?"

He shook his head. "No. Thankfully."

"Family drama with God as the mediator. There's no winning."

Ryan started to laugh, and with that, Salena found a smile. His hand brushed a strand of hair from her face, and the air charged with something other than tension.

"What are the chances of me being able to drag you out of here later?"

His question didn't surprise her. If anything, she expected it.

Her answer, on the other hand, frustrated the ever-loving crap out of her. "And explain my absence to the ice king for the next six months?"

A brief wave of disappointment flashed on Ryan's face. He glanced away, then back quickly. "We're being watched."

She closed her eyes and held still, forcing herself not to look over her shoulder, knowing her father was likely lurking. "You see my dilemma."

He sighed and dropped his hand to his side. "Are you leaving tomorrow?"

"I'm on first shift. I told Mari and Luca I'd open so they could take their time coming back tomorrow."

Ryan nodded toward the parking lot all over the front of the property. "You expect that car to get you there?"

Salena appreciated the change of subject and rolled her eyes at Ryan's comment. "She'll be fine. I have this oil additive thing that limps it along."

"*Oil additive thing*?" His words were slow.

"It's this stuff that saves me from spending good money after bad. It will make it. It always does." Okay, that was a full-on lie. The car had left her stranded on several occasions, hence the reason she didn't go far from her neighborhood unless someone else was driving. The oil issue was new. A leak somewhere, according to the last guy she dated . . . or saw twice, as it stood.

"How about I follow you back to San Diego to make sure you get there?"

She stopped thinking about her car and stared at him. Surprised by his suggestion.

"You wouldn't want another reason for your parents to give you a hard time. Breaking down on the freeway with everyone you know here busy with the day-after activities," Ryan added.

Salena's mouth gaped open. "You want to follow me back to San Diego."

"Make sure you get there safe."

And what else? "I promised Luca I wouldn't bring men back to my place."

Ryan's smile grew bigger. "I was suggesting making sure you got home. Not making sure you were late opening the restaurant."

It was her turn to grin. "You would drive all the way back to San Diego just to—"

"Yes."

"And that's all?"

"Yeah." He looked to the side and back. "And talk you into giving me your phone number."

She wanted to give him a hell of a lot more than her phone number. But since he was asking so nicely . . . "That's more than a fair trade."

"Good." He glanced over her shoulder again.

"He's still there, isn't he?" she asked.

"Yup."

Salena pulled her shoulders back and sighed. "Shouldn't they be cutting the cake by now?"

He offered her his arm. "Let's go find out."

CHAPTER SIX

Salena's eyes opened to quiet and the early-morning sun.

The kind of silence that normally made you think the world wasn't right. The kind of silence she never experienced living in Little Italy.

Reality crashed back in. It was the day after the ball, and her pumpkin needed to be driven home.

She stumbled out of bed and straight to the shower.

Once the sleep was pushed away by hot water and shampoo, Salena tiptoed through the sleeping house to the kitchen, in hopes of making some coffee before she had to leave.

Those dreams dashed to a halt when she took in the scene on the living room sofa.

Luca was sound asleep with Leo snuggled up next to him, a pacifier completely forgotten and lying to one side of Leo's cheek.

It was so damn adorable, Salena found herself staring for a solid minute as father and son pulled in deep, restful breaths.

So much for coffee. Making it would wake them up, and Salena didn't have the heart to do that.

Instead, she backtracked through the house and packed her bag. Instead of leaving through the front door, she exited from the back and walked around the house.

Ryan was already there, standing over her car with the hood propped open.

"Good morning," she said as she sauntered his way.

He looked up, an easy smile on his lips. "Morning. How did you sleep?"

"I didn't want to get out of bed. Everyone is still asleep in there."

"How late was it when the last guest left?"

"It wasn't too bad. Midnight or so."

Ryan had taken off a half hour before the last of the guests found their cars. Her parents being part of that group. It was like they didn't want to leave until Ryan was long gone.

She nodded toward the car. "You know your way around an engine?"

"The basics. I'm better with motorcycles."

Salena opened the back door and tossed her bag in. Then she popped the trunk and removed one of the three bottles of oil she had and one smaller container with an additive that helped stop leaks.

"This should be all it needs."

Ryan took the bottle from her hand and looked at the label. "I've heard of this stuff but have never seen it in use."

She rounded to the trunk again and found the funnel she kept close by and a greasy rag. "Put that in first and then the oil, if it's low."

"You do this all the time?"

"Often enough."

Ryan grasped the funnel and proceeded to pour the additive in.

"We need to stop at a Starbucks or somewhere before we get on the freeway."

"Not a problem." He finished with the additive and then checked the oil. "You're really low."

"Think it will take two quarts?" As she asked the question, she moved back to her trunk.

"How much do you have in there?"

"Four, but it never takes that much. I buy them by the case."

Ryan looked at her from around the hood. "Did you ever stop and think about the cost of oil versus the cost of the repair?"

She shook her head. "Every time anyone looks at this car, they tell me I'm wasting my money fixing it."

The half smile on Ryan's face suggested he agreed.

"And . . . I'm told it needs a dozen things that I can't afford to fix." Salena handed him a second quart. "So, I dump that stuff in it, top off the oil after any significant drive, and voilà. I'm good to go."

He put in the second quart before telling her to turn over the engine.

Salena slid behind the wheel and turned the key.

It hesitated for a moment and then fired up.

The engine coughed a couple of times before finding its rhythm. The smoke that had come out of it when she arrived had dimmed significantly. "See?" she called from the driver's seat.

Ryan closed the hood and wiped his hands on the rag she'd handed him. "I'll still feel better following you home."

"I'm not sure why you want to spend your morning on this, but who am I to argue?"

"Arguing is a waste of time. I'll lead us to coffee, and then I'll follow you."

"Okay."

Salena watched as Ryan got into a 4Runner and smiled at her from behind the windshield.

As promised, they found a coffee shop, where Ryan bought her a double cappuccino and himself a plain black coffee.

When they hit the freeway, Ryan followed a couple of car lengths behind and endured the occasional puff of smoke that exited her tailpipe.

Her oil light had eased off on blinking, but the check engine light, which never really went out, kept her on her toes.

Sunday-morning traffic was light, and the drive into San Diego took just over an hour.

But more importantly, the car made it without having an asthma attack.

She pulled into her parking spot behind the restaurant, and Ryan took up Luca's space beside her.

Little Italy was coming to life with the restaurants that offered breakfast. The D'Angelos had always been a lunch and dinner place that had a few brunch items on the menu for those that needed eggs until noon. Still, the cooks and opening staff would be there by nine thirty for a ten thirty opening, which gave Salena plenty of time to get ready for the day.

Ryan stepped out of the car and looked up at the building. "So . . . this is D'Angelo's?"

"You've never been here before?"

He shook his head. "I've been meaning to."

"Let me show you."

"You sure I'm not cramping your time?"

Was this guy for real? He'd just spent his morning babysitting her drive back from Temecula and now was suggesting he take off without so much as a glass of water. "We don't open until ten thirty. I just need to be here for the morning staff to get in the door." She pulled her bag from the car and walked to the steps leading to the back entrance. There, she set her bag down and fumbled with the keys.

Ryan stepped up beside her and took possession of her bag.

She glanced at him, her bag, and back to him. Without a word, she smiled and let them in.

An alarm instantly started to chime. She moved to the control panel to turn it off. It was only the second time she'd actually had to turn the alarm off since she'd moved in. There was almost always family around—or trusted employees in the mix, getting things ready for the day.

"You can leave that here," she said, pointing to her bag. "That's the door to the apartments upstairs." She pointed a thumb behind her. "This is the way to the restaurant."

Turning on lights as she went, she spread her arms wide. "Obviously the kitchen."

They walked through to the restaurant, lights flickering.

"Mari's father ran this before she and her late husband took over. A lot of the newer restaurants have a modern, more San Diego vibe. A few, like this, keep a traditional Italian feel."

Ryan walked past her, ran his hand along the bar top. "Emma said it felt like Italy."

"Have you been?"

"Once, when I was like ten. All I remember is wineries and pasta . . . and my mom complaining that she was going to gain weight."

Salena laughed.

"What about you, have you been?" he asked.

"Once when I was too young to remember, and again when I was twelve for an aunt's funeral."

Ryan pointed to his left. "What's in there?"

"The Grotto." She walked into the smaller room. One they used for intimate parties and special occasions. With low lighting and a wine cellar feel, it was hard not to enjoy.

"This is nice."

"Friday and Saturday reservations for this room are months out."

"It must have been a big hit to stay closed for the wedding," Ryan mused.

Salena knew firsthand the kind of financial loss a closed Saturday meant for the D'Angelos. "According to Mari, the day she puts money in front of her family is the day she's closing her doors."

Lost in his own thoughts, Ryan shook his head. "I wish everyone thought like that."

"Italian families seem to."

"Huh . . ." Ryan glanced around the room and settled his eyes on hers.

"Let me show you the best part."

"Lead the way."

They meandered through the restaurant and back to where her bag stood at the doorway to the stairs that led to the apartments. Using a keypad, she opened that door with a number lock and turned off yet another alarm.

"You guys take security seriously."

"This is new. Now that Luca is the only man here, he thought it was important to add another layer of security for the family." She shrugged. "I'm good with it."

"Me too."

Salena blinked in his direction. "What?"

He shook his head, grabbed her bag. "Nothing. I'm following you."

She led him up the stairs, pointed at the door on the second floor. "Mari's place." They rounded the corner to the third floor. "Luca and Brooke's."

Finally, the fourth floor, which had two doors. One for her apartment and the other door for the terrace. She opened the door without a key. "My place."

"You don't lock it?"

She laughed and started holding up fingers for each of her points. "One key, two alarms, and a keypad . . . I think I'm good."

"But you can, right?"

"It locks."

Inside, she told him to leave her bag by the door and crossed to the sliding doors that opened to the terrace. She stepped outside and walked to the edge of the building. A view of San Diego's bay stretched out before them. "This upstairs apartment was mainly a guest room when company came for the family. The terrace is used for family dinners and sunsets."

"It's fantastic."

"Great digs for San Diego. Chloe and Dante rent a condo between here and Point Loma. Close to the marina." She pointed across the bay.

"Boats are his business, right?"

"Private charters. Yeah." She thought about her friends, how Dante was working his business and Chloe was entering a whole new world of online yoga courses, collaborating with women of like-minded vision.

Unlike Salena, everyone around her seemed to be figuring out what to do with their lives . . . and here she was just now getting out from under her parents' thumbs. Only this weekend proved that maybe even that was an illusion.

"When did Mari lose her husband?"

"Oh, God . . . uhm . . . we were in high school. Eight, nine years now. She's a pretty remarkable woman. I don't know if my mother could have done what she has."

"Your mom seemed capable."

"And you got that from what? 'Hello'? Or 'nice to meet you'?" Not that Salena thought less of her mother, but she'd never seen the woman do much of anything other than raise her kids and accept whatever her father made for money. No outside hobbies or even close friends. It was strange when you looked at it from an outside lens.

Ryan narrowed his eyes. "You don't think much of them."

She sighed. "I love my parents. I do. I'm just over being the little girl they feel the need to helicopter over. This weekend was a prime example. Mari wanted to assure them I'm fine, so they ended up at the wedding. I had to raid your sister's closet to put something on over my shoulders just to keep them from damning me over my choice of dress. I was told no less than three times that I didn't need to have another drink. I was asked twice where I was sleeping, and then they left with a promise from me that I'd be by later tonight for a Sunday dinner."

Ryan blinked several times. "That's a lot."

Salena shook her head. "Whatever. That's all my drama."

They headed back into her apartment. "I have a friend in town that owns a shop. If you want, I can take your car over and have him take a look at it," Ryan said.

As much as she liked the sound of that . . . "I can't afford the repairs right now."

He opened her front door and turned to her. "He mentors students from the local high school. They do a lot of labor for free. All you have to do is buy the parts."

"Wait, what?"

"High school automotive programs are hard to come by these days." Ryan smiled. "It can't hurt for him to look."

She hesitated, crossed her arms over her chest. "W-why are you doing this?"

"Doing what?"

"Being so . . . helpful." Considering he was headed out the door and hadn't made one suggestive comment, or even put a finger on her since their dance the night before . . . she was starting to wonder what his motive really was.

A slow smile split his lips, and Ryan leaned against the door frame. "In case you missed it, I think we have a connection. I want to see you again."

She hesitated. "What? Like friends?"

He laughed. "What about a date?"

Salena thought of the warnings Chloe had voiced. Ryan was a part of her extended family, and Salena was living in said family's home. "Dating can lead to emotional attachment. And that gets messy."

He looked like he wanted to question her logic further but decided against it. "What about friends with a possible benefit package?" he asked.

Okay, now he was talking her language. She found her footing and smirked. "That depends on the package."

Ryan tossed his head back and laughed. He held out his hand. "Give me your keys, *Trouble*."

Much as she liked the idea of telling him she didn't need his help with her car, Salena wasn't an idiot. Parts and not labor was probably her best bet in keeping her piece of junk on the road a little longer.

She grabbed her keys from the counter and handed them over.

His fingers grazed hers, with a physical zap. One made by static electricity.

Looking up at him, she half expected him to take that opportunity to make a move to kiss her. And maybe, for a moment, he considered it, by the look in his eyes.

Instead, he lifted the keys from her fingertips and waved them in the air. "I need your phone number."

Sly . . .

She put her hand out, palm up, and he gave her his phone.

Salena typed in her number and hit call. With one ring from her phone in her back pocket, she knew they now had the ability to call and text.

"I'll be back later."

She lifted her chin. "Thanks."

He smiled. "No problem." And then he turned and left. "I'll lock the door behind me," he called out.

"It does it automatically." She moved to watch him walk away.

"Even better."

Only once his footsteps left the stairwell and the door from the living space to the restaurant closed behind him did she walk away.

CHAPTER SEVEN

Ryan dialed a number, put the phone on speaker, and dropped it in his lap.

It took four rings for Mateo to answer. "Hey, buddy. You're up early."

A traffic light went red, and Ryan hit the brakes. The damn things didn't respond at first, so he hit them again.

"Early and in town."

"Wait . . . didn't your sister get married yesterday?"

"She sure did. Great guy this time."

"And you're already in San Diego? Did the party fizzle with all those stuffy wine people?"

"No. Emma married into an Italian family. They know how to party, believe me."

The light turned green, and he hit the gas. When he did, no less than three lights started blinking on the dashboard. "Really, Salena?" he said under his breath.

"Who's Salena?"

Ryan hit the dash, and one of the lights went off. "A woman. You wouldn't happen to be at the shop, would you?"

"Wasn't really planning on it. Sunday and all."

That's what he thought would be the answer. "Are all the lifts being used?"

"One is free. What's up?"

"Mind if I use it?"

Mateo laughed. "Considering you're my silent partner, I don't know why you're asking."

Ryan eased onto the freeway and really hoped the car would make it a few miles. The thing was seriously jacked up. "Common courtesy."

"There can't possibly be anything that wrong with your 4Runner."

"No . . . it's a . . . friend's car."

"A female-type friend . . . Maybe her name is Salena?"

Ryan paused, confused that Mateo knew her name. "How do you know about her?"

"Dude, really? You just said her name."

The car hiccupped, and the oil light went back on. "Jesus, woman, how do you drive this thing?"

Mateo started laughing. "Let yourself in. Give me thirty minutes."

"You don't have to—"

"If you're cussing out a car, you're in over your head."

The man wasn't wrong. Ryan's wheelhouse was motorcycles. And yeah, he understood the basics behind the engine of a car, but fixing them was never his strong point.

"Thanks, man. I owe you."

"Don't break anything."

He slapped at the dashboard again. "I don't think there's much left here to break."

Mateo was laughing as he hung up the phone.

Ryan didn't dare push the speed limit on the car. The fact that Salena was driving this—only thirty minutes or so before—and reaching seventy-five on the drive back from Temecula was shocking.

Mateo's shop was in Chula Vista above the 805 freeway, which put it in a slightly better part of town. This did two things for the business. First, it was simply safer. Even though Ryan had to unlock a chain-link fence and then go through a deadbolt and alarm system to get into the shop, they had yet to have a break-in. The cameras on the building helped deter vandals and anyone wanting to tag the building. And the second, it brought in business from those who could afford repairs, and sometimes modifications, as well as those like Salena who didn't have a cushion in their bank account to keep their cars on the road.

Mateo did, in fact, help a lot of the local kids learn about cars and offered them use of the shop as he supervised their work. Mainly, the kids worked on their own beat-up pieces of crap. Because of Mateo's desire to pay it forward to the teenagers, this also kept the shop crime-free.

Inside the building, there was a small reception area with five whole chairs, a table filled with magazines that dated back at least three years, and a television mounted on the wall. The space was functional . . . not fancy.

Ryan pushed through the door leading into a hallway that split off to an actual office, a break room, and of course, the door to the shop itself. A storage room in the back of the building was under yet another lock and key. While Ryan had keys to everything, he couldn't remember if there was a time he'd actually needed to use any but those for the gate and front door.

He headed to the break room first and went through the motions of brewing a pot of coffee. Only first, he needed to pour out something that looked like crude oil, complete with a film floating on top.

More than once, Ryan had seen one of the mechanics pour cold coffee into a cup, pop it in the microwave, and take it back to whatever they were working on.

Mechanics were a different breed. They ate with a percentage of engine grease as part of their diet. They ended their days with beer, sometimes before they left the shop, and started the day with a Red Bull or the before-mentioned rot-gut coffee that made your hair stand on end.

Ryan never interfered with anything at the shop. He was, as Mateo put it . . . a silent partner.

Mateo did all the heavy lifting.

Ryan was an investor. Basically, he helped finance Mateo to start up the shop. The banks were less than enthusiastic to help, so the Bank of Ryan stepped in. Easy enough to do when you had a trust fund the size of his.

He and Mateo had found the building, and Ryan purchased it. Commercial real estate wasn't on Ryan's radar, but he'd learned through his dealings with Mateo how lucrative it could be. So much so that Ryan seldom dipped into his trust fund these days. The older he got, the less he wanted to depend on his father's money to live his life. Arguably, he would always live off his father's generosity since it was that money that was initially invested, but it was Ryan's business sense that was growing that portfolio instead of just depleting it.

Apart from Mateo's place, Ryan owned a small industrial building with four shops in Temecula. All of them rented. Rent on two of the units paid for the mortgage, insurance, and cost of keeping the place up. The other two units were gravy.

Funny, though . . . with all the real estate he owned, he rented his apartment. He didn't see himself buying something in Temecula. But he hadn't moved out of the area since his mother and sister were there. But now Emma had Giovanni. And technically, Ryan's mother had always had his father. But Robert spent the majority of his time at their Napa home. And again . . . there was now Gio. A thought that had run through Ryan's head several times when it became apparent that Emma and Gio were going to marry. All any of that amounted to was Ryan now had choices. Stay in Temecula, or move to the city?

After Ryan cleaned the carafe and put on a fresh pot of coffee, he left the break room and entered the shop.

Fluorescent lights flickered to life with a hum. One of the work bays on the far end of the shop was empty, so he walked down to it and pulled on the chain to open the massive metal door leading outside.

Light from outside filled the space and helped release some of the stale air.

He considered pulling Salena's car in but thought Mateo would get a better idea of the magnitude of the car's problems by driving it around the block.

Instead of lingering outside, Ryan went back in and poured himself a cup of coffee.

It wasn't long before he heard Mateo pull in.

A jingle of keys and heavy footfalls followed the man through the door. "Where are you?" he called out.

Ryan stepped into the hall, coffee in hand. "Made it fresh."

"It's no good that way, man."

Mateo dropped a pink box on a table and reached for Ryan's hand. "Can't believe you're dragging my ass in here on a Sunday."

They shook hands before Ryan stepped to the side so Mateo could fill a cup of coffee. "I didn't drag—you volunteered."

"The thought of your pretty hands in an engine is physically painful for me to think about."

"I'm not that bad."

Mateo stared at him, lips unmoving for several seconds. "You're not that good."

Ryan chuckled. "I'll fix a motorcycle any day of the week."

His friend relented. "I'll give you that."

Ryan flipped open the lid of the pink box and pulled out a glazed donut.

Mateo stood at five ten. His frame looked as if the daily donuts were catching up to him. Or maybe it was the burrito truck that stopped by the industrial area every day at noon. The food that came out of those things was tasty, but it also kept the local cardiologist in business.

"We can't possibly eat all of these," Ryan said, looking at the dozen donuts of all shapes and varieties staring back at him.

"Day-old donuts go great with day-old coffee."

"You might want to hold off on these things, m'friend." Not that he heeded his own words. Ryan took a big bite and savored the sweet. The last time he ate a donut was the last time he stopped by this shop.

"Yeah . . . I know." Mateo reached in, snagged a maple bar. "January first will be here before you know it."

They laughed and ate the fried-flour-and-sugar goodness anyway.

"So, who's the girl?" Mateo asked between bites.

"She's a friend of Giovanni's."

"How long have you two been—"

"We aren't . . . haven't *been*." Ryan let the *been* speak for itself.

Mateo narrowed his eyes. "How long have you known her?"

Ryan knew how his answer would sound, but he said it anyway. "About forty-eight hours."

"I'm confused. Is this a favor for your sister?"

"No. Emma has no idea about this. Or Giovanni. Salena showed up at the wedding driving this thing. Smoke blowing, engine coughing. It took two quarts of oil just to limp it back here."

"That doesn't sound good."

"Take it around the block. See for yourself."

They both walked toward the front door and out to the car, holding their coffee cups. "Is this woman hot?"

Ryan held nothing back. "As fuck!"

Mateo started to laugh. A slow, low amusement that had them both laughing in no time.

~

Sometime after one, Salena found a message on her phone from Ryan asking if she needed her car anytime soon.

With a couple of questions, *soon* was defined as the next week. And since the most she'd driven it in the last month had been to the wedding and back, she assured Ryan that her life wouldn't end without a car for seven days.

She had plenty of questions, but the lunch rush was still clicking, and she was running food and seating customers to make up for the waitress they were down.

Even with a little missing help, D'Angelo's ran without many bumps. Sundays in Little Italy were busy. Lots of tourists no matter what time of year . . . and locals that didn't have to punch in at work on the weekend.

Around two thirty, Salena was able to break away from helping customers and went into the office to catch up on a few things there.

Soon after sitting at Mari's desk, a knock on the open door had her looking up.

Ryan stood there with a smile. "Hey."

"Hi." She looked beyond him, saw the hall empty. "Did you come in the back?"

"No." Ryan pointed a thumb behind him. "Sergio, is it? The bartender . . . said you were back here. I hope it's okay."

"Of course."

"There's a lot of familiar faces out there from the wedding."

Salena nodded. "Yeah. Just about everyone on staff was invited. Then again, most of these guys have worked here since I was a kid." She indicated the seat across from the desk. "Have a seat."

"Your car . . . ," he started.

"Is a mess, I know. But I can't afford a newer one, so please don't tell me it's not worth fixing."

After sitting, Ryan leaned forward with his elbows on his knees and stared at her.

"If you run it much longer with that oil leak, you won't be debating between repairs and new, since you'll likely freeze your engine and kill the thing. Your oil filler fix is not supposed to be permanent."

"What's that gonna cost?" The last time she'd heard the number, it was out of her range.

"Parts. My buddy is compiling a list now."

"You left the car there?"

He nodded. "It's up on a lift with lots of pieces removed to get to the biggest issues. Every dashboard light was blinking."

Salena probably should have been embarrassed, but she was too broke to give that much thought. "It's always Christmas in my car. Lots of red lights blinking on and off."

Ryan didn't look amused. "Your brakes are shot."

"But my tires are good," she countered.

"Your starter is going out."

"The heater works."

"The passenger-side window doesn't roll down."

"There aren't that many passengers in my car."

He pointed a finger her way. "I asked him to find the most critical issues."

Salena sat back in her chair and sighed. "I can't afford an overhaul."

"Mateo knows that. He should have most, if not all, of the answers in the next day or two. And so long as you don't need it anytime soon, he can work on it with his students and save the money from a professional mechanic."

"Isn't Mateo a professional?"

"Yeah, but he won't be doing most of the work. He directs the students, oversees, and checks everything. Experience for them and cost-effective for you."

Salena knew on the way up to the wedding that she was driving the car into the ground. And as much as she hated the timing, she really didn't have much of a choice in fixing a few things. "Fine."

Ryan slapped his hands on his knees and stood. "Good. I'll keep in touch with Mateo and let you in on his findings."

She tilted her head. "Wouldn't it be more efficient for me to have Mateo's number?"

"Probably. But what better excuse to call you than to have information about your car?"

"Do you need an excuse?"

He hesitated. "Probably not. But I'm going to use it anyway."

Salena liked his conclusion and, even more, liked the way he smiled at her.

"I should let you get back to work," Ryan said.

She stood. "Might be a good idea."

He waved to the back door. "Mind if I go this way?"

"I'll walk you out."

They passed the kitchen and the door leading to the apartments and walked outside. Unlike when they arrived, the music of people talking on the streets lingered in the air.

Salena turned to Ryan the moment they reached his car. "You do know that you didn't have to do any of this to get my phone number, right?"

"I didn't *just* get your phone number." His smile was a hair past wicked. "I guaranteed myself the opportunity to see you again."

"Ah . . ."

"And . . . maybe put myself in the 'trusted men' category. There's a lot of assholes out there. Women can't be too careful."

"Did having a sister teach you that?" Salena asked.

"Pretty much."

A gust of wind blew Salena's hair into her eyes. She brushed it away and tilted her head to the side.

Ryan's gaze met hers, his eyes drifted to her lips and back up.

He took a step closer.

She lifted her chin. A sample of his "benefit package" lingered between them.

One corner of his mouth lifted. "You sure you're going to be okay without a car for the week?"

She leaned forward, his body well into her personal space but not close enough. "I'm positive. Are you going to kiss me, or just think about it?"

Ryan held back a laugh and looked up at the sky. "Ah, man. You are something."

"I know."

That made him laugh. But when his eyes met hers again, his mirth subsided slightly. "If I kiss you now, then everything I did today counts as some kind of transaction. And that's not why I did it."

"Liar." The word came out of her mouth so fast she couldn't stop it.

He glanced to the side. "Okay, maybe it's a little why I did it." He squeezed his thumb and forefinger together and made an inch of space between them. "But I'm better than that."

Ryan leaned back, ending the possibility of that lingering kiss.

She was disappointed, and a tad impressed by his restraint. "Okay, then . . ." Salena stood tall and pulled her shoulders back. "I'll get back to work."

His eyes followed her as she walked around him.

"I'll call you," he said with a lift in his voice as she walked away.

Salena raised a hand and two fingers in the air while his chuckle followed her inside.

CHAPTER EIGHT

Some people went to gyms to keep fit.

Chloe spent her time bending and balancing on a yoga mat and taught others to do the same.

Salena, on the other hand, wrapped her limbs around a pole and channeled her inner stripper.

Ashlynn's Goddess Within was a ten-minute Uber ride away from Little Italy. As much as Salena would have no problem owning her desire to pole dance and tell the world, that world would get back to her parents and require a loud and chaotic conversation.

Or maybe just yelling and screaming.

Either way, only a handful of her girlfriends knew she spent her time learning all the moves and keeping her body in shape by dancing with a pole.

The Uber driver dropped her off across the street from the studio, five minutes late for her class.

Salena did a double take on the traffic and jaywalked in a half jog to her destination.

A bell rang on the door as she dashed in.

The warmth of the studio made it easy for her to pull the light sweatshirt from her shoulders as she hustled past the empty reception desk and around the corner to where everyone was already warming up.

"There you are. I was wondering if you were going to make it." Ashlynn stood in a tight spandex top that covered her barely-there breasts and boy shorts that were at least one size too small. Her blonde hair had a streak of purple that framed her face and the ice-blue eyes that everyone noticed first about her.

"Car is in the shop," Salena commented as she kicked off her shoes and tossed them to the wall with everyone else's backpacks and purses.

"You need a sugar daddy to buy you a new one," Elsa, one of the other advanced dancers, teased.

Salena pulled off her loose-fitting pants and added them to her mess on the floor. Next, her hair came up into a high ponytail. Finally, she blew out a long breath and felt her pulse returning to normal.

There were three empty poles in the room, so she took up residence beside one.

Sultry music you would expect in a smoky bar, if they still had those, filled the room.

Salena moved into a series of stretches to help warm up the muscles in her body.

Ashlynn clapped her hands over the music and took up her position in front of the class. "It's time to add on to the routine we started on the first of the month. And since I haven't seen many of you during my open pole time, let's recap."

Ashlynn looked directly at Salena with her comment on missing free pole sessions for practice.

"There was a wedding," she said in her defense.

Ashlynn smiled and started to call out the positions on the pole as she moved through the routine.

As she did, the other students went through the motions as well. All while Salena continued her warm-up.

By the time the class had gone through the choreography one time, she felt limber enough to join in.

She started like everyone else, flirting with the pole, moving around it in slow, thoughtful strides. With a grip of one hand on the pole, she hooked one foot and spun around to the other side. Each move lent itself to the next, like chords on a piano.

When she first joined the studio, she memorized all the names of the moves they put together to make the dance. Hook and Arch, Fireman Spin, Cupid, Chair Spin, the Gemini. The list was longer than she expected, and each one took skill, style, and more importantly, strength to make the person watching think there was no effort in the dance. Now the names were only a passing thought as she put them together.

The studio was filled with women of all ages, sizes, and skill levels. Some were brought there by the novelty of it all and stayed because of the way pole dancing inspired them. No one stuck around because it was easy. It wasn't. The physical strength and stamina it took to gracefully move your body up and down a pole, to music . . . in time wasn't for the weak. This wasn't the kind of class you could pop into once in a while and get a good workout. This was a skill, one mastered by practice.

Salena loved it.

An hour later, Salena's arms were tired, her core felt like it was on fire, and she had at least one more bruise on her shin from wrapping her leg too fast on a backward spin.

But she felt good. Unlike lifting weights or running on a treadmill, this workout was something she never felt forced to be a part of.

Two of the women in their group scattered the second the class was over, rushing home to their husbands and kids, while everyone else took their time throwing clothes over their skimpy outfits and putting on shoes.

"What's wrong with your car now?" Elsa asked as they walked out of the studio and into the lobby.

"Everything, sadly."

Elsa snorted a short laugh. "I was serious about the sugar daddy."

"I know you were."

"Reynaldo is sexy as hell and pays for my BMW."

"And married."

Elsa shrugged. "The last two guys I dated, who I thought were single, were both married. All I got from them was headaches from crying over them when I learned the truth. This way, I date someone, know what's up, and he buys me expensive things." She hiked her purse higher on her shoulder. "This way, I'm winning."

"And it doesn't bother you that they have someone waiting for them at home?"

"That's a *him* problem, not a *me* problem."

And boy, wouldn't a therapist have fun with that statement. "I'll figure it out on my own," Salena said.

Ashlynn was checking in her beginner-class students that were making their way through the door as Elsa bid her goodbyes and left.

Salena pulled out her phone to order a ride.

"Salena?"

"Yeah." She popped in her home address on the app and looked up at Ashlynn.

"Can you come for the open pole night?"

"Thursday?"

"I need to come in late but don't want to have to cancel it."

"I get a free week like last time?" Salena bartered her time for free sessions any chance she could.

"Of course."

"I need to look at the schedule, but I think that will work. I'll text you when I get home."

"Great. You know, the offer still stands if you want to work here."

Salena made her way to the counter and rested her arms on it. "If I had the time, I would. But to be honest, I need to find a job that pays a hell of a lot more than what you can offer or the D'Angelos can afford."

"That bad?"

"My car needs so much work it's starting to look like Frankenstein. Even with only paying for parts, I'm going to max out my credit card and end up paying twenty percent interest for the next decade to pay it off. Elsa's sugar daddy solution is starting to look inviting."

Ashlynn shook her head. "Don't go there. I've seen a lot of Elsas pass through this studio, and the guy that wants that is never dependable. The next shiny toy comes along, and that BMW is repoed."

"I'm not serious about the married guy with money. But I could use a side hustle that pays a few bills."

Another beginner student passed through the door, the bell chiming in her wake.

"I might have a solution for you," Ashlynn said. "Stay late on Thursday and I'll let you in on it."

"Legit?"

"Completely."

Salena's phone buzzed, indicating her ride was pulling up.

"See you Thursday."

~

"Are you serious?" Ryan listened to Mateo's numbers with one eye shut and the other trying not to cringe.

"Dude, this car should have been put out of its misery five years ago. The bubble gum holding it together has caused cavities everywhere. Parts alone are already over two grand, and if I was billing this out, we'd be way over six at this point. And we haven't found the cause for the overheating yet."

"Is the block cracked?"

"Not that I can see. We have the cooling system torn apart, and while the thermostat needs a part thrown at it, I'm not convinced it's going to fix the problem. All the hoses, belts—"

"I get it," Ryan cut him off.

"This chick is throwing money away."

"She doesn't have money to throw."

Silence filled the line. "What do you want me to do?" Mateo asked.

Ryan wasn't about to make the decision without her. "Let me talk to her and I'll call you back."

They disconnected the call, and Ryan stared at his phone.

"I can't afford a newer one, so please don't tell me it's not worth fixing." Salena's words rang in his head.

"Fuck."

Ryan walked into his kitchen, grabbed a beer from the fridge, and kicked the door shut. Instinctively, he knew Salena wasn't about to accept any help he offered, but that wasn't going to stop him from trying. His thoughts drifted briefly to another woman . . . a long time ago.

Ryan sucked in a big breath and blew it out, along with the memories, and looked at his phone.

Having zero clue as to Salena's schedule, Ryan sent her a text asking her to call when she had time to discuss her car.

He had no sooner sat on his couch than his phone rang. "That was fast," he said when he picked it up.

"Oh . . . are you expecting a call?"

It was his mother.

"Sorry, yes. Hi."

"Is it a woman?"

"Is *what* a woman?"

"The call you were expecting?"

"You had a fifty-fifty chance of getting that right."

His mother cooed. "Who is she?"

"Good God, you're starting to sound like Gio's mother." Mari had asked Ryan no less than three times if he was seeing anyone and asked why he wasn't married.

"She's a lovely woman."

"I didn't say she wasn't. But asking about my personal life is new for you."

His mother sighed. "Fine. I won't ask about the woman whose call you were expecting."

"Good."

"But if you need to hang up because she does call, I'll understand."

He rolled his eyes. "Good."

"Now that we have that out of the way. Your father would like you to come over for dinner tomorrow night."

"Why?" He and his father barely got along when there were other family members in attendance to put out the flames of their arguments. Ryan knew for a fact that Emma was out of town . . . her being on her honeymoon and all. And Richard had fled back to Napa the day after the wedding. Which meant a solo audience with dear old Dad.

"Does he need a reason?"

"Seriously, Mom?"

"Okay, fine. I don't really know why. But he is asking, and he's been trying."

"With Emma." So far, Ryan and Robert's relationship was exactly as it had always been . . . strained.

"Maybe he wants to with you, too."

Ryan rubbed his forehead. "I just saw him on Saturday."

"Ryan!" Beth used her *Mom* voice.

"Fine. What time?"

"Six."

Another call buzzed through. This time he looked at the name on the screen, saw the word *Trouble*, and smiled. "I have another call."

"Oh, good. I can't wait to hear about her."

"See you tomorrow."

Ryan clicked over to Salena's call before saying goodbye. "Thank you" was how he answered the phone.

"For what?"

"I was just talking to my mother, and she was . . . never mind. How are you?"

"I don't know. That depends on what you're going to tell me. I figured since we haven't spoken since you left, I'm assuming the worst."

"I didn't really know anything more until today."

"Don't tell me it's not worth fixing."

Ryan took a swig from his beer. "You want to talk about the weather?"

"C'mon, Ryan." Her voice was all stress.

"As things stand, we're looking at a minimum of two grand just in parts, probably closer to three."

"Shit."

"Even then, there is a heating problem Mateo can't guarantee these parts are going to fix. You could get it all put back together with pretty new pieces, and the whole thing could die on you and need the junkyard in weeks or, if you're lucky, months. Mateo says you need a new engine, and considering the shape of the car, that would be like using a bucket to empty a swimming pool in the rain."

She started cussing under her breath. "Can't we put the old parts back in and I can drive it the way it was—"

"Doesn't work that way. Rusted parts require force to remove. They don't go back in."

"Ryan, I can't afford this."

He didn't know this woman well enough, or long enough, to feel the stress in her voice, but he did. "I wish I had better news. You can spend the two grand you were going to have to throw at parts and put a down payment on—"

"I would have had to max a credit card for those parts. I don't have two grand."

"I'm sorry." And he was. "I can lend you—"

"No. I barely know you. It was generous enough of you to use your connections for free labor." Once again, she cussed under her breath. "I guess I can cancel my car insurance. That should pay for a few Uber rides."

In a million years, Ryan couldn't imagine the solution for his car being out of order was to simply live without one. Knowing that she needed his help and he wasn't close enough to her to insist triggered a tic in his head.

"Tell me where the shop is so I can go and clean out the stuff I have in it. I guess it needs to be towed to a junkyard. Goddammit."

"I'll pick you up and take you over there."

"That's not—"

"I'll take you out to dinner. Give you an opportunity to say good-bye to your car and pay for your drinks to mourn the loss after."

He heard her laugh, and that brought a smile to his face.

"Friday," she said.

"Isn't that a busy night at the restaurant?"

"It is. But the waiters had last Saturday off for the wedding and need the tips."

"Don't you need the tips?" Wasn't the bulk of her issues financial?

"I'm management. I get the leftovers, which is what I signed up for."

"I'll see you Friday."

CHAPTER NINE

"My car is officially dead."

Salena sat on the balcony of Chloe and Dante's condo overlooking the San Diego harbor. The temperature hovered in the midseventies, and they were wearing tank tops and flip-flops. Fall wasn't even hinting at an appearance, and summer was just yesterday. Only it was October.

"Oh no! I thought Ryan found someone to fix it." Chloe sat across from Salena, a bottle of water in her hand.

"He did. Except the fix was cost prohibitive."

"You've been hearing that for a while now."

"I know. It's a hard pill to swallow," Salena said with a sigh.

"What are you going to do?"

"Do without a car, apparently. It's not like I've saved anything and have the money to get a replacement." Living with her parents and using their backs—and financial security—had aided in Salena's lax attitude toward saving for a future. Which served as an exclamation point for her desire to break away from them. For better or for worse . . . she'd figure out what to do about a car without their help.

Chloe moaned on Salena's behalf. "You're welcome to borrow mine."

Salena met her bestie's eyes. "Thank you. But I hope to never have to take you up on that."

"We've had a car since we were sixteen. Or at least access to one. Doing without now is . . ." Chloe's voice trailed off.

"Unimaginable." Salena looked away from her friend. "I live in the city, and everything I need is close by."

"It's San Diego, not Manhattan."

"I've never been to New York."

Chloe moaned. "New York City has public transportation, the subway, and you can always walk or grab a taxi."

"We have buses."

"When was the last time you were on a bus?"

Salena cringed. "San Francisco. Remember the bass player I dated for five minutes?"

Chloe started to laugh. "I rest my case."

Salena put a hand in the air. "I get it. But the truth is, I didn't drive that much."

"Because your car sucked."

"Because I didn't need to," Salena corrected. "Besides. We have Uber. And with gas prices the way they are . . ."

Chloe sighed as silence stretched between them. "You're making excuses."

"I know." Their eyes met. "What else can I do? I wanted my independence from my parents, moved into the apartment . . . and now I need to figure out a car situation. Just like everyone else I know that is five years younger than me."

"You make it sound so bleak."

Salena ran a hand through her hair and pulled the bulk of it over to one shoulder. "I'm just mad at myself. Do you know how much money I blew when I lived with my parents?"

"Can you call it blowing it if you were enjoying your life?"

"Yes." She waved a hand in the air. "All the tips, all the paychecks. And zero to show for it. Outside of a closet full of clothes, a cell phone, and a laptop, that car was my only possession. I have no one to blame for my situation but myself. If I'd gone with my gut and moved out of my parents' home years ago, I would have realized how ill prepared I was to make it alone."

"You're beating yourself up for nothing. We were both told that marriage was the way out of our family home." For Chloe, that worked out.

"You and I both know marriage was never on my immediate list of things to do. If at all. I'm the girl that hooks up with strippers in Vegas. You were the serial dater who held out for her childhood crush."

"You make it sound like I was a virgin."

"Okay, not a virgin, but not me."

Chloe sat forward in her chair, hands waving. "I've always admired how you own your sexuality. Don't make that strength out to be something less now."

Salena released the lock of hair that she'd been twirling around in her fingers with a heavy sigh. "I'm not. Only I realize now that my pursuit of honing that sexual strength may have gotten in the way of me figuring out how to navigate life better. Look at you. Even if you and Dante weren't a thing, you knew you wanted to make a living with yoga somehow . . . or at least take that passion and do something with it. Restaurant management is not a life goal."

"It's a stepping stone. I understand that more than most. Ask yourself what you're good at."

"Picking up men is not a career path."

"No, but motivating women to own their sexuality can be." Chloe twisted in her chair. "When I went to Bali, before Dante showed up and convinced me to give us a chance, I did a whole lot of contemplating. What did I want to do with my life? How did I want it to look? Who did I want to be in it? I did what you're doing now. Maybe not the regrets of living at home, but I had every intention of coming back and setting boundaries with my brothers, my mother . . . so I could live my life the way I wanted to. I'd tell you to meditate on this if you'd listen."

Salena cringed. Meditating, or trying to, was her personal hell. "We tried that, remember?"

"Less than three minutes in, you were tapping your foot and checking your phone."

"Exactly."

"Meditating can be watching the waves on the beach. It can be listening to music that makes you forget where you're at and turn inward. It can be a state of silence in your mind you get on a run."

"When I run, all I can think about is how long until it's over." Running was her second circle of hell. Right next to meditating.

"Ughhh!" Chloe leaned over, pushed Salena's shoulder in frustration. "Give yourself some time. Hardship makes you stronger."

"Okay, Yoda."

Chloe lifted her middle finger in the air with a smile.

~

"Hi, Christy." Ryan walked through the front door of his parents' home and greeted their housekeeper.

"How are you?" she asked.

"I don't know." He lowered his voice. "Is *he* in one of his moods?" Ryan nodded toward the interior of the house, knowing Christy caught on to the *he* Ryan was referring to. The fights Ryan and his father managed to get into were never quiet.

"C'mon, Ryan. You know I can't answer that."

He regarded her with a sideways glance. "I'll take that as a caution light and tread lightly."

She smiled and took his jacket.

Requested family meetings always took place in the formal living room. One designed for conversation and not a quiet evening watching something on the TV.

A massive family portrait hung above the fireplace. All their smiles perfectly synchronized. The shot was originally taken for a magazine cover, one that highlighted California wineries and the families behind them. Ryan remembered the hours it took for the perfect picture to happen, and how much he hated being in the spotlight. His father loved being the center of attention and, in fact, expected nothing less when he was in a room. Add wine and the people that surrounded themselves with the beverage, and Robert Rutledge considered himself royalty among the crowd.

"I thought I heard the door." Beth met him halfway in the room with a quick hug. She patted his chest. "You look nice."

"It's just a sweater."

"Well, I like you in sweaters."

"It's cold tonight."

"Don't tell me you rode that motorcycle," she said.

He shook his head. "It's tucked away at home. You don't have to worry."

Beth crossed the room to the bar. "You know I hate that thing."

"And here I was hoping you'd change your mind." His mother never gave up an opportunity to express her distress about his Ducati.

"Never." She paused. "Beer or something stronger?"

Ryan moved to her side, reached for the beer. "This is fine." He pried off the cap and took a swig. "Where is he?"

"Finishing up a call."

"At six o'clock at night?"

"He's a busy man."

"I bet his staff just loves the late hours."

Footfalls announced his father's arrival before he reached the room. "Oh, good, you're here" is how his father greeted him.

"Hello, Dad. Keeping your employees on the clock after five?"

"Some people are dedicated to finishing their tasks before going home."

"Or the fear of getting fired makes them stay late."

Robert narrowed his gaze and stopped whatever words wanted to escape from coming out.

"Okay, you two, that's enough." Beth sat in one of the side chairs by the fireplace and stared them both down.

Ryan took an end of the sofa, set his drink down. "Not my business."

"No, it's not. You never wanted anything to do with the family business." Robert made his way behind the bar.

"Good thing you have other family to carry on your legacy."

Out came a bottle of whiskey. "It would be a shame if everything I built couldn't continue through your generation."

Ryan sat back. "I can't argue with that."

His dad looked up. "You would if you could," he said with a hint of a smile.

"True."

Robert managed a huff that sounded a little bit like a laugh. A sound Ryan didn't hear very often.

"Speaking of legacies . . . that's why I wanted you to come by tonight."

Thinking he knew exactly where this conversation was going, Ryan cut his father off before he had a chance to begin. "I'm not interested in R&R Wineries."

Robert emerged from the bar, a splash of amber liquid moved around in his glass. "I didn't think you changed your mind."

"Good."

"I want to talk about your own."

"My own what?"

"Legacy. What you're creating."

Ryan took a drink from his beer. "I didn't realize I was creating anything."

"You're acquiring real estate. That's creating a legacy."

He shook his head. "Investing in commercial property where others produce products is not the same as making something from nothing."

"Maybe not, but you are securing your future and acquiring something that can be passed down to your children one day. That can be considered a legacy."

Much as Ryan wanted to argue the vast difference, in his mind, between what a legacy was and what he was doing, he gave his father a pass and nodded. "If you say so."

His father took a seat. "Do you have anything new coming into play?"

"More property?" Ryan asked.

"Yes."

"No. Nothing's come up."

"Have you considered apartment buildings?"

Ryan shook his head. "Dealing with people attempting to make a living is much easier than individual people and families struggling to make the rent. I'm going to stick with commercial."

"I can't imagine having to evict a family," Beth chimed in.

"I don't want to evict anyone."

"Have you had to evict any tenants?"

"No. I had one that was falling behind, but he decided to close up shop instead of going further into debt. We came up with our own agreement on payments and skipped bringing in attorneys. Next month is his last payment."

"Avoid the lawyers as long as you can," Robert suggested. "They'll suck you dry."

"I seem to remember you saying that before."

"And you listened?" His father sounded surprised.

"You were probably yelling it," Ryan said, his tone teasing.

"I'm sure you're right," Beth said.

"What about buying a house to live in?"

"What about it?"

"You own *two* commercial buildings and rent an apartment. Where is the logic in that? You understand more than most the value of letting your money appreciate and not be given to someone else while they get richer. When you rent, you're just throwing your money away."

"I'm not sure where I want to be."

"What do you mean? What's wrong with Temecula?" Beth asked.

"Nothing. But you know me, I prefer a city over grapevines."

"Yet you're still here," Robert said.

"Because you haven't been." The words were out of Ryan's mouth before he could stop himself.

For a long moment, Ryan stared at his father without apology.

Beth broke the silence. "Are you saying you stayed in Temecula out of loyalty to me?"

"You and Emma were both here." He glanced to his father, who was studying the contents of his glass. "Dad spends most of his time in Napa. I know you and Emma can take care of yourselves, but I've felt better knowing someone was close by."

Robert pulled in a breath and dropped the foot that was resting over the opposite knee to the floor. "Dinner should be ready."

Without another comment, Ryan's father stood, set his glass on the coffee table, and exited the room.

"Is it something I said?" Ryan asked under his breath.

"I think you surprised him."

Ryan took a swig of his beer. "If my dedication to you and my sister comes as a shock, then he doesn't know me very well."

CHAPTER TEN

Salena used the key Ashlynn had given her months before to let herself into the studio.

The alarm inside beeped until Salena punched in the numbers to turn it off. She arrived fifteen minutes early to make sure the lights were on and the room was set to a bearable temperature.

Even though Salena was simply doing a favor for a friend, she took on the responsibility of the place as if she were a paid employee. She'd covered this night for Ashlynn more than once and understood the assignment.

Salena clicked on all the lights before moving to the sound system to put on some music. The slow kind that one might find in a strip club. It really was all about setting a slow pace so that the students weren't attempting to keep up with a fast beat and hurt themselves in the process. After a quick walk through the locker room and a scan of the single shower, which was seldom used, to make sure there were towels and soap, she made her way back to the front desk and woke up the computer.

A sticky note sat in the middle of the screen with a message. *I'll be back in time to lock up.* It was signed *Ashlynn*.

Slowly, women made their way into the studio. Using a key fob, they signed in. Their pictures and names flashed on the screen, giving Salena the ability to put faces to names. Not that she needed it for most of the ladies. The students that came to open pole night were almost never newbies. These were the diehards, the women who either had a pole in their homes or wished they did.

The greeting was similar with all of them.

"Hey, Salena."

"Oh, is Ashlynn not here?"

"Covering again?"

At ten minutes past the hour, Salena was fairly certain the last of the women that were coming were there. Leaving the key in the door so that anyone that was inside could get out, but no one else could walk in undetected, she abandoned the desk and joined the group. Everyone that worked out at the studio knew to buzz the bell from the outside if they showed up late.

Salena channeled Ashlynn by walking around, offering suggestions, or spotting someone who needed help. Three of the women were working on the routine the advanced class was learning. The intermediate-level students were less about routines, and more about individual moves. Either way, the women were talking, laughing, and cheering each other on.

One of the students was struggling with an inversion, and Salena stood by to spot her.

"Once you get your hips up, the rest will fall into place."

The woman, blonde, probably in her midthirties, gripped the pole again.

Salena stepped in, guided the blonde's lower hand to give her a better angle, and waited.

"What's your name?" Salena asked.

"Kate."

"You got this, Kate. Remember, engage your core."

Kate narrowed her eyes and kicked.

Salena stepped in, got under Kate, hands on the other woman's hips, and helped her into position.

Kate tangled her leg with the pole with a tiny sigh and a big smile.

Salena stood back, hands at her sides. "Come down. Let's do that again."

Ten minutes before the session ended, the door chime went off.

Salena peeked into the hall to see Ashlynn walking her way.

"Everything good?"

"Only the A team tonight."

She stopped at the registration desk and pulled her sweater from her shoulders. "I appreciate you covering."

"I'm always willing if I'm not needed at the restaurant."

The students were slowly wrapping up, some slipping into pants while others opted to wear their athletic shorts out the door.

"You're all dressed up," Salena said. "Did you have a date?"

Ashlynn answered with a grin.

"Ohhh, who is the lucky guy?"

"Just a guy, and no, he didn't get lucky."

Salena laughed. "First date? Second?"

"First. We met for happy hour."

"How happy was that hour?"

Ashlynn shrugged. "Eh . . . I'll give him a second date. He seemed nervous. Said he doesn't date a lot. Too busy with work."

Salena didn't hide her frown. "The work excuse is a red flag."

"I don't think so. Work keeps me from dating."

"Does this guy own his own business or work nine to five?"

"Nine to five. Works downtown . . . wears a suit."

Red flag! "Has evenings and weekends off and doesn't date. Does he have kids?"

Ashlynn shook her head. "He said he's never been married and doesn't have kids."

"Do you have a picture?"

Ashlynn removed her phone from her purse and pulled up a profile picture from a dating app.

"He's good-looking." If you liked blonds.

"I thought so."

Salena handed the phone back. "Let me know how it works out."

One by one, the women in the studio filed out until it was only Ashlynn and Salena.

"Can you give me a ride home?" Salena asked.

"Is your car still in the shop?"

"My car is in the graveyard," she said with a long, exasperated sigh.

"That sucks."

"Tell me about it. It's going to take me a while to save up enough money to buy a newer one."

Ashlynn locked the door and walked toward the back. "I know a way you can make good money in your spare time."

Salena followed. "I'm all ears."

Ashlynn stopped at one of the poles, tapped it, and looked directly at her. "People pay good money to watch women on this."

"I'm not taking off my clothes for money."

"Nobody said anything about getting naked."

Salena thought she knew where Ashlynn was going with this. "Vegas is too far away, and the clubs and casinos nearby are seedy as fuck."

Ashlynn laughed and waved a finger in the air. "None of that. I'm talking about OnlyMe. It's for more than just strippers and people with a foot fetish."

"And porn."

"Right. There are a lot of us on there collecting a monthly subscription check from people who want to watch pole dancers in the privacy of their own homes."

Salena narrowed her eyes. "Us?"

Ashlynn nodded. "*Me.*"

"You're on OnlyMe?"

"Yup. I had to do something to keep afloat during the recession. The government handouts only helped so much for small business owners. It was *find another source of income* or *close the studio.*"

"You've been on OnlyMe this whole time and haven't said anything." Salena had known Ashlynn for years. They weren't super close, but a secret this big was hard to keep.

"Anonymity is key. Fake names. No links to this business. The last thing I want is a fan finding out my address and showing up here. The less people that know your true identity, the better."

"You have fans." Salena laughed at the thought.

"I do. And they're growing by the week. Things have really taken off."

"Good money?"

Ashlynn shook her head. "Not good. Great. I've made more money in the last six months than this place makes in a year."

Salena's jaw dropped. "How much do you post?"

"I film a couple of hours a week, break it into pieces, and upload it. The more I put out there, the more subscriptions come in."

Salena glanced around the empty studio, her mind racing with the possibilities. "And you keep your clothes on."

"I don't flash even a nipple." Ashlynn winked. "No less than a bathing suit that keeps all your shit in."

"And no one knows you're doing it."

"Did you?"

Salena huffed. "No, but I'm not on that site."

"Exactly my point. You keep what you're doing to yourself, and no one knows to look for you."

"How much time are we talking?"

Ashlynn leaned against one of the poles. "I film a few hours of content. Spend another few hours editing. A few more hours managing my site. I have it streamlined now, but I can show you. It will take you a while to build a paid following, but I can help with that. We can create a duo routine and help grow your page with mine."

Salena smiled into the thought. "Like a guest appearance?"

"Exactly. Bonus content for subscribers. We'll film some stuff for the free content and get the grittier stuff for subscribers. My stuff will sell yours, yours will sell mine. It's a win-win."

Salena found herself nodding. The thought of making money without coming in contact with the people watching her sounded too good to be true.

She waved her fingers in a way that beckoned Ashlynn her way. "Show me your page."

~

Ryan parked on the street a couple of blocks from the D'Angelos' restaurant and home and walked his way through the crowds in Little Italy to pick up Salena. Even though it was October, San Diego's weather hadn't gotten the memo that it was fall yet. Only a few clouds filled the sky, but the temperature hovered in the seventies.

He walked up to the doors of the now-familiar restaurant and smiled at the hostess. She looked familiar, but he didn't remember her name. "I'm here for Salena."

The girl smiled. "She isn't on tonight."

"Yeah, I know."

"Ryan?"

He looked across the room with the sound of his name.

Mari D'Angelo walked his way, a smile on her face.

"Hello."

She walked up to him with open arms, kissed the side of his cheek with a hug. "What are you doing here? Did we know you were coming? Are you here for dinner?"

So many questions.

They moved out of the way of the front door and farther into the restaurant so the hostess could seat a party of four.

"I'm taking Salena to get the belongings from her car," he explained.

Mari stopped, turned, took a breath. "One of us could have done that. You didn't need to drive all the way from—"

Ryan placed a hand on his chest. "It was my idea."

"Oh . . . *Oh!*" Slowly Mari started to smile. "Oh."

"Ryan?"

Another voice . . . another D'Angelo. "Luca."

Wearing a chef uniform, minus the hat, Luca walked over and extended a hand. "What brings you to town?"

"He's here for Salena," Mari explained, her smile more than a little suggestive.

Luca's eyes narrowed.

"I'm helping her with her car," Ryan quickly added.

"I thought her car died."

"It did."

"What's to do, then?"

Mari nudged her son's shoulder.

Luca glanced at his mother, then Ryan, then his mother a second time. *"Oh. "*

Ryan was starting to feel like he was picking up a prom date. "No, really . . . it's just that her car is at my buddy Mateo's shop, and she needs to get her things she left inside."

Luca wasn't buying that. "Right."

"I think that's very kind of you," Mari said.

"Really *kind*." Luca smiled like a man with a secret.

Mari motioned toward the bar. "Would you like something to drink while you're waiting?"

"No." He glanced at his watch. "I'm sure she'll be down soon."

For a few awkward moments, the three of them stood there in complete silence, staring at each other. If there was one thing Ryan had learned about the D'Angelos in the short time he'd known them, silence was not their normal state of being.

Ryan found himself shuffling from one foot to another. "I don't want to keep you," he said.

Luca simply smiled and stood his ground.

"How is your mother doing? Recovered from the wedding?" Mari asked.

"I think so."

Another moment of silence.

With a sigh, Ryan looked over Mari's head and found Salena watching him from the back of the room.

He must have made a sound because both D'Angelos turned to see what he was looking at.

"There she is."

Salena walked up to them, wearing tight jeans and a button-up blouse. Her hair was draped over one shoulder, and she only wore a dusting of makeup on her face. The high heels dressed up the outfit and added the perfect amount of sexy to the look.

Ryan kept his expression neutral as she walked his way.

She tucked the phone she was carrying in her back pocket when she stopped in front of them. "Hey."

"Hi." He smiled.

"You didn't tell us Ryan was coming." Mari's words were just short of accusing.

"No, I guess I didn't. Must have slipped my mind." Salena spoke to Mari but stared at Ryan.

"I should get back to the kitchen." Luca glanced at Salena, then Ryan. "Good to see you again."

"Likewise."

Luca said something to his mother in Italian and walked away.

Mari raised both hands in the air, said something in return that Ryan didn't understand. "You sure you don't want something before you leave?" she asked Ryan one more time.

"No. We should get going before the shop closes."

"Okay, okay. Next time." Mari patted his shoulder, turned to Salena and raised a silent finger in the air, and then walked away.

He couldn't help but think there was a whole lot that was said in that one gesture that he didn't completely understand.

"Shall we?"

Salena took the lead as they exited the restaurant and dumped out onto the sidewalk.

"That was painful," he admitted the moment they were outside.

"Be happy it was Mari and Luca and not my father and mother."

"You're a grown woman."

She moved beside him, looped her arm through his. "And they know you, or it would have been worse."

Ryan felt his brain short-circuit with how quickly Salena melted into his side.

He looked up, stopped, and turned. "My car's the other way." He pivoted and caught her hand to pull her in the right direction.

CHAPTER ELEVEN

She'd bought the car with her tip money from her first job.

Now Salena sat behind the wheel, sucked in a breath that was filled with the scent of stale leather—or maybe that was plastic—and years-old french fries lost within the seats.

It didn't matter.

The car had been hers.

The freedom it represented at the time of purchase was somehow being stripped away with its last farewell to the graveyard for cars.

Over the dashboard and beyond the hood, Ryan and Mateo stood watching her with confused expressions.

She looked like a fool, but that didn't stop her from taking a moment to remember.

"You were like a boyfriend," she whispered to the steering wheel. "Exciting when it began. Reliable for a short time . . . and disappointing in the end." And like any temporary thing in her life, Salena opened the compartments, took what might serve her in the future, and pushed out of the car.

Ryan and Mateo spoke in hushed tones as she popped the trunk and filled a duffel bag with the crap she carried with her. An unused umbrella, a flashlight . . . and a handful of reusable bags that she almost never reused. Everything else in the trunk could go to the junkyard with the car.

Much as she wanted to hate the thing for dying on her, she rested her hand on the trunk one last time and sighed.

Then she kicked the tire.

Damn thing should have waited a few months for her to save up enough for another beater.

"You okay over there?"

Salena looked over at Ryan and rolled her eyes.

"I'm sorry I couldn't put her back together without spending a fortune," Mateo said.

"It's not your fault." Salena dropped the bag filled with what she wanted to keep to the floor and reached into her back pocket for her phone. "Do you have Venmo?"

Mateo glanced at Ryan, then back at her.

"For what?"

"You have to tow it to the junkyard, right? That has a cost."

"Uh . . ." Another look to Ryan.

"Junkyards pick up cars that have scrap value," Ryan told her.

Mateo's expression called bullshit.

Salena indicated her car behind her with a thumb. "Nobody wants a piece of that."

"I have a buddy . . . ," Mateo started.

Ryan looked at his friend. "Right."

"He'll take it for next to nothing."

Salena waved her phone in the air. "Next to nothing isn't zero. I know you spent time on the piece of crap, and that's worth something. Give me a price."

"It's okay, Salena—" Ryan started.

Salena snapped her eyes to him. "What are you? My sugar daddy? I don't think so. I might be broke, but I'm not without some reserves." She directed her attention to Mateo. "How much do I owe you?"

"A hundred bucks will get it to the junkyard," Mateo told her.

"And your work?" she asked.

"Another fifty is fine."

She knew she was getting off cheap, but it wasn't like she had the bank account to toss out dead presidents like they grew on trees. "Fine. Bring your family to the restaurant and I'll make sure your meal is on the house." That she could do. So long as the group wasn't thirty deep and they didn't ring up a massive bar bill, Salena was at liberty to comp a meal or two . . . or three.

"My wife would like that."

She took Mateo's Venmo information and sent him the money he requested.

Salena didn't look back as she and Ryan walked away from the shop.

"Did you get everything you needed?" he asked once they were alone.

"Yeah."

"What do you want to do now?"

She looked over her shoulder. "I need a drink."

Ryan started his engine. "I can take care of that."

Less than an hour later, they were parked in the sand on Fiesta Island, with In-N-Out burgers, Animal Fries . . . and a bottle of whiskey they picked up from the grocery store.

"When I suggested dinner and drinks, this isn't what I had in mind."

"I work in restaurants," she said as she opened the door of his car. "This is better."

A firepit sat on the banks of the shore of Mission Bay. In the distance, the sounds of Sea World filled the air.

Ryan walked to the back of his car. "Next time I'll bring chairs." He pulled the bundle of firewood they'd gotten from the store from the car and tossed a single beach towel over his shoulder.

"That would be way too organized."

"Yeah, you're probably right."

He handed her the towel and placed the wood to the side of the firepit.

Salena spread the towel out before dropping to the ground.

Ryan stood over the firepit with his hands on his hips. Silent.

"What?" she asked.

"I don't smoke."

"Okay . . . that's a good thing."

He slowly moved his head until he was looking directly at her. "I don't have matches."

She started to laugh. "Were you a Boy Scout? Can you rub sticks together?"

He shook his head. "Not a chance."

She laughed harder.

Ryan looked over her head, focused on the group of people a campsite away. "I got this."

While Ryan went off in search of a flame, she unscrewed the cap on the whiskey and poured a generous portion inside her cup of soda and did the same for Ryan's.

A few minutes later, he returned with a lighter and a small stack of newspapers.

"Making friends?" she asked.

"San Diego is a friendly place."

It didn't take long for him to get the wood to catch fire and return the lighter to the people at the adjacent campsite and then take a seat beside her.

Salena lifted her red and white disposable cup in the air. "A toast . . . to the passing of my car and the end of the money pit that it has been for the last year."

Ryan tapped his cup to hers. "Only a year?"

She drank, felt a little fire as the liquid slid down her throat. "Maybe two." She used her straw to stir in the liquor.

Ryan dug into the bag with their burgers, handed one to her. "What will you do now?"

"Save money. Bum rides off my friends." She pulled down the wrapper and took a bite of her double-double with grilled onions, then chased it with another sip of her drink.

"Have you considered getting a loan to buy something else?"

"Mmm . . ." She swallowed her food. "The only financial thing I have going for me is my lack of debt."

"No one escapes debt for long." He opened the box with their fries and pulled a few away from the cheese and sauce that stuck them together.

"Oh yeah? You have payments on that?" She nodded toward his car.

"Yup."

"And it doesn't stress you out?" She took another bite of her burger.

"No. My income supports it. Besides, I use it as a tax write-off."

"How?" she asked around the food in her mouth.

"I, ah, own a couple of pieces of commercial property. I need to visit the properties on occasion, maintain them. That requires me to drive." He waved a fry in the air. "Tax write-off."

"Commercial, huh?"

"Yeah."

"How did you get into that?" Salena chewed as Ryan spoke.

"It wasn't wine. And it wasn't something my father was an expert on."

"Let me guess, your dad preaches his way of life on any subject he deems himself an authority."

"You've met him," Ryan said, smiling.

"Only briefly. Gio says he's a stubborn man."

Ryan laughed. "Gio is too kind if all he says is Robert Rutledge is *stubborn*."

"What would you call him?"

"Unbending with narcissistic tendencies. Ego driven and just short of a dictator."

That made Salena chuckle. "You've given his title some thought."

Ryan shrugged. "I used to call him a narcissistic dictating asshole, but then Emma ended up sick . . . well, not sick, I guess, but had that health scare, and that rattled my dad's cage. I've softened my view on the man."

"Gio said he's trying."

"That's what everyone is saying."

"You don't see it?" Salena asked.

Ryan pulled the rest of his burger from the wrapper, tossed the paper into the fire. "I do. I also have years of being the black sheep of the family and therefore on the negative end of his spite and anger. I'll hold my final opinion on the man until the newness of the leaf he's turned over has gotten old."

"The bar for black sheep is high for your family. You own property and can write off your car. In my family, I'm covered in dark wool because I want to live on my own."

"That's nuts." He put the remainder of his burger in his mouth.

"My parents are going to have to get used to things this way. It's taken my car dying for me to realize how unmotivated I've been about securing a financial future. I can blame my parents for not encouraging me to do more. Truth is, I've been fine living paycheck to paycheck. Only now I look back and realize how much money I blew, with nothing to show for it."

Ryan leaned back on his elbow. "Adulting sucks."

"So does staying a child under the thumb of your parents."

Ryan lifted his cup to hers. "True story!"

She took a drink, looked over her shoulder at Ryan's car. "I can't use a car as a write-off. My shoes, maybe. It's not like I have a commute to my day job."

She thought of the potential of earning money pole dancing. What kind of write-off could she use for that? A phone? An internet connection. The Wi-Fi at the D'Angelos' was part of the building and not something she paid separate for. Besides, write-offs were for people who itemized their taxes. The most Salena had ever filed was an EZ form that always resulted in a refund.

"Someone got quiet," Ryan pointed out.

Salena shook her head, took a drink that started to give her head a little buzz. "I'm just trying to figure out how to write off a car I can't afford."

"Start your own business. One that requires you to drive."

"Uber?" she said quickly.

Ryan winced. "Ohh. I mean, that would do it, but do you really want to drive people to and from the bars and airports?"

"No." But she would have to drive to Ashlynn's studio if she started her side hustle. Thinking about her future without a car was giving her a headache. Salena finished her burger and watched the paper it came in burn in the fire.

~

Ryan mixed the two of them a second drink as dusk fell over San Diego.

Fiesta Island was slowly clearing out of the families that came for the day to use their Jet Skis on the bay or simply entertain their kids in the water.

Some, like he and Salena, were chilling by a campfire and watching the sky.

The more Salena drank, the more she talked. Not that Ryan minded. She had a handful of friends. At the top of that list was Chloe and the D'Angelo family.

"What about you? Who do you hang out with?"

"Mateo. We've known each other for a few years. I have a friend that lives in the complex, his name is Yuri. He owns a motorcycle, too. Sometimes we drive up the coast."

Salena leaned on one elbow, traced his arm with one manicured finger. "Tell me about these."

Ryan looked at the image inked into his skin, rolled up his sleeve to show her the whole thing. "Soon as I turned eighteen, I found an artist. I knew my mom was going to be pissed and my father disappointed . . . which was what I was aiming for."

"I know that feeling," Salena said.

"Luckily, the artist pegged my reason for ink the moment he saw me. I wanted a full sleeve. Skulls, bikes . . . all the things."

Salena lifted his arm, looked around the back. "I don't see any of that."

Ryan cleared his throat. "He talked me out of it. He pulled out dozens of pictures of what my arm would and could look like. The guy could have sold me on just about anything. But Archie . . . his name was Archie . . ."

Salena laughed.

"Archie showed me something that looked like this." Ryan traced the middle of the ink on his bicep.

"It looks like thorns."

"It is. Thorns emerging from empty grapevines. It passes as a tribal tattoo, but it means something different to me."

"Rebellion."

"Exactly. I was eighteen. My mom was *disappointed.* Pissed to the point of not even looking at it. Dad, though, he recognized the tangled vines immediately."

"What did he say?"

"He said, 'At least I know you'll never forget where you came from.'"

Salena's jaw dropped. "My God. What an ass."

"I looked him in the eye, all eighteen years of piss and anger, and said, 'No, Dad . . . this will remind me what to never be.'"

"Oh, snap."

Ryan shook his head. "But he was right. It does remind me of that angry time in my life, and I'm forever grateful that Archie talked me out of skulls and bikes."

Salena traced the ink. "You've added to it."

"I did. More tribal, less vines."

"I like it."

And he liked how she petted his skin as she explored it. "Do you have any?" he asked.

She shook her head, let her hand drop. "I want to, though. These things cost money, and I was never committed to a design enough to pull the trigger. If I did it when I was eighteen, it would have been nothing but regret. Piss off my parents and end up with a fucking teddy bear on my ass."

Ryan tossed his head back with laughter.

"I think Chloe talked me out of it."

"Good friends are worth their weight."

Salena shrugged. "Older, wiser . . . when I see something that moves me, I'll make it happen."

Ryan opened his mouth to ask another question when the familiar sound of fireworks shooting in the air drew their attention to the sky above Sea World.

"I thought these only went off during the summer," he said.

"And weekends during special events."

"What's special?" It was October.

"They have their Haunted Halloween gig going on."

Another pop, then another flash of brilliant lights in the sky.

Salena stood and moved closer to the fire, her eyes to the sky. She sipped her drink and folded her arms over her body.

While she watched the fireworks, Ryan walked to his car and found his jacket.

Back at the campfire, he placed it over her shoulders and was rewarded with a smile.

He started to drop his hands. Salena took hold of one and held it to her shoulder.

Ryan stepped a little closer and placed both hands on her arms.

She ohh'd and ahh'd a couple of times, the lights flashing on her face.

Like any theme park, the show was over much faster than something put on for an Independence Day celebration or welcoming in the New Year.

The family he'd borrowed the lighter from clapped when it was over, and the kids ran in circles while the parents picked up their belongings and filled up the car.

"That looks like a lot of work," Salena said, indicating the family.

"Those kids will be asleep before they make it onto the freeway."

"You're probably right. I don't remember a lot of late night car rides, just having to wake up and walk to bed."

Salena turned away from the people they were watching and faced the fire. The movement dislodged Ryan's hands and left him missing the warmth of her body. "Do you have places out in Temecula where you light a fire and stargaze?"

Ryan scanned the sky. The marine layer was starting to roll in, obstructing any searching of the cosmos from their vantage point. "Does a firepit by the pool count?"

"Why not?"

"Then yes."

She sucked in the last of her drink and rattled the ice in her cup. "That did the trick." She tossed the empty cup into the fire.

"What trick was that?"

"Made me forget about my lack of a car."

Only he could see by the look on her face that the mention of it brought those memories back.

Ryan stepped closer and placed a hand on the side of her face.

Their eyes met.

"Can I distract you another way?"

Salena looked at his lips and smiled. "I was starting to wonder if you were ever going to make a move."

He curled his fingers around the back of her head, stepped into her space. "Friends first . . . benefits second."

She licked her top lip and placed a hand on his waist.

Ryan didn't need another invitation. Their lips met at the same time a snap from the firewood cracked the air with sound. Salena tasted like whiskey and sin . . . and Ryan was way past thirsty.

She wasted no time in melting her body with his, their open-mouth kiss ignited the fire he'd felt from the moment he'd set eyes on her. Their tongues met and tangled until they were both breathless and looking for more.

He started to back away, only to feel her teeth catch his lip. The lava that shot straight to his cock had him pressing his hips against hers.

"Nice," she whispered.

Ryan opened his eyes, found her hooded gaze, and went in for more. He pushed his hands inside the jacket he'd tossed on her shoulders and captured her waist. The feel of her purr against his lips made it hard to think.

"The car," he heard her whisper.

"The what?"

Her breath brushed against the lobe of his ear.

Cold air rushed in when she stood back and pulled him toward his car. Salena opened the door to the back seat and slid inside.

For a brief second, he questioned the decision of doing this here and now. But Salena was no sooner in the car than she tossed the jacket to the side and started to undo the buttons on her shirt.

"Damn, woman."

She chuckled, and Ryan slid inside.

For a precious few moments, the dome light of the car illuminated her skin as she exposed a lace bra covering her breasts. He reached for her, brushed her hand aside, and finished the last buttons as the light in the car went off. "This is crazy."

"Do you have a better idea?" she asked. "You live in Temecula, and my place is off-limits."

He kissed one nipple through her bra.

Salena arched into him.

"A hotel?"

"Too far away."

Her nails bit into his back.

He reached behind her and started fumbling with the clasp of her bra. He felt one clasp free and fought with the other until they were both laughing. "I swear I'm better at this."

Salena sighed when the material was free, and he cupped one breast and gave it a squeeze.

"God, you're beautiful."

"And flexible," she boasted right before she wrapped her free leg around him and pulled him closer.

He abandoned her breast and kissed her again. The kind of hungry kiss you dream about long after the encounter is over. She matched his energy, move for move.

Her hands explored his body as he attempted to do the same to her without crushing her between the seats and the weight of his frame.

When her fingertips brushed his erection, his body stilled, and little fireworks went off in his head.

"I think I'm gonna like this benefit," she said, teasing. The snap on his jeans was freed, and one of her hands pushed inside.

Somewhere in the back of his head, something was knocking. Maybe a warning. Damn, she felt good.

"Ryan."

His hips pushed toward her hand.

He heard the knocking again.

Only this time, it wasn't in his head.

Ryan's eyes sprang open to see a bright light flashing into the window of his fogged-out car.

"Oh, shit."

Scrambling, he moved off Salena almost as fast as he'd jumped in the car.

"What the?" It took Salena a moment longer to catch on that there was someone at the door of the car.

Knuckles rapped on the window. "Police."

"Oh, come on," Salena moaned.

Ryan looked at Salena, her shirt half-off, bra hanging at the wrong angle. "Just a second," Ryan yelled to the man standing outside the door.

He picked up his coat from the front seat where Salena had tossed it and shoved it back at her. At the same time, he leaned over the seats and pressed the button on the car, turning on the power so he could roll down one of the windows. In doing that, the dome light turned on, illuminating the scene.

He cracked the window just enough to talk to the cop.

"Hello, Officer."

Ryan glanced at Salena, who was pushing her arms into his jacket.

The flashlight beamed in, first catching Ryan, then moving toward Salena.

"Really?" the man said. "I was expecting teenagers."

"We were just—"

"I'm sure you were. There are families out here."

Salena scrambled over the seat and across Ryan's lap, looked straight up at the officer, and said, "How do you think those families started?"

Ryan half laughed, half hushed her.

The cop wasn't nearly as amused. "Step out of the car."

Ryan's pulse jumped. "We will leave."

"Step out of the car." This time, the man's voice lowered, and he stood back.

"This is ridiculous," Salena said under her breath.

"I got this," Ryan told her.

He opened the door and climbed out first, then reached for Salena's hand and pulled her beside him.

The flashlight once again illuminated their faces.

Salena put a hand in the air to shield her eyes. "Is that really necessary?"

"I need to see your ID."

"Why?" Salena asked. "We're obviously adults. There isn't any crime being committed."

Ryan reached for Salena's hand and tugged.

"You seem to think you're the authority on the law. Have you heard of lewd conduct?" The officer's gaze moved to the jacket she was wearing, which wasn't completely zipped up and exposed a half-open shirt. "Indecent exposure and public indecency?"

The cop, a good ten years older than Ryan from the looks of the man, had a receding hairline and a belly that suggested he ate at far too many fast-food restaurants. If Ryan had to guess, the man hadn't had sex in quite a while, let alone in a car.

"No one saw anything," Ryan told the man.

"Making out in a car isn't against the law," Salena said in solidarity.

The flashlight moved up and down Salena's frame.

The cop's eyes narrowed.

Something in the look the cop gave Salena had Ryan stepping in front of her.

"Two adults, nice car. I can't imagine you both don't have your own place. If you're cheating on your spouses, that's none of my business . . ."

"That's not—"

The cop stepped to his side, narrowed his eyes. "ID," he said again.

Ryan lifted a hand in the air. "It's in my back pocket."

A single nod from the cop and Ryan reached for his wallet. He pulled out his driver's license and handed it over.

The man glanced at it but didn't give it back. "Now yours."

Salena rolled her eyes. "I don't have it on me."

Ryan glanced at her.

"I only brought my phone," she told him.

The officer scratched his palm with Ryan's ID and smirked. "A woman that doesn't carry a purse."

"Is that illegal?" Salena's tone matched the cop's, and Ryan couldn't help but feel that it wasn't going to end well.

"I need you to step over to my car," the man told Salena.

Ah, fuck.

Salena sighed, looked at Ryan, and said under her breath, "I bet he thinks I'm a hooker."

The cop pointed to his car. "I'm not asking twice."

"We should probably do as he says," Ryan said to her softly, all the while wondering if she had a point.

She stepped out from behind him and stumbled slightly.

"Have you been drinking?" the cop asked.

"Am I under arrest?" Salena asked.

"Not yet."

Instead of answering the question, Salena turned toward the squad car and started walking.

"You stay here," the officer instructed Ryan.

All he could do was run his hands through his hair and watch as Salena was led to the car and patted down before being pushed into the back seat.

CHAPTER TWELVE

Nothing sobers you up faster than sitting inside a police car behind the cage with a door that only opens from the outside.

The cop had asked her for her full name and whether she knew the number on her driver's license. Where she lived . . . all those things.

He moved to the front seat of the car and started typing into a computer.

She placed her hands at her side, her right one touched something sticky. "Ewhh."

"You make a habit of leaving home without your ID?"

"I take it with me when I'm driving or going someplace I get carded. Purses get stolen."

The cop spoke into his radio, and within a few minutes, another squad car pulled up, lights flashing.

Looking out the window, she could see a small crowd of people watching. In the distance, she saw Ryan leaning against his car, his arms folded over his chest.

The officer that had put her in the back of the car stepped out, closed the door, and approached the second cop.

The thought of how this night could go snuck in.

Even though she was convinced that she and Ryan hadn't done anything so bad as to warrant being arrested, if the police wanted to, they could take the both of them in. She wasn't completely sure if there were rules against drinking on Fiesta Island. She'd been doing it since she was a teenager, but that didn't make it okay with the law.

As for sex in the car . . .

Wasn't part of the excitement the fact that they could get caught?

Only having her hand in something sticky in the back of a police car put a seriously cold shower on any excitement she'd experienced.

And who would she call to bail her out of jail? Would they call her parents? Or go to the restaurant since she gave them her current address? She could call Chloe.

Through the window, she watched as both cops stepped up to Ryan, the three of them talking.

The smell of the back seat was starting to get to her. It reminded her vaguely of a bar room floor, topped with a dose of body odor.

Much as she hated to admit it, losing her cool with the cop was probably what prompted her being where she was.

After what felt like forever, the officer returned to the car and opened the back door.

"You can step out, Miss Barone," he told her.

Trying to do so without touching the door took effort.

"Thank you."

"I have a couple of questions."

She folded her hands in front of her and stayed quiet.

"What were you doing before coming here?"

She glanced over at Ryan, who was still talking to the other cop. "Ryan took me to a shop to get a few things I had in my car before it's towed to the junkyard."

He nodded. "And then?"

"We grabbed some burgers and firewood and came here. Watched the fireworks."

"Anything else?"

"No."

He stared at her.

"Listen, I'm sorry. I've had a shitty day but shouldn't have been disrespectful to you."

He regarded her with a tilt of his head. "No. You shouldn't have. But you're not in the system, and I want to believe you are who you say you are."

"I swear."

"Don't let me find you out here like this again."

Her lungs sighed in complete relief. "You won't."

When he moved to the side, she started walking back to Ryan.

By now, the fire in the pit had completely burned out, and the people gathered around began to disperse.

He reached for her.

She stopped short, lifted her hands in the air. "There was something sticky in there."

He shook his head.

Salena moved to the side of the shore and knelt to wash her hands in the salt water.

Behind her, Ryan held the beach towel they'd used to sit on. "I really thought he was going to take you in."

"So did I." She reached for the towel to dry her hands.

Back in the car, they watched as the police circled around and left the island.

"Let me get you home."

Halfway there, Ryan started to laugh.

"What's so funny?"

He glanced at her and said, "'How do you think those families started?'"

Salena laughed with him. "That was pretty good."

"Almost landed you in jail."

"But funny." She made light of it even though she wanted to toss up her burger with the thought of explaining the situation to her family.

Ryan laughed harder. "You're living up to your name, *Trouble*."

The whole ordeal had taken up a big portion of their night. There were still people living it up in Little Italy. And likely, the bar was still hopping at the restaurant, not that Salena had any desire to be a part of it.

Ryan parked in her spot in the back lot behind the building and cut the engine.

"The D'Angelos can't know about what happened tonight."

"It didn't cross my mind to tell them."

"Yeah, but if you mention it to Emma, and Emma to Gio . . . Not that I think Mari or Luca will think less of me. Well, maybe they would. But word would get to my parents—"

"I get it. You and I can laugh about it later."

Salena nodded and got out of the car.

Ryan walked her to the back door.

She turned to him and suddenly felt a wave of uncertainty. "I can say without a shadow of a doubt that you took my mind off of my missing car."

He chuckled and reached for her hand and pulled her into his arms.

Strong arms wrapped around her, his chin rested against the side of her head.

This felt good, she realized. His warmth, his support.

And when Ryan pulled back enough for her to look up at him, he pressed his lips softly to hers. Even though the passion that had coursed through them earlier wasn't there, that didn't make this kiss any less effective. If anything, it moved Salena more.

"Isn't this what got us into trouble?" she said against his lips.

"You're worth it," he whispered, then kissed her a second time and pulled away. "I'll call you."

"Men that say they'll call, never do," she pointed out.

"Then you've picked the wrong men."

There was no arguing that.

"Good night." Salena turned and walked into the building.

~

Yuri was Russian . . . from Russia. How the hell he ended up in Temecula and living in the apartment next door to Ryan was a story Ryan had never gotten right since most of the time he and Yuri talked, there was a copious amount of alcohol involved.

"She mouthed off to the police?" Yuri asked from his Adirondack chair, a glass filled with vodka and ice in his hand.

Twenty-four hours later, Ryan needed to vent.

"The guy was a dick." The more Ryan replayed the scene in his head from memory, the more he realized how ridiculous the night had turned out.

"Maybe getting naked in a family park was a bad idea."

"It wasn't a family park. And no one was naked." Yet.

"You said Sea World."

Ryan shook his head. "An island across from Sea World."

"You said there was a family."

Okay, so maybe Ryan didn't explain the situation well, or maybe . . . just maybe, Yuri had a point.

Ryan's silence had Yuri continuing. "I have a three-year-old. I'm biased."

Yuri's daughter visited every other weekend. And if Ryan had to guess, she was the only reason the man stayed in Temecula.

"Getting mouthy with a cop and not having your ID on you is a bad combination," Ryan said.

"You forgot the naked part."

"We weren't . . . Never mind."

Yuri laughed.

"It was hard watching her in the car and knowing there wasn't a damn thing I could do about it. I could have gotten in the man's shit. He really didn't have to give Salena a hard time like that."

"Then you both would have ended up in jail. How you handled it was perfect. You both went home, no one with a criminal record."

"But—"

"Yes, your fragile ego took a hit. Get over it."

Ryan took a swig from his beer and leaned his head against the back of his chair. "I hate that you're right." Gone were the days of swinging first and thinking later.

The firepit by the apartment pool was all the company they had.

The residents of the building were long since in bed, and the community area was occupied solely by the two of them.

A few moments of silence stretched in front of them when Yuri ended it. "I would have mouthed off to him."

Ryan started to laugh and called him out. "And if Anika was there?" Anika was his little girl.

Yuri winced before shaking his head no.

"I didn't think so."

"Fuck . . . this growing older shit is not okay."

"Proof that wisdom only comes with age," Ryan said.

Yuri took a long drink and reached for the bottle at his side. "Are you going to see this woman again?"

"Absolutely."

"You said that quickly."

"She's different." Ryan wasn't exactly certain as to why, but he knew in his gut she was.

"A woman you wanted to get in your bed the night you met her is different . . . how?"

"I, ah . . ." He sighed. "She's tough. Unapologetically beautiful and knows it. And is surprised when someone offers her kindness." That's when Ryan paused and started piecing together his thoughts and feelings toward her. "I knew our naked options were limited, and I didn't book a hotel room. I'd have happily driven home with a promise of a second date."

Yuri looked him up and down.

"You were caught by the police screwing in the back of a car."

"Making out, at best," Ryan defended.

"Only because you were interrupted."

Ryan shook his head, then nodded. "I want more than that from her."

"You've known her a week."

"I know." Ryan propped his legs on the side of the firepit. "Crazy, right?"

~

Salena cocked her head from one side to the other as she walked through her apartment at the end of her Saturday-night shift.

Mari had gone to bed by eight . . . Luca finished his shift with the last meal served, and Salena had locked the doors after the staff had finished the cleanup and gone home.

She was exhausted.

A hot shower and bed were all she needed.

Much like leaving her purse and ID at home when she didn't think she'd need it, she'd left her phone in her room during her shift.

It wasn't as if anyone who knew her didn't have a second phone number to use to call her if there was an emergency. Besides, how was she going to set an example of telling the employees to leave their phones in their lockers if she was constantly on hers?

That didn't mean she didn't find her phone within seconds of walking through her apartment door.

A missed call from her mother awaited her. *"Oh, I bet you're working late tonight. I wanted to hear your voice. It's been so long."*

The mom guilt was thick.

Salena looked at the time . . . knew her parents had gone to bed at least three hours before, and sent a quick text saying it was late and they could talk tomorrow.

In her text messages were two from Ryan.

He'd been silent the whole day. Not that she expected a "good morning" from the man, but she would have secretly liked it.

The first message had come in midafternoon. After she'd gone downstairs for her shift. Have you recovered from last night? was his question.

The second text was sent at eleven. You said you were working tonight. Call me. It doesn't matter how late.

Salena looked at the time and dialed.

The phone connected, and the noise of someone fumbling with a phone followed.

"You called." Ryan sounded half-asleep.

"You're demanding."

He laughed. "How was your night?"

The question felt foreign to Salena's ears. "More eventful than yours. Did I wake you?"

"No . . ."

Was that a yawn?

"No. I'm wide awake," he said with a sigh.

"Liar."

Ryan chuckled. "Busy night, Trouble?"

"Saturdays are always busy. Thankfully we don't have bands and two a.m. closings."

"Fun for patrons, sucks for staff."

"Exactly." One of the many reasons she'd taken a management position with the D'Angelos. "How was your night?"

"Much quieter than yesterday."

She laughed. "That wouldn't have taken much."

He yawned again, this time Salena found herself reaching for her next long breath as well.

"When can I see you again?" he asked.

"Because you had so much fun the last time?"

He didn't comment on that. "Next Friday?"

She hesitated. "I have plans."

"Thursday night? Saturday for lunch?"

"You want to meet for lunch?"

"If that's the time you have . . . that's the time I'll take."

Salena rubbed her forehead. "Lunch?"

"I'll pick you up at eleven, get you back to work by two . . . is that okay?"

"My shift starts at three on Saturday."

"You have an hour to get ready, then."

"You're going to drive all the way down here for a three-hour date in the middle of the afternoon?" she questioned.

"Ah-huh. Wear comfortable clothes and walking shoes."

"You're serious."

"I'll pick you up at ten."

She narrowed her eyes. "Okay."

"Great." He sounded excited.

"Ryan?"

"Yeah?"

"I'm exhausted."

"Get some sleep, Trouble. I'll text you tomorrow."

What the actual hell was this?

"Good night."

"Night, babe."

Salena stared at her phone as if the object wasn't something she'd seen before.

CHAPTER THIRTEEN

Was Sunday really Sunday without a family dinner? This was a question that Mari lived by. And apparently, that family now extended to Salena in a very real weekly way.

Salena attempted to get out of interrupting the D'Angelos' weekly gathering by suggesting she work.

Mari wouldn't have it. And to make things even better . . . at least in Mari's eyes . . . she invited Salena's parents to join them.

Salena should have been grateful. Having her parents over with a group of people would take some of the pressure and spotlight off her.

Or so she hoped.

The rooftop terrace was set up with a long family-size table, space heaters, and strands of lights to illuminate the area once the sun started to fall. There were plants and lounge chairs mixed in the space, giving everyone a place to land even before the meal was served.

With the exception of Giovanni and Emma, the entire D'Angelo family, including Dante's mother, Rosa, slowly made their way onto the terrace.

Baby Leo moved from one lap to another, enjoying all the attention.

Franny ran around to help set the table.

Mari and Luca slowly brought food up from their apartments, and Dante took over the job of arranging the space heaters to keep everyone warm.

Salena played hostess and made sure everyone had something to drink.

When her parents arrived, a dish in hand, it was added to the mounds of food on the table.

"It's a good thing Mari arranges these dinners, or we'd never see you," Brigida said as she kissed Salena's cheeks.

"Mama, please don't start."

"What? I'm not starting anything. I'm stating fact."

"How about some wine?" Salena refused to argue with her mother and turned toward the table to get her mother a glass.

Chloe moved in and greeted Salena's parents with hugs and smiles. "I'm so glad you guys could make it."

"Look how happy you are," Brigida said. "Married life is agreeing with you, no?"

"It is."

Salena's mother turned and looked directly at her. "See, it's not all bad."

"She's married to Adonis, Mama." Salena smirked.

Dante heard the compliment and called from a few feet away. "They broke the mold with me, Mrs. Barone."

"My son, the joker," Rosa said, playfully hitting him with the back of her hand while holding Leo in the other.

Brigida looked at the glass of wine in Chloe's hand and frowned. "You're not pregnant yet?"

Salena laughed.

"We're waiting for a while."

"What? Why? You're married now. No need to wait, sì?"

"I know, Brigida. I ask the same thing." Rosa moved closer as if the older women in solidarity would change Chloe and Dante's conviction to wait a couple of years before starting a family. "Who wouldn't want one of these? Isn't that right, little Leo?"

Leo was half-asleep, a pacifier in his mouth.

"They haven't even been married a year," Salena argued.

"What does that matter?"

Salena and Chloe exchanged looks. "Is this always the subject of conversation on Sundays?"

Brooke was folding napkins and setting them on the plates. "No, sometimes we lay bets on how soon Emma will be pregnant."

Salena rolled her eyes.

Mari walked through the door leading into the building, her hands filled with a serving tray.

"Chloe, Salena, go help bring the food."

Salena looked at the chore as a blessing to escape the marriage-and-baby inquisition.

"That has to get old," Salena said to Chloe the moment they were out of earshot of the others.

"Mama isn't so bad, but Rosa is anxious for a grandbaby."

"Why? I mean, it isn't like she's old. She should be out living her life instead of thinking about babysitting."

"I say that to her all the time."

"Is her divorce final?" Dante's father hadn't been in the picture for years, and yet it had only been in the last year that a divorce was filed.

"We wish. Trying to divorce someone who lives in Italy isn't as easy as you would think."

"I'd ask about it to get the spotlight off me if she wasn't so sensitive," Salena said.

"Don't do that. She still cries."

"What a waste."

They worked their way down two flights of stairs to Mari's apartment, where Luca was finishing up.

Luca stripped the apron from his frame and clapped his hands. "Perfect timing."

The three of them marched back up to the terrace, platters in hand. A well-choreographed dance ensued.

Brooke retrieved Leo, who was fast asleep, and took him into Salena's apartment, where a playpen had been set up for him to sleep and be close by. Drinks were topped off, and everyone found a seat as the food was passed around the table.

Mari asked that Luca say grace, which they all took a silent moment to be a part of, and then the conversations began again.

"Has anyone heard from Gio or Emma?" Mari asked.

"If they are worried about what's going on at home enough to interrupt their honeymoon, they're doing it wrong," Dante teased.

"Gio's not sharing Emma until he has to," Luca added.

"I bet she's pregnant by Christmas." Rosa passed the bread to her right.

"It was Thanksgiving last week. What changed?" Brooke asked.

Rosa lifted her fingers in the air. "My gut."

Salena stared at Chloe and blinked several times, her expression a straight line.

"Every week."

Salena's father looked at Dante. "How is the boat business?"

"A little slow right now, but we have lots of bookings in December."

For a few minutes, the subject moved from babies to boats.

"How is Daniella?" Mari asked. "We haven't seen her and her family in so long. Are they coming for Christmas this year?"

"We don't know yet," Brigida replied. "Aldo and I were just talking about going to visit them."

"For the holidays?" Rosa asked.

"No . . . well, maybe. But we are talking about driving over and spending some time with the grandbabies."

Salena sat taller. "I think that's a great idea."

Her father offered a disapproving look.

"What? I've been encouraging you to go there more. You're retired. Nothing is stopping you."

"Not to mention the empty nest," Chloe reminded them.

Salena shot a look at her best friend, would have kicked her under the table if she could reach her. "I've been grown up a lot longer than I've been out of the house."

Aldo huffed.

"Your daughter has a point," Luca said.

"I'll come by and water the plants," Salena offered. "Think of all the worldly advice you can hand out at Daniella's." With four grandkids, they could be dictating someone else's life in a few hours with the right travel plan.

Her father softened his stare and put another forkful of ravioli in his mouth.

"Salena? How was your date with Ryan?"

Mari's question came at the same time Salena was trying to swallow her wine.

She half coughed, half choked on the liquid and had to grab her napkin quickly to avoid spitting all over her plate.

Dante laughed, and Chloe covered her smile.

"Who is Ryan?" Brigida turned to Salena and asked.

"Emma's brother," Franny answered. "They went out Friday night."

Salena recovered well enough to contradict the youngest D'Angelo. "It wasn't a date."

"He picked you up. You had dinner, yes?" Mari asked.

"Kinda."

"Kinda? What is kinda? You ate or you didn't," Rosa said.

"Is this the man you were talking to at the wedding?" Salena's father asked.

"Yes."

"He's a nice young man, Aldo. And the Rutledges are a lovely family."

Salena thought of Ryan's opinion of his father and wanted to argue but kept her knowledge to herself.

Brigida stared at her. "Is this serious?"

Salena dropped a hand to the table. "It was one date. Not even a date. No, it's not . . . He was just helping me with my car."

"And you had dinner," Mari said with a smile.

"And he kissed you." All eyes swung to Franny, who shoved food in her nine-year-old mouth as soon as she said the words.

"How do you know that?" Brooke asked.

With a full mouth, she said, "I saw them from the window."

"You shouldn't spy on people," Brooke scolded.

Salena felt heat fill her cheeks.

"I wasn't spying. I was looking out the window."

"Watching other people is spying," Chloe corrected.

"It wasn't my fault they were kissing when I was looking."

"Don't argue," Luca scolded Franny.

Salena dropped her head in a hand.

"Dinner and kissing sounds like a date to me," Rosa said.

"Me too," Mari agreed.

"Are you seeing him again?" her father asked.

Salena wasn't about to answer the question. "Okay, let's lay bets on who is going to get pregnant first . . . Emma or Chloe."

Dante laughed.

"Don't toss me in the hot seat," Chloe teased.

Mari lifted a hand in the air. "Okay, okay. I like the boy. That's all I'm saying."

"Does he help run the winery?" Rosa asked.

"No," Luca answered. "He has rental property."

"Houses?" Aldo asked.

"Commercial," Salena found herself answering.

It was Brigida's smile of approval that prompted Salena's next words. "He has tattoos and drives a motorcycle, Mama. Don't get too excited."

"But he's employed," Aldo said.

"Everyone I've dated has been employed."

"DoorDash driver doesn't count," Dante teased.

Salena broke off a piece of bread and tossed it at him.

He and Chloe started laughing.

"If this is what it looks like to have a big family, remind me never to have kids," Salena told them.

Luca joined Dante and Chloe in laughter until it spread to everyone at the table. Even Salena had a hard time keeping her lips from splitting into a smile.

Finally, the subject was changed, and Salena was able to finish her dinner.

~

"How *was* your date with Ryan?" Chloe asked just above a whisper as they worked together to wash the dishes.

Salena looked over Chloe's shoulder toward the door leading outside, where everyone was still talking over shots of *limoncello* or coffee.

"Unexpected."

"How so?"

"We picked up In-N-Out and went to Fiesta Island."

Chloe winced. "What? Why?"

"My idea. I wasn't in the mood for waiters and a bar. We grabbed some whiskey and watched the fireworks."

Chloe shrugged. "That doesn't sound bad. Was he boring?"

"No. We found a lot to talk about."

"So, what was *unexpected*?" Chloe asked.

Salena rocked her head from one side to the other. If there was one thing about her best friend that she understood, it was that Chloe could not keep a secret. "We were getting cozy . . ."

"Was he good at 'getting cozy'?"

Salena blew out a breath. "Yes. Other men could take lessons."

It was Chloe's turn to look over her shoulder. "What happened?"

"We were in the car . . . you know, making out."

"Ah-huh."

For the briefest of moments, Salena almost told Chloe everything.

But then she'd tell Dante, who would let it slip to Gio, and Gio to Luca . . . and Luca already gave her sideways glances when she talked about her escapades. Now that she was living there, those big-brother disapproving looks were digging deeper.

"We got caught."

Chloe gripped the side of the sink and started laughing. "Holy crap. Were you guys in the middle of—"

"No. Most of our clothes were still on. It was dark. Nobody could really see in unless they were right there."

"Who caught you?"

Salena shrugged and came up with an easily believable lie. "The guy next to us. Knocked on the car, said his kids could see."

"Could they?"

Salena took the fork Chloe had just washed to dry it. "No. Some people just like to kill the joy . . . you know?"

Chloe laughed again. "Then you guys didn't . . ."

"No. Sadly." She'd been nothing but thirsty for the man ever since.

Chloe passed another plate. "How about you go to Ryan's place next time and avoid a car?"

"In Temecula?"

"Oh . . . good point."

"Yeah, and here is out of the question. I can't believe Franny saw us."

"Kissing by the back door isn't the end of the world."

"If she'd seen more, Luca would have my ass."

Chloe agreed with a nod. "So, get a hotel."

"I guess."

"I'm sure you've done that before."

"Hotels when I'm already out of town, yeah. I don't have that kind of money. Neither have the DoorDash drivers in my past."

Chloe giggled. "Ryan isn't broke."

"I know. Whatever."

"You are going to see him again, right?"

"He's going to take me to lunch next Saturday."

"Nooners are fun."

"Not that kind of date. In fact, he didn't allude to us hooking up at all. Just a date."

Chloe turned to her and paused. "Only a date."

Salena shrugged. "I think so."

"How do you feel about that?"

"Confused. You know me. I'm the girl guys want to play with, not get to know."

Her best friend lifted her chin. "You do that to yourself."

Salena couldn't argue. "It's safer."

Chloe returned to the soapy water. "Maybe this is a good thing. Have a few non-naked dates and get to know each other first."

Ryan's image floated in her memory, his laughter and tenderness when they'd arrived back after the run-in with the cop. "He has his shit way too together to be interested in me for long."

"Shut up. That's my friend you're talking about. And she's incredibly amazing."

Salena rolled her eyes. "I was only looking for a wedding hookup."

"Yeah, well . . . maybe fate has more to say on that."

"Listen to you talking about fate."

"All I'm saying is take it slow. You said it yourself. The guy is hot *and* put together. That isn't an easy-to-come-by combo."

"He's rich, and I don't even have a running car."

"His dad is rich. That doesn't mean he is."

True. "He's not hurting."

Chloe turned off the water, handed the last plate over. "All that is crap anyway. Try him on for size, you never know."

"I am trying," Salena said with a grin. "We never got there."

"Ahh, you're all kinds of sexually frustrated."

"I am!"

They both laughed. "If your parents go to Daniella's, you can always go to their place instead of a hotel."

Salena paused and then grinned. "Good point."

CHAPTER FOURTEEN

Salena Ubered her way to the studio on Thursday night. This time she showed up a little late and used the public time to warm up.

She and Ashlynn exchanged knowing glances but kept everything they'd talked about the previous week a secret.

Once everyone cleared out for the night, Ashlynn put the "Closed" sign on and locked the main door and dimmed the lights in the reception area.

Salena followed her into the office, where Ashlynn unearthed several tripods and iPhones.

"You do all this with iPhone cameras?" Salena asked.

"I tried a professional camera at first, but this is much easier. As long as the phone is a ten or newer, we're golden."

"I thought for sure you had someone here to record for you."

"Nope."

Ashlynn rolled out a privacy curtain that she explained she had in several different fabrics and colors to change things up.

Salena had spent some time watching Ashlynn's work and had started to get a general sense of what she needed to do.

Tonight was about watching Ashlynn's process and coming up with a sexy duo routine they could film to get Salena's page up.

There were marks on the floor that she was just now noticing where Ashlynn set up the tripods. Tape indicated the height of the stands.

"I record from all of the cameras at the same time and splice it together later." Ashlynn moved to the sound system and turned it on only high enough to give her a beat, then she lowered the lights slightly. "You can fix the lighting in edits, too. Sometimes, when I don't have time, I use what the camera picks up."

"Why is the music so low?"

"I overlay the music after. Otherwise, outside noise gets picked up, or if I'm out of breath. The phone rings."

"Makes sense."

Ashlynn pulled off the tank she'd been wearing in front of the other women that night and revealed a sexy red lace bra that matched the tiny red briefs she had on and walked to the pole in the frame of the cameras.

Salena stood back and watched through the center camera.

"How am I framed in?" Ashlynn placed her hand high on the pole. "You should see above my fingertips."

Salena adjusted the angle a tiny bit.

"There."

"This is the one part that takes me some time. I have to go back and forth and fiddle to get them perfect. With us working together, we can get done even faster."

Salena moved around the room and tilted the cameras to Ashlynn's specifications.

Once they were ready, Ashlynn applied a fresh layer of lipstick and slowly walked back to the pole, this time as if she was walking onstage. "I'll talk a little through this and then do it again in silence just so you see my intentions."

Salena pulled up a chair and watched.

"Sometimes I walk into the frame, sometimes I start at the pole. No different than how we do in class." Ashlynn reached for the pole and slowly ran her hand up one side. "Slowly get friendly with your equipment." She did a half turn, her back against the pole. "A little tease." She arched her back, pressed her breasts to the sky. "Easy moves, nothing too fancy, just set the mood."

"No different than a basic approach," Salena said.

"Right. A little walk-around . . . a sumo squat." Ashlynn's mouth was half-open, her eyes half-closed as she moved to the beat of the music. She moved out of her wide leg squat, gripped the pole and inverted, wrapped a leg around the pole, and slowly slid down. Her dismount was grace and skill. "More teasing." She ran a hand down her own chest, fanned her flat stomach, and wrapped around the pole again.

Salena had seen Ashlynn perform so many routines over the years, nothing here was new . . . just put together and seamless. After about fifteen minutes, she reset the music and did the whole thing a second time, this time in complete silence, her body on point, her facial expression all kinds of sex and desire. Pure female power and femininity. Yeah, some might think this was over the top, but for the women and the few men that dared to join, they loved this.

When she was done, she ended with a direct stare into one of the cameras, her hair disheveled in her face.

"That was hot."

Ashlynn got up much faster and walked away from the pole. "Your turn."

"What do you want me to do?"

"Anything."

She moved to the center tripod, and Salena switched places.

"You're taller than me, so hold up." Ashlynn moved from one camera to another.

"Your first couple of videos will be free. And you'll put new free stuff out that isn't as sexy but sets the mood to pull in your subscribers. Tonight, we'll just play. If we can use it, great, if not, we'll get more on Monday."

Just as Ashlynn did, Salena moved to the pole and treated it like a familiar lover. "I'm going to need to buy better outfits."

"Worth the investment," Ashlynn said.

"I hope so."

Salena closed her eyes and listened to the music and simply started to move. Wearing a tight and skimpy tank and a modest pair of shorts and high heels, Salena put more effort into the flirting and dance, using her hands to draw whoever watched to her ass and chest. All moves taught to beginner students and perfected by years of practice. If there was one thing Salena knew how to do, it was capturing the attention of the opposite sex. Pole dancing was an extension of that power. She combined a routine she'd perfected in the summer with a little of what they were practicing currently.

The memories of her first trip around the pole surfaced in her head. The impossible act of lifting her body onto the static object . . . no matter how strong she thought she'd been at the time, she couldn't do it. It was the fact that she wasn't physically able to that prompted her to show up for class again and again. Taking a regular dance class, one filled with men and women, sounded more like a club without the dim lights and alcohol. Pole dancing felt energetic and taboo at the same time.

Like a weight lifter would approach a barbell, Salena engaged her core the moment her grip settled on the bar, and she inverted her legs. She closed her eyes, concentrated on what her legs were doing, with her hair dangling toward the ground. The muscles in her abdomen and back worked together as gravity helped her do the splits in the air. Slow, thoughtful movements, almost as if she were walking down steps, brought her to a ninety-degree angle to the ground. She hovered, felt muscles engage in her waist and hips she hadn't known existed before discovering pole.

She worked her way up and down the pole with precision until she was breathless and tired. Unlike Ashlynn, when she finished, she hid her face from the camera and walked out of the frame.

Slowly, Ashlynn started to clap. "You're a natural."

"My last spin was too slow."

"It won't show on camera."

The music was turned off, they both pulled on sweatpants and T-shirts and headed to the office with the phones.

Two hours later, Ashlynn had a five-minute tease and a fifteen-minute routine completely sliced, edited, and dubbed over with the music she wanted, ready to upload to her site.

And much to Salena's surprise, her routine was easily clipped into two ten-minute videos.

"This is actually going to make me money?" Salena asked.

"Stay consistent with content, and yes."

"And the doubles routine?"

"It's gonna be a game changer."

"How soon before I get these videos out there?"

"I had a half a dozen videos before I launched my page and slowly put them out. That way, if I got tied up and couldn't film, I had new stuff. And since we'll be feeding off each other's content, you'll get on your feet much faster than I did."

"I hope this works. Not having a car sucks."

Ashlynn pushed back from the desk. "Let's clean up. I'll give you a ride home." They walked back to the studio and put everything away. "I'll send you some links where I've found some sexy, inexpensive outfits that you can order online."

"I'll bring my laptop on Monday and try and do these edits on my own."

Ashlynn patted her on the back. "It's nice to have someone to talk to about this."

"I still can't believe you've kept this a secret this whole time."

"It's better this way, you'll see."

Salena left the studio with a chest full of hope and excitement. And that felt good.

~

"You're taking me to the zoo." It was more a statement than a question. She looked up at the signage directing visitors to the parking lot of San Diego's zoo while Ryan maneuvered his car in the traffic.

"I was considering a hike up in La Jolla, but since it might rain, I thought this would be better. Besides, who doesn't like animals?"

Salena couldn't remember the last time she'd walked around the zoo. "The zoo?"

Ryan caught her eyes, his smile falling slightly. "You hate the idea."

"No. Shocked, maybe." Stunned was more like it. "Men don't take me to the zoo."

He regarded her with a turn of his head before the person behind him honked their horn.

Ryan pulled into an empty spot and killed the engine. "After the excitement of our last date, I thought this would be about as safe as we can get."

That put a smile on her face. "I'm sure I could get us kicked out of here if I tried hard enough."

Ryan closed his eyes and shook his head with a grin. "Of that, I have no doubt."

They climbed out of the car and started toward the gate.

Ryan jockeyed his position to stand between her and the way traffic was headed toward them and, at the same time, he reached for her hand and wove his fingers with hers.

Salena glanced at their joined hands, then to him. "What's this?" Holding hands was what couples did.

"I don't want you to get lost."

Should she say something? *I don't hold hands. Do I?* Men put suggestive hands on her back, her hip . . . they slung an arm over her shoulders. But holding hands? What was that saying about whatever it was that they were doing? Going to the zoo, yes, but what else? Dodging arrest for indecent exposure . . . for mouthing off to a cop. Naked possession Salena understood. Hand-holding, not so much.

"Someone got quiet."

"I'm trying to remember the last time I was at the zoo."

"C'mon. This zoo is world-famous. It's in your backyard."

"You come here a lot?"

The answer was in the fact that they passed the ticket booth and went straight to the entrance.

Ryan pulled a card from his wallet, along with his driver's license, and presented it to the kid checking passes.

"Thanks," the kid said and waved them both through.

"You have an annual pass?"

He shrugged.

"Seriously."

"The animals need to eat," he said as if that was the proper answer to her question.

They paused at the crossroads of the park. Parents pushing strollers with screaming kids, vendors selling everything from cotton candy to helium balloons walked around them.

"What's your favorite animal?"

"Men," she said, deadpan.

Ryan split into a grin, licked his lips, and rephrased. "Non-human."

She hadn't thought about it before that moment. "Predators."

"That's a category."

"Who wants to watch a bunch of animals grazing when they can watch a giant cat take down something double its size?"

He blinked . . . twice, and then tugged her to follow him.

"You know where you're going?"

"Nawh . . . I'm going to wander around until we come across a meat eater and pretend I know where I am."

Only he kept walking . . . past the alcoves of birds and small animals.

"I'm calling bullshit."

He shrugged. "Believe what you want."

"Does Emma like the zoo?"

"I have no idea," Ryan responded.

"Your mom?"

"Probably."

They kept walking until he stopped in front of the dwarf mongoose exhibit.

Salena looked left, then right. Not one lion, tiger, or bear in sight. "What are we doing here?"

"You said predator."

Her eyes narrowed on the tiny rodent-looking animal popping its head up from a clump of dirt. "That's a rat."

"Arguably, it will happily eat garbage . . . Its desire, however, is to hunt and chow down on flesh."

Salena did a double take back to the thing with tiny ears and short hair. "It's cute."

"There are a lot of cute animals that eat meat." Ryan gave her a sideways glance that made her laugh.

"Okay, Mr. Zoologist. I was picturing something bigger."

"Fine." He tugged on her hand and started walking.

"Did your parents have animals when you were growing up?"

"No. You?"

"No. I lived in a condo."

"Did you want pets?"

They paused in front of the monkeys to watch as their bored faces took in the humans.

"I wanted a kitten."

"And your parents said no."

"My father said I was allergic."

"Are you?" Ryan asked.

She shrugged. "No idea. No one I know had cats."

"Did you have a reaction as a baby?"

"Couldn't tell you. My father said no, gave me a reason for his answer."

"And you didn't question him?"

"Oh, I questioned him. And when I didn't like the answer . . . I went on a hunger strike."

Ryan started laughing. "You're serious?"

"Yeah . . . I didn't eat dinner at home for four days. My mother thought I was going to starve."

"Only dinner?"

She could tell by the look in Ryan's eyes he knew there was more to the story. "You wouldn't expect a teenager to not eat all day . . . even on strike."

"Heaven forbid."

"Someone at school posted a picture of me eating lunch, and my parents found it. That night, my mom stopped threatening to find the strays on the street so I wouldn't starve, and my parents didn't bother setting a place for me at the table. The great hunger strike ended six days after it began."

"And no cat."

"No cat."

Ryan lifted her hand to his lips and kissed the back of it.

A twist and a turn later, and they were standing in front of a lioness stretching out in the late morning sun. Several yards behind her, a lion stood long enough to find a better spot before curling into a ball and plopping on the ground with an undignified thump.

"This is more like it."

"He'd make one hell of a pet," Ryan said before leaning his arms on the fence separating them from the animals.

"Ha. You'd only forget to feed him once."

"True."

Salena studied the lioness that lifted her head and looked at the crowd with disinterest. "Did you know that when the female wants to mate, she demands sex thirty times a day?"

"I like the sound of that."

"And if the male is tired or not in the mood, she's known to bite the balls of the male to get him to perform."

Ryan glanced over. "For someone who doesn't frequent the zoo, you seem to know a thing or two about the animals that live here."

She shrugged. "I saw it on TikTok."

"Then it has to be true."

He grabbed her hand and pulled her away from the exhibit. "I think I need to introduce you to animals that aren't involved in fifty shades of kink."

They snacked on popcorn as Ryan wove her through the winding paths of the zoo. They laughed at the turtles that had no desire to find privacy as they attempted to mate. The red pandas ran around their habitat, entertaining the guests with their fuzzy ears and perpetual smiles. Ryan knew more than the average person when it came to the animals they stopped to watch.

His easy grin and charm as he pulled her around the zoo, trying to get as much in as they could in the few hours they had to explore, was engaging.

Lunch was in a sit-down restaurant he'd made reservations for, giving them the opportunity to cut past the dozen parties all waiting.

The décor was straight out of Africa. Animal print, dark wooden masks, colorful baskets . . . the food was a step up from what was offered in the park, but not by much. The draw was likely the availability of cocktails, a waiter, and air-conditioning. It gave the two of them the opportunity to quietly chat.

"Have you been on a safari?" she asked.

"No."

"I'm surprised."

"That's not a trip you take solo."

"You can't get your buddies to go along?"

He laughed. "Maybe if hunting was involved."

She winced. "Do you hunt?"

"No. I guess if I was hungry, I could, but that's not my angle."

Salena leaned forward on the table, rested her chin on top of her folded hands. "I'm sure you could have talked a woman into that trip."

He matched her gesture, leaned in, his lips spread in a smile. "When do we leave?"

Her laugh was a short staccato. "Yeah, right."

"It was your idea."

"I need to buy a car. Plane tickets to Africa will have to wait."

His eyes drifted down her and back to her eyes.

"What?"

A soft lick to his lips. "I'm picturing you in a colorful dress, the setting African sun at your back . . . hair blowing in your face."

The comment had her speechless. An uncommon event for Salena.

"You don't like that idea?"

"Most men only picture me naked."

Ryan regarded her with a sideways glance. "I'm not most men."

"All men say that."

He lost his frown. "Why do you do that?"

"Do what?"

He lowered his voice. "Assume the only thing I want from you requires nakedness?"

"At your sister's wedding, that's all you were thinking." Of that, she had no doubt.

"True."

"There you go." She sat back.

He kept staring.

"What?" His unrelenting gaze had her squirming in her chair.

The waiter arrived, took their order, and left them exactly where they left off.

Ryan stared.

Salena squirmed.

"Who was he?" Ryan finally asked.

"Who?"

"The guy who convinced you that all men were the same?"

The answer wasn't instant. There wasn't a name attached to her belief. "There isn't an ex, if that's what you're thinking."

"Something shaped your thoughts."

"History."

"So . . . an ex."

She shook her head. "No one broke my heart. I haven't gotten close enough to anyone to allow that to happen."

"Not even in high school?"

"No."

"Your first?"

The memory of that day made her wrinkle her nose. "God, no. Did your first girlfriend break your heart?"

He paused. "A little."

"She broke it off?"

"Summer came, and my mother made us go to Temecula. When I went home, Brittany had moved on."

"Brittany?" The name conjured the image of the cheerleader type with a posse of girls, dictating everything the others did by pure pressure.

Ryan's gaze drifted for a moment; his lips fell into a straight line. Then, as if catching himself, he smiled and lifted his eyebrows. "She had really big . . ." He left off the rest.

"I'm sure she did."

"Have you ever considered that the reason you've never gotten close enough to suffer a broken heart is because you've set boundaries before giving a guy a chance?"

"Is that what you think I'm doing?"

"It's not what I think. It's what you're doing."

Salena leaned in again. "Are you suggesting I let down my walls, Ryan? For you?"

"Yes." His answer was quicker than a skate striking its prey.

"So that you can be the first to break my heart?"

His playful smile fell. "That wouldn't be my intention. And not on purpose."

"But it's a possibility."

"There is always a risk."

What game was this man playing?

The question must have played on her face.

Ryan reached for her hand that lay on the table and stroked her finger.

She stared at their hands, an unfamiliar knot formed in her throat. "You've already nicknamed me *Trouble*."

"A name you've lived up to," he said with a soft laugh.

Their eyes met and held. Was that sincerity she saw staring back? Was it a man gifted in deception?

Fear tasted like bile in the back of her throat.

"I'll get back to you," she said.

"On?"

"Lowering my walls."

One corner of his mouth lifted in half a smile. "I can work with that."

CHAPTER FIFTEEN

Gathering information about another person without seeming overly excited about the answers never really worked. Doing it as an adult was just as awkward as it had been as a teenager.

Emma and Giovanni returned from their honeymoon, and within two days, Ryan found an excuse to show up on their doorstep.

"I'm thinking about moving," he announced once the pleasantries were over. They sat on the back patio, Gio and Emma held glasses with wine, Ryan opted for beer.

"How far?" Emma seemed to hold her breath.

"Just to San Diego. I was talking to Dad, and he made a few good points about owning my own place. I'm bouncing the idea around."

Emma blinked several times. "You and Dad had a congenial conversation?"

"Hard to believe, but yeah."

Gio reached for Emma's hand. "Are you thinking house or condo?" he asked.

"I have no idea." Ryan lifted a hand to the air. "This is all new for you both. What are your thoughts on living without neighbors on the other side of the wall?"

"You guys didn't argue?" It seemed Emma didn't grasp Ryan's question.

"No. I think Dad was just as surprised as you are."

Gio stuck to the topic. "The condos downtown or overlooking the bay will run you almost as much as a single-family . . . more even."

"When was the last time you and Dad didn't get into it during private family time?"

Gio and Ryan both turned to stare at Emma, who was wrinkling her forehead with enough force to need Botox to smooth out the lines.

"I think I was ten," Ryan said. "Can we move on?"

Emma shook her head. "Sorry."

"I personally like the space," Gio told him. "I also lived the exact opposite of the two of you my entire life. I guess it just depends on what you like."

"I didn't mind condo living when it was just me. I was traveling all the time and could always escape the small space and visit Mom," Emma replied.

Ryan and Emma had always considered the Temecula family home their mother's and the Napa home their father's. Even though Ryan had the same option, he didn't exercise it often. Only when he had too much to drink or someone needed him in the next room had he stayed in the family home after his short stint in college.

"Apartment living works. It doesn't feel like home, though," he confessed.

"If you owned a condominium, that would change." Gio sipped his wine.

Ryan tried to picture how things would change in a high-rise condo in San Diego. A barbeque grill on a small patio or a back porch like the one sitting next to the pool. He didn't desire a pool . . . but maybe a hot tub. A private hot tub.

The thought of Salena in a bathing suit . . . hot bubbling water . . .

"If you got a house, you could finally get that dog you've always wanted," Emma interrupted his thoughts.

"What dog?" he asked.

With a tilt to her head, Emma chided him with only a look. "Please. You've wanted a dog for as long as I can remember." She turned to her husband. "You should have seen the fights he'd get into with our dad about not owning a dog. Every year at Christmas, he'd beg for a dog and was convinced that Santa would bring one if Mom and Dad didn't relent."

"You had all that land . . . why not have a dog?" Gio asked.

"Dad said no. That was the end of that."

"He probably didn't want the responsibility when Mom took us down here."

"Probably."

Gio reached for the wine bottle and topped off his and Emma's glasses.

"I'm sad you'll be leaving the area," Emma told him. "I'm kind of surprised you stayed around as long as you did."

"I haven't left yet. Besides, I'll bum off your guest room before Mom's, so don't worry about missing me too much." He smiled at his sister. Of the three Rutledge children, he and Emma were the closest. Probably because their father favored their older brother, and the two of them always felt in second place.

"I don't know . . . you and Dad are becoming chummy."

Ryan waved his beer in the air. "There is a long-ass way from a conversation without fighting to *chummy*."

Gio slapped his thighs and stood. "Let's throw something on the grill. Ryan, you want another beer?"

He stood. "I'll get it."

As Ryan walked into the house to fetch another beer from the refrigerator, his decision on what type of dwelling to purchase was made.

Twenty minutes later, Emma was inside putting together something to go with the steaks Gio put on the grill when Ryan brought up Salena.

"So . . . ah," he started.

Gio glanced at him from the corner of his eyes.

"I've gone out with Salena a couple of times."

Gio had a slight smile on his face but concentrated on the grill. "Gone out?"

"Yeah . . . a couple of dates." Ryan lifted his beer to his lips. "She's pretty closed off."

The smile on Gio's face faltered. "How do you mean?"

"I don't know . . . like closed off. Walls. Did she have a douche ex or something?"

Gio laughed quickly. "Salena doesn't get involved enough to blame any of that on one person."

Ryan wasn't sure if that was comforting or not. "Why, then?"

"That's a question for Chloe. I mean, if you want a direct answer. I've known Salena a long time, I love her . . . like a sister."

Gio paused.

"What?"

"I kissed her once."

Ryan's back straightened. An uneasy swell in his gut started to reject his beer.

"We were young . . . someone suggested spin the bottle. I wanted to puke. She and Chloe had been friends for so long I never realized how much like a sister she was."

Ryan felt the air enter his lungs again.

"Only not exactly a sister. I mean, I gave her hell for some of the choices in guys she made. Told her she was too good to go out with just anyone." Gio turned over the steaks with one hand, drank wine with the other. "You know what she said to me?"

"No."

"She called me a fucking hypocrite. She was right. No one ever questioned who I dated, or . . ." Gio let his words fall off. "She told me once that if she ever settled for one guy, it would be on her terms. Not because someone dictated it was time. Not because of a biological clock. Not because society told her." He paused. "How is that any different from any man you know?"

"It's not."

149

Gio pointed his glass at Ryan and sighed. "Listen, if you're still in the picture this long after you've slept with Salena, she obviously likes you. Even with those walls."

"I haven't slept with her." *Not for lack of trying.*

Gio lost his smile. "Really? I thought—"

"We just ah, . . ." *Almost got arrested for trying.* "It hasn't happened."

"Huh."

A spark from the grill had Gio turning his attention away.

Emma poked her head out the back door. "How long?"

"Anytime," Gio told her.

Emma ducked back into the house.

"Salena's good people. Loyal. I love her like a sister and would protect her as if she were family. But I don't coddle her. She's more independent than most men I know and seems to understand exactly what she wants in life. Some of that might be an act, but who knows . . . maybe she does. One thing I do know is she isn't searching for a forever guy."

"No one said anything about forever."

Gio shrugged. "We're all looking for something until we find it. The question is what."

Was he looking? Ryan never felt like he was on a quest to find the perfect woman. Not that Salena was perfect. Hell, she was as flawed as him. The image of her mouthing off to the cop flashed. Strong women like Salena didn't stick around for long, and Ryan avoided weak and needy women like the plague.

"I don't know." And Ryan didn't.

"Funny, I feel the need to say something like, 'If you hurt her, I'll be forced to deal with you.' But I know Salena well enough to suggest that you should be the one on guard."

That was at least the second time Ryan felt warned away from getting deeply involved with Salena.

And here he was . . . already planning their next date.

~

"It's Halloween. It's a costume party on the boat."

"And last minute," Salena chided before moving her phone from one ear to the other. The restaurant was packed, but thankfully, they were fully staffed. She was jumping in where she was needed but wasn't running plates to tables. Hence the reason she was on the phone with Chloe discussing costume parties.

"How many Halloween parties are you doing this year?" Chloe asked.

"Zero."

"And when was the last time you did one on a private boat?"

"Never." The thought was appealing.

"I've already spoken to Mama, so you can't say you have to work."

Except the D'Angelos' restaurant wasn't her only source of income these days. She and Ashlynn had a busy schedule for filming content that took up nearly all of Salena's free time.

"I don't know."

"What?" Chloe gasped. "Salena Barone is passing up a party? Are you feeling okay?"

"I've been busy."

"Yeah, busy hanging out with Ryan . . . who already said yes, by the way. You can make him and your best friend happy at the same time."

That certainly felt like a perk. "What time?"

"Good God, that took some serious effort." Chloe told her a time.

"I'll be late."

"You can't be too late, it's on the boat. We'll take off in time for sunset."

"Shit, that's right." She'd have to juggle the schedule with Ashlynn to make it work. If Salena didn't go, questions would be asked, and that wasn't something she wanted to get into right now. Not without a paycheck to back up her choices. "Okay, fine. I'll make it work."

"Do you need a ride?"

"I'll Uber."

"You sure? I bet Ryan would be happy to pick you up."

Salena paused. "I'll work it out."

"Awesome. We thought it would be fun to pick a theme. Do you still have that roaring twenties dress from a couple of years ago?"

"Somewhere in a box."

"Well, dust it off. We're doing a Gatsby motif and want to take pictures for the new brochure. Film some content for the website."

Salena's shoulders straightened at the thought of filming in a 1920s-style dress. How many pole dancers were there in the '20s? She could Uber from Ashlynn's already dressed and ready to go. "Sounds good."

The sound of one of the chefs barking orders caught Salena's attention and drew her away from the conversation. "I've got to go."

"We'll talk later. Ciao."

Salena ended the call and went to find out what the raised voices in the kitchen were all about. When she got there, Luca was already there, arguing with another chef in Italian. Something about too much salt in a sauce. Either way, the subject was out of her lane, so instead of offering a taste test, she quietly made her way to Mari's office, where the woman was working on payroll.

"Sounds like Luca and Fausto are at it again."

"I can hear them." Mari rolled her eyes.

"Want me to tell the staff to announce the ravioli as a special? Or omit the vodka sauce from the menu?"

Mari stood up behind the desk. "Ravioli for now."

Salena patted the frame of the door and left to give the staff the update.

CHAPTER SIXTEEN

Midweek, the restaurant closed its doors by midnight at the latest. The beautiful thing about a family-run business was the ability to close the place early if customers stopped showing up. Salena had worked more than her share of closing-the-bar hours, not collapsing into bed until nearly three in the morning, in many of the places she worked. The D'Angelos didn't run that kind of business. The noisy bar scene was farther down the block, and that was perfectly fine with her.

Salena locked the door behind the last employee that left for the night and set the alarm. The D'Angelos were already in their apartments and likely in bed. As she made her way to the top floor, her cell buzzed in her back pocket with a text message.

Ryan's name appeared on her screen and put a smile on her face.

Still working? he asked.

Done for the night, she texted back.

Salena pushed into her apartment at the same time her phone rang.

"That was quick," she said to Ryan as she answered the phone.

"I hate texting. It's much better to have a conversation."

She closed the door behind her and kicked off her shoes before walking around her space. "I don't think I knew my phone could be used for calls the first five years I owned one."

"We're not twelve anymore," he told her.

"Still, there are times talking isn't appropriate."

"Name three."

She strode into her bedroom and put her phone on speaker so she could use both hands to strip down for a shower.

"A doctor's office."

"Okay."

"An airplane."

"Yeah, that's annoying," Ryan agreed.

"When you're saying something about the person beside you and don't want them to know what you're gossiping about."

"That sounds like high school."

"Still applies. I bet you text Emma to bitch about your family during holiday dinners." She knew enough about Ryan to understand the dynamics of his parents.

"Well—"

"When you're with one guy and another one is texting your plans for later in the week."

"Fine." Ryan blew out a breath. "Maybe there are more than three reasons to text instead of talk on the phone."

"When it's too noisy to talk or be heard." Her shirt landed on her hamper; her bra fell to the side.

"Do you text other guys when we're on a date?"

She sat on the edge of her bed to remove her socks. "No. I've only done that when I knew the date was going nowhere and I wouldn't see the guy again. Even then, I've tried to hold off a conversation until I was alone."

"I guess that means I'm still in the running for future dates."

She smiled, unbuttoned her jeans. "We'll see," she teased.

"Is that right?"

She wiggled out of them, kicked her panties to the hamper, and walked to the bathroom.

"People are starting to ask about you when they talk to me," she said.

Was that a hum coming from him?

"I like that."

"We've been on two dates."

"We know the same people."

"Hold on." She placed her phone on the counter and turned on the water for the shower.

"Is that water?" he asked.

"I'm about to take a shower."

"You're naked?"

Salena smiled at her reflection in the mirror. "Bummed you didn't FaceTime me?"

"Yes." His answer was instant, and that made her smile even bigger.

Steam started to billow, and for fun, Salena pressed the button to turn their phone call into a video call and left the phone on the counter, pointing to the ceiling.

Ryan picked up the video on the first ring. His image filled the screen, his face close to the camera.

Salena, on the other hand, was nowhere to be seen.

"Where are you?"

She stepped into the tub, pulled the curtain closed, and spoke up so maybe he could hear her. "Just a minute."

A few cuss words escaped him.

"I can't hear you. Hold up."

She went ahead and took her time soaping up and rinsing off. She'd wait for the next day to wash her hair. For now, the desire to rid her skin of marinara and wine was high on her list.

When she cut the water off, the room filled with silence.

"Are you still there?"

"Is the pope Catholic?"

Laughing, she toweled off before wrapping the cloth around her body. When she picked up the phone, Ryan was still glued to the thing, hoping for a peep show.

"Damn," he said. But he was smiling.

"Disappointed?"

"Is there a mirror in your bathroom?"

She glanced again at her reflection. "Of course."

"See that?"

"See what?"

"The beautiful, wet woman staring back at you?"

Salena stopped looking at herself and smiled at the camera. "You're good, Rutledge."

"I know."

She liked his cocky smile. Back in her bedroom, she dropped the phone on her bed, the towel to the floor, and put on clean panties and a long T-shirt.

"You're naked again, aren't you?"

"Wanna see?" she asked with no intention of showing.

"No, no . . . the texture of the wall is fine."

"Are you frustrated yet?"

"Is that the goal?" he asked.

The T-shirt went over her head, and she pulled at the tie holding her hair back to let it loose. "Maybe if I tease you enough, you'll plan a date that lasts well into the evening."

"You're the one that only had time for a long lunch."

"True."

"Can I pick you up on Saturday? I'm told we're both going to the same party."

Back in front of the camera, she walked back into the living room and sat on the sofa. "I'll have to meet you there."

"You sure?"

"I have some things I need to do. Did Chloe tell you this costume party had a theme?" Salena changed the subject quickly to avoid questions.

"Speakeasy 1920s."

"You're good with dressing up?"

"Why not? When men wore hats and hard-sole shoes, and women were being liberated."

"I'm not sure how liberated they were. A woman didn't have the right to have her own bank account until the '70s . . . but hey, she could wear pants."

Ryan's eyes narrowed. "Really?"

"Yeah, look it up. I imagine having the choice of putting on pants felt pretty freeing at the time."

"I never thought about it."

Salena curled her legs under her on the couch and switched the phone to her other hand. "Chloe took a Women's Issues class in college. I helped her with her homework. There were a lot of fascinating things I learned. You know how women went to work during the war effort during World War II, right?"

"They had to."

"Yeah. But did you know that after the war, these women who had become largely independent were told to go back home to the kitchen and make babies and were denied jobs they held during the war?"

"And given to men."

"Exactly."

"That sucks."

"I'm glad I was born when I was. My personality in that time would have made me a Bonnie to someone's Clyde."

Ryan smiled. "You do have a way with the authorities."

Salena leaned her head back on the couch. "You almost get arrested one time and you never live it down." She opened her mouth to a wide yawn.

"You're tired."

"Hospitality is busy work."

"That you can do in pants," Ryan added.

"Spandex makes me more tips." Not that she'd exercised that choice in clothing since taking the management position with the D'Angelos. That was strictly the bar room scene.

"Isn't dressing sexy to earn better money against the feminist movement?"

Salena shrugged. "Probably. But since I alone can't change the world, I might as well use the system to my benefit."

"You're straight up, Salena. I'll give you that."

"I've never been angry that I'm a woman, just with what society thinks I should and shouldn't do because of my gender." She yawned a second time.

"Okay, I'm going to let you go before you fall asleep on me."

"I'll see you at the party."

"If you change your mind about needing a ride . . ."

"I'll let you know."

His voice lowered. "Good night, Salena."

"Good night, Clyde."

Ryan smiled before ending the call.

Salena stared at the dark screen with a grin.

~

"If you guys fly, I can use your car when you're gone."

Salena stood in her parents' living room with a list of instructions for things she already knew needed to get done. Pull the mail out of the box daily to avoid it overfilling, water the plants, and rotate what lights were on and off so if anyone was watching, they'd think someone was home.

"It's cheaper to drive," her father pointed out.

"It used to be cheaper to drive, then gas prices went over five bucks a gallon."

Her mother waved at her father. "Papa hates to fly."

"And you don't like long road trips."

"Only when you were a child. Kicking the seat, whining about the long days."

It wasn't just that, but Salena wasn't going to drill her point home. Her father avoided airplanes as much as he could, and her mother put up with the alternative form of transportation to avoid an argument.

"I'd suggest you stay over, but I know how much you hate it here." Her father's words were meant to cut, and they did. Although Salena wasn't about to show it.

"It was time for me to move out, Papa." She thought of Ryan and the possibility of having breakfast with him. "If it makes you happy, I'll stay over a couple of nights, throw off the neighbors."

Her mother huffed. "If you can do that when we're away, you can do that when we're here."

"Never mind, then. I'll play with light switches instead." Salena grabbed her purse and swung it over her shoulder. "Have fun and drive safe."

"You're mad," her mother pointed out.

Salena placed a hand on a hip. "I'm disappointed that every time we see each other, you guys both want to berate me for my choices."

"We're not yet used to your absence," Aldo said.

"Get over it, Papa. I'm not moving back." Instead of driving the moot point home, Salena leaned over to her mother, kissed her cheek, and walked to the front door.

"We'll call you when we get to your sister's," her mother told her.

Salena turned, looked at the two of them. "Love you both."

Her mother returned the sentiment, and after a swift smack to her father's arm, her dad did the same.

The oppression of being in her parents' space lifted once she reached the street.

The weather in San Diego was taking a turn. Cold wind blew off the bay, prompting her to pull the collar of her jacket higher on her neck.

She donned a pair of dark sunglasses and took wide strides as she crossed traffic to get to the side of the street she now called home.

Before walking into the restaurant, she pulled out her cell phone and dialed her sister.

They weren't terribly close. When they were young, their age difference was their biggest hurdle. After Salena's first nephew was born and Daniella moved away, the miles kept them from getting close right about the time the two of them had something in common. She sent gifts for birthdays and holidays, but they didn't get much time together face to face.

"Hello?"

"It's me," Salena said. "I just left our parents'."

"You sound frazzled."

"I am. I don't have a lot of time to chat, I just wanted to remind you that you owe me."

Daniella laughed. "For what?"

"Making our parents the neurotic mess that they are. When they get to you, keep them there."

Her sister moaned. "They're threatening to stay through Christmas."

"Good! By New Year's, they might be used to my absence and stop giving me a hard time."

"I don't . . ." Her sister started to waver.

"Daniella, please. I'm stuck with them all year. I get to hear about your teenage drama on the regular. The least you can do is make them comfortable." Salena ignored the passing crowd.

"Salena."

She felt a *no* coming. "Please."

"Matt and I are having trouble."

That stopped Salena's pleas. "What kind of trouble?"

"We're seeing a counselor."

"Shit."

The word escaped without permission. The hard truth was, Salena wasn't at all surprised by her sister's confession, and the *shit* was more about the timing than the event. Her sister's marriage being on the rocks was, in Salena's opinion, a good thing. She and Matt never were right for each other. They married because they were told to and continued having kids every time things got rough. More bad choices after bad.

"Maybe Mom and Dad being there will give you and Matt the opportunity to get away. Just the two of you."

"Since when do you advocate for my marriage?"

"You have *four* kids."

"I know. I know."

Salena rubbed her forehead. "That was a shitty thing for me to say. I'm being selfish. Kids are no reason to get married or stay married. If you're unhappy, get out." Not that her sister could afford to live on what she made as a single mother. "Move back in with our parents." That wasn't a half-bad idea.

"There is no way I'm taking my kids out of their schools. Besides, the cost of living is cheaper here."

Salena saw the icing on the shit cake. She pulled her sunglasses from her face and stared across the sea of people traversing Little Italy. "So, get Mom and Dad to move to Arizona. When you and Matt split, you have built-in babysitters."

Her sister stayed silent.

"Think of what's next."

"I hate that what you're saying might make sense," Daniella said.

"I know."

Salena released a long sigh. "I have to get to work. Call me if you need to talk."

"What if I need you to come and get our parents?"

She rolled her eyes. "Call 911."

They ended the call, and even though Salena felt bad for what her sister was going through, the fact that she managed to come up with a solution that fit both her and her sister felt fantastic.

Five minutes later, she was in the restaurant, grabbing her duffel bag filled with the laptop and costumes she'd bought online. She'd stashed them in the office on her way out earlier that day to avoid the three flights of stairs to get to her apartment.

Greeting employees and customers, she worked her way to the back office with the hopes of slipping out without too many interruptions. Salena wasn't sure how the D'Angelos separated work and their private life, with work being in such close proximity. She hadn't managed it very well with the move. When the employees saw her, they assumed she was on duty. *"Did you see my schedule request?"*; *"Did you order X, Y, or Z?"*; *"Did you hear that so-and-so did such-and such?"*

The office was empty, giving her hope of a clean getaway.

With her bag swept over her shoulder, she turned and bumped right into Mari.

"I'm so sorry. I didn't notice you."

Mari pointed to her sunglasses. "You might want to take those off inside."

"I was running out."

Mari eyed the bag. "To the gym?"

"Yeah."

"Why do you wear makeup if you're going to the gym? That's bad for your skin."

Salena placed a hand on her own cheek. "True . . ."

"Unless the gym is not the whole truth . . . Maybe you're meeting Ryan?" A hopeful smile gave a spark to Mari's eyes.

Salena tilted her sunglasses to make sure the oldest D'Angelo saw her expression. "Are you trying your hand at matchmaking again?" It was common knowledge that Mari was somewhat responsible for Brooke and Luca's relationship. And if she could have pushed Dante and Chloe together, she would have.

"I didn't introduce you to the man. I honestly wouldn't have thought of it."

A strange wave of insecurity, a foreign feeling, washed up Salena's spine. "Why is that?"

"I don't know him well. And I haven't yet figured out who suits you best. I don't remember any of the men you've dated."

By design . . . since Mari and Salena's mother were cut from the same cloth.

"I'll give you a hint. Motorcycles and tattoos make me smile."

Mari scowled. "Motorcycles . . . dangerous machines. Giovanni took years off my life when he bought that thing."

"He is careful." Salena's memory jolted to a time when Mari would have disagreed if she'd seen the speed Gio pushed his bike to.

Mari clicked her tongue, narrowed her eyes. "I don't want to know."

"Probably not."

A finger ended up in Salena's face. "And no tattoos. I promised your parents I'd watch out for you as if you were my own."

"Yes, ma'am."

"Okay . . . go to your gym. Take that makeup off before you sweat."

"Will do." *Or not.*

Salena started toward the back door.

"Wait."

She stopped midstride.

Mari reached into the top drawer of the desk and jingled her keys. "Take my car. Those Ubers are expensive."

"I can—"

"You can take my car. I don't need it today."

Salena moved back into the office, took the offered keys, and kissed Mari on the cheek. "Thank you, Mama D'Angelo."

"You're welcome. Don't drive like my Gio on a motorcycle."

Salena winked. "I won't."

Mari muttered about children, motorcycles, and gray hair as Salena left the building.

CHAPTER SEVENTEEN

After they'd filmed another hour of content, Ashlynn's studio filled with a late afternoon class with one of her instructors while the two of them sat in the office.

Salena's page on OnlyMe, or OM as those that used it called it, stared at her from her laptop. A picture of her with a stage name, one she used to open a second Facebook, Twitter, Instagram, and TikTok page, all tied up with pictures and information to push this new adventure. Salena really wanted to keep this to herself. Her parents would not understand. She'd have to show them that she wasn't taking off her clothes to make money, but that didn't mean they would approve of the sexy images she was putting out there.

Anytime Salena started to question her decision, she looked at the printout of earnings Ashlynn made in the last month and pushed on.

"Are you ready for this?" Ashlynn asked as they both stared down at their computers, both set up on their respective pages, getting ready to upload and publish their content.

"Ready to make money with my secret hobby?" Salena pressed the "Enter" key. "Hell yeah."

Ashlynn smiled and did the same on her page. "Don't expect a whole lot right away. I'm sure my page will generate interest in yours, and when you get going, that will come back to me. As much as you want to check the page constantly to see your views or subscribers, set a time to do it, or you become consumed by the site."

"Like any other social media platform."

"Exactly."

"Keep it classy and keep it clean. And when someone sends you a private message asking for that one picture you really don't want to give them—"

"You mean naked pics."

"Yeah, or more. Believe me, they ask. Remember the first rule."

"Keep it classy and keep it clean," Salena repeated their mantra. She pointed to her image on the screen as the video she'd just posted played. "That's slightly dirty."

Ashlynn rolled her eyes. "Suggestive and sexy. You only think it's dirty from what they feed you at church on Sundays."

Lord knew Salena avoided that at all costs.

She glanced at her watch. "I've got to go." She closed her laptop and shoved it in her bag.

"We'll talk tomorrow."

She tossed a jacket over her shoulders. "Thanks again for suggesting this. Even if it doesn't work out."

Ashlynn raised an eyebrow. "Let me pick the color of your new car."

"That's a deal."

Hours later, after the restaurant was closed and the till was counted . . . Salena dragged herself to her apartment and showered off the night's work. One of the waitresses called in sick, putting her on the floor to cover a station during their busy time. Then she needed to jump behind the bar and help Sergio out as a party in the Grotto did its best to drink every last ounce of tequila and red wine they had. Salena cringed at a similar memory. That was a hangover she remembered quite vividly. Patrón tasted like regret to this day.

She tipped out to the cooks, the bus staff, the bartender, and the hostess, which left her with an extra fifty bucks for the night. She cleared a lot more in tips in previous jobs, but she was management now. Better hourly pay, more flexibility, health benefits. Still, if she was honest, it wasn't a whole lot more in her bank account than when she worked a bar job in a high-end establishment.

There, she had to dress the part . . . wear the spandex, or the less-than-modest top to show some skin. She'd flirt with the men, compliment the women, and tips flowed. It was a hustle. One that would work in her youth, but not forever.

At least with OM, she didn't have to see or have a face-to-face conversation with the people that wanted something from her.

It was cleaner, somehow. Yet when you talked to the public at large about the site, everyone thought it was porn. It wasn't. Hell, there were comedians, exercise enthusiasts, podcasters. And yeah, a whole lot of explicit material, but so long as Salena kept her space classy yet sexy, suggestive but not indecent . . . she could do this.

She settled into bed and pulled her computer onto her lap to check out her site.

Her eyes widened as she looked at her stats. Her one video had over three hundred views and fifty comments. But more, she had ten subscribers who went on to watch the private content exclusively for them. For that video, she had two tips and one private message.

A grin the size of the city spread over her face.

She clicked over to the monetizing page that calculated her earnings for the day and coughed on her own saliva.

Salena pushed the laptop aside, grabbed the bottle of water by her bedside, and cleared her throat.

Back on the money screen, she started to laugh. She'd earned $230 in less than eight hours.

Her chest filled with the possibilities and excitement of what this could mean for her. Ashlynn warned her not to get overwhelmed . . . that subscribers paid for a monthly plan, so consistency meant retention. Otherwise, they fell off.

Salena pulled up the notes and tips Ashlynn had provided and went through the process of commenting on people's messages, thanking her subscribers personally. And then looking at the request.

Sure enough, it wasn't something classy or clean.

"I'd like to see if the carpet matches the drapes." The user offered her a hundred dollars for a picture.

Salena would have been offended if the request wasn't something she'd heard before . . . on more than one dating site.

Her knee-jerk response would be something to the tune of . . . "I personally like hardwood floors, but you'll have to ask your wife for a picture of hers." Or, "Men that need to see pictures obviously never see the real thing."

Instead, Salena referred to her notes and picked the best response from a list of standards Ashlynn had already perfected. "Thank you for your request, but this isn't content I provide. I'll let you know if this changes."

This response did a couple of things. It gave the person requesting their answer . . . and hope that maybe Salena was desperate enough to take the man's money. And according to Ashlynn, it helped retain the subscriber for an average of two months if, in fact, they were only interested in nudes or sexual content. Mouth off to them, and they'd unsubscribe before their next payment was due.

She jumped on her other social media sites, responded to the few people she picked up interest from . . . likely those on OM crossing platforms . . . and encouraged them to subscribe to her OM page.

In less than an hour, she was done.

Her mind buzzed. The potential of this was off the charts. For the first time in forever, she thought of other things. Outside-the-box things that she could do to earn a living. Didn't people have Amazon stores? Or resell other people's products on Etsy or something? She was getting ahead of herself and cautioned her thoughts.

Still . . .

Salena removed her cell phone from the bedside charger and pressed on Ryan's picture to text him.

Are you still up?

She was about to abandon the idea of a conversation with Ryan when three dots filled his message screen, and she awaited his reply.

I am.

Are you alone?

Her answer was in the ringtone she'd applied to Ryan's name filling her bedroom with song.

Salena answered to Ryan's sleepy eyes. "Hi."

"You're in bed."

"I am." He positioned himself higher in his bed, the sheet around him fell.

Salena hadn't seen much of the man the night she almost got arrested, but what she did remember . . . she liked.

"Are you naked?"

His eyes drifted south, then slowly back to the screen. "Is this one of *those* kind of calls?"

"No." *Yes.* "I mean . . . you look like you might sleep naked."

"I might."

"You might? Or you do?"

"I do when I'm in my own bed."

"So not at a hotel."

"No." He rubbed his eyes. "How was your night?"

Dollar signs flashed in her head. "It was great."

"*Great?* That's a first."

Dollars, dollars, dollars. "I got a big tip."

"That's awesome."

"Tell me about it. Mari is feeling so bad for me, she's loaning me her car to go to the gym." Salena had been calling Ashlynn's studio "the gym" for the entire time she'd gone there. The white lie slipped from her lips without thought.

"She seems like a great woman."

"She is."

Ryan yawned.

"I'm keeping you up."

He didn't disagree. "I like talking to you before I fall asleep."

His confession put a fuzzy feeling in her chest.

"Did you get your costume for the party?"

"I did. How about you?"

"I'm reusing an old one."

"Do you go to these kinds of parties often?"

She shook her head. "Nawh . . . I just like playing dress-up."

That had him staring at her . . . past the sleep in his eyes. "French maid?"

Salena tossed her head back with a laugh. "Cliché much?"

"I mean—"

"I'm Italian." And to prove the point, she told him she wanted to see every square inch of him at the earliest convivence . . . in Italian.

"Not sure what that was, but I liked it."

"I'm sure you did."

His eyes drifted closed. "I'm fading."

"I'll let you go."

"I'll call you tomorrow."

"You don't have to. I'll see you Saturday." Which was only two days away.

Ryan stared at the phone. "I'll call you tomorrow. You work nights again, right?"

"Someone is paying attention." She'd told him her schedule earlier that week, and he remembered.

"Good night, Trouble."

"Good night, monsieur." She faked a lousy French accent.

He wrinkled his nose. "I like the Italian better."

"Buona notte, a domani."

"Much better." Ryan blew her a kiss before their call ended.

~

Ryan arrived at the marina within five minutes of the start of the party. Normally he wouldn't be so prompt, but since the event was on a boat that was expected to tool around the bay once everyone arrived, he thought it was best to be on time.

Signs with glittering letters led him down the path, through the gate, and onto the dock where Dante and Chloe kept their boat.

There was no need for anyone to spell out which vessel the party was on since it was decked out in gold lights from bow to stern, with music reminiscent of the 1920s floating from its deck.

Ryan saw Dante on the back deck, arranging cushions on the bench seats.

"Permission to board?" Ryan called out. "I brought provisions." He held a bottle of sparkling wine and waved it in the air.

"Ciao!" Dante greeted. "You look great."

Ryan stepped onto the boat, felt the sway under his feet. "I can say the same to you."

Dante wore black pants, a plain white shirt with the arms rolled up. Suspenders and dress shoes that fit the time . . . and a hat that looked like those worn by boys that delivered the newspapers back in the day.

"I'm early." Ryan handed him the bottle.

"Not at all."

"Can I help with anything?"

"Yeah, actually. There are bags of ice in the galley that fill these coolers."

"I'm your guy."

Dante went back to his task, and Ryan moved deeper on the boat, through the open glass doors and into the space that held the kitchen.

Chloe walked through a hallway with a huge grin.

She wore a long 1920s-style gown, less flapper and more elegant. On her head was a beaded band with a feather sticking up one side. On her neck was a long rope of fake-looking pearls. Ryan was sure he'd see a lot of those before the end of the night. "Don't you look fantastic!" he boasted.

She waved a hand his way with a toss of her fingers. "This old thing?"

Moving to her side, he kissed the side of her cheek. "I've been put on ice duty."

Chloe pointed to a tub half-hidden under a table. "It's right there."

The decorations they'd adorned the space with were black, silver, and gold. Plenty of sparkle and lights illuminated the room.

Ryan lifted two bags of ice at a time and took them to Dante.

"Thanks, man."

"I'll get the rest."

Footfalls and laughter sounded on the dock as others arrived. Ryan could tell by the high-pitched squeal that it wasn't Salena coming his way.

He continued to schlep ice until the coolers were full.

Grabbing Chloe's attention before she greeted the new arrivals, he asked, "Where do you want the tub these were in?"

"Take it to the front and just set it on the side of the dock."

"You got it."

He worked his way around the side of the boat, which he had to think was much closer to being a yacht. Not that he knew what the definition of either technically was. Even on the bow, the hosts didn't skimp on setting the mood. More lights and large black and gold pillows filled the area where people could sit to feel the salt air as they glided over the water. Though it was getting close to sunset, and that space wouldn't be used for long once the temperature dipped.

Back at the stern, Ryan recognized his sister's hair before she turned around. Dressed all in white, with tassels flowing past her knees—the dress was very flapper style and might even have doubled for a wedding gown at the time. Her red curls were straightened so completely, her hair looked like it had grown three inches since the wedding. "Who is that dame?" he called out behind her.

Emma turned, batting her eyelashes. "Little ol' me?"

He moved in for a hug, kissed her cheek. "This is fabulous."

She straightened the bow tie on his neck. "You clean up, too."

"Hey, hands off my girl."

Beside her, Gio wore a short-waisted 1920s tux. Very much the groom to her white dress.

"You guys should have done a theme wedding and you could have recycled your outfits." Ryan shook Gio's hand.

Dante and Chloe were both waving their guests on board as couples continued to flow in.

Men popped open beers as many of the women opted for champagne flutes.

This was definitely a help-yourself crowd, with many assisting the hosts with the job of making sure everyone had what they needed.

Ryan was introduced to new people, and some of those that had attended the wedding, but the names escaped him. All the while, his eyes were glued to the dock, wondering what was taking Salena so long.

A photographer moved around the crowd, taking pictures of some of the elaborate and unique outfits people chose. One couple wore 1920s swimsuits, the kind that covered everything. Another dressed like someone selling cigars and cigarettes, complete with shallow boxes that they hung from their necks with long straps. The boxes held candy cigarettes and mints . . . and doubled as a table for their personal drinks.

Most men, as expected, wore pin-striped suits and fedoras or derby hats . . . while the women were classic flappers with beads and fringe, fake fur, and feathered boas.

Just about the time Ryan was going to give up on Salena making it, he heard her voice. "Now the party can get started!"

He turned to see her staring down from the dock.

Laughter choked from his throat as more than one person whistled out their approval.

There were no frilly pieces of string hanging from her outfit . . . no fake beads on her neck.

Salena wore a man's jacket that was long enough to hang past her butt, but just barely. The dark gray pinstripe had been altered enough to plunge down her chest to reveal a hint of her breasts. Fishnet stockings that stopped midthigh caught his eye, and the high heels she wore would bring her height to his . . . if not make her taller.

She wore a fedora . . . and carried a plastic tommy gun.

Their eyes met and held.

"You forgot your gun, Clyde," she told him.

Ryan moved to the edge of the boat and lifted his hand for her to take.

"Shouldn't a lovely little thing like you carry a Derringer?"

Sure enough, they were eye to eye with the impossible height of her shoes. "Why have something small"—she placed a hand on his chest—"when you can have something big?"

His whole body jumped to attention. The smile on his face too big to miss. His eyes traveled down her body. "Damn."

"You're too easy, Clyde."

When she turned to walk away, Ryan snaked his hand to the back of her neck and pulled her close to his frame. He gave her a breath before capturing her lips for a quick kiss.

Yup . . . she tasted like trouble.

Those cocky, and now stunned, eyes stared back at him when he released her.

She placed a hand on his face, wiped his lips with her thumb, which came back red from her lipstick.

"Laying your claim?" she whispered.

Looking the way she did . . . "Damn straight."

"Holy shit, Salena . . . did you forget your pants?" The question was from Gio, who was laughing.

She turned his way.

"What happened to reusing an old costume?" Chloe asked.

Salena glanced over her shoulder at Ryan. "I had a better idea."

CHAPTER EIGHTEEN

Ryan wore a light gray double-breasted pin-striped suit, white hat and shoes. But the red lipstick she'd placed on his lips was the best part.

Salena's outfit had been Ashlynn's idea. The only thing Salena had added to it was the fishnets, which didn't work when dancing with a pole.

Either way, their Halloween material had been filmed, and Salena had Ashlynn drop her off at the dock to avoid an Uber in her outfit.

Now it was time to sit back and enjoy the party.

And the man who branded her with a kiss the second she boarded the boat.

The last time someone had done something like that to her, she ignored him for the entire night, danced with anyone but him . . . and never answered his calls again.

Not with Ryan.

And she couldn't exactly put her finger on the why of her actions.

Hadn't she brought the fake gun as a prop for the joke they'd passed between them since her near arrest on Fiesta Island? A toy she had every intention of having Ryan hold so everyone knew he was with her?

Who was laying claim to whom?

When it was time for Dante to pull up anchor and move out of the slip, Ryan joined him and Giovanni at the captain's seat.

Salena mingled with her friends and helped Chloe and Emma bring out food, preprepared and in warming bags.

"You and Ryan seem to be getting along," Emma said when they were both in the galley.

Salena hadn't had many private conversations with Gio's bride and wasn't sure of her response. "Yeah . . . I hope you're okay with that."

"I am. Not that you need me to be. My brother's a great guy, and Gio and Chloe are good judges of character."

Her words felt like an expectation. "I'm usually the one causing trouble."

"A perfect match, then. Ryan spent more time in the principal's office than a classroom."

Chloe walked in from behind. "What are you two whispering about?"

"Ryan," Emma said quickly.

"Ohhh, do tell."

"We're just dating," Salena said.

"It always starts with 'just dating.' Then it's more than dating," Emma replied.

Salena looked between them. "Don't, ah . . . ." There was a hopeful spark behind both sets of eyes. "Yeah, uh . . . okay." Salena picked up a tray of food and started toward the outside deck.

As soon as she set the food down, she reached for a beer.

"Hot as ever," a male voice said from behind her.

Tim, who she never dated but knew he always wanted to. He was there with his long-term girlfriend, Cindy, who was not at his side. Hence the comment.

"Thanks." Salena took his words as a compliment and refrained from the snarky reply she'd usually deliver.

"I heard your new toy is rich."

"My new what?"

"Toy. That's Emma's brother, right? Lots of money in that family."

The hair on her neck stood up. "I don't need his money. I have my own." And frankly, she never even thought of it. "And he's not my toy."

Tim laughed. "Right . . . okay. Good one."

And before she could lay into him and cause a scene, Tim turned and walked away.

The cool wind caught her hair with a shiver.

She took another swig of her beer. How many people thought the way Tim did?

"That outfit is epic."

A friendly face distracted her from Tim's words. "You look great, too."

~

Something had changed.

Somewhere between Ryan happily flirting with Salena and then joining Dante on the bridge of his boat, Salena's smile faltered.

To anyone watching, maybe they wouldn't notice. There were snarky retorts and fake-innocent comments meant to singe her targets. Only these people knew her and batted off her meaningless insults as a personality trait.

When the shots came out and the music moved out of the 1920s theme and into the modern age, Salena seemed to relax.

"C'mon, Barone," someone egged her on.

She shook her head. "Tequila and I broke up a long time ago."

"Good thing we have vodka."

Salena lifted her hands in the air and pointed toward the person holding a giant bottle. "Now we're talking."

Gio pushed his shoulder into Ryan's. "Glad she's not driving."

Salena took her first shot.

"I'll make sure she's good."

Gio patted him on the back.

Salena and Chloe encouraged each other to take another shot, putting Ryan and Dante in the same corner, chatting.

"That's going to hurt in the morning." Dante had his arms crossed over his chest, a smile on his face. One of his employees that captained the boat was at the helm, giving Dante a chance to join his guests.

Salena appeared a little steadier on her feet than her best friend. "And Salena's tolerance?"

"Let me put it this way. Chloe had two older brothers playing Dad, limiting her party life growing up. Salena's parents were in bed by ten, and no one told her no. They didn't drink the same."

Ryan stood back, watching and hoping Salena didn't regret her life choices in the morning.

This was the woman he'd met at his sister's wedding . . . who wasn't completely who he'd been dating and talking to ever since. It was as if Salena Barone was two sides of the same coin. One that took her job and responsibilities seriously . . . and still acted careless and free of adult responsibilities on the other.

A few hours and several shots later, the boat was docked, and people were working their way home.

Salena held her shoes in her hand . . . the fake gun lost somewhere on the boat. Ryan steadied her when she swayed into him. "I should get you out of here."

"Good iddeeea." Her speech slurred.

"Maybe that last round wasn't a great choice," Gio ribbed.

Salena spouted off something in Italian that had several people around them laughing.

"Do I want to know?" Ryan asked.

Dante shook his head. "Just make sure she finds a pillow and not another bar."

"I'm fine." She swayed into him again. "Damn boat."

Only they weren't rocking.

"Okay, Trouble . . . let's go."

After a round of goodbyes and thanks for having them, Ryan led Salena to the shore of the harbor and opened his phone to hire a ride.

"The restaurant is still open," Salena informed him. "I'm a little drunk."

He pinched two fingers close together. "Maybe a bit more than a little."

"I don't want to walk by those people."

"I have a room at the Hyatt."

Her eyes lit up. "That's a great idea."

Much as he would have loved to take her up on the look she was offering . . . "And you're drunk."

"Then it's an even better idea." The hand that wasn't holding her shoes patted his chest. Even flat-footed, she stumbled into him. "Damn boat."

Ryan laughed, sobering up faster with his responsibility of making sure she was safe.

The Uber pulled up, and Ryan poured Salena into the car.

Her head hit his shoulder the second they pulled away from the curb.

"Don't let her get sick in here," the driver said from behind the wheel, his eyes glued to the rearview mirror.

"I don't get sick." Salena's eyes were trying to close. "Unless I drink tequila. I didn't drink tequila, right?"

"No, baby. You stuck to vodka." Ryan encouraged her head to stay on his shoulder.

Less than a mile down the road, she was purring.

Thankfully, once the car stopped, she opened her eyes. He had no qualms with carrying her through the hotel lobby but wasn't sure the outfit she was in would cover all the important parts that others might see.

The attendant at the hotel opened the door of the car and stood there while Ryan helped Salena. "That was fast," Salena said.

"You fell asleep."

With her shoes in one of his hands, his hat skewed on his head, and one arm around her waist to keep her steady, Ryan wrangled them both into the hotel.

The staff at the registration desk didn't give them much attention as they worked their way through the lobby. He could only imagine what they looked like. Wearing costumes and unsteady on their feet . . . Ryan laughed to himself.

"What's funny?"

"Just a couple of drunks stumbling home from a party."

"I-I'm not drunk." Her head bobbed forward.

"Ah-huh."

The forward momentum ended in the elevator, and Salena became heavier at his side.

He used that moment to pull his room key from his wallet.

One step out into the hall to his room, Ryan gathered her legs under one arm and carried her the rest of the way.

"Ahhh, you're strong."

"Ah-huh."

Down one hall, and then a second, his room came into view.

The card key opened the door without much effort. Ryan pushed in, dropping her shoes almost immediately.

He attempted to lay Salena down on the bed without losing his balance.

Only she kept her arms around his neck, pulling him down with her.

"This is better," she purred.

"Ah-huh . . ." No. If there was one rule Ryan always followed, it was never to sleep with a woman for the first time if she was drunk. Didn't matter that he knew in his heart it would be consensual. Didn't matter that both of them had discussed said encounter from the first day. He didn't go there.

Ever.

He pried her fingers from the back of his neck and leaned over her. She was smiling . . . and half-asleep.

"I'm going to use the little boys' room," he said before kissing her nose and standing up.

"I'll be right here."

"Ah-huh."

In the bathroom, Ryan ran the water on hot and used a cloth to wipe his face. He studied his image in the mirror for a good two minutes before poking his head out the door.

Sure enough, Salena was out.

He went ahead and took a quick shower to wash the salt spray off his skin before returning to the room. In a clean pair of briefs and a T-shirt, he pulled a second shirt from his suitcase and walked to the purring woman in his bed.

She was stunning, even asleep. Way too much makeup, but that seemed to be the theme at the party.

Lucky for him, her costume wasn't filled with sequins and strings, or getting her out of it so she could sleep off the vodka would be impossible unless she was awake.

The fishnets were first.

While he would have liked to be the kind of man that didn't look as he removed them from her legs one at a time. Yeah . . . he wasn't that righteous.

And Salena was sexy as hell.

A golf-ball-size bruise on her shin, one that looked new, caught his attention and made him wonder if he'd banged her into a wall as he'd juggled her in his arms.

The jacket was next and buttoned up the front.

Her breasts, neatly packaged in a lace bra, were just as beautiful as he remembered from the back of his car. He left the lace bra on as he slowly pulled one of her arms free, rolled her onto her side, and did the same with the other.

Salena murmured something and started to curl into a ball.

"No, no . . . let's do this."

Ryan pulled his extra T-shirt over her head and pushed her arms through.

Twice she attempted to bat his hands away with hers.

Chuckling at just how dead asleep she was, he finally managed to get her under the covers, where she could drool properly on a pillow.

"Not exactly how I pictured our first night together," he said to the quiet room.

He considered himself a gentleman but wasn't about to drag a pillow to the floor.

No sooner was he under the covers with the light in the room off than Salena curled up next to him and placed a soft hand on his chest. Fast asleep, she kept purring like a kitten and muttered something he didn't quite catch.

He kissed the top of her head, whispered good night, and closed his eyes.

CHAPTER NINETEEN

The boat was still rocking.

Everyone at the party was wearing normal clothes except Salena.

She was dressed for pole dancing. Skimpy shorts and bare arms . . . Her top was too tight, almost cutting off her circulation.

On some level, Salena knew she was having a dream.

The colors weren't quite right, and even though she was on Chloe and Dante's boat, they were nowhere to be seen.

Ryan sat in a round booth, arms spread along the back, watching her. Expecting something of her.

Only there wasn't a pole, and the music was all wrong.

And besides, the sea was choppy, making it difficult to stand, let alone dance.

He stopped smiling and turned to stare at a woman beside Salena. Who was she? And why was Ryan looking at her like she was his next meal?

Jealousy coursed through her veins, and that's when Salena knew, without a doubt, she was in a dream.

Just wake up, *she told herself.*

The boat tilted hard, and Salena started to slide across the deck. The water was going to be cold . . .

Her eyes opened with a jolt.

An unfamiliar room stared back at her.

She lifted her head just enough to see who she was tangled up with.

Ryan's face brought relief. His eyes were open, his lips held a soft smile. "Good morning."

Salena rested her head back where it had been with a sigh. "Do I need any details about last night?"

He chuckled. "You were wild. Kept telling me to call you Jane and wanted me to play Tarzan."

She remembered the ride to the hotel . . . or part of it. Getting to the hotel and, at some point, Ryan lifting her. Once in the room, though . . . not a whole lot. "I fell asleep."

"Before your head hit the pillow."

One of her legs was draped over his, their skin warm against each other. She glanced down, saw the shirt she'd slept in.

"You undressed me."

"I made you comfortable," he corrected.

She glanced under her shirt. "Next time, take off the bra. Wearing them to bed gives me bad dreams."

"I was trying to be a good guy."

Once again, she glanced up to meet his eyes. "You have my express permission to remove the vise around my girls."

Ryan rolled onto his side, positioned himself to look directly at her. The move sandwiched her knee between his legs, which she secretly loved.

His hand slid around her waist and back, snaked up the T-shirt, and started to play with the clasp of her bra.

It took him three tries to get the thing free.

"Much better," she said. "Hold that thought." Salena pushed up from bed. "I need the bathroom."

As soon as her feet met the floor, she pulled the T-shirt from her shoulders and let the bra hit the floor. A quick glance over her shoulders confirmed Ryan's attention.

She went into the restroom and took care of her needs. A quick stop at the sink to wash and put a finger full of the toothpaste sitting there across her teeth helped get rid of the sins of the previous night.

Salena smiled at herself in the mirror, approved of what she saw, and walked into the doorway to the room.

Ryan watched, his eyes drifting to her bare chest. She wore regular panties, not the thong type, considering the costume she'd worn the night before.

He'd pushed away the covers, which left him in the clothes he'd slept in.

Salena took her time moving from the frame of the door to the bed. A slight sway of her hips. One free hand traced a finger down her chest, past one nipple, and lingered at the edge of her panties.

Ryan watched her hand as if she'd told him to do so.

A trick Salena had learned on day one, class one, of pole dancing. If a woman touched herself anywhere provocative, men watched. The slower the movement, the more erotic it became. Too bad the hotel didn't have a pole in the middle of the room, she'd give him a show he would never forget. Instead, Salena settled on climbing on top of him from the bottom of the bed, one catlike step at a time on her knees.

A fingernail slid along his thigh, making him jump, and stopped just shy of his briefs.

She met his eyes.

Ryan's hips bucked slightly.

"Damn, Salena."

That teasing fingernail moved closer and closer.

Ryan's lips parted. "I could watch you all day."

She touched him now, through the thin layer of cloth. One finger, then two.

He went from a little swollen to let-me-out erect in five seconds. For Salena, that was power. The kind she was familiar with.

Ryan reached for her hand and stopped her. "C'mere," he said, his voice a hoarse whisper.

He leaned forward and hauled her up onto him. Then reached for her lips with his.

She sunk into his kiss. The man knew what he was doing. Open mouth with a hesitation before his tongue found hers. This was so much better than in the back seat of a car . . . much more room to move, touch, and taste.

Salena settled with one of his legs firmly planted between her knees. Her hips tilted, and her body filled with pleasure.

Ryan moaned, and with one swift move, Salena was under him, his body pressing her into the mattress, and his hungry kiss moved from her lips to her neck. "I have wanted to touch you from the moment you got out of that broken car," he told her as his teeth grazed her skin, nibbled, and then kissed before he found another spot.

"I haven't said no."

She pulled at his shirt, which he impatiently dragged from his back and tossed to the floor.

Salena managed to pull one leg out from under him and wrap it around his waist and filled her palm with the cheek of his ass. Every inch of him that touched her felt like fire. Either the room was cold, or there was something chemical happening.

Teeth found one of her nipples, with a slight sting before Ryan moved to the next. Her back arched to get closer. "I like that."

His response was to pinch a little harder before sucking away the sting. "I want to learn everything about you. What you respond to, what makes you crazy." His hand slid between her legs, his fingers under her panties.

"Waiting makes me crazy," she confessed.

His hand stopped.

She moved her hips against his. "We've waited long enough."

Just as one long finger found the wetness between her legs, Ryan came back to kiss her at the same time he slipped inside.

"Yes," she gasped. The feeling, next to perfect.

She gasped and squirmed, encouraging him to continue.

"So hot," he told her, his lips next to her ear.

He increased the pressure and circled her clit at just the right speed, when he changed his angle, she protested. "No. Keep doing that."

"Tell me what you want."

He found the right spot again. "That. Right there."

All the muscles in her body started to tighten and feed into where he touched. He was kissing her again, only she couldn't concentrate with an orgasm so close.

"Yes, Ryan . . ."

She did. A hot cry of pleasure rolled through her in waves. His name repeated for the people in the next room to hear.

His dark eyes stared into hers when she could see again.

"I needed that."

His hand slipped away, and he lifted them to his lips and tasted. "Yum."

The smile on her lips would take an army to remove. Salena reached for him. "Your turn."

This time, he let her touch her fill and lifted himself so she could shed the briefs that kept them apart. He, in turn, tossed her panties to the floor, giving them both the room they needed.

"You're so beautiful, Salena," he said softly as he settled between her thighs. The tip of his erection seeking the warmth of her body.

She placed a hand on his cheek, liked the tickle of the morning hair on his face.

The hard planes of his shoulders and chest hovered just above her body, giving her a glimpse of the tattoos on his skin. Tattoos she wanted to lick and kiss and learn about. But right now, all she wanted was him.

All of him.

"Ryan . . ."

He started to push into her, and her eyes rolled back.

"No. Look at me."

She did. Saw the heat in his gaze as they both felt each other for the first time. "Fuck . . ."

Yeah, it felt that good.

An unfamiliar feeling tightened in Salena's chest. Maybe it was the way he was looking at her, or certainly the way their hips rose and fell together. Whatever it was, she knew it wasn't something she'd felt before. Like maybe Ryan would stick around for a while. Hope that she could have more than just this with the man.

She mentally told herself to get out of her head and stay in this moment.

Nothing killed an orgasm faster than thinking about the morning after in the middle of the act.

Slowly, she closed her eyes and released all her running thoughts, giving in to the sensations.

He was kissing her again.

"I want you in the shower."

"Yes." That was a favorite of hers. "Over the counter."

"In front of the mirror, so I can watch you."

He was moving faster now.

The bed moved with them, their gasps and breath too short to speak.

She pulled his hips close and tightened her legs around him as they both searched for release.

"Damn . . . I'm so close."

"Not yet . . . just a little—" And there it was, a wave of heat that uncoiled in a breath.

Ryan's hand moved to her face and neck, forcing her eyes to his. And somehow, that made her orgasm all the better.

"Baby?" His single-word question made all the muscles inside her clench.

"Yes."

His tempo quickened before his body arched and a strangled cry announced his orgasm.

All the while, Ryan's eyes, hot, lava, and electric, stared deep into her soul as he released inside her.

~

Ryan gathered Salena into his side as they both reclaimed their breath.

He could get used to this.

With his eyes closed, he kissed the top of her head.

Moisture dripped from the tip of his cock, and Ryan's eyes shot open. "Fuck."

"What?" She jumped.

Ryan slapped his hand to the side of the bed where he'd placed a condom and brought it in front of them both. "I didn't put this on."

Salena looked between the prophylactic and him. "I see my doctor every year. You don't have to worry."

"Not me . . . you."

"Is there something you need to tell me?"

He shook his head. "No. I'm good. It's up to both of us that you don't get pregnant."

For one moment, she paused. "I get the shot every few months."

There was relief in that. "I'll remember next time," he told her when she settled.

"It's not a problem. Trust me. The last thing I would let happen is pregnancy."

Words he'd heard before, but that didn't mean he left things up to chance.

And yet he had.

Salena started to squirm. "I'm going to take a quick shower."

"Want company?" he asked.

Her eyes drifted to the bedside clock. "I want to make it back home before any employees show up for their shift. That outfit sounded great last night, but in the light of day, it will look like I lost my pants."

Ryan's eyes drifted to the costume tossed on the back of a chair.

"I have a pair of lounge pants with a drawstring. They'll be way too long and look like pajamas, but . . ."

She smiled. "I'll take it."

He sat up in the bed. "So . . . that shower?"

Salena pressed her palm against his chest and pushed him back on the bed. "Order coffee. Contrary to popular opinion"—she waved a hand over her midsection—"that hasn't happened for a while, and I want to walk today."

That was probably the best thing she could have said.

Ryan watched her ass as she walked away before reaching for the phone to order room service.

CHAPTER TWENTY

Salena refused to let Ryan drive her home. First off, his car was still in the marina parking lot from the party, and that was in the opposite direction of Little Italy. Truth was, she could have walked if she'd brought a pair of shoes that didn't come right out of a pole dance studio.

She was keenly aware of how ridiculous she looked in men's lounge pants, a T-shirt that was three sizes too big, and high heels. The fishnets were shoved in the pockets of the jacket she slung over her shoulders to ward off the morning chill. Her phone, completely dead after a night of not being charged, at least made it back from the boat with her.

It was midmorning, and the streets of Little Italy were buzzing with activity.

Salena jogged from the side street where the Uber dropped her off to the back door of the building.

The key she had tucked in a small pocket of the case holding her phone was unleashed and used, giving her hope that since the door was still locked, no one would see her dressed as she was.

As soon as she slipped past the door, she locked it behind her and slid off her shoes.

The door leading up to the apartments was open slightly, which cautioned her to move as slowly and quietly as possible.

Someone was up and about; the question was who.

She made it up four steps before Mari's voice had Salena's heart jumping out of her chest.

"I thought I heard someone."

Salena turned, looked behind her.

"You scared me."

Mari didn't apologize and didn't explain. Her eyes traveled up and down Salena's body, her smile steady. "Did you have fun at the party?"

"Yes. Yes. Chloe and Dante know how to throw it together."

Mari stayed silent.

Salena wanted to disappear.

"Was that your costume?"

She looked down at herself, pulled at the jacket. "This was . . . and the shoes."

Mari stared at the shoes. "Interesting."

"Didn't Chloe have something more appropriate for you to wear home?"

There was no way in hell Mari believed the clothes she wore belonged to Chloe. Even the T-shirt wasn't Dante's style.

Salena didn't confirm or deny . . . and didn't offer a deeper explanation. Instead, she patted the rail in the hall and said, "I need to change."

"That's a good idea."

By the time Salena made it to the first landing, Mari had moved out of the stairwell and back to the restaurant.

The door to Mari's apartment, however, was wide open.

"I've seen the walk of shame before, but this one is classic." Gio stood, one shoulder against the doorjamb, his arms folded over his chest.

"Shut up."

He started laughing.

"What are you doing here?"

"Emma and I stayed the night. Mama wanted us for Sunday dinner."

"Where is Emma?"

"She and Brooke went for a walk."

Salena looked up the stairs. "Is Luca going to jump out at me, too?"

Gio simply laughed. "Tell Ryan I like the pants. Great Christmas gift idea."

She waved a middle finger in the air and continued to her rooms.

Luca, thank God, wasn't waiting to pounce.

The first thing she did was plug her phone in before dumping the shoes and jacket on her bed. In her own bathroom, she took a good look in the mirror.

She'd combed her hair but didn't have a tie to pull it back, and yeah . . . it looked like a woman who'd spent the night doing what everyone assumed. Or in her case, the morning.

The clothes she was swimming in reminded her of those video clips of the most poorly dressed customers of Walmart. But at least her ass was covered, which her Bonnie outfit from the party barely did.

She ran the hot water, used her makeup remover to swipe away the mascara that her earlier shower didn't get rid of.

It was when she was brushing her hair into a clip that she noticed a mark on her neck.

She swiped at her skin several times and moved closer to the mirror. "Damn him."

Ryan had given her a hickey.

As if the pants and walk of shame weren't enough. "You have it coming, buddy."

A quick change of plans, and she plugged her straightening iron in to warm it up. No updo today.

Ryan's clothes made it into her hamper, and her own settled on her body.

Back in her kitchen, she reached for her phone, which had charged enough to reveal a few text messages.

Chloe had snapped a picture of Salena's location last night, and again in the morning. Along with the photograph, she said, I want details.

Beyond that, Ashlynn had sent a message earlier that morning. Good stuff is happening. Check your subscriptions. CALL ME.

Salena pulled her laptop onto the counter and turned it on before searching out another cup of coffee. Even though she may have deserved a hangover, she didn't have one. But that didn't mean she wasn't wicked tired and in need of another cup of coffee . . . or a gallon.

Her one-cup-at-a-time coffee maker had the magic bean juice in her hand in no time.

A cup in one hand and logging into OM with the other, Salena was ready to see what Ashlynn was going on about.

The number next to new subscribers stood out in bold print.

Salena's jaw slacked. "Holy shit." Pushing the coffee aside, she called Ashlynn.

"Did you see? Did you see?" was how she answered the phone.

"Is this right?"

"An hour ago, you were at sixty-eight new subscribers."

"It says seventy-two now. How did that happen?"

"The video we posted last night took off." The sexy little outfit that wasn't fit to stroll around in on Sunday morning was a hit on OnlyMe.

"Posting part one on my page and part two on yours worked!"

"Did you get new subscribers?" As far as Salena saw this, she was the one getting the better end of the deal. Ashlynn was the one with fans funneling people to her.

"I pick up a few every day, but I'm up eleven since last night. Four are returns."

Salena found the video and looked at the views. The free tease was in the thousands, the paid stuff was in the hundreds. And since her fans weren't at the century mark yet, that meant they were being watched over and over.

"That's over fourteen hundred bucks overnight, lady."

The monetizing page confirmed what she guessed based on how the week was going. "Seventeen fifty. More tips." That was more money than she made in two weeks at the restaurant, including tips. "This is crazy."

"It's fantastic."

"It can't possibly continue at this rate."

"It absolutely can."

"Can I cash out anytime?"

"Twenty-four hours from the time the money goes in. If you do it on a weekend, you'll see the money in your account on Monday."

Salena rested her head in her hand and started to smile. "I'm going to be able to buy a car." And not a broken-down piece of scrap metal with an engine . . . but a car she could be proud to drive.

"I get to pick the color."

They both squealed.

For the next ten minutes, Ashlynn reminded her of Uncle Sam's take and the risks involved with spending money she hadn't yet earned. All things Salena had heard before and needed to hear again. Seeing the monetization screen had her bursting with excitement.

Her phone pinged.

I miss you already.

Ryan's text added to the joy of her day.

"I think we should hit it hard over the holidays. Lots of men are lonely, want to spend time online and not with their families. I'll start shopping for costumes."

"I can't thank you enough for bringing me in. I keep waiting for the catch."

"People are making thousands selling pictures of their feet, Salena. Used panties. We're just marketing what we love to do. There is no catch. Remember . . . keep it classy—"

"Keep it clean," Salena finished for her.

"I need to respond to these messages and get to work."

"We'll talk later."

She disconnected the call and silently bumped her fists to the sky. "Oh! My! God!"

She couldn't stop smiling.

She carried her phone back to her bathroom to finish getting ready and texted Ryan back.

You sure know how to wake a woman up in the morning.

Did you make it to your apartment without a welcoming squad? he asked.

No! Mari was nice enough to not state the obvious. Giovanni wants a pair of your pants for Christmas.

She ran the straight iron through her hair.

I'll put that on my list.

She glanced at her phone and realized this was the longest amount of time that they'd sent text messages. Normally, Ryan just picked up the phone and called. You're not texting and driving, are you? You usually call.

It took a moment for him to respond. No. There is someone with me.

A slight wave of doubt ran down her spine. Who is she?

Salena stared at her phone now, waiting for his reply.

Only he didn't.

A minute went by . . . another.

Her heart started to pound.

And why? She didn't have a leash on the man. He did say he wasn't one to talk to one woman while with another . . . or was she the one that said that?

"Fuck."

He's not that guy.

She blew out a breath and rushed through putting on her makeup.

Her phone rang.

It was him.

"Hey," she answered, gulping down the insecurity dancing in her veins.

"The only woman with me is the one whose scent still lingers on my skin after spending the morning with her." His voice was low.

Salena closed her eyes and started to smile. "I'm not a jealous woman."

"Liar."

"You don't know me well enough to call me that."

"I'm with a real estate agent looking at property."

"I didn't ask."

"You did." He sighed. "When are you off tonight?"

"I don't know. One of the waiters has been hit-and-miss this week. His mom is ill."

Someone called Ryan's name.

"I'm keeping you," she said.

"You're worth it."

There he was, making her smile again. "I need to get downstairs."

"We're good?" he asked.

"We're good," she replied.

He promised to call her later and ended the call.

"Nothing like channeling the strong, confident woman you are, Salena!" she scolded herself in the third person to an empty room.

～

Ryan stepped in the front door of D'Angelo's and smiled at the hostess. "I'm looking for Salena."

It was just after four thirty, and only a smattering of tables inside the establishment were taken. The outside didn't have a table available.

"I haven't seen her in a while . . . She might be in the back."

The hostess looked between him and the flower he held in his hand.

It had been a long time since he'd cared enough about a woman to stop by her work just to tell her she was on his mind. The fact that a streak of jealousy had translated in their earlier conversation suggested maybe . . . just maybe, Salena was on the same page.

"Ryan!"

He heard his name from across the room.

Sergio waved him over from the bar.

They shook hands. "Good to see you again."

"You too. Is Salena around?"

"She's upstairs. Go on up."

Ryan gave the man a thumbs-up and started toward the stairway to the D'Angelos' residence.

It felt out of place walking into the family and employee section of the restaurant, but no one stopped him.

Someone he vaguely recognized nodded his way before Ryan rounded the corner and moved into the stairwell.

At the top of the stairs, there were two doors, one for Salena's apartment, and the other that spilled onto the rooftop terrace . . . and that one was wide open, and voices carried with a mixture of Italian and English.

Ryan worried that maybe a private party was taking place and he was interrupting. He poked his head out the door and heard his name.

"Ryan?"

A long table sat under strings of lights, holding the entire D'Angelo family, including Emma and Gio.

Several chairs slid against the terrace as people jumped to their feet.

His gaze met Salena's, and he smiled. "I don't mean to interrupt."

"Interrupt? Who's interrupting?" Mari called out. "Gio, go get your brother-in-law a chair."

"That's not . . ." Ryan sheepishly lifted the flower in his hand in the air. "I was just dropping this off."

Gio placed a dramatic hand to his chest. "Ryan, you shouldn't have. I'm so flattered."

"I don't think that's for you, Zio Gio," Franny said.

Her words had everyone laughing.

"Why are you standing in the doorway? Come, come!"

Salena pushed out of her chair.

"Salena, grab another setting. Franny, move down next to your papa. I want our guest to sit right here next to me."

Dante walked past him, patted him on the back. "Sorry, buddy."

Oh, shit . . . was that a bad thing?

The family moved as if they'd choreographed his arrival. One place setting was moved, Salena returned with dishes from inside her apartment. A glass was instantly filled with wine and put by the top of his plate.

And saying no was not an option.

Of all the ways he envisioned what was going to be a *brief* encounter with Salena during her workday, this was not one of them.

Salena stood by the seat for him that hadn't been there a minute before and tapped the edge of the chair.

Ryan made eye contact with his sister. "It's getting cold," she teased.

That had his feet moving.

Salena passed him to take her seat on the opposite side of the table, sandwiched between Franny and Gio.

Before she sat, Ryan handed her the single red rose in cellophane.

Her eyes said thank you before she whispered the words.

"Ahh . . . and I thought that was for me," Gio said again.

"Zip it, Gio," Salena said from the side of her mouth.

Ryan had no choice but to take a seat. "Thank you," he said to his hostess instead of repeating his remorse for showing up without an invitation.

Mari snapped a command in Italian, and plates of food were passed his way.

He put a small forkful of pasta on his plate, and Mari clicked her tongue. "Are you on a diet? What is this? Emma, does your brother not eat?"

Okay, another forkful.

Mari shrugged.

A third, and she smiled.

"We were talking about last night's party. Chloe said they went through enough alcohol to shame a Friday night at the restaurant."

Another plate, this one piled with prosciutto and cheese. Ryan took his fill. "Several cars were still in the lot when I picked mine up this morning," he said.

"Good. Have a good time, but don't get arrested," Mari said.

Ryan cleared his throat, his eyes found Salena's.

"I don't think anyone got in any trouble," Dante told her.

"I didn't see one cop car," Salena added.

"I'll show you the pictures, Mama. The costumes were fantastic."

"Giovanni and Emma's were darling. I wasn't sure about yours, Salena." Mari pointed her fork at Salena.

"It was better last night, Mari." Salena picked up her wine, took a sip.

"Hmmm." Mari didn't sound convinced.

Ryan sat back with a full plate and picked up a fork.

"Do you have friends here in San Diego?" Mari asked him.

His fork stopped halfway to his lips. "A few."

"Did you stay with them?" she asked.

Someone to his right chuckled.

"No, ma'am, I got a hotel." Ryan took his first bite. The ziti was just this side of heaven.

"Save your money next time. There's always room here. I have two extra rooms in my apartment. And if they're full, there's always the couch."

Ryan once again met Salena's gaze.

She was trying not to laugh.

He swallowed his food with a dose of wine. "I wouldn't want to impose."

Mari lifted both hands in the air. "*Interruption . . . imposition.* These are not words Italians use. If we don't like you, we tell you we're out of food and wine. Then you leave."

He looked at his full plate. "I guess I'm okay, then."

"We like you," Franny chimed in. "You're family."

Ryan took another look around the table.

Brooke was holding Leo in one arm, eating with the other. Franny was sitting on her knees, even though she was tall enough to sit normally. Chloe and Dante beside each other, nudging each other in silent communication. Luca refilled his wine, handed the bottle to his brother.

And Emma caught his attention and grinned.

This was nothing like a family dinner at the Rutledge estate.

"Crazy, right?" Emma asked.

He was at a loss for words.

"What's crazy?" Mari asked.

"It's all good, Mama. In our family, dinners are . . ."

"Strained," Ryan finished for her.

"I've had dinner with your family, and they're wonderful," Mari countered.

"Papa says Mr. Rutledge has a stick up his—"

"Franny!" Brooke and Luca yelled at the same time.

Ryan started to laugh. "He does."

"We haven't found the right doctors to get it out, Franny," Emma said.

Brooke shook her head. "I'm sorry."

"I like you, Franny. You say it like it is." Ryan shoved more food in his mouth.

Franny didn't look the least bit embarrassed by her comment.

"She's willful, that one."

"I like willful." Ryan's eyes settled on Salena once again.

The click of Mari's tongue had Ryan finding another place to rest his eyes.

Dante asked Gio if he could stop by the harbor before heading back to Temecula, and Brooke and Emma were saying something quietly to each other.

Mari asked Salena about her parents' trip and when they were coming home.

The noise on the terrace became a hum filled with utensils touching plates, and the sound of the gulp of air that hits the back of the bottle of wine as more is poured into glasses lifted above it all. Food passed by as seconds were dished up.

And most of the time, Franny spoke in Italian, bringing to Ryan's attention Salena's ease with the language.

Dante sat to his right and leaned in. "Franny practices her Italian on Sundays. Before Brooke and Luca met, no one spoke English at this dinner."

"You do this every Sunday?"

"Most."

"I avoid family dinners," Ryan admitted.

Dante patted his back. "I've met your family."

"Mr. Ryan?" Franny called from her perch at the table.

"Just Ryan is okay."

She rolled her eyes. "Are you a hair person?"

"A what?"

The conversations around them got softer.

"Someone who cuts hair?"

Several confused faces stared at the girl.

"No."

"Why do you think that?" Ryan asked.

"Because I heard Zia Chloe ask Salena if she burned her neck with a curling iron, and Salena said you did."

Gio choked.

Chloe spat wine onto the table.

Salena rested her face in her hands.

Brooke was trying to tell Franny to stop but laughing so hard she couldn't get the words out.

Dante nudged him, repeated Ryan's words from earlier. "She says it like it is!"

And Mari . . . her silence would have provoked a confession out of him if he was twelve.

"Did I say something funny?"

Mari lifted her wineglass. "Did your parents ever take you to church on Sundays?" she asked.

Ryan glanced at his sister. *Help!* He silently mouthed the word.

CHAPTER TWENTY-ONE

Ryan never drank wine.

He didn't like it.

Yet in the course of two hours . . . a two-flippin'-hour dinner in the middle of the day that he had no intention of having when he woke up that morning, he'd consumed half a bottle.

Next came *limoncello* shots, then espresso with dessert.

All he wanted to do was assure Salena that the morning had meant something to him. He'd thought about her all day. The unexpected comment about being with another woman told him, without question, that Salena wasn't as tough as she pretended to be.

Ryan wanted to share even more with her. Like searching for a house.

He didn't know how to go about choosing a home for his future. He wasn't into the brick-and-stucco villa style that mimicked his parental homes. The style Emma and Gio lived in as well. It was undeniably beautiful, but for Ryan, it came with memories of his childhood that he'd just as soon forget.

That left so many other options, and San Diego was filled with them. Bungalows or colonials . . . those weren't on every corner. Modern and classic, farmhouse, or ranch . . . or even a Spanish hacienda. He wanted a woman's opinion, and the first one he thought of was Salena.

He wasn't an idiot.

How would it look if a man, after only knowing a woman for a few weeks, and sleeping with her once, started asking her what kind of house she liked?

Wasn't that why he hadn't even told her he was looking?

He didn't volunteer the information during their conversation that morning over room service. And he let her believe that the "property" he was looking at was commercial.

Now he was sitting in front of a fire on the terrace of the D'Angelos' building, drinking more wine because someone filled his glass . . . again . . . and wondering how he got here.

"You okay over there?" Gio asked him.

Salena, Emma, and Chloe were running plates back to the kitchen. Luca and Brooke were putting the baby down and letting Franny "babysit," with the intention of coming back to the terrace. And Dante was talking on the phone on the other side of the rooftop. Mari had run downstairs to check on the restaurant.

"Your mother hates me."

Gio's staccato laugh made him look above the flames. "No, my friend. If my mother hated you, you'd know it."

"She doesn't approve."

"I have an Italian mother who hasn't had sex since my father died . . . and likely won't ever again."

Ryan found that hard to believe. "What is she, sixty?"

"Fifty-four. She had us young."

Maybe the gray in her hair was throwing off his ability to judge her age. Ryan's mother wouldn't be caught dead with a single silver strand. "And you think she'll never have sex again?" Ryan planned on having sex until it didn't work, and even then . . .

"And your mom and dad are going at it right now."

Ryan snorted. "I don't even get to say that my parents had sex three times." Ryan had just learned that Robert wasn't his biological father . . . that the title belonged to some sperm donor in a clinic. None of which should have mattered, but the family lie had been kept his entire life up until that year. And if there was one thing Ryan honored over all else, it was honesty.

"Point is, Mama wouldn't be doing her job in life if she didn't make all of us squirm a little."

"Or a lot."

"The more you squirm, the more she likes you. And if she pulls you aside and gives you a firm warning, that's her love language."

"How does she get rid of people she doesn't like?"

"Exactly how she said she does. She doesn't feed them or give them wine." Gio waved toward the glass in Ryan's hand.

Ryan took a sip. "If this is how she is, how would Salena's parents be?"

"Worse. Aldo and Brigida have been trying to get Salena to settle down since she was seventeen."

"You're kidding."

"Wish I was." Gio leaned forward. "Imagine meeting the parents for your senior prom and having them genuinely talk about you as if you were their future son-in-law."

Ryan shook his head.

"Salena stopped introducing the guys she dated to them."

Gio sat back. "I'll tell you this. Salena's good people. She's not vulnerable to anyone," Gio hedged.

"What about asking for help if she needs it?"

Gio shrugged. "Not her strong point."

Ryan swallowed hard. "If it was dire?"

"What do you mean?"

"If things were really bad. Would she ask for help?"

"I think that depends on the help. She'll ask for a job before asking for money. She'll offer to help you move but won't request the same in return."

"Emotionally?" Ryan's gaze traveled to the entrance of Salena's apartment but didn't see her.

When Gio wasn't quick to answer, Ryan returned his gaze to his.

"I honestly don't know. I've never seen her cry . . . and certainly not over a guy."

Ryan sighed. "I don't intend to make her cry."

Gio crossed one ankle over his knee and paused. "Actually, I hope you do."

~

"You know they're out there talking about me," Salena announced.

"God, I hope so," Emma said quickly.

Salena glanced at the ceiling, thinking about where they'd left Ryan and the others. "He's your brother . . . I don't think I should be talking with you about—"

"Yeah, he's my brother. Nice hickey, by the way."

Chloe laughed, and Salena gave up on trying to guard her words around Ryan's sister.

"I about died when your mama suggested Ryan stay on her couch."

"She did that to see how he would react. You know full well Mama only interrogates the guys she likes," Chloe said.

They were in Mari's kitchen, running dishes through the water in the sink and filling the dishwasher. The big serving dishes were taken to the restaurant, making cleanup twice as easy. Mari's plates, however, were a family heirloom the staff couldn't be trusted with.

"Is Ryan staying at the hotel tonight?" Emma asked.

"I have no idea. I thought he was going back to Temecula today. I was shocked to see him here."

"And with flowers."

Salena thought of the single bud in a vase in her apartment. "That was sweet."

"It was one flower." Chloe wasn't impressed.

"A whole dozen brought into your place of work screams you just had sex. One flower says something entirely different," Emma told them.

"How do you figure?"

Emma leaned against the counter, drying one of the wineglasses with a towel. "My father always buys big bouquets for my mother every year for Valentine's Day . . . her birthday. Their anniversary. He sends them to her. Doesn't hand them to her. A man who has the money to buy expensive bouquets who hands a woman a single flower . . . or even picks one for her as they're walking in a field. That's different."

Salena felt a punch in her solar plexus. "He brought me a single rose."

Emma slowly smiled. "Yeah. We have the same parents."

The fork she was cleaning slipped from her hand. She made eye contact with Chloe. "How do I do this?"

"What?"

"This?" Salena shot her eyes to Emma. "Don't say anything to Ryan."

"Do what, Salena?"

"Guys don't bring me flowers, Chloe. We both know this. They stick around until we hook up, and then tap a few times before getting bored. Or they don't bother. They don't have all-day dinners with family that isn't theirs . . . Oh, wait." Salena looked at Emma. "Maybe he stuck around for you."

"Stop right there. My brother doesn't put up with his own family for anything. He certainly wouldn't have felt obligated to be here tonight just because of me. He's skilled at making excuses as to why he needs to leave. He'd fake a kidney donation if he had to."

Chloe chuckled.

"He was here for you."

Salena met Emma's eyes. "I don't know what to do with that."

Chloe handed her a dish. "You do what any of us do. Enjoy it."

"Can I give you a little advice?" Emma asked.

"Please."

"Keep things real with him. Be honest about what you are or aren't feeling. He's a big boy. He can take it if you're not into it."

Salena looked at her. "I am. I'm just new . . . at flowers and family dinners."

"I think he is, too."

"You think?" Chloe asked. "Hasn't Ryan dated anyone seriously before?"

"There was one, but . . ."

Salena grinned. "Brittany."

Emma narrowed her brows. "Who is Brittany?"

"High school. He told me about her."

Emma shook her head. "No. Not Brittany."

Salena stopped what she was doing and stared. "Then who was she?"

Emma closed up. "It's really not my story to tell."

"Really, Emma?" Chloe asked with a huff.

"If I tell you, then I'm betraying his trust. Trust and honesty are important values to my brother." Emma looked at Salena. "If you ask him about it, he will either tell you or say he isn't ready to share. But he won't lie."

"Did he love her?" Salena hated that she asked.

"I honestly don't know. I do know that how he is with you isn't something I've seen."

Salena wanted to bring down the intensity of the conversation. "We're just dating."

Chloe went back to the dishes. "Has to start somewhere. Just don't get scared and tell him to get lost."

The hair on Salena's neck stood up. "I don't do that."

"Yeah, you do. Every single time."

You can't lie to a best friend.

They know you too well.

～

"You're walking me to my car."

"I'd escort you to the hotel if the fact that walking into an Italian restaurant on a Sunday meant you weren't leaving until dawn had occurred to you."

Ryan stopped drinking hours ago in preparation for his long drive home. "This Italian thing is new to me. I'll learn. I thought you were working."

"I was. But since I moved here, Mari refuses to let me work during our Sunday dinners."

Ryan was starting to understand how difficult it would be to live under Mari's roof and not abide by her rules.

He'd slipped his hand in hers the moment they left the restaurant, and now he squeezed it. "I hope tonight wasn't too bad for you."

"Me? You were the one in the hot seat."

"You have the hickey."

She pulled away slightly. "About that."

"Not intended."

"Good. Don't make it a habit."

"Kissing your neck? Sorry, that's going to be a habit. Leaving a mark, I'll work on."

Her strides picked up. "You're awfully confident over there."

"You don't like my lips on your neck?" He lowered his voice.

A couple walked by, smiled.

"I didn't say that."

They turned up the street where he'd parked. "Good."

The quiet street left them alone.

Ryan took advantage of that the moment they reached his car. He turned Salena to face him and nuzzled the spot on her neck that Franny had been so gracious to point out.

"Now I know why this is here."

He felt her hand on his hip, the other on his chest. "Oh . . . why?"

His tongue darted out, tasted . . . "I want to bite."

She leaned back, tilted her head.

Damn, damn, damn. He settled for a kiss, one that put his body on alert and damned him for not booking another night at the hotel. A mistake he wouldn't make twice.

Finally, because he had to, he pulled away. "When can I see you again?"

"My schedule is crazy."

"Give me a day." He didn't care. His schedule was open.

"Wednesday. Or—"

"I'll see you Wednesday."

"That drive is stupid. I'm off Friday."

"The whole day?"

"Yeah. All day Friday."

"Then rest on Wednesday and make excuses for not coming home on Friday night."

She smiled. "You're going to keep me all day *and* night?"

"I am."

He kissed her again, made sure she felt it.

Salena pushed him away. "If you don't go, we're going to have to explain to Mari why the local cops are walking me home."

Ryan pulled himself together, ignored the swell in his jeans. "I'll call you tomorrow."

"Drive careful."

He got into his car, rolled down the window. "I can take you back."

She shook her head. "I've been walking this neighborhood my whole life. But thanks."

"'Night, Trouble."

She liked her nickname. "Thanks for the rose."

He just smiled and pulled away from the curb.

CHAPTER TWENTY-TWO

The holidays rolled in like the tide.

One minute everything in the city was decorated for Halloween, and the next, it was Christmas lights and artificial trees. Almost as if Thanksgiving wasn't a thing.

For three weeks following the elevation of Salena and Ryan's relationship from friends to friends with benefits, Ryan had become a regular at the Hyatt. In turn, so had Salena. As much as she could, in any event, with how crazy her schedule had become.

Her parents had returned from Arizona for Thanksgiving but were planning to go back for Christmas. The slight reprieve from them was a blessing.

The weather was showing off why so many flocked to San Diego this time of year, and Salena was happy to see Ryan standing in the doorway of the restaurant, carrying a helmet.

He'd told her to wear jeans and a jacket, and now she knew why.

"This is a treat."

He kissed her and led her outside on the sidewalk.

"It's too nice of a day to be cooped up in a car." He handed her a helmet. "I bought this for you."

She took it from him, turned it around in her hands. "Bought it?" She glanced at his bike that was parked at the curb, noticed his helmet strapped on.

"Mine is too big. Helmets need to fit."

"For me?" Salena couldn't quite grasp the fact that he'd bought her an accessory for his bike.

Ryan smiled, lifted an eyebrow. "There's a com system in it so we can talk as we're driving."

"What?"

"Try it on."

Salena loosened the band she had holding her hair back and lowered it so her hair gathered at the base of her neck before placing the helmet on her head.

The noise of the street instantly dimmed by several decibels.

Ryan helped her adjust the strap until the helmet sat securely on her head. Like a glove.

He lifted her chin with a finger and pursed his lips. "Sexy."

Once his helmet was on, he flipped a switch, and his voice sounded as if he were speaking right next to her ears. "Can you hear me?"

"Wow. That's awesome."

He tossed a leg over the bike and turned it over.

After he backed it out of his spot, he nodded for her to get on.

"You'll have to teach me how to drive this thing." She straddled the bike . . . him and leaned over his shoulder.

"Just wrap your legs around me, babe. I'll do the work."

She loved it when he talked like that. "Don't threaten me with a good time."

He revved the bike before pulling into traffic.

"Where are we going?"

"I hope you don't mind, but I have to run a couple of errands before we go for a ride."

"What kind of errands do you run on a bike?"

He darted down the road, turned onto Harbor Drive. "I need to check out a few houses."

Houses? Did he say *houses*? "You need to *what*?"

"Remember a while back I told you I was looking for property?"

She'd completely forgotten about that. "Yeah. Did you find a building?"

"I wasn't looking for commercial property. I want to buy a house."

"Oh!" She didn't expect that. "Wait, here? In San Diego?"

"Yeah."

They stopped at a red light, and she leaned forward and looked at him from the side. "You're taking me with you to look at houses."

He nodded once. "I need a woman's perspective. I'm having a hard time picking."

"My perspective?" What did she know about buying a house? "Why me?"

He rubbed her leg. "Why *not* you?"

The light turned green, and she held on.

"You're awfully quiet back there," he said as they buzzed through traffic.

"I'm still in shock."

She felt another pat on her thigh as they passed into Point Loma and over to the ocean side of the peninsula.

They stopped in front of a house with a "For Sale" sign in front of it, and Ryan cut the engine.

He pulled his helmet off, and she followed.

"Houses?" She climbed off the bike and looked up.

"I've been thinking about it for a while. Now that Giovanni is in Temecula with Emma, and Mom has a man close by, it's time for me to move."

Salena narrowed her eyes. "That's a bit sexist."

He shrugged. "I don't care. I worried about my sister and my mother being out there alone. You call it sexist. I call it being protective."

Okay, when he put it like that. "And you want to move to San Diego."

A car pulled into the driveway of the house.

Ryan waved.

"I do."

"Have you been looking every time you come and see me?"

"Yes. I didn't want to say anything."

"Why?"

"I didn't want to scare you off."

That was not the answer she was expecting.

The man from the car walked toward them.

"Tobias, this is Salena." Ryan introduced them. "Tobias is my real estate agent."

"Hi," she said in a daze.

"Great to finally meet you."

Finally?

She smiled at the man, lifted a finger in the air. "Can you give us a second?"

Tobias looked between them, smiled. "Yeah, sure. I'll meet you inside."

"Thanks."

When he was gone, she turned to Ryan. "Scare me off?"

He regarded her with a tilt of his head. "Bear with me here . . . You meet this guy. This amazingly good-looking man who drives a motorcycle and who pushes all your sexual buttons."

It was hard to keep a straight face. "Okay."

"And within a month of meeting this guy, he tells you he wants to move to your town. What's your first thought?"

"He's moving for the girl."

Ryan pointed a finger at her. "Right. Only it's timing, and not really the girl. But the girl definitely makes the move more inviting."

"But the guy is asking the girl to look at houses."

"Because the guy can't make up his fucking mind. Tobias is starting to think I'm never going to squeeze the trigger." He sighed. "I need help, Salena. Maybe not so much help, but someone else's perspective. Someone whose opinion I trust."

"You've known me for less than two months."

"And I trust you. So, are you helping me or not? You know this city better than I do."

"Huh!" Salena turned toward the house. "Okay."

~

Why hadn't he done this sooner?

Salena knew San Diego. Had a story for nearly every neighborhood they looked in.

Ryan had kept his search limited to the neighborhoods that stretched from the beach cities to those that overlooked the bay. If he was going to spend the money, he wanted a view of something other than his neighbor's yard.

The airport that sat in the center of the city was a concern, along with flight patterns for the commercial airlines, as well as the military bases that had air traffic.

They followed Tobias from house to house, privately talking through the com system in the helmets. Buying her one had been his best idea to date.

At least two of the homes Ryan had viewed the week before and were still on the market. Interest rates were through the roof, giving him time to sit on a property instead of having to compete with twenty other buyers and being forced to make a quick decision.

"Pacific Beach is great. But if you want a view of the water, you're going to have to get close. It gets busy in the summer, but the city has a great vibe."

"All I know about it is the bars."

Salena patted his thigh. "That, too."

They pulled up to the house, which sat several blocks from the ocean, with the only view being a glimpse from a roof patio. The yard was way too small, so they never got around to even discussing the things they liked about it.

It wasn't until the fourth listing that their excitement spiked. This one sat up on a hillside overlooking the bay in Point Loma.

"Wow!"

They walked into a modern home with floor-to-ceiling windows, tile floors, and a sleek open kitchen that spilled into a living room, dining room, and billiard space with a separate bar.

"You could throw one hell of a party here." Salena's approval was obvious.

"I viewed this last week," he confessed.

She walked toward the massive window. "This is a door, right?"

Tobias moved to her side and slid the sliders open, making the wall disappear, and the patio outside seamlessly became part of the room.

"The view of the city at night is spectacular." Tobias handed her a brochure on the house that had a photograph of what he was talking about.

"Wow!"

Ryan enjoyed watching her expressions. "That's what I thought."

They both walked out on the patio and stood by the railing. "What are your concerns?"

"I've never lived in a modern home."

"Two out of the four we've looked at have been this style."

He nodded. "I keep gravitating that way."

Tobias held back as they walked through the rest of the house. It had three bedrooms, three and a half bathrooms, along with an office.

"It's huge," Salena commented as they stood in the primary bedroom on the second floor.

"The room or the house?"

"Both."

Another balcony extended past the sliding wall of windows and offered an even higher view.

"It is bigger than I was looking for. But it does have a garage, and the backyard is big enough for a hot tub and a dog."

"You really like this one," Salena said.

"It's also one of the most expensive."

Her smile fell. "If it's out of your budget, why tease yourself?"

"It's on the high end of my budget." A self-imposed amount since his prequalification gave him a much higher number . . . thanks to the money in his trust fund. Some of which he would use for a down payment. The mortgage, however, he would swing on his business income.

"Let's keep looking and use this as the one to beat."

And they did. For the next three hours, Tobias pulled them from one end of San Diego to the other, including Coronado.

"Too dark." This was one that needed a few hundred thousand in updates to remove the 1980s oak and rock-wall fireplace. Even though the ocean view was spectacular and the lot bigger than the others.

"Emma and my mother would love it." This one was more Spanish than a modern Mediterranean. Wood floors, a kitchen that Salena shook her head at, and way too many small bedrooms.

"It could work." Modern, and a smaller version of the original. The sliders didn't open all the way across, but according to Tobias, that could be done. The kitchen, like the house, was smaller. Three bedrooms, without the office, and while the floor plan was open, it didn't feel as spacious with the low ceilings.

"Room for a hot tub and a dog," Salena pointed out as they stood in the backyard. "And it's cheaper."

They added this one to the small stack of maybes and moved on.

Once they exhausted the listings, Tobias left them with the promise of Ryan calling him later.

They sat on a bench in a massive park between Liberty Station and the bay. They'd picked up some street tacos and were eating off their laps, discussing his options.

"This was a lot more fun than I expected it to be," Salena said. "I like shopping with other people's money."

Ryan started to laugh. "I've yet to meet a woman who didn't."

"Nawh, nawh . . . Not the same. What you're thinking of is a woman using your wallet to buy something for herself." She paused, tilted her head. "Which still doesn't suck."

He laughed harder.

"You have a definite style."

"Modern," he admitted.

"Yeah. Glass and tile and not a lot of fuss. Clean. But not black and white. Soft colors with maybe a pop of surprise in a corner."

Ryan brought his taco to his mouth. "I didn't know you had interior decorating ambitions." He took a bite.

"No. I'm just observant. Which is easier when I don't have a dollar in the pile."

"What if you did . . . have money at stake. Which would you pick?"

"A small three-bedroom without a view that could be managed on a waitress salary. It doesn't exist. Not in San Diego." She put a chip in her mouth. "There is a reason my parents have always lived in a condo. They're cheaper."

"You prefer them."

"No." She shook her head. "If today taught me anything, it's that I need to work harder to have a house. At the D'Angelos', it's quiet. No crazy party downstairs that's keeping you up."

He laughed. "Yeah, they do that upstairs."

"Mari hears the bulk of the noise from the restaurant. If the baby is crying, no one is pissy about it 'cause it's family. At my parents' place"— she rolled her eyes—"neighbors fighting, someone burning breakfast, a dog left alone and barking at all hours. You live in an apartment right now; you know what I'm talking about."

"I liked the noise when I first moved in. Silence felt stuffy."

"Move into the bay-view modern, and it won't be silent for long. You'll have to tell your houseguests to leave."

Ryan could see that future. "You liked that one."

"I did. But what I like is irrelevant. *You* loved it."

He sat back, brushed the crumbs off his lap. "You were a huge help today."

"Good," she said with a grin. "I'll let you return the favor soon."

"Oh? With what?"

"I'm almost ready to get a car."

He paused. "That was quick. You made it sound like it was going to be months."

She grinned. "I've made some decent tips. And this guy I'm seeing pays for all our dates."

"Sounds like a great guy."

She shrugged. "He'll do."

Ryan laughed . . . She joined him.

"Are you going to buy new or used?"

"Certified preowned, I think. I'm not sure the tips will continue and don't want to overextend my budget."

A budget she obviously had. He'd never had a used car, even when he was sixteen. His parents considered that a slight on their reputation. And hell, he was sixteen. Who didn't want something new right out of the gate?

"Anything bought at a dealership with a warranty is going to be pretty clean. I doubt you'll need my help with the shape the engine is in."

"I wasn't going to ask about the engine."

"Make and model?"

She shook her head. "I know what I want."

Ryan scratched his chin. "So how am I going to help?"

"The color."

God, she made him laugh. "I'm only good for the color."

She wadded up the paper that had held her food and shoved it in the bag. "Just kidding. I know what color I want, too. I just didn't want you to feel left out."

"Thanks for saving my feelings."

She pushed off the bench, brushed down her clothes. "You're welcome. As much as I'd love to look for cars today, I need to get to work so I can pay for it."

Ryan looked at the time.

Twenty minutes later, he was double parked in front of the restaurant, and she was trying to hand him the helmet.

"It's yours. No need for me to take that home."

He reached for her, pulled in for a kiss. "Thanks for today. You were a tremendous help."

"You're going to put an offer on that house, aren't you?"

He looked into her bright eyes. "I'm considering it."

She leaned in, kissed him again. "For luck."

Ryan licked his lips as she moved away from the bike.

A car horn behind him motivated him to stop staring and let traffic move.

CHAPTER TWENTY-THREE

It was Thanksgiving, and as much as Ryan tried to talk her into joining him, Gio, and Emma on their trip to Napa for the holiday, there was no way in hell Salena was ready for a Rutledge family dinner.

Instead, the typical Sunday-dinner crowd, complete with her parents, as well as Dante's mom, sister, and family . . . and a few stragglers on staff that had nowhere else to go, gathered for a traditional turkey with all the trimmings.

Salena stood in the back parking lot with her parents at her side and pointed. "I bought a car." Technically it was a Jeep. Two-door Wrangler that even preowned cost more than she ever thought she would be able to afford. Spending only her OM money, she managed a hearty down payment, with reasonable monthly payments that she had every intention of paying off should things with OM continue the way they were.

"What?" her mother said as she walked closer to the car.

"Where did you get the money?" her dad asked right away.

"I've been saving." Which wasn't a lie.

"Salena, I can't believe you did this." Her mama sounded excited.

"Can you afford it?"

"The payments are less than a week's pay, Papa."

That seemed to appease her father slightly. "How does it run? Used cars have problems."

"It has a warranty."

Both her parents turned to her. "That's very responsible of you."

"Thanks, Mama. I'm trying."

Salena pressed the button on the remote and unlocked the Jeep and watched as her father inspected the vehicle.

~

"You bought a what?"

Ryan stared across the table at his father, who seemed surprised by what he'd just heard.

"Where?" Emma asked.

"It's in Point Loma. I just opened escrow. It's nowhere close to being a done deal."

"That's amazing, Ryan," Giovanni said. "Congratulations."

"I'm glad you're finally taking my advice," his father added from his perch at the top of the table.

Ryan lifted his wineglass to his lips. "Much as it pains me to say this, you were right."

For the first time in years, Robert cracked a smile at something Ryan said. "I'm sure that hurt."

Ryan put a hand on his chest. "You have no idea."

Richard, his brother, added his congratulations. "Do you have pictures?"

"After dinner," his mother suggested.

"Does Salena know?" Gio asked.

"Who is Salena?" Beth asked.

Ryan looked between Emma and Gio. "She does. Actually, she was pretty instrumental in helping me make a decision."

"And Salena is?" Beth asked again.

A friend?

Girlfriend?

Would Salena be okay if he gave her a title to his parents?

No. *Trouble* would not be all right with him calling her anything without her permission.

223

"The woman I've been seeing." Ryan drank his wine, put the glass down.

"Interesting," Richard said with a smirk as he nudged his wife's side.

"When are we going to meet this woman?" his mom asked.

"You already have," he said.

"At the wedding," Emma added. "She's a longtime friend of the family."

His mom and dad exchanged a long look. "I don't remember . . . Oh, wait. She was at the rehearsal dinner."

"She was?" Robert asked.

Beth waved his question off, turned to Ryan. "Do you have a picture for your father?"

He lifted his fork instead of his cell phone. "After dinner."

Emma laughed. "Maybe the one at the costume party isn't the best picture to share."

That was the one he liked the most.

~

"Was it awful?" Salena asked Ryan as she settled into bed after a long and gluttonous day of family and food.

"Surprisingly, no. What about yours?"

"Same. My parents were shocked silent when I showed them the Jeep." She'd video-messaged Ryan when she was comparing two cars and teasing about the color difference. Ashlynn was with her at the dealership and had already decided that red was the best choice if it was available. "It's hard for them to keep going on about what a huge mistake moving out was when I'm getting ahead in the world."

"The sooner you can let go of the weight of their opinions, the faster you'll be happier."

"Have you done that? Shed that parental weight?"

"Maybe not a hundred percent."

She appreciated his honesty. "Did you show them pictures of the house?"

"I did."

"Did they like it?" Salena twisted the edge of the blanket on her bed.

"Dad did. Mom wanted to hear more about you."

She went still. "You told them about me?"

"Yes."

"What did you say?"

He chuckled over the line.

"Why are you laughing?"

"Because every once in a while, the strong, willful woman inside of you looks aside, and the inquisitive, cautious one steps forward."

She wasn't sure she liked the sound of that. "Never mind, then, talk about me all you want."

He laughed harder. "Gio . . . or maybe it was Emma, asked if you knew about the house. I told them you helped me pick it out. At that point, my mother needed details."

"Hmmm." What details?

"What, *hmmm*?"

"Nothing."

He laughed again. "Dad wanted pictures of the house. My mom wanted pictures of you."

They'd only taken a couple of pictures with each other, and maybe a couple that shouldn't be shared.

"I guess that's okay."

"You're adorable."

She wrinkled her nose. "Hot, sexy, sinful . . . but adorable? No. The nickname is Trouble. You'd be better off remembering that."

The sound of his low laugh warmed her. "When are we getting you that tattoo?"

"I haven't decided on a design yet." She hadn't given it much thought. Tattoos weren't something you did on a whim.

"I'll start looking for you."

"This I'd like to see."

"Don't tempt me, Trouble."

"Challenging you. Not tempting you." She pulled her knees to her chest.

"Accepted."

This could be fun. "When are you coming home?"

"Sunday. Emma, Gio, and I are on the same flight."

"Dinner here, then?"

"We just had Thanksgiving."

"Like that matters. Let me give you a heads-up of what every Italian mother in this neighborhood will say to you. 'You eat every day.'"

"Yeah, but your meals are two and three hours long."

"If you think you can get out of Sunday at D'Angelo's when you're flying into San Diego, you might want to ask Giovanni what the odds of that are."

"Okay, but no wine for me. I need to get back to Temecula."

"Since when do you drink wine?" He always ordered beer or whiskey when they were out.

"I don't know."

It was her turn to laugh. His bitter tone said he wasn't happy about the switch.

"Maybe it's R&R wine you dislike."

He growled. "I'm blaming my Italian girlfriend."

She caught her breath. "Your Italian *what*?"

"Too soon?"

"Depends . . . who is she?"

"I like the title," he told her.

She dropped her knees to the bed. "And if I don't?"

"Give me another one I can use."

"Italian summer. Italian night. Italian holiday." There were so many.

"Let's see how that rolls off the tongue. 'Hey, Mom . . . let me show you a picture of my *Italian holiday* that helped me pick out a house.'"

That made her laugh. "Probably not."

"'The woman I'm seeing' is a mouthful. *Girlfriend* is easier."

She mulled the thought over, found herself squirming. "I'll think about it."

"What do you call me?"

The image of her pulling up in the Jeep for the first time and a neighborhood friend asking her who bought it for her flashed in her head. "Sugar daddy."

"Excuse me?"

"I call you Ryan."

"Let's back up."

"Let's not."

"You won't let me take you to someplace nice. It's always street tacos or burgers. How can I be considered a sugar daddy?"

"It's a joke." She closed her eyes, felt a weight in her chest. "A bad one."

"Okay."

"Okay." The night pushed in, and the need to curl in a ball and sleep outweighed continuing this conversation. "I'm tired."

There was silence. "I'll see you Sunday, Trouble."

That title she could accept. "I'll bring the wine."

~

"This place is unbelievable."

Ryan walked beside Giovanni on a hillside that overlooked the R&R vineyards, estate, and winery. Grapevines spread out for as far as the eye could see. All of it belonged to Rutledge.

"That's what everyone says." Ryan wasn't impressed.

"Does nothing for you, does it?"

"No. This is someone else's dream." Ryan glanced at his brother-in-law. "Yours?"

Gio shook his head. "Not if it means being disconnected from your family."

"You're a good man, Gio. I'm glad Emma found you."

"That means a lot."

They walked in silence until Gio broke it. "You wanna tell me what's on your mind?"

A glance at Gio, then the horizon. "Salena."

Gio let out a single sound that sounded like a laugh. "That can't be easy."

"Actually, it has been."

"Until?"

Ryan took a breath. "Last night, she said something to me that I wasn't expecting."

"That's Salena." Gio didn't sound surprised. "What did she say?"

"She called me a sugar daddy."

Gio stopped walking, turned toward him. "Did you buy her that car?"

Ryan winced. "No!"

Gio put his hands in the air. "I had to ask."

"Is that what everyone is thinking?"

The answer wasn't instant. "Salena isn't the type to save. The weekend, the party. No one expected her to have the money to buy something nice."

Fuck. "I had nothing to do with it. She didn't even ask my advice on the color."

That made Gio laugh. "That sounds like her."

"The only thing I spring for is a hotel. We both know my presence at her place isn't acceptable."

"Maybe not at first."

Ryan doubted Mari would be any more okay with it now than she was a month ago. The woman was as old world as they came. "Our first date was In-N-Out Burger. To go."

"Her suggestion?"

"Yeah. Said she worked in restaurants and didn't want fancy."

They continued walking. "Fair."

"I suggest a lunch place on the bay, she says street tacos on a bench. I'm not her sugar daddy."

Ryan could think of at least two women he'd dated in the past he'd spent more money on in the week of their dating than he had the whole time with Salena.

"If the title doesn't fit, why is it bothering you?"

"When this is your backyard, you grow up with many people expecting you to foot the bill. Friends, relatives . . . women."

"I can imagine."

"She doesn't look at me like that. I hate that, somehow, that title was put in her head. It does strange things to women." Ryan pulled the jacket he was wearing closer to his skin as the autumn wind blew over them.

"What do you mean?"

He hesitated for only a minute and then started to tell Gio what really sparked his reaction.

"It was the first year out of my parents' house. I was living in San Diego, going to college . . . well, pretending to go to college. I partied more than attended classes."

"Sounds like a lot of people I know."

"Yeah, well. I met this girl. Young. Eighteen."

"How old were you?"

"Nineteen."

Gio laughed.

"We were at a party, hooked up. I was happy getting away with underage drinking. Helen . . . God, she hated that name. HP. That's what she wanted to be called. HP partied hard."

"Drugs?"

The memory of her passed out on his couch, completely unable to move, flashed in his head. "Yeah. I didn't realize how much the crap she was taking was messing her up. Most of the time around me, she just drank. I told her I'd have nothing to do with supporting her habit."

"Was it . . . a habit?"

Ryan nodded. "She never asked. In fact, she was the first to call out people that wanted to use my deep pockets when we were out together."

"No one's sugar daddy." Gio's assessment was spot-on.

"Exactly."

"What happened?"

The cold whipped around Ryan. He shivered. "I knew she was in some trouble. When we met, she had a car, a part-time job. Was juggling a full schedule at the college we both went to. She started ditching classes at the same time I did, so I thought nothing of it. The job went next. She didn't tell me. Lied about where she was."

"Were you exclusive?"

Ryan shrugged. "Yeah, no. It wasn't really like that. We slept with each other, but I only thought of her as a friend. A friend I wanted to help."

"She didn't ask."

Ryan shook his head. "Never. And I offered. Not to give her money but help her get a job. A place to stay. It was always 'No, I'm fine. I've got this.'" He paused. "She didn't have it."

"Where is she now?" Gio asked.

"In an urn on her parents' mantel."

Gio moaned. "Ah, fuck."

"She'd disappear for days, weeks at a time. She'd text sometimes, say she was fine. I knew she was lying, but . . ."

"What could you do?"

"A year after we met, almost to the day, I got a call from her friend. They found her in a car at the bottom of a cliff up near Arrowhead. The guy who was driving was a known dealer. Her real sugar daddy."

"Damn, Ryan. That's awful."

"Would have been really awful if I'd loved her." Ryan stared off across the empty vines. "I felt guilty for not caring more. Not trying more. Not forcing her to clean up. She kept so many secrets."

"You were kids."

"I know. Felt guilty just the same. I told Emma all about it, after."

Gio hesitated. "Not your parents?"

"No. We don't have that relationship."

They started walking again.

"Have you told Salena this?"

"No."

"Why?"

"It's a heavy subject. I'm used to keeping things light with women."

"You still feel that way about Salena?"

No. And that was the problem.

He shook his head.

"Remember when I warned you that Salena wasn't easy?" Gio asked a few seconds later.

"At the wedding. Yeah."

"She doesn't do drugs."

"I know that." That wasn't a question.

"She is exceptionally good at holding her cards close to her chest. You have a secret, she's the one to tell. Things don't slip from her."

"Meaning?"

"If the sugar daddy comment came up, and you both know it's bullshit, someone said that to her. Normally, Salena would blow that off. Tell whoever to fuck off. But she repeated it to you. So the comment stung."

Ryan blew out a long-winded breath. "You even assumed I bought her the car."

"I'm sure I'm not the only one. You have money. She isn't known to have any. Less sensitive people would flat out ask her if you did."

"That sucks. She's working her ass off, and people think it's given to her."

"The whole interaction proves two things."

"Which are?" Ryan asked.

"The comment hurt. And you've penetrated her walls enough that she let you know. I don't know that she's ever let a man in like that."

"I'm not sure I'm *in* anywhere."

Gio laughed. "Emma and I have been married for seven weeks."

"Yeah."

He patted Ryan's back. "You're in."

CHAPTER TWENTY-FOUR

Salena sat back in the massage chair and sighed. There was a woman pampering her feet while another fixed the mess that she called fingernails. Beside her, Chloe moaned. "We don't do this enough."

"I say we make this a girl date every three weeks," Salena suggested.

"Deal. We haven't been spending as much time together."

"You're married to the hottest Italian this side of Italy who keeps you exhausted."

A woman sitting in a chair beside Chloe laughed.

Chloe glanced her way. "She's exaggerating."

Salena snorted.

"Okay . . . maybe not."

"You're busy. I'm busy. It's not a big deal."

"Girl time is important," Chloe insisted.

The woman to her left chimed in as if the conversation included her. "Never forget that. Marriage, kids . . . those things make you forget. Don't let it." The woman looked as if she was in her forties and likely spoke from experience, and Salena lent her an ear.

"Life gets busy."

"It does. Nothing wrong with that. Next thing you know, you haven't had a mani-pedi in years and your kids are off having a life and the girls you once hung out with are all disconnected and you have no idea how it happened."

The woman at Salena's feet pointed the bottle of polish at her. "She's right."

"That won't happen to us," Salena insisted.

"Really?" Older and Wiser asked. "What was your friend doing last week?"

Salena met Chloe's eyes, came up completely blank. "Working."

"What are her thoughts? What is she worried about? What is she excited about?"

Salena couldn't answer.

"You guys are best friends, right?"

"Yeah," they both answered at the same time.

And yet Salena couldn't answer a single question this stranger posed. What were Chloe's thoughts? Was she worried about something in her life? What was going right in her world?

Chloe offered a sheepish grin.

Twenty minutes later, Salena insisted on paying for their spa treatments, claiming a lost birthday gift.

They climbed into Salena's new car, and before she could turn over the engine, Chloe started. "What's going on?"

"What?"

"You heard that lady. What's going on with you?"

"Nothing."

"We don't pay for each other's nail polish."

"I can't treat a friend?"

Chloe shook her head. "I know the kind of money you make at the restaurant. I know you were close to broke when you moved in."

"It was a pedicure."

Chloe tapped the dashboard of the Jeep. "And this?"

There were many things Chloe was good at. Keeping a secret wasn't one of them. "I've been helping out Ashlynn at the studio. The extra income has been a huge help."

Not a lie . . . not the whole truth.

"Oh." Chloe sat back against her seat.

"What about you?" The question was meant to be accusatory. "Is Dante pressuring you to have a baby?"

Chloe shook her head. "No. We agreed on a couple years. We're not ready. Want to buy a house first."

"So nothing has changed?"

"No." Chloe sighed. "I just . . ."

"What?"

"Get the feeling you're hiding something from me."

Guilt played in Salena's chest as she scrambled for something other than her OnlyMe truth to spill. "Daniella and Matt's marriage is on the rocks."

Chloe's eyes widened. "What?"

"Don't say anything to your mom. It will get back to my parents."

"What happened?"

"Growing apart? I don't know. I'm not sure they were ever emotionally together."

"And your parents don't know?"

"My parents only see what they want to see. They were there for three weeks, came back talking about what a lovely married life my sister has. They're going back for Christmas, and Daniella is going to encourage them to look at houses."

Chloe's jaw fell open. "To move there?"

Salena nodded. "If her marriage is over, she's going to need help."

"Whoa. I can't imagine."

"I feel bad."

"Yeah, of course you do. Divorce sucks."

"Not about that." Salena waved a hand in the air. "I didn't think it would last as long as it has. Daniella is still young. She deserves someone who adores her."

"That isn't Matt."

"I know."

"Then what do you feel bad about?" Chloe asked.

"I'm totally taking advantage of the situation. If my parents move there . . . no more helicopter here. And if her relationship falls apart, it will be really easy for me to toss up the situation to them every time they go on and on about the sanctity of marriage."

Chloe started to laugh. "Yeah, you should feel like shit about that."

"I know. I suck." The truth was, Salena did feel bad about how she felt, but she wasn't about to lie to herself.

Chloe placed a hand on Salena's arm. "You've lived under Daniella's shadow your whole life. You can't help the way you feel."

Salena turned over the engine of the Jeep and patted the steering wheel. "I went into a little debt buying this, but it's worth it if my parents see that I'm doing okay, and they can move on."

"Are you going to struggle to make the payments?"

Salena hedged, knowing she was going to be fine but not wanting Chloe digging deeper into where the money was coming from. She wasn't ready for the world to know or her parents to worry.

Or Ryan.

The closer they got to each other, the more she cared about his opinion of her. And no matter how she spun the OnlyMe bottle, the organization had a bad reputation.

"I'll be okay."

"You'll ask for help if you need it, right?" Chloe asked.

"Yeah."

"Good."

~

There was something about sitting on a rooftop terrace, the Sunday after Thanksgiving, with a gas firepit on for more show than warmth, that just didn't suck.

Ryan stretched out next to Salena and pulled her legs to rest on his thighs as she relaxed. If anyone in the group objected, they didn't say a thing.

Mari was talking with Rosa, Dante's mother, in one corner while Giovanni, Emma, Dante, and Chloe were huddled around the fire with them. Luca was down in the restaurant kitchen, and Brooke was settling Franny and Leo, likely going to bed early.

"I can't get a grasp on your brother and his wife." Giovanni was sharing the Rutledge family dynamics with those who weren't there. "They seem happy."

"You could tell that through the plastic smiles?" Ryan asked.

"I keep telling Richard if he doesn't stop acting like Dad, he's going to end up divorced," Emma said.

Ryan huffed, "Kristen isn't leaving him."

"How long have they been married?" Chloe asked.

"Right out of college."

"And no children?" Dante asked.

Emma shook her head. "I hope they figure out their marriage before bringing kids into the mix."

"Not everyone wants kids," Salena said.

Ryan nodded. "Richard does. Told me a couple of times."

"Kristen wants to be a size four her whole life."

Gio dismissed this notion with a wave of his hand. "Baby weight comes off. Look at Brooke. And even if it doesn't, who cares?"

"Well said, bro." Dante gave him a fist bump.

Salena laughed, pointed between Emma and Chloe. "Don't listen to them. They have ulterior motives."

"Having babies doesn't make you gain weight," Mari said from the side. "Raising them does."

"I thought that was gray hair, Mama," Gio said.

Rosa lifted her wineglass in the air. "Those, too."

"Speaking of," Ryan said. "Did you get your hair done, Mari? I meant to comment on how flattering this new style is." He wasn't sure if wearing it down was the new part, or maybe less of the gray they spoke of.

Several sets of eyes took in the oldest D'Angelo with concentrated gazes.

"Yeah, Mama . . . did you get it dyed?" Chloe asked. "It looks fabulous."

Rosa nudged Mari. "I told you."

Mari touched the edges of her hair as color rose to her cheeks. "I thought it was time for a new look."

"Why?" Gio asked straight-out.

Emma swiped at his arm.

"Ouch."

"It looks great, Mama," Emma said.

"Thank you, *cara*."

Gio stood, crossed to his mother, and kissed her cheek. "You're always beautiful."

She patted his arm. "Nice save."

Dante chuckled, and Gio found another bottle of wine and topped off everyone's glasses.

"I thought you weren't going to drink tonight." Salena nudged Ryan with her leg.

"Tell that to the man that can't stop pouring."

Gio lifted the empty bottle in the air. "I'm Italian. It's in my blood."

Ryan took another sip. "I'll get a room at the hotel."

"That's ridiculous," Mari said with a click of her tongue.

"It's fine."

Mari switched her gaze from Salena to him, him to Salena. "You don't think I know where Salena spends the nights when she's not here?"

Someone cleared their throat.

"I was young once. And since I'm not an idiot . . . and I like you, you're welcome to stay." Mari turned to Salena and held up one finger.

Ryan wasn't sure what the gesture to Salena was, but he knew he'd passed the Mari D'Angelo test somehow.

Rosa stood. "I'm going to go."

"I'll walk you home," Dante told his mother.

"I'll grab my sweater and go with you," Chloe said.

Everyone got to their feet and said their long goodbyes.

Everyone but Emma, Gio, Salena, and Ryan left the terrace. Once they were alone, he asked, "What was the finger all about?"

"Salena's been given her one hall pass," Gio told him.

"Luca made it abundantly clear, no men in this apartment," Salena said.

"And Mama just overrode him."

Ryan puffed his chest out. "I'm the chosen."

Salena rolled her eyes. "Don't let it get to your head, Rutledge."

Emma giggled and leaned close to her husband. "You might want to inform Luca of the situation. I'd hate to wake up to a misunderstanding in the morning."

"Good idea."

Ryan glanced at Salena. "You okay with me staying?"

She grunted like it didn't matter either way. "Just make sure you put the toilet seat down."

Emma and Gio took their leave, giving Ryan and Salena the terrace.

"And then there were two," he said.

Salena shook her head. "I never thought that would happen."

"You heard the woman. She likes me."

Salena grabbed their wineglasses and headed inside. "Why don't you turn off the fire. I have a better idea of how we can spend our evening."

Ryan did not need to be told twice.

∼

Ryan ran a lazy hand up and down her leg, his lips close to her ear. "I'm sorry I have to leave so early."

They were still catching their breath from their morning workout. "The consolation prize was worth it," she teased. "Besides, I need to get to the studio early."

"Studio?"

Salena held her breath. "I mean gym."

"Your gym is a studio?"

She hadn't meant to say that. But maybe if she eased what she was doing into the conversation, Ryan would better understand her choices when and if he found out about her side gig.

"Like a yoga studio?"

"Downward Dog is not my thing. That's all Chloe."

"Downward Dog is kinda hot," he teased.

"Pfft!"

"What?"

"My workouts are a lot hotter than that."

Ryan hiked her knee higher on his legs. "What's hotter than a woman bending over with her ass in the air?"

Salena couldn't help herself. "When she does it on a stripper pole."

Ryan snorted. "Yep. That would do it . . . Wait. What?"

"I work out in a pole-dancing studio."

Ryan leaned back enough to look her in the eye. "No shit?"

She lifted her leg, pointed to a bruise on her shin. "I didn't get this dropping a weight on it."

"A stripper pole?"

She patted his chest. "With my clothes on. Don't get excited. It's not that kind of studio."

"No shit?" He started to smile. He licked his lips. "My girlfriend pole dances."

"Here you go with that *girlfriend* thing again."

"Why didn't you say something before?" he asked.

"It didn't come up in conversation."

"You talk about going to the gym all the time."

"*Gym* is code for the studio. My parents would not be okay with it. I saved their feelings by telling them I was going to the gym."

"When do I get to see this workout?"

Subscribe to my OM page.

The words sat on her tongue, ready to be spat out.

She held them in.

"The studio is for those participating, not spectating."

He groaned. "I guess that's probably a good thing."

Yeah . . . exactly what she thought he'd say. Keeping OM to herself was the right call.

"I know the owner, though. I'm sure I can sneak you in for a private lesson. You know, for a special occasion." She ran her hand down his chest.

"My birthday is coming up."

"Really? When?"

"April."

She started to chuckle. "April it is, then."

"Wait. No. I meant next week."

Salena pushed him away and scrambled off the bed. "Driver's licenses don't lie." She bent over at her waist to retrieve his jeans and grabbed his wallet out of the back pocket. Ryan was watching her with his mouth open. "April twenty-ninth."

"Christmas is coming," Ryan suggested.

Salena tossed his wallet on the bed and turned toward the doorway to the bathroom. There, she stopped and ran her knee up the wall as if it were a pole. "I might be convinced."

Ryan swung his feet off the bed and jumped toward her.

Salena squealed and ran so he could give chase.

CHAPTER TWENTY-FIVE

December rolled in with a steady climb of OnlyMe subscriptions. As Ashlynn had predicted, a few fell off. Mainly those who requested nudes and were denied.

She and Ashlynn were in a back room that they had set up for the sole purpose of filming. They'd invested in a fog machine, studio and spot lighting, and better cameras. Most of the investment was Ashlynn's since her page significantly outweighed Salena's. But Salena did help with what she could.

"You know what would really take this to the next level?" Ashlynn asked.

"No, what?"

"A cameraman."

They did spend a ton of time editing to make things look good.

"That cuts into profits. And gives people access to what we're doing."

"We can demand discretion."

"That still leaves profits."

Ashlynn pointed at her. "If you double your subscriptions by the New Year, we hire a cameraman."

"I can agree to that."

It was after midnight when Salena pulled into the parking lot. The restaurant was closed, but there were still lights glowing on the main floor.

She walked through the back door, heard voices from the main dining room.

The kitchen staff was in the finishing touches of cleaning up for the night. Salena greeted them in Italian, asked about the shift.

Mari's voice drew her into the dining room.

Salena found her and Luca huddled over some papers at one of the tables. "Oh, good, you're here," Mari exclaimed when she saw Salena walk in.

"Is everything okay?"

Luca shook his head. "Craig quit tonight."

"No!" Craig was one of their full-time night-shift waiters, well known and well loved. "Why?"

"Better job at a bar downtown." Mari scowled.

Salena slid into the booth beside them. "I didn't even know he was looking."

Luca shrugged. "Happens."

"Leaves us really short for the weekends." Mari pushed the schedule toward Salena.

"I'll post an ad in the morning that we're hiring." Salena looked at the staffing, saw the gaps. "What's going on here?" There were extra empty slots, those that didn't have Craig's name and color code on them.

"Niki gave her shifts away to Craig. She has plane tickets." Luca sat back, rested his head against the back of the bench. The man was exhausted. A new baby and late nights did that.

"I'll figure it out," Salena announced.

"You can't be two people on a shift," Mari said.

"That would be one hell of a talent. I'll plead with the staff to step up, try and hire, and if all else fails, ask Chloe to cover a shift or two."

Mari scowled. "I hate to do that. She just stepped away from all this."

"I'll figure it out. It's why you hired me. Don't worry."

For the next two days, Salena held team meetings at the beginning of each shift to speak to everyone on the wait and hostess staff. After getting permission from Mari and Luca to get the funds to implement her plan, she got to work.

"Anyone who volunteers to take an extra shift will be the first one to flex off, if they want it, on any day they work. If more than one of you are stepping up, we will rotate that flex. Anyone who recommends a friend as a waiter, who we hire and retain, will be given a three-hundred-dollar finder fee after the second week in January if they are working out. We all know how hard it is to find good staff." That got a few people mumbling. "On nights that we are unavoidably understaffed and people are complaining, we will be extending our happy-hour rates throughout the night. This won't be advertised but happily enforced."

"That's a great idea."

"Tipsy customers complain less."

"I'm going to do everything I can to make this as painless as possible. If you need something, say something. If you see something that needs to get done, and you have time, do it."

"And where will you be?" The person asking had come on right before Salena was hired. And if Salena could afford to fire her, she would. Not because she wasn't efficient at her job, just that her attitude didn't suit what the D'Angelos had created.

"Right here, Brynn. If we're short-staffed, I will be on the floor. Any questions?"

A muttering of *no*s traveled through them.

"Great. Now who wants to pick up a shift and make more money for the holidays?"

Two of the waiters stepped up to look at the schedule.

After doing everything she could, Salena pushed the schedule to the side and rested her head in her arms. She'd penciled her name in every blank she could, and they were still short every weekend. Holiday parties, family coming in from out of town. This was not the month that staff wanted to pull favors.

As for Sunday dinners, those were out . . . at least for her.

A knock on the office door had her popping her head off her arms. "Wine shipment is here."

Salena pushed away from the desk and got to work.

~

"I can't."

It was the first time Ryan had heard those words from Salena's lips.

"What about next week?" He was trying to plan an overnight trip up to the mountains. Just the two of them, crisp air . . . a change of scenery. A break before escrow closed and Christmas.

"I'm open sometime in January," Salena told him with a laugh. "We're down one and a half employees, and we were already struggling going into December. Not to mention we're moving into flu season. It's gonna suck."

"Well, shit." Ryan scooted the empty box with the toe of his shoe and sat on his sofa.

"It's not like I can call in sick. I live here." She sighed. "If we manage to hire someone, they still need to be trained."

"Has anyone applied?"

"No. There are so many ways for people to make money from their computer. No one wants to do this kind of work anymore. I can't say I blame them."

"At the risk of being completely selfish, when can I see you?"

Salena snorted. "I'll have Sergio hold a corner seat at the bar. You can see me running my ass off every night."

Ryan thought of that ass and grinned.

"There's an inspection on the house on Tuesday morning. Do you think you can—"

"I promised Ashlynn I'd help at the studio."

"Can you get out of it?"

"I need the money. The down payment on the Jeep put me back. I need to—"

"I can help with that."

"What? Pay my bills?"

He knew how he sounded. "If things get tight. Don't struggle."

"If things get tight, I'll work more." She was starting to sound angry.

"I get it." Ryan pushed himself off his sofa and grabbed an empty box. "Tell Sergio to hold me a seat on Tuesday."

~

"Don't worry, I'll take care of it" turned into each day running into the next without a single break. If Salena wasn't at the restaurant, she was at the studio. If she wasn't physically at either place, she was on her computer, editing, uploading . . . engaging with the people putting cash in her pocket. Ashlynn constantly pointed out that the money Salena was making on OnlyMe was three times her hourly rate at her day job. And not nearly as sticky. No one spilling drinks on you . . . no burning your fingers on hot plates or smiling at an asshole customer when all you really wanted to do was shut them up with a fist.

"Up until last year, Giovanni and Chloe split the job I'm doing. And they took a few shifts a week. I can do this." Salena sat with her back against a pole after they'd finished filming.

"I know you can, but do you have to?"

"You're one to talk. How long have you been doing OM again?"

"Over a year."

"I don't see you hiring a bunch of employees to run this place." Salena patted the floor of the studio.

"I've thought about it. I've even considered opening a second place."

"Where?"

"Oceanside. Maybe even La Jolla."

Salena pushed up off the floor. "If you can't find good instructors for this place, you won't find them for two."

"I'll need to figure something out or pay out my ass in taxes next year if OM continues to climb."

"Sounds like a first-world problem to me," Salena said.

"One you're going to have, too."

Salena grabbed her jacket off the floor and shoved her legs into a loose pair of jeans. "If I'm sitting on as many subscribers as you next year, I'll go in with you on a second studio." She looked at the time. "I've gotta go."

She hit the back door running.

The good part about living where you worked was you didn't have to commute very far, the bad news was . . . you never left.

Salena had enough time to shower, toss her hair in a thick ponytail, dust some makeup on her face, and run downstairs for the lunch rush.

She zipped between seating customers, bussing tables, and running food. By two, the lunch crowd fizzled, and the early shift staggered out while the evening shift slowly came on.

It wasn't uncommon to be out a bartender during the quiet time, and Salena would take her paperwork back with the alcohol to kill two birds with one stone.

Salena was filling a drink order when she heard a familiar voice behind her.

"Damn, Sergio. You look a lot better than I remembered."

She shot a smile over her shoulder and wiggled her hips.

Ryan blew out a whistle and took a seat.

She finished the order, put it on the counter for the waitress to pick up, and moved to Ryan's side.

He patted her butt and leaned in for a brief kiss. "Hi," he whispered.

"Ciao."

"Does a kiss come with every order?" a guy on the other end of the bar asked.

Ryan scowled and death-glared at the customer.

"Settle . . ." Salena moved back behind the bar, laughed off the customer's comment. "Only if I call them Daddy."

The guy talking laughed. "You can call me anything you want."

Ryan stood up.

The man quickly backpedaled. "Just playing around. You're a lucky guy."

Salena grabbed a cold glass from the fridge and poured Ryan the beer he liked from the tap. "How did the inspection go?"

He was still snarling at the wiseass. "The house is in good shape."

Salena handed him the beer, moved between him and the other guy. She pointed a thumb behind her. "That happens all the time. I know how to take care of it."

"That ass is for my eyes only."

"Oh, really? When did you turn into a caveman?"

"When someone is flirting with you right in front of me."

She reached across the bar, placed her hand over his. "That wasn't flirting, that was a compliment. And the difference between a two-dollar tip and five. Now . . . tell me about the house."

Ryan's shoulders started to relax. He reached for the beer. "Minor, chickenshit things. Garden hose faucets weren't current code because they didn't save water . . . stuff like that."

"Nothing to break the deal," she concluded.

"Nope. Roof is in good shape, all the appliances work, the heating and air ran great. No leaks in the outside fireplace or the one in the living room."

He was smiling again.

"You're excited."

"I am. I offered to buy the pool table."

"One less thing to shop for."

An order came up on the computer behind the bar. She told Ryan to hold his thoughts.

Day drinkers were easy. Lots of spritzers, wine, and beer. Bloody Marys and mimosas. The easy stuff. She completed the order, checked on those sitting at the bar, which was the guy Ryan glared at and a woman huddled behind a book and a glass of chardonnay.

Fast footsteps announced Hurricane Franny as she burst through the front door with a beeline toward Ryan. Her backpack slid to the floor with a crash. "Hi."

"Francesca!" Brooke called her name as she pushed a stroller inside. Franny made a face but didn't look the least bit sorry.

"Late day at school?" Ryan asked.

"We went to the park after. What are you doing here?"

"Visiting Salena."

She climbed onto a barstool.

Ryan stood and said hello with a hug to Brooke. Leo was kicking his feet and looking around from his chariot. "He gets bigger every week."

Another order came up, and Salena had to walk away to fill it. By the time she was done, Brooke had funneled Franny out of the restaurant.

"Franny is a handful."

Salena placed a hand on her chest. "A girl after my own heart."

A bell from the kitchen rang out several times, prompting Salena to grab a hot order that was waiting too long. "Hold on."

She piled the plates onto a tray and ran it outside to a table on the patio. The waitress that had that station was nowhere to be seen. Back behind the bar, she refilled their drink order and caught Noleen as she was walking by. "This is for patio four. They wanted more bread."

Back in front of Ryan, she took a breath.

"I caught you at a busy time."

"Are you kidding? This is nothing. Give it an hour."

He did. For the next hour, as the restaurant started to slowly fill, her conversation with Ryan happened one sentence at a time.

The bartender came on right as the workday ended and happy hour picked up.

Mari emerged from the kitchen and perched beside Ryan. On occasion, she would go to the front of the restaurant and seat a party or welcome someone she knew . . . but she returned to Ryan's side and kept him company.

All this, Salena watched as she ran. Every once in a while, Ryan's gaze would meet hers, and he'd smile.

"So that's your boyfriend?" Brynn asked at the prep counter as they picked up orders.

"You could say that."

"I thought we weren't supposed to have our boyfriends here distracting us on our shifts."

This girl was nails on the chalkboard. "When you can keep up with me, even with a distraction, we can revisit this conversation."

One of the cooks heard her through the window and chided Brynn in Italian. An insult that the girl did not understand.

Brynn closed her lips and left with her order.

Salena sighed.

~

Mari placed a plate of food in front of Ryan.

"How do you make money if you keep giving food away?" he teased.

"You're family. Paying me is an insult."

Ryan dug his fork into the pasta, took a first bite. "So good," he said.

Mari patted his back. "I'll leave you to it."

Ryan quietly ate in the noisy restaurant.

"Is it always this busy on a Tuesday?" he asked the bartender, who was not Sergio.

"It's the holidays."

Salena would flash by, run her palm along his back, and rush off again.

Luca emerged from the kitchen and shook his hand. "How was it?"

"You guys can't make a bad meal." Ryan pushed his plate aside.

"You haven't had Chloe cook for you."

Salena snuck up behind them. "I'm going to tell her you said that."

"She'll agree with me."

Luca nodded toward the room. "I thought we had staff tonight?"

"Not enough to fill in for breaks."

The familiar bell sounded from the kitchen. Something that apparently only went off when Salena was needed, because she shot away without a nod.

"We're trying to hire. It's hard this time of year," Luca told him.

"That's what Salena said. I was trying to plan a night out of town, but it will have to wait."

Luca looked around. "There's got to be a way to make that happen."

Ryan suddenly felt as if he was overstepping. "It's all good. Escrow should close before Christmas. I plan on kidnapping her as much as she'll allow it."

Luca tilted his head. "You guys are really getting along."

"I think so. We don't have matching tattoos yet, but I'm working on it."

Luca's approval was a nod and a pat on the back. "I'm going to say hello to a few people and get back to work."

"Nice talking with you."

Finally, after four hours of sitting at the bar and getting snippets from her, Salena took a seat beside him and blew out a long breath.

"Do you have time to pee?" he asked.

She laughed. "Not always."

He kissed her briefly. "You work too hard."

"I have to. Nothing is worse than a manager that's sitting around while the staff is running. I hated that when I was on the other end."

The bartender filled a half a glass of red wine and put it in front of her.

"Drinking on the job, huh?"

Someone walked up from behind, put the same plate of food Ryan had eaten in front of her. "Eating dinner without wine is a sacrilege around here. Besides, I never leave."

He watched as she plowed into her plate. "You look tired, babe."

"That's accurate." She washed the food down with wine. "I can't believe you sat here all night."

"If this is how I have to see you, this is what I'm going to do."

One of the waitresses walked by and scowled at them. "Ouch."

Salena glanced out of the corner of her eye and lowered her voice. "If we didn't need every staff member with a pulse, that one would be gone."

For twenty minutes, Ryan watched Salena eat faster than he'd ever seen her consume a meal as they talked about the house and his move.

"The place is going to look empty until we go shopping."

"We?"

"I'm not a designer."

"And I am?"

He nudged her. "You said you liked spending other people's money."

She grinned over her forkful of pasta. "I do."

"Good. That's settled. After-Christmas and year-end sales might be the key."

"Something tells me you're not a bargain shopper."

"Depends on what you call a bargain."

She pushed her plate away with only half of it gone. Same with the wine.

He glanced at his watch. "I guess that's my cue to go."

Salena placed a hand on his thigh. "I'm glad you came by."

"Walk me out?" he asked.

She took his hand.

At the end of the block, he pulled her into his arms and kissed her like he'd wanted to all night.

People flowed around them like water around a rock in a river. Neither of them paid attention.

He pulled away to see the Christmas lights dancing in her eyes. "I'll call you tomorrow."

She wrapped her hands around her bare arms and rubbed them. "Drive careful."

The light turned, and he joined the crowd crossing the street, headed to where he'd parked his car.

When he looked back, Salena was rushing into the restaurant.

CHAPTER TWENTY-SIX

Relief came from the most unexpected source. One week before Christmas, two days before Ryan's move date, Elsa waltzed into the restaurant.

Salena saw her from the bar and smiled at the familiar face in an unfamiliar environment. "What on earth brings you here?"

Elsa plopped down, tossed her designer handbag on the counter, and scowled. "I need a job." She said *job* as if it were a dirty word.

She couldn't help it. Salena started to laugh.

"It's not funny."

"What happened to the sugar daddy?"

"His wife wants to go to *therapy*. As if that's going to work." Morals aside, Salena had to agree with the eye roll. Any man who spent as much money as he had on Elsa just to have a side chick was destined to cheat on whoever his wife might be. "Ashlynn said you were desperate."

Salena wasn't sure if she was that desperate. "When did you ever wait tables?"

Elsa was an expert at rolling her eyes. Salena could take lessons. "I hustled tips before men. How do you think I met them?"

"Bars?"

"Working them. Listen, I don't like this any more than you do. But I have rent to pay as of the first, and I really don't want to sell my shit." She picked up the bag that likely cost more than Salena made in a week. Even with OnlyMe.

"I need nights and weekends."

"Can't do Thursdays. Ashlynn hired me for open pole."

Salena glanced around them, made sure no one was listening. "I don't talk about that here."

"What? It's a secret?"

"I'm the manager. I don't want the questions or attention."

Elsa laughed. "Whatever. Am I hired or what?"

Salena could count on two fingers how many jobs she'd gotten with that line.

"Final decision isn't mine. Mrs. D'Angelo is an Italian Catholic woman who would send you to church if she knew how you earned that bag."

"Okay."

"We don't talk about Ashlynn's; we go to the *gym*."

Elsa nodded. "Okay."

"You don't pick up your next sugar daddy in this establishment."

"Okay."

"And you're honest about how long you think you might need this job. If you're not cutting it, or plan B rolls around, you give notice. Ghost me, and I'll have your ass."

"You drive a hard bargain, Salena."

"Wait here."

Salena left the bar, half jogged to the office, and returned with an application.

An hour later, Salena pushed the application in front of Mari and leveled with her. "I already called her references. They said she showed up on time and the customers liked her. Asked for her section."

"She hasn't worked for a year."

"A man told her she didn't have to."

Mari clicked her tongue.

"I know her," Salena admitted.

Mari tossed the application. "Then why are we talking? Hire her."

"I appreciate that. However . . ." Salena cleared her throat. "I don't think she'll be around for long. Maybe a season."

"Kids get jobs for the summer. We're used to that."

Salena hadn't thought of it that way.

"I've never worked with her."

Mari placed her elbows on the desk. "Is she trustworthy?"

"She's never given me a reason to think otherwise. Another friend of ours hired her to work a shift at the gym we both go to."

"Hire her. You train her, and if she doesn't work out . . . you fire her." Mari sighed. "We need the help. And you haven't had a day off in two weeks. You think I don't notice."

"I promised you I'd handle it."

"Handling it is taking a chance on someone else to pick up the slack. You're no use to anyone sick. Call your friend, tell her she has a job. She starts tomorrow. If she balks at that, no go."

"Thanks, Mari."

"For what?"

"Trusting me."

Mari took off in Italian. *Are you serious? Get out of here. Trust you? You're like a daughter.*

Salena lifted both hands in the air and backed out of the office with a huge smile on her face.

～

"Babe, that's awesome."

The video call with Ryan that night was the cherry on the top of her ice cream. "I start training her tomorrow. And Chloe is going to cover so I can help you with the move."

Ryan scoffed at that. "You need a day to sleep."

"Yeah," she said. "With you. In your new house. Don't wear yourself out. I have plans."

He rolled his head back. "Fuck."

"That, too. I've been getting it on the regular, and I miss it."

"It? Or me?"

Him . . . but she wasn't about to admit that. "Yes," she said instead.

He laughed. "I have a bunch of guys helping out. I'll call when we're on our way, and you can meet us at the house."

"I can do that." Which gave her the morning to sleep in. Thankfully, she and Ashlynn had filmed enough when things were calm to keep pumping material out, even though Salena hadn't been in the studio for a couple of weeks. Subscriptions were growing, and tips came in. Salena was exhausted.

"We're doing Christmas at Emma and Gio's, right?"

"Yeah. My parents are going to Arizona to be with my sister and the grandkids. But let's plan to come home. Giovanni's is going to be packed with D'Angelos. Your parents—"

"Say no more. Two glasses of wine, that's it."

She pointed through the screen. "Deal."

"Damn." The word came with a huge smile.

"What?"

He shook his head. "This is going to come out wrong."

"Say it anyway," she encouraged.

"I can't."

"Say it!"

"I'm." He coughed. "I'm really glad you were more than a one-night stand."

If his statement wasn't the absolute truth, she would have been offended. "Be sure and put that on my Christmas card."

Ryan lost his grin. "Shit."

"What?"

"Christmas. I haven't done a damn thing."

A tiny artificial tree sat on a corner table in her apartment, one Mari and Franny had brought to her room because *"It isn't Christmas without a tree."* Other than that . . . nothing. She hadn't so much as bought a single present for anyone. "Who's had time?" she asked.

"It's okay. I do my best shopping under pressure."

"Leave me off your list."

He shook his head. "Are you crazy?"

"I mean it. I don't have time for the mall."

"What kind of boyfriend am I if I don't give my girlfriend a gift for Christmas?"

She ran a hand through her hair. "Fine, *that's* my gift."

"What?"

"You can call me your girlfriend. You do it anyway, so I guess it doesn't really count, but I'll stop giving you shit about it."

"What?" Ryan peered into the camera.

"I don't have time to shop, Ryan. My gift to you is helping you unpack. Your gift to me is being my boyfriend."

"That makes no sense."

"It does in my head."

"No."

She released a frustrated sigh. "Fine. Then refer to me as 'the woman I'm seeing.'"

He laughed.

"You're infuriating," she snarled.

"You're adorable."

"Fuck you."

"Okay."

She bit her lip, tried not to smile.

"Anything else you want to add?" he asked.

"Yes."

"What?"

"Nothing."

"You sure? I think there's something you want to say."

An idea emerged. "What's your favorite color?"

"Blue."

"Fine."

"Why do you want to know?"

"No reason."

"You're a terrible liar."

She winced. "That's just mean. Take that back."

Ryan bit his lip. "I'll see you in two days."

"Don't wear yourself out, Rutledge."

~

Salena leaned against the back of her Jeep in Ryan's new driveway when he pulled up in his 4Runner, followed by an open-bed truck. Someone navigated a box U-Haul, and Gio and Dante pulled up in the SUV that Luca normally drove.

Ryan jumped out of his car, a twenty-four-carat smile on his face. "Hey, Trouble. I hope you weren't waiting long."

"I just got here."

He slid a hand around her waist and kissed her hello.

"Someone's excited." She traced a dimple on his cheek with an index finger.

"Beyond."

"Hey, Salena?" Dante called to her as he jumped out of the car.

"Yeah?"

"Let's move your car so I can back in and unload."

She pulled her keys from her pocket and tossed them to Dante. "Do what you gotta do."

Mateo joined them from the U-Haul, gave her a hug hello. And Ryan introduced her to his neighbor from Temecula, Yuri. He kissed the back of her hand. "Damn . . . you are beautiful."

She was all smiles.

"Hey!" Ryan teased.

"Why are you with this loser?" Yuri said.

She gave him a once-over, cocked her head to the side. "You guys all go to the bathroom together. You know what I get to play with."

Mateo blew out a whistle.

Ryan slung his arm over her shoulders. "You tell 'em, Trouble."

Gio joined them, looked up at the house. "Let's get a tour before we get started."

Ryan led the way and unlocked the front door.

The house looked huge without furniture or things on the walls.

As Ryan gave the tour, Salena stayed behind, putting her focus on the status of the kitchen. Not because she felt particularly at home in that room of a house, but she knew from working in restaurants her entire adult life that keeping that space clean was imperative. She opened cabinets and cupboards and checked the appliances to see how the previous owners left the space.

Except for under the sink, the kitchen was spotless, as if they'd hired a professional to do that job.

She darted out to her car to bring in the bare necessities of cleaning supplies. She had garbage bags, paper towels, and toilet paper. Cleaning rags, grease killers, and disinfectant sprays. Glass cleaners and abrasive sponges . . . Basically, she raided the supply closet at D'Angelo's.

The guys walking down the stairs sounded like a herd of elephants. She had the strange desire to tell everyone to take off their shoes. But that wouldn't be practical, considering it was moving day. The floors would just have to be cleaned after.

"If you are all done freeloading, let's get to work," she teased.

"What are we doing for food?" Dante asked. "We've already been at this for hours."

"Mari is sending a runner with pizza at noon," Salena informed them.

"Sweet."

Mateo clapped his hands. "Okay, let's get cracking."

The doors to the house were all opened, as was the garage . . . and everyone scrambled.

Boxes were hauled in, each labeled for the room in the house where it was destined, making it easier to unpack.

A cooler was placed in the center of the kitchen, which Salena opened. It was filled with what had to be the contents of Ryan's refrigerator from home.

Condiments and beer.

That was it.

Mustard, ketchup, with all their cousins . . . and beer.

Next were grocery bags that rounded out his pantry. The usual suspects, open peanut butter, some canned goods. It was when her hand hit the plastic bag with ramen noodles that Salena paused. She held up the desperate college food as Gio and Ryan were walking by, boxes in hand. "What the hell do you want me to do with these?"

Gio made a noise that didn't sound human.

"What?" Ryan asked.

"Don't let my mama see that."

"Hey. Sometimes—"

"No, dude. No time. Mama sees that in your kitchen, she'll have an apron on your ass and you'll be elbow-deep in flour and eggs before you can blink."

Salena held the ramen noodles over a garbage can and exchanged a look with Ryan.

A knock on the front door, followed by Mari's voice singing from the porch, made Salena drop the ramen faster than a snake strikes its prey. "Ciao!"

She shooed them off to greet Mrs. D'Angelo and quickly rid the kitchen of any pretend pasta Ryan might own.

"Hey, Mama . . ."

~

A man had his priorities.

Ryan's massive television was mounted on the wall. His bar was aptly appointed and ready for use. And his bed was put together for the night.

The rest could wait.

Mrs. D'Angelo brought enough pizza from the restaurant to feed the block . . . or Dante, who Ryan thought was a human garbage disposal. And more beer.

Even with every item Ryan owned inside the house, the place looked empty.

The guys had all gone home, leaving Salena and Ryan alone for the first time in what felt like months. It had only been a couple of weeks, but damn, he was getting used to her being around.

He grabbed a couple of beers and walked out onto the patio, where she stood looking over the railing as the city lights started to flicker to life once the sun had set.

"Here."

She smiled at him, took the beverage. "This view will not get old."

He patted her ass with his free hand. "Sure won't."

"Not that view."

"Oh, right. The city."

She chuckled, blew out a breath.

"It's been a long day," he said, took a drink.

"It's been a long month." She turned to look back into the house. The front room was completely empty. "You have some serious shopping to do."

His table for four looked dwarfed in the dining area adjacent to the kitchen. The TV room, which held his furniture and the pool table, looked relatively complete. "I don't know where to start."

"Patio furniture," Salena announced. "You'll spend a lot of time out here and upstairs."

"Noted."

She nodded several times and looked up at the house. "It's great, though."

"I like it."

"I hope so. You spent a fortune."

She'd shopped with him, so it wasn't like he could keep the price from her. Not that he felt the need. "And will continue to for the next thirty years."

"Does it scare you? That commitment? I had a hard enough time with the Jeep."

He shrugged. "If this was the first time I'd ever bought something, then maybe. It's property. If you buy right, it appreciates. Things get tough, I can sell."

"Ouch. You haven't even spent your first night here, and you're talking like that."

"Keeping it real. Houses only become homes by who you spend time in them with. I've lived in two spectacular places growing up yet felt more grounded in my two-bedroom apartment."

"Will you miss Temecula?"

He slid his arm around her waist, pulled her against him. "Maybe. But I have something here that's much more appealing than vines and heat."

"Hmm, oh yeah. I almost forgot your housewarming gift."

"I thought you said you didn't have time to shop."

Salena twisted out of his arms and started walking into the house.

She turned toward him and undid the first button on her shirt. "I didn't go shopping."

Ryan's mouth went dry as the second button let loose to the top of a black bra. "Giving the neighbors a show already?"

"I can't help it if people are watching through these massive windows." Salena backed into the empty living room, and Ryan followed her inside.

CHAPTER TWENTY-SEVEN

Christmas rolled in on them like a storm blowing in from the sea.

One minute Salena was driving her parents to the airport, promising that the next year she'd figure out a way to be with them, and the next, she and Ryan were driving to Temecula with gifts piled in the back seat.

"I thought you didn't have time to shop," Ryan had said when she started transferring packages from her car to his.

"It's amazing what you can find at midnight with online shopping," she'd explained.

The closer they came to Gio and Emma's house, the more Salena found herself fidgeting.

She wore a long sweater that covered her ass with black leggings and boots. An outfit she'd bought thinking it was festive and slightly conservative at the same time. Officially meeting Ryan's parents as his girlfriend put her on edge.

This was new territory.

As much as she didn't want their opinion of her to matter . . . it did.

"Why are you pulling at your sweater?" Ryan asked when they turned off the freeway and started snaking their way through the Temecula hills and vineyards.

She stilled her hands and rested them in her lap. "I'm not."

Ryan patted her thigh. "My dad's an asshole, my mom's cool . . . stuffy at times, but cool."

Salena balled her hands into fists. "I'm fine."

They pulled through the gates and up the tree-lined drive to the house. Garlands with lights wrapped around each pillar of the patio, with a pine wreath on the front door. Festive and elegant and everything Salena thought it would be.

With gifts in hand, they walked up the steps as someone opened the door before they could knock.

"There you are. We were starting to think you got lost." Chloe stood with a glass of wine in her hand.

"Salena changed outfits . . . twice."

"I did not." Once. She switched out the sweater once.

Chloe looked her up and down. "Super cute. Is that new?"

"Yeah."

Inside, the house had transformed into a wonderland of holiday cheer. A Christmas tree sat center stage in front of the largest window in the living room. A flickering of flame came from the fireplace, even though it wasn't cold enough outside to warrant a fire. Candles and garlands, lights and presents . . . it was beautiful.

Franny ran over from where she'd been sitting on the floor by the tree. "Are those for me?" she asked, looking at the gifts.

"Maybe one," Salena told her.

"Hey, guys." Gio set his glass down and joined them at the door. "Let me help with that."

He took Salena's armful from her, kissed her cheek. "Merry Christmas."

"Merry Christmas. This place is gorgeous."

"It's all Emma. I just nod."

"Merry Christmas!" The chorus erupted from everywhere.

The great room and open kitchen were packed with people. Plates of food spilled out everywhere, and the scent of dinner cooking lingered in the air.

Their gifts were placed under the tree, and Ryan and Gio took another trip to the car to retrieve the rest.

Salena spotted Ryan's mother, Beth, first. Probably because the woman was attempting not to stare.

Chloe closed in and handed Salena a glass of wine. "I know what you're thinking, but they're going to love you."

She sipped the liquid courage and whispered, "This is exactly why I don't date. It's nerve-racking."

"You're a grown woman."

"Who hasn't *met the parents* since high school," Salena reminded Chloe.

Chloe looped her arm through hers and walked her toward Ryan's mom. "Let's get this over with."

"Where is the dad?"

"I don't know. He was here a minute ago."

They stopped in front of Beth, and Chloe put on a hostess hat. "Beth, I'm sure you remember Salena."

"Merry Christmas," Salena said with a painted-on smile.

"Yes. And we've been hearing so much more about you."

Salena's eyes widened. "Don't hold it against me."

Beth laughed and took a long look. "Where did my son run off to?"

"There are more gifts in the car."

Emma walked up behind her mother. "Did I hear you say my brother has gifts? He's notoriously bad when it comes to shopping."

"That hasn't changed," Salena said. "Whatever he bought, he did it in the last four days."

"He just bought a house. He doesn't need to be buying anyone anything," Beth said.

"I heard it's fabulous," Chloe said.

"It is," Salena confirmed.

"And you helped pick it out?" Beth asked.

"I wouldn't say that."

"Ryan did," Emma said.

"I was with him. I didn't make the choice." The way Emma and Beth were watching her had Salena covering her unease with a healthy swig from her wine.

"I'm sure it was mutual."

Salena shook her head, but before she could deny that Ryan's home purchase was in any way her doing, Robert stepped out from the hall and walked straight toward them.

"Everything looks amazing, Emma. Gio says it's all you." Salena changed the subject.

"He's lying. We moved that tree three times before settling for in front of the window."

Salena glanced over her shoulder, wondering what the hell was taking Ryan so long.

"Robert. You remember Salena." Beth did the introduction this time.

"Hello, Mr. Rutledge." God, that sounded pathetic. Like not-even-her-voice pathetic.

"You're the girlfriend."

Emma nudged her father.

"I keep telling Ryan to call me his Italian fling, but he refuses."

Chloe and Emma burst out laughing, and Beth smiled.

Now Salena was feeling a bit more like herself. "I'm going to go find out what swallowed him."

With wineglass in hand, she fled the Rutledge scrutiny and knew her two-glass maximum was never going to fly.

~

"You bought running boards for her Jeep?" Gio asked.

"That's really romantic, bro," Emma chided.

Salena held up the picture Ryan had taken of the gift that sat in his garage. "I love it."

"What is that?" Beth asked.

267

"They're a long step that mounts onto the car so it's easier to climb into."

"You bought her a car part?" His mother wasn't impressed.

"It's practical, Beth," his father said.

His mother rolled her eyes. "You two are more alike than I thought."

Ryan wasn't happy to hear that.

"Considering I told him not to buy me anything . . . this is perfect." Salena shot him a smile.

It was his turn to open his gift from Salena.

She watched him with a snarky smile on her face, one that made him look under the wrapping paper before ripping it off. Inside the box were two items, both in tissue paper. The first was a blue scarf. Which he had to admit was about as practical as his gift had been . . . only they lived in San Diego, and scarf-wearing wasn't really a thing. "It's soft."

"Do you like it?"

That sly smile put him on edge.

"It's great. Thank you."

Chloe reached out, touched it. "Is that cashmere?"

Salena shrugged.

Ryan dug into the second layer of tissue paper and pulled out something much more his speed. Black leather, zipper up the front, with pockets and silver accents. He recognized what it was for immediately. Something to protect him when he was on his motorcycle. "Wow." He pushed the box off his lap and stood to put it on.

"I tried to find it in blue, since that's your favorite color."

"Ewhh," Dante said.

Now the scarf made sense.

And it fit like a glove. "It's perfect."

"Looks great," Emma said.

"And you bought her car parts." His mother wasn't letting that go.

Ryan tossed the scarf over the jacket, leaned over, and said thanks with a kiss.

He kept his jacket on and watched as everyone else opened their gifts. Once the room looked like a bomb hit it and they were cleaning up the mess, Chloe cornered him. "That's a really nice jacket."

"She has great taste."

"Mind if I look at it? I might want to get one for Dante for Valentine's Day."

Ryan shrugged out of it and handed it over.

The first thing Chloe did was look at the label. "It's heavy."

"They need to be able to protect you from the asphalt."

"I bet it was expensive."

They usually were. "I'm sure Salena can tell you where she found it."

"Yeah. Huh . . . Thanks." She handed it back.

Ryan packed it up with the rest of the gifts they were taking back with them and put them by the door.

Two hours later, they were kicking off their shoes in his bedroom, and Salena was pulling the scarf she'd bought him off her neck and tossing it on the bed.

"Thanks for driving."

"You never have to thank me for driving, babe."

"It's a long way."

"And worth it." Neither of them had any desire to wake up to a house full of people. "I almost forgot. I have a little something else I wanted to give you."

"Really? I have something else I wanted to give you, too."

He smiled. "Does it involve you naked?"

"Not completely."

That smile turned into a frown.

"Sit there. I'll go get it."

While she left the room, he reached into the nightstand and tucked her gift under the pillow.

"Close your eyes," she called from outside the bedroom door.

Ryan did as he was told, imagined her almost naked behind his closed lids.

"Okay, open them."

His gaze slid from her smiling face to what she held in her hands.

A dark side-view silhouette of her arched and leaning against a pole, wearing next to nothing and high heels . . . a scarf dangling from her fingertips. The entire image was in black and white, clouded with smoke . . . except for the cobalt blue scarf she'd given him earlier.

He shuffled to the end of the bed and took a closer look. He knew it was her, because he knew her, but if someone saw it on the wall, they'd have to ask who the model was.

"Fuck."

"A bachelor pad like this needs good art for the walls."

He looked up at her, then back at the image. There was no way he was going to let his friends see this.

"I'm speechless."

"You like it?"

He took the picture from her and held it out. "It's incredible. You're incredible."

Ryan moved to his dresser, pushed a bunch of stuff cluttering the top to the floor, and leaned the frame against the wall.

He stood back and stared.

When his brain cells started firing again, he was at her side in two strides, her face in his hands, his lips on hers. "Thank you," he whispered between them.

After another long-lingering kiss, he sat her on the edge of the bed and told her to close her eyes.

He retrieved her gift from under the pillow. "Put out your hands." She did.

"Don't open your eyes until I say."

He carefully placed the ruby and diamond tennis bracelet around her right wrist and hooked the clasp. The contrast against her olive skin was stunning and everything he imagined. "Okay. You can open your eyes."

She looked at him before looking down.

Salena covered her mouth with her left hand with a gasp. "Ryan."

"You didn't really think I only bought you car parts."

She started shaking her head. "This is . . . this is too much."

Probably, but he didn't care. He saw it and immediately thought of her. "It looks good on you."

"I can't accept—"

"Yeah, babe. You can."

Her eyes never left her wrist. "I thought you were putting handcuffs on me."

The picture of her in the back of the cop car flashed in his memory. "Because you miss them?"

She finally looked up. "I don't know how to accept this."

For a moment, he thought she was going to tell him she couldn't. He knelt in front of her, gathered her hands in his. "You say thank you, and you kiss me."

Moisture gathered in her eyes before she blew out a breath. "Thank you," she whispered.

His lips hovered over hers, their eyes locked. "You're welcome."

CHAPTER TWENTY-EIGHT

Salena parked around the block from Ashlynn's studio on open pole night for the sole purpose of practicing. Something she hadn't had time to do in weeks. Stepping down from the Jeep and locking the doors put a smile on her face. The financial picture the New Year brought in was night and day compared with what it had been the previous year.

OnlyMe was giving her a future. On some level, she understood that things on that site could die tomorrow. But the money she was making today did something that waiting tables had never done. It gave her insight into what it was like to be an entrepreneur. She was creating something from nothing and turning a profit. It might take a year to earn enough money to truly consider a partnership or her own studio, but the possibility would never have happened if she hadn't taken Ashlynn up on the chance.

It was liberating . . . powerful. It made Salena crave more.

She pushed into the studio and swiped her key fob to check in, then followed the noise into the back.

Two weeks into the year, and the place was busier than it had been before Thanksgiving.

"I'm guessing the Groupon Ashlynn ran worked out," Elsa whispered to Salena from the front of the room.

"A lot of new faces."

"All gyms are filled in January. Let's see if they're around next month."

Salena swathed her palms with dry grip to keep from sliding on the pole before she got started. "Remember when you first started?" she asked Elsa.

"Been a while, but yeah."

"The thing that kept me coming back was how damn good Ashlynn was. How effortless she made it look."

Most of the newbies in the room were practicing beginner moves and having fun cheering each other on.

"I saw her really shine on open pole nights. Where she helped the intermediate and advanced dancers."

"That's us now."

Salena gripped the pole. "Yup. And we want Ashlynn to retain these women." She circled the pole twice, reverse-gripped her free hand, and inverted using just about every muscle in her body. The strength in her upper body kept control as she managed a midair split before wrapping her legs around the pole and turning. Slowly, she worked her way higher, giving herself room to gracefully spin down.

By the time she planted her feet on the ground, many sets of eyes were focused on her.

Without stopping, she did the opening move again, dismounted, and repeated it . . . over and over until she was happy with how steady she kept her legs in the air.

While she worked, Elsa walked around the room, helping the others.

An hour later, Ashlynn walked into the studio as the place was clearing out. "How did it go?"

Elsa slid her arms into her jacket, nodded toward Salena. "Show-off here helped two of your trial ladies sign up for the next three months."

"It was a group effort," Salena said.

"You guys are awesome."

"Same time next week?" Elsa asked.

"If you're up for it."

She rolled her eyes. "No papa paying the bills, so I'll be here."

Ashlynn and Salena smiled at each other as Elsa made her way out the door.

"How is she working out waiting tables?" Ashlynn asked once Elsa was gone.

"Better than I expected. She does flirt . . . a lot."

"Looking for the next guy?"

"Oh, I'm sure. At the end of the day, it's better tips."

"That's fair."

Salena glanced at her wrist and the gift Ryan had given her. "It's nice to break away from that routine."

"What do you mean?" They walked from the front desk to the office, where Ashlynn took a seat and shuffled through a few papers.

"The hustle for tips."

Ashlynn paused, looked at her. "If a man is buying you jewelry like that, I'd say your waiting-tables days are coming to a close."

"Working in restaurants is limited because of what we're doing on OnlyMe . . . not because of this." Salena held her wrist in the air and gave it a shake. "Do you have any idea how many people have suggested that my life is gravy now that I'm with Ryan?"

The Elsas of her world. Neighborhood friends . . . people like Tim.

"There are no guarantees." Ashlynn had been married once, for about five minutes, right out of high school. Her husband had come from a family with money, and to him, the whole wedding thing was just something to do. Monogamy was a surprise stipulation for him, and the divorce was filed before the ink was dry on the marriage certificate.

"I know."

"Listen, I never want to be Debbie Downer, especially when I see someone light up your face the way Ryan does for you."

"I hear a *but* coming."

Ashlynn smiled. "But . . . you two can get married, have the kids . . . do all the things, and then he gets hit by a bus. Now what do you have?"

The thought literally made Salena's throat swell. And not because of the "what she would do," but the thought of Ryan being gone.

"Or that bus isn't literal but someone new, and he wants out."

"We're not teenagers. And no one is talking about marriage."

"Didn't you tell me he told you to pick what sink you wanted in the bathroom?"

Salena smiled into the memory. The first night at the house, he stood in the bathroom and pointed. *"Which one do you want?"*

"I don't live here."

"I don't need two sinks."

His logic was so matter-of-fact, Salena dropped her brush on one side of the counter, and that became her sink.

"He did."

"And what about a place for clothes? A drawer?"

"Yes."

"Does it not occur to you that this relationship might be headed in the direction of promises and commitment?"

"I'm already committed." Salena ran a hand over her face. "I haven't even looked at someone else since we met." A completely foreign state for her.

"That's what happens. You're going along, and suddenly this person shows up and changes things." Ashlynn sighed. "I know. I'm one hundred percent jaded after my brief marriage; I know that. That's not my point. Every powerful woman you've ever heard of or met has one thing in common. They've retained their power. They've kept their jobs, their ability to provide for themselves and the families they create even if they are married. A lot of what I see here are women who don't keep that power. Elsa is a great example. She doesn't even want her own way in life. Happy to jump from one man paying the bills to the next. Eventually, that doesn't work."

"It's not in me to be financially dependent on someone else." Salena wanted to be more like Mari, a woman who partnered with her husband so that when his unexpected death happened, she didn't financially crumble. "I understand where you're going with this. I will always have my own income, regardless of what happens between Ryan and I."

"Good," Ashlynn said. "What does he think about OnlyMe?"

Salena looked up with a shake of the head. "He doesn't know."

"What?" Surprise laced the question.

"You know the photograph I gave him for Christmas?"

"Yeah."

They'd both worked on creating the perfect seductive shot exclusively for Ryan.

"I can't convince him to hang it. It's leaned up against a wall, and when people come over, he hides it in the closet. Says he doesn't want his buddies gawking at me."

"Ouch."

"I was hoping the picture would bring out the conversation organically."

"Is he the jealous type?"

Salena found herself more and more uncomfortable with this conversation. "Aren't all boyfriends, to a degree?"

"What degree, though?"

"I don't know. I've seen him a little up in his shit if someone comes on to me in front of him, but he isn't busting beer bottles over heads." She sighed.

"Not violent."

"God, no. That wouldn't fly for five minutes."

Ashlynn paused, took a breath. "Do you think he'd ask you to quit?"

The thought had crossed her mind. "He could ask, but that doesn't mean I would. Especially now that I'm making decent money."

"All money is decent."

"You know what I mean."

Ashlynn logged off the computer and flipped off the light. "Before that drawer and sink become half the closet and the same street address, you might want to bring up the conversation on how you really afforded that Jeep."

They walked out of the office and through the lobby, turning off lights as they went. "I will."

~

Salena had put off lunch with her parents since they returned from Arizona.

Twice her mother had walked into the restaurant and cornered her about picking a day to set aside for her family.

The day arrived on a Friday, only because Mari had overheard the conversation and had insisted that the staffing was under control enough for Salena to go.

So here she was, mixing a salad while her mother ladled homemade soup into bowls and her father sat at the table, waiting to be served.

Salena found herself comparing and contrasting Ryan and her dad. There was no way Ryan would sit around when others were working. They'd only had the opportunity to cook together a handful of times, but none of those involved anyone doing it alone.

Yes, she could cook her share of Italian meals. It would have been impossible to grow up without some of that rubbing off. Even though she skipped out on those lessons as often as possible, many things sunk in by pure osmosis. Almost like high school algebra. When it came to mixing drinks, she took the lead . . . when it came to grilling a steak, Ryan took over. As far as gender roles went, that was the extent.

Salena wasn't sure her father knew one thing about the kitchen. If it wasn't for her mother, her father would starve.

"I'm surprised Mari could spare you on the weekend," Aldo said from his perch.

"Considering how short-staffed we've been, I am, too," Salena told him.

"You manage to spend time with your friend." Her father was looking for a fight. Salena had sensed it the moment she walked in.

"You mean Ryan?"

"Is that his name? We wouldn't know. It's not like you've introduced him to us."

She knew that was coming.

"Aldo. Please."

Salena walked the salad to the table. "Maybe if I knew you weren't going to interrogate him, I'd bring him around." Back to the kitchen for the bread.

"I don't do that."

"True. I haven't given you the opportunity in years."

"We're curious, *tesora*. Any man who buys you such nice things must have good intentions. Right, Aldo?"

"Or he thinks he can buy you."

Salena set the bread on the table and stood tall. "No one is buying me, Papa. It was a Christmas gift. I bought him something nice, he bought me something nice." Nicer, but who was counting?

Her mother set the soup in front of her father, went back for more. "And the car?"

"*I* bought the car."

"You say, but how?" Aldo asked.

Salena took her seat. "I work. Remember that thing you did before you retired? You get a paycheck, and you buy things."

"If you marry this man, you won't have to work so hard." Her mother set a bowl in front of Salena.

And there it was . . .

The reason she hadn't blended Ryan with her parents. Salena was used to their set dialogue. Had a comeback for nearly everything that came out of their mouths. "Working gives me purpose, Mama. If I won the lottery tomorrow, I'd still find something to work toward." Ashlynn's voice mixed with Salena's in her head.

Her father picked up his spoon. "It wouldn't be waiting tables."

"Probably not. Unless I owned the restaurant."

Her mother sat. "You want to own a restaurant?"

"No. That isn't my passion." Salena looked at the meal. "This looks wonderful, Mama. Thank you."

Brigida patted Salena's hand with a smile.

Her father started eating without so much as a glance at his wife.

Absolutely nothing had changed since Salena had moved out.

"You can't keep him from us forever," Aldo said.

Salena wanted to argue with him. Tell him she had no intention of forever with Ryan. But the comeback would have been a lie that even she wasn't prepared to say. Instead, she changed the subject.

"Tell me about the houses you looked at in Arizona."

An hour and a half later, Salena walked into the restaurant, mentally exhausted from the time she'd spent playing verbal volleyball with her parents.

The noise inside stole her thoughts and had her turning a full circle.

The place was packed.

No one stood at the hostess counter, and Sergio was running behind the bar.

"Did someone let a bus out?" she asked him when she was close enough for him to hear.

"Pretty much."

It was closing on two in the afternoon, when things normally slowed down.

That was not the case.

Salena walked back toward the kitchen, poked her head in, and saw Mari barking orders. "I'm back."

"*Allora*, Brynn has sent two plates back, customer complaint. Check on that."

Salena turned around, went back through the restaurant. First, she noticed Elsa standing at a table with three guys, laughing, an empty plate in her hand.

Looking farther, she saw Brynn rushing back from the outside patio with empty wineglasses.

Salena approached her. "Which table had the problem with the food?"

"Where've you been?"

The question surprised her. "Off. What table? What happened?"

"Patio three, and it was cold. Sat in the window too long. I thought you said if we were understaffed, you'd be around."

The bell from the kitchen rang.

Brynn turned and rushed away.

Salena headed toward the patio, noticed Elsa still chatting. Out on the patio, she found a party of five. Two sat without a meal in front of them, the other three were picking at their food. "Hello. I understand there was a problem with your order."

"Ours was cold," one of the men said as he pointed between him and the other person without food.

"I'm sorry to hear that. Mrs. D'Angelo is working on it now. Is there something I can do? How about some more wine? On us since you've been so patient on this busy day."

The customers looked at each other and shrugged. "That would be great."

Salena asked what they were drinking and headed back toward the bar.

Brynn hustled by, presumably with the two plates that were in question.

After pouring the refills herself, Salena took them to the table. Brynn was already at another, taking plates away.

"Better?" Salena asked since their food had arrived.

There was steam coming off the pasta.

"Much."

She set the wine down. "Can I get you anything else?"

The woman sitting at the end of the table motioned for Salena to lean in. "I know our waitress is busy, but she was kind of rude."

Not what Salena wanted to hear. "I'm sorry. Was it something she said?"

"Annoyed that we complained. We weren't being a *Karen* about it," said the woman with the new plate of food.

"Food should be hot," someone else at the table said.

"Absolutely. I'm sorry that's been your experience. We're unexpectedly busy, but that's not an excuse."

"It's okay. Maybe she's having a bad day."

Salena smiled. "We all have those. And thank you for being so understanding. I'll have a chat with her."

Before Salena left the patio, she walked around Brynn's station to see if anyone needed anything. She helped take away plates and took a refill request.

Back inside the restaurant, Brynn was at the workstation putting in an order.

Salena pulled one of their beers on tap and handed it to the hostess to take outside.

Elsa was back at the table of men.

Was that a hair flip?

With a forced smile, Salena walked up behind Elsa to dislodge her from her spot. "I think you have an order in the window."

"What? Oh, okay."

She scurried off, and Salena asked the guys at the table how the meal was.

"Wasn't mine," Elsa said a couple of minutes later at the workstation.

"Do you know those guys?"

"Table fifteen?"

"Yeah."

Elsa leaned in. "No. But the guy on the right owns a shipping company, and he paid with a platinum card. He wanted my number."

"We're crazy busy, and you're picking up men."

"My tables are good."

Two of which were empty.

"You've worked the patio. It's a nice day, Brynn is swamped out there."

"She didn't ask for help."

Salena just stared, let her look of disappointment do the talking.

"Fine." With a roll of her eyes, Elsa walked away.

For the next hour, Salena helped where she could.

Once the day leaned into normal and the customers cleared out right at the time the staff flexed off before night shift started, Salena sought Brynn out.

"Hey."

Brynn looked at her as if she knew what was coming but didn't say a word.

"You want to tell me what happened with that table?"

She didn't have to be told which customers Salena was talking about. "I don't know. The food was cold."

"I'm not talking about cold food. That happens." Plates came up staggered, and sometimes they sat in the window too long while waiting for other dishes at the table to be completed. Most of the time, it came together like peanut butter and jelly. Sometimes it didn't.

"I was busy."

"They said you were rude."

Brynn looked at her, blinked twice. "I was busy."

Salena had been there. As much as she didn't like Brynn, she wasn't going to drill her about one complaint. "Next time, when you're that crazed, ask for help."

"You weren't here."

"I'm not the only one who can step up. The staff inside wasn't nearly as swamped. And if that doesn't work, offer a glass of wine. We've already said you can."

"Customers only tip on the total of the bill."

"When they're unhappy, they don't tip at all."

Brynn let out a sigh. "It was a bad day."

"Okay."

Salena left Brynn in the break room and moved into the office.

The clock said she wasn't supposed to really begin her shift for another thirty minutes, yet she'd been running since her annoying lunch with her parents.

She was tired already, and the night hadn't even begun.

Mari walked by the open door. "I'm going to rest before the dinner rush."

"Luca isn't here?" It wasn't often that Mari worked the kitchen two meals in a row.

"No. He needs to spend time with his family."

"Go. I've got it covered."

Mari smiled, walked away . . . and Salena rested her head on her arms.

She'd hardly closed her eyes when a knock sounded on the door.

"Yeah?"

Elsa stood there. "Did I wake you?"

"No." But damn, she was tired.

"Good." Elsa walked in and closed the door halfway.

"What are you and Ashlynn doing?"

"Excuse me?" Hearing Ashlynn's name in the office of D'Angelo's felt out of place.

"I might have overheard you two talking."

Salena's mind scrambled to recall the conversation.

Then it hit her.

"What did you hear?"

A sly smile hit Elsa's face. "OnlyMe," she whispered.

Salena sat back, motioned toward the door for Elsa to close it.

"What the hell?"

Elsa forged innocence. "Much as I just love tossing pasta around, it sounds like you have a better way of making money."

"It's not what you think."

"I'm sure it's exactly what I think. Believe me, I've thought about it. But you two are doing it, and I want in."

Salena sighed. "Elsa."

"You and I both know this isn't my dream job."

And this was not the place to be having this conversation. "I can't talk about this here."

Elsa looked pleased with that. "Thursday, then. At the . . . *gym*?"

"Yes, Thursday."

Elsa smiled, opened the door.

"And stop looking for your next conquest while you're on the clock."

"What, this isn't where you found Ryan?"

Elsa knew damn well Ryan was nothing like her sugar daddies. "Get out of here before I'm forced to fire you."

"See you tomorrow, *Saint* Salena."

Salena lifted her middle finger.

Elsa laughed.

Salena rested her head in her hands and silently screamed.

CHAPTER TWENTY-NINE

"How did this happen?" Salena stood in front of *her* sink in *Ryan's* bathroom, holding a toothbrush.

"What?" Ryan spoke around a mouthful of toothpaste.

"This. How did I end up with a sink at your house?"

He laughed before spitting out the foam in his mouth and rinsing with water. "I told you to pick one."

She opened the drawer closest to her assigned space. "All this stuff is mine."

He glanced at the contents. "Yeah, that's not my shade of pink."

Salena swatted at him. "Mari asked me today if I was moving out."

Ryan leaned against the vanity and crossed his arms over his chest. "Huh."

"Wait. No, that sounded like I'm asking to move in. I'm not. But this is crazy, right?" Salena pointed at the drawer again. "I didn't even pack a bag tonight when I came over. Is that weird for you?"

"Is it weird for you?"

"No." She tossed the toothbrush into the drawer and closed it. "And I don't know why."

Ryan reached over and pulled her to stand in front of him, her hips resting against his. "I know why."

"Well, can you tell me, please. Being in a man's space for more than a night has never appealed to me. Knowing that he folds his T-shirts but hangs his jeans . . . and makes his bed every morning are things I've never wanted to know."

"You roll your panties and stack your bras."

"That's deep stuff." And the truth was, she looked forward to learning all the things that made Ryan do what he did.

Ryan shook his head. "No, babe. That is a layer of icing. The cake is in the why."

She placed her hands on his shoulders. "Why?"

"Because you're falling for me."

She couldn't help it, she laughed. The expression of innocence on his face, along with how casually he'd told her how she felt, was pure comedy. "Oh, am I?"

"You are. I'd say my master plan is working." His fingers rounded over her hips as he spoke.

"Master plan?"

"Yeah."

"What else is in this plot of yours?"

He squeezed her hips. "Ah, now. I can't tell you that. It would ruin it."

"You can't make someone fall for you."

"I'm charming."

"Sometimes."

"Devilishly handsome."

She bit her lip to keep her laughter back. "Humble."

Ryan shook his head. "No. But we both have that in common."

"True." Humility didn't come easy to either of them.

"I'm employed."

"Technically, you employ yourself."

"But still make money."

She rolled her eyes.

He leaned in and whispered next to her ear. "I know how to do this." The nibble on the lobe of her ear shot straight to her core.

"I do like that."

"I rub your back after a hard day."

"For about five minutes before you start the ear-kissing thing." As she spoke, she leaned her head to the side, offering him her neck.

"And you hate that."

He ran his tongue along her neck before kissing it softly.

"*Hate* is a strong word."

"I make you think about me several times a day."

Text messages, voice mail. "A little stalkerish if you ask me." Salena was smiling.

Ryan leaned back, wrapped his arms around her waist, and pulled her even closer. "I'm giving you all the time in the world to fall. And I'm catching you with sinks in bathrooms and drawers filled with girlie stuff and space in the closet."

"Garage space," she said. Her Jeep was parked next to his 4Runner and bike.

"Exactly. Mari's question deserves some consideration."

Salena stopped thinking about the garage space as her gaze shot to Ryan's. "What do you mean?"

"Moving in."

Was he serious?

She felt her body lean away. "Ryan, it's—"

"Too soon. I know. But we should consider it, don't you think? You're here all the time. You said yourself that you never feel like you can get away from the restaurant since you live above it. Which makes sense for the people that own it, but not for a workaholic employee."

"I'm not a workaholic."

"When was the last time you had a full day off?"

The answer wasn't instant, which proved his point.

"Maybe the timing of this conversation isn't great, but we're here, and I want you to think about it."

A drawer was one thing . . . felt natural. But not having somewhere else to go if things got sticky? Counting on Ryan for a roof over her head made her swallow hard.

"I know what you're thinking," he told her.

"I don't think you do."

"Maybe not everything, but I'd bet my left nut that you're worried that by moving in with me, you're somehow dependent. Or you lose some of the autonomy you've been working so hard toward if we cohabitate."

She just stared at him.

"And I'd bet that when you had lunch with your parents today, and the subject of us came up . . . they harped on you for us to all get together so they can meet me."

"I told you that was going to happen."

"Yeah, but you haven't talked about it since. And the reason you haven't brought it up tonight is because you know me meeting your folks as your boyfriend is going to happen. And when it does, your dad's going to ask all the questions dads ask when their daughters are in serious relationships."

She looked into his eyes.

"Drawers at the boyfriend's house, relationships."

"My father will put pressure on you."

Ryan half laughed. "Yeah. I know. I mean, he can try. But have you met my dad? The man tried to pull me into the wine business for years. College-prep classes in high school, wanted the *Rutledge and Sons* thing. I learned to deal with dad pressure when I was sixteen."

She grinned. "Me too."

"I'm saying I can handle it, babe. Your dad isn't going to press us to move any faster than we want to." Ryan squeezed her hips again. "And he isn't going to scare me away."

It was those last words that put moisture in her eyes. On some level, she realized that was a fear. Even if unfounded.

Ryan's eyes searched hers, and the smile on his face grew.

He traced a thumb under her eye and then kissed the tear. "And if you move in, I'm putting the electric bill in your name. You like it way too hot in here."

She coughed out a laugh, found more tears following the first.

"There're things about me you don't know."

"I bet. I'm looking forward to learning about all of them."

"Things you might not like." *Like how I sell pictures of myself on the internet.*

"I know what I need to know. You're honest, trustworthy, and loyal."

"But . . ."

He stopped her by placing a finger over her lips. "It's after midnight. We don't have to solve all our puzzles in one night. Let's go to bed. I'll rub your back."

Salena let out a sigh. "For five minutes."

"Three, tops."

The next morning, Salena woke to the sun rising, the hues catching on the window that spanned the entire wall in Ryan's bedroom.

Her head rested on his chest, and she felt the rhythmic movement of his hand as he stroked her hair.

She made a sound that mimicked a purr as she stretched beside him.

Ryan's voice was a hoarse whisper. "Move in with me, Salena. I want this every morning."

It was in that moment she knew Ryan's plan to make her fall for him had totally worked.

"Our families need to meet first. Maybe a Sunday dinner with reinforcements."

His palm cupped the back of her head. "Sounds perfect. I'll have you here before Valentine's Day."

Salena lifted her head to find him staring.

Staring and smiling like a kid on Christmas morning.

~

It was almost an intervention.

Elsa stood with folded arms in the empty studio after open pole.

Salena and Ashlynn explained, as carefully as they could, what they were doing and why they didn't think their pages could be linked to anything Elsa might start up.

"I'm happy to show you the ropes," Ashlynn said. "But we know how you are."

"What is that supposed to mean?"

"The first time someone offers you a grand for a picture of your boobs, you're going to send it," Salena told her.

"Someone offered you a thousand dollars for a picture of your tits?"

"All the time."

Elsa looked at Salena like she was crazy. "And you don't take it?"

Salena looked at Ashlynn, then back to Elsa. "That's not what we're doing."

"You're humping poles, I get it."

They weren't . . . well, yeah, maybe a little.

"We don't advertise that we're doing this. Not here. We have online aliases and keep it clean."

"And if I promise to keep it clean?"

Salena exchanged glances with Ashlynn a second time. Their look said one thing . . . never gonna happen.

Elsa waved her fingers in the air. "Show me."

Salena pulled up her page and ran the last video she posted for her subscribers.

"That's pretty close to naked."

She knew her outfits were getting smaller and had even questioned the last one she posted, thinking maybe she needed to pull back.

"It's more than a bikini."

Elsa rolled her eyes.

A second video with both Ashlynn and Salena together had Elsa blowing out a whistle. "You sure you guys don't play on the side?"

"A big part of the reason Salena's page grew so fast is this. I've been doing this for a while and have a following, she's getting there."

"I want in."

"I'm not linking my stuff with anyone selling skin pics or naked videos." Salena was insistent.

"Fine. But I'll need to film here."

"You can't tell anyone," Ashlynn said.

"I heard you the first time. When do you record the videos, and who does the editing?"

"It depends on our schedules, and we do our own editing."

"How?"

"It's not hard, just time-consuming," Salena told her.

"I need to see the videos before you post them," Ashlynn insisted. "Make sure nothing in the background points to this studio. The last thing anyone wants is a subscriber waiting at the door when we leave at night for a personal show."

"I get it."

"It's hard work," Salena said.

"You're not going to talk me out of it. I'm just as good as you are on that pole."

Yeah, Elsa knew what she was doing.

"I'll give you a list of things you'll want to set up before we start filming. We have our whole schedule for the next couple weeks. We'll help you get going mid-month."

"Fine." Elsa reached for her purse.

"I'll see you at work. And nothing about this."

"I'll keep your dirty little secret."

Elsa left the studio, and this time Ashlynn locked the door behind her.

"I don't like this," Ashlynn said once they were alone.

"I don't either, but what are we going to do? If you tell her you don't want her using the studio, will she advertise what we're doing?"

"That's why I don't like it. I'm not sure what she'll do."

Salena had gotten to know Elsa a little better since she started working at D'Angelo's. She knew how to wait tables and did okay. But as predicted, she spent more time flirting than running that extra mile to make people happy. "Maybe she'll land another guy and she won't want to work that hard."

"True. She wants instant success, and that doesn't happen on this platform without huge pushes."

They both walked away from the conversation hoping to put Elsa off long enough for her to find another, less labor intense, way to make money.

CHAPTER THIRTY

"Oh my God, you're going to ask her to marry you."

Ryan stared into his phone with a look of disbelief. "How did you jump to that?"

Emma's smile fell.

They were on a video call where he was doing what he could to get Emma and Gio to come to the jumbo Sunday dinner.

"You're not."

"Salena is moving in. But before she does, she wants me to meet her parents, have our parents meet. She's expecting some serious resistance when we announce that she's moving in. And since you and Gio were living together before you got married, Salena thinks that will soothe any tension. Especially with her dad."

Emma's dropped smile quickly returned.

"What did I say?" Ryan asked.

"Living together *before* you got married."

"Em!"

"Fine, whatever. Yes, we'll be there. This is next Sunday, not this one, right?"

"Yeah. The great and powerful Mr. Rutledge can't ever do anything last minute. He agreed to next week."

She started to laugh. "You know what's funny?"

"What?"

"If dinner runs long, Mom and Dad might have to stay with you instead of drive home."

Ryan lost his grin. "Thanks for the nightmares."

"You read my diary when I was in sixth grade."

"That's a long time for you to pay me back."

"Ha ha." Emma giggled. "For the record, I like Salena. You guys really work together."

"We do."

"Nobody thought it would last." He and Emma had always kept things real, and hearing this was no exception.

"I know."

"I'm glad it is."

"I am too, Em. She makes me happy."

"We'll see you in just over a week."

~

Salena met with Chloe for their every-three-week date the Tuesday before the meeting of the families.

The temperature in San Diego had dropped enough to put the flip-flops away, but that never stopped the two of them from getting pedicures.

"I can't believe you're moving in with him."

Salena pointed a finger at her bestie. "No one knows that yet. Don't go blabbing."

"Most of us already guessed."

"My dad is going to freak."

Chloe shook her head. "No. He's going to quietly say a few things and keep his cool since there will be too many people liking the idea. Then maybe by the time you talk to him alone, he will have gotten used to it."

Salena laid her head back and closed her eyes. The woman doing the pedicure was massaging her tired feet, and it felt wonderful. "That's what I'm hoping. Not that his opinion really matters. I'm doing it anyway. We'll have this dinner. I'll make sure Ryan knows all my shit before the move, and yeah."

"Shit? What shit? He doesn't care about your past."

"Not that." She opened her eyes and remembered that Chloe knew nothing about OnlyMe. "There's something else I need to talk to him about."

"Do I know what this is?"

Salena shook her head. "You suck at keeping secrets. You know that, right?"

"Only when I drink."

"D'Angelo Sunday dinners require a minimum of four bottles of wine. And Dante pulled me aside and asked about Daniella . . . asked if she's getting a divorce."

"He's my husband. I don't keep things from him."

"Exactly. And I don't need him pulling Ryan aside to blurt out mine if I tell you." This was a circle Salena knew was coming if Chloe heard so much as a whisper about OnlyMe.

Chloe's shoulders fell back, there was no denying her epic fails in keeping secrets.

"This has something to do with the money, doesn't it?"

"What money?" Salena feigned ignorance.

"New car, new clothes. I looked up what that leather jacket you bought Ryan for Christmas ran. And if you try and say it's tip money, then what the hell was I doing wrong all those years working there?"

Salena squeezed her eyes shut. "You're right . . . there's something."

"I knew it!"

"But I can't tell you yet. Let me come clean with Ryan first."

"I'm your best friend."

"Who sucks at secrets. I love you, but no. Trust me, once I move out and Ryan is good, I won't be so worked up about how this will go down."

Chloe switched to Italian to ask her next question. "Are you doing something illegal?"

"No." Salena's voice rose. "But my parents most definitely won't approve. Mari would try and drag me to church each week, and Luca . . . I don't know what he'll do."

"And it's not illegal?" Still in Italian, and Chloe's face was a sea of confusion.

"No."

"You think Ryan is going to disapprove?"

Her heart sped in her chest at the thought of him having a huge issue with it. "I hope not."

"That didn't sound convincing."

"If I was a hundred percent convinced, he'd already know, wouldn't he?"

Chloe moaned. "Why do I have a bad feeling about this?"

"Because you're smart."

"Gio said honesty and keeping things real with Ryan was key."

Salena agreed . . . but how did Chloe know that? "I guess Gio and Ryan have talked."

Chloe nodded. "He told us about Helen. That had to suck."

"Helen?"

"The girl that died."

Salena blinked a few times. "A girl died?"

Chloe stopped, looked at Salena. "Oh, shit. Never mind."

Salena sat taller in her chair. "Oh, no. You don't blurt that out without an explanation."

"I didn't know it was a secret."

"Did Gio tell you it was?"

"No."

"Then it isn't. Keep talking."

Chloe looked around the nail salon and kept talking in Italian. "She was a girl he knew early in college. She got involved in drugs. He tried to help, but she didn't let him."

"Overdose?" Salena asked.

"Car accident."

"Oh. Was he serious about her?" Salena didn't like the thought of him keeping that from her. When she'd asked about a broken heart, he'd only brought up the high school girl. How serious could that have been? It was high school.

"Gio said no."

That made her feel a little better.

"I'm surprised he hasn't told you."

"I am, too." She replayed some of the conversations they'd had. "He does ask me if I need his help a lot."

"What? Like money help?"

"Yeah."

"I guess that would be expected . . . considering."

As much as she wished Ryan had told her about this Helen, Salena felt a little better about the secrets she was keeping from him. At least now, when she asked him about Helen, and he had to explain why he hadn't said anything to her, Salena could open up about OnlyMe.

She smiled, finally seeing a gateway to open up the conversation.

~

If things didn't slow down in the restaurant, Salena wasn't going to have time to shower and change before the family Sunday Funday began.

Of all days for the sky to open up and dump rain, it had to be this one.

No one wanted to sit on the patio.

The Grotto was set aside for the family dinner since the terrace was out of the question because of said rain and the inside of the restaurant was packed.

Elsa wasn't even slowing down to flirt, which proved the crazy state of the restaurant wasn't just Salena's nerves talking. To make matters even more charming, Brynn had turned up her bitchy card with Salena all day.

Salena stood in the doorway to the Grotto and once again did a chair count to make sure there were enough places set. *Luca and family is four but only really three. Chloe is two more. Gio is two. Rutledge two. Mari . . .*

Someone behind her bumped into her.

"I could use some help. There're more things to do than worry about dinner with the family."

Salena turned to find Brynn once again seeking her out. She'd just come from taking drinks to one of her tables, and when she walked away, everyone in her section was settled.

"What do you need, Brynn?"

"Table nine wanted more bread, and seven didn't like the wine."

Salena narrowed her eyes. "Do you have hot food coming out? A new table?"

"I have to get some side work done before the dinner rush. And since you're going to be in here all night, you might want to step up now." Without waiting for Salena's response, Brynn walked away.

Elsa stopped at Salena's side and stared at the exiting Brynn.

"Who peed in her Cheerios this morning?" Salena asked Elsa. "It's like she's asking to get fired."

"We were talking last week. I think she's looking for another job."

"She might want to hurry up. She won't keep this one for long with that attitude." If Mari had heard the woman, she'd already be gone. Firing her midshift on a busy Sunday would only mean Salena would have to step up. Today was not the day for that.

"She's a crafty one."

"What do you mean by that?" Salena asked.

"When I first got the job, she asked how we knew each other."

Salena sucked in a breath.

"Don't look at me like that. I said we went to the same gym."

That was a relief.

Elsa leaned in. "She told me yesterday that she saw both of our cars at Ashlynn's."

"She followed us?"

Elsa shook her head. "It's *you* she doesn't like. Made a shitty comment at the beginning of today's shift."

Fuck! "You don't think she knows anything about—"

"Not sure how she could. But she knows what *gym* you're going to."

Salena told herself to calm down. Pole dancing wasn't new.

"Do you have time to check her tables?" Salena asked Elsa.

"Yeah."

"Thanks."

Elsa went back to the dining room, and Salena sought out Brynn. She found her in the stockroom.

"There is time for this at the end of your shift," Salena pointed out.

Brynn rolled her eyes.

Salena looked behind her, made sure no one else was around. "And a little advice. If Mari or Luca hears you talk to me the way you just did, or roll your eyes the way you are now, they won't hesitate to let you go."

She full-on expected a snarky comeback . . . Instead, Brynn pasted on a sappy smile, turned on her heel, and walked out of the stockroom.

Salena knew a temporary employee when she saw one. First thing in the morning, instead of moving into Ryan's house, she'd be juggling the schedule to cover Brynn's shifts.

Chloe and Dante walked through the back door, shaking rain off their coats.

Salena glanced at her watch. "Shit."

"It's a mess out there," Chloe said when she saw her.

Without explanation, Salena took one look at her friend and darted up the residence stairwell.

She was going to be late for her own party.

~

Ryan stood under the balcony awning and out of the rain of his new home with his parents on each side of him.

"It's a good piece of real estate," his father said. "Decent neighborhood. Keep it for a few years, and you can turn around and sell it. Make some good money."

Ryan placed a hand on Robert's back. "That was almost a compliment, Dad. But I didn't buy it to turn around and sell it."

"I half expected a Harley to be sitting in the living room," Beth said.

"Maybe a few years ago. Besides, Salena wouldn't like that."

His mother looked through the corner of her eyes. "She's here a lot?"

Ryan turned and led his parents back inside and out of the cold. "She's moving in," he told them.

"Really?" Beth asked.

"Yeah. That's kinda what tonight is all about."

"There's no way you're seeking our approval," his father said.

"I haven't done that since I was a teenager, Dad. I'm not starting again now."

"Then why?"

"Salena is expecting some flak from her parents."

Beth sighed. "Ahh, she cares what her parents think. It's been so long."

Ryan shook his head and smiled. "I care what you think. I'm just not going to base my life decisions on your thoughts. Anyway, Aldo and Brigida are Italian, Catholic, and old-school. They didn't want Salena to move out of their home until she got married. Moving in with me before we get married is going to cause some tremors. I'm hoping that your easy acceptance of it at dinner tonight . . . when they find out . . . will help keep them calm while reality sets in."

"You're going to marry her?" His mother was smiling.

Ryan didn't say yes.

Didn't say no.

"It's wise to try the grapes before you buy the vineyard, son."

"She's not a grape, Dad."

Robert shrugged.

Beth squared her shoulders. "Well . . . I'll keep my hopes up and my mouth shut. I know she's loved by Giovanni's family, and they're a very good judge of character."

"As opposed to me."

His mother sighed. "They've known her longer, honey." Beth reached out and dusted something from the jacket he was wearing. "Clearly she's good for you."

"How did you deduce that?"

"We're standing in your home. You never once invited us to where you lived after you moved out."

"Dad called apartments 'hovels.'"

Robert shrugged. "I stand by that."

"Your arrogance is showing. Might want to drop it a notch."

His father narrowed his eyes. "That arrogance put a roof over your head."

Hair on Ryan's neck stood up.

Beth moved to stand between them. "Okay. We are not doing this tonight." She turned to her husband. "We're going to your son-in-law's family home tonight. Family that live in the building above the restaurant." She then turned to Ryan. "And you'll avoid saying anything that might provoke an argument with your father. You wouldn't want to make a bad impression on your future in-laws."

"No one has bought any rings yet, Mom."

Beth patted his shoulder. "We're going to be late."

CHAPTER THIRTY-ONE

Salena showered, redid her makeup, and threw on a dress. A sweater dress that went below her knees and fell into a pair of boots she'd been dying to wear since she bought them.

She turned to the side to catch her appearance in the full-length mirror and approved. Then she reached for some lipstick right as a knock sounded on her door. "Come in."

"Hey?"

It was Ryan.

"Back here."

"Chloe said to come and get you." Ryan walked around the corner and caught her looking at herself in the mirror. "Wow."

"Is it okay? Not too sexy, not too conservative?"

Ryan blew out a breath. "You can't wear anything without looking sexy to me, so I'm the wrong person to ask."

She shook her head. "You're not helping." Her nerves were jumping. She probably shouldn't have had that last shot of espresso.

"You're beautiful."

"It's crazy down there. I thought I'd have more time to—"

Ryan stepped up, placed his hands on her shoulders. "Deep breath."

She tried and failed. That deep-breath shit worked for Chloe, not her. "Are my parents here?"

"Dante said they were walking in, so I darted up here to get you."

"Your parents?"

"Gio is pouring them wine. It's all good, babe."

"Okay. Okay." Another look in the mirror, a little more lipstick. She turned and faced him. "I'm ready."

Ryan took her hand as soon as they were at the bottom of the stairs, and she led them through the restaurant.

"Sexy mama."

"Zip it, Elsa."

Elsa stepped in front of them, looked up. "You must be Ryan."

Unable to avoid the introduction, Salena stopped. "Ryan, Elsa . . . Elsa, Ryan. Now . . . don't you have something to do?" she hissed.

"No. Not really. You're a lot hotter than the picture I found of you on the internet."

"There's pictures of me on the internet?" Ryan asked.

"You have to be living under a rock to not have pictures somewhere."

Salena wasn't happy with how Elsa was eyeing him. She stepped forward, placed one finger on Elsa's shoulder, and pushed. "I think you have food in the window."

Elsa laughed. "Fine. Have fun."

They walked away. "Who is that?"

"We go to the same"—she lowered her voice to a whisper—"*studio*. She needed a job, we needed the help."

Ryan looked behind them. "I really do need to see this studio."

Salena nudged him. "Don't ruin my Valentine's gift for you by asking for it sooner."

Ryan made a humming noise in the back of his throat.

She really hoped that once he saw what she did, he'd accept the job that was really making her money.

They walked past the sign that said "Private Party" and into the Grotto, where all the familiar faces were standing around chatting.

Unlike their everyday Sunday dinners, everyone was dressed a little bit nicer, and the atmosphere was a bit more rigid.

Salena's gaze immediately went to Ryan's mother, who seemed to notice them the moment they walked in. Her smile put her at ease.

Ryan leaned down and whispered in her ear. "They already know you're moving in."

She squeezed his hand.

Chloe breezed by them. "Incoming."

Salena turned to see her parents walking toward them. "Mama." She kissed her cheek and moved to her father. "Papa." Another kiss.

She stood back, placed a hand on Ryan's shoulder. "I know you've kind of met. But this is Ryan. My *boyfriend*. Ryan . . . Aldo and Brigida Barone."

Ryan extended a hand. "Mr. Barone. A pleasure."

Salena watched as her father and Ryan shook hands for several long seconds.

"I saw you eyeing my daughter at the wedding."

Ryan cleared his throat. "Guilty, sir. But I see by your lovely wife you understand my infatuation."

Salena stood back and took that breath Ryan had talked about upstairs. The man definitely knew what to say. She'd never seen her mother blush the way she was now.

Ryan stepped toward Salena's mother and moved in for a hug. "I see where Salena gets her eyes."

"They *are* from my side of the family."

Ryan glanced at Salena briefly with a look that said, *See, everything is going to be okay.*

"Dinner without wine isn't dinner." Giovanni swooped in with two glasses already filled with something red and handed them over. "Your parents brought in some reserves."

"They did?" Ryan asked as he looked across the room to where his parents stood.

Salena glanced at him. "Is that a big deal?" She lifted the glass to her lips.

Giovanni laughed, leaned over so only she heard his words. "Last market check, it was six hundred dollars a bottle."

She stopped herself from sipping with a tiny cough. "Oh."

Gio handed her parents a glass as well.

Salena watched as Ryan took a drink.

Their eyes met.

"It's good," he said.

She took a sip. Rich, not too heavy, not too light . . . oak, berries, and that's all she got. Better than good. If someone complained about this wine at a table, she'd tell them to leave. "Really good," she admitted.

"I like it," her mother offered.

"It's not bad."

Gio laughed at Aldo's comment.

Ryan smiled. "Mr. Barone, you and I are going to get along very well."

Franny ran into the room, followed by Brooke. "Zio Gio." Her arms were wide.

Gio caught her, talked to her in Italian. "Stop growing. You're going to be taller than me."

Salena smiled.

"What did he say?" Ryan asked.

"He's complaining about her growing so fast."

"You don't speak Italian?" Salena's father asked Ryan.

Ryan sipped more wine. "I can learn."

Franny looked up at him. "I can teach you. Mama's learning, and Zia Emma is, too."

Ryan knelt to Franny's level. "Sign me up. I need to know when she's talking smack about me."

That had Franny laughing.

His parents took that moment to walk over to their side of the room.

Franny scurried off with a wave of Brooke's hand.

The ease in Salena's shoulders stiffened the closer Ryan's parents came.

Another sip of courage, and she put on a smile.

It was her turn.

Ryan took the challenge of meeting her parents like a champ. She could do this.

Gio looked between them. "You've all met, right?"

"Briefly," Aldo pointed out.

Gio leaned in, looked at Aldo, and said in Italian, "They're my in-laws. Be nice."

Salena tried not to laugh.

Ryan placed a hand on the small of her back as they stopped in front of them.

"Mom, Dad . . ." He turned to Salena. "You remember Salena."

"Hi."

"Christmas was only a month ago, hon." Beth broke any tension. "I love your dress. God, I remember being able to wear those things."

Salena looked down at herself and finally felt like she'd made the right choice in outfits. "You still can."

Beth sighed. "I wish."

Salena gave Beth a hug. "I'm glad you could come tonight."

Salena stood back, glanced at Robert, unsure if she should try and hug him . . . shake a hand . . .

He stood there, unmoving.

"Beth and, ah . . . Robert, these are my parents, Aldo and Brigida."

Ryan's father wasn't quite as animated. "Our children are dating," Robert said to her parents.

"So we've heard," Brigida said.

"He's a handful."

Beth smacked Robert's arm.

Aldo laughed. "She is, too."

Another smack, this one from Brigida to Aldo . . . and harder.

Gio simply stood there and laughed.

Salena stood taller, lifted her glass in the air. *"Salute."*

"Hey, Salena?"

She turned toward the entrance of the private room, saw Brynn standing there. "If you'll excuse me."

"Babe?" Ryan turned to her.

"I'll just be a second." Three strides, and she was standing beside Brynn. "What?"

"The people at table nine are complaining."

Salena didn't want to hear about what. "All server issues tonight are supposed to go to Sergio."

"He's busy. And according to the schedule, you're on."

What the actual hell! "Mari took me off. I'm not here. I'm invisible. Ask Sergio to deal with it."

The dirty look on Brynn's face had Salena's fingers balling into a fist.

"You suck at this, you know that?" Brynn looked at the wine in Salena's hand. "Enjoy your party."

Brynn walked away, and Salena rolled her shoulders back.

Chloe walked up behind her. "Is everything okay?"

"I don't know. A problem with a table."

Chloe set her glass down. "I'll deal with it."

Luca walked in with a massive plate of food in his hand and waved. "Gio!"

Gio moved to help with the food, and Salena surged forward to help.

"Can I do anything?" Ryan asked.

"Yeah, make sure your parents and mine aren't sitting next to each other."

Salena left the Grotto and did her level best to ignore the busy restaurant as she made her way to Mari's apartment to help retrieve the family's dinner.

She and Gio passed Mari on the stairs. "There're three more plates."

"Got it, Mama."

In Mari's apartments, Gio turned to Salena. "Is everything okay on the floor? I saw you talking to a waitress."

"Brynn." Salena rolled her eyes. "She's crossed the line one too many times."

Gio's expression said he'd been there. "Mama and Luca will support you in any decision."

"I know. It's timing." Salena grabbed the larger dish while Gio grabbed the remaining two. "We need more staff."

"It always works out."

Salena agreed.

Back in the Grotto, Gio announced the food with a boisterous call of "It's time to eat!"

Ryan stood in front of an empty chair, presumably hers . . . His parents sat across from them with Gio and Emma at their side, while Salena's mother and father were next to the empty chair.

"It smells lovely," Beth said before she sat.

"I'm just sorry we can't eat upstairs," Mari told them. "Next time."

"This room was designed for family dinners," Gio said. "My father . . . our father"—he looked between Luca and Chloe—"said that if you're going to own a restaurant, you need to have at least one table to fit everyone in your family."

"So, he carved this room out of the old storage space," Chloe said.

"You remember that?" Luca asked.

"Even I remember that, and I didn't live here," Salena said.

"He did that right after you were born," Luca said to Franny.

"I don't remember him."

"You wouldn't, *tesora*. You were a baby."

Mari lifted her glass. "Your father was a good man and is certainly watching us all now."

"*Salute.*"

The conversation about Mari's late husband stopped as they started to pass food around the table.

The noise from outside the room was a low roar, but there, and if Salena was honest, more distracting than she'd like it to be. She wasn't quite sure how any of the D'Angelos tuned it all out.

"How are your grandbabies, Brigida?" Mari started the conversation on one end of the table as Luca asked Gio about the winery. Emma said something to her parents, and Salena took another deep breath like Ryan had suggested earlier.

That's when she heard her name.

Again.

Brynn stood in the doorway.

Dammit!

She started to scoot her chair back.

Chloe reached across Dante and tapped Salena's hand. "I can—"

"Salena!"

Several eyes turned to the door.

Mari shifted in her seat. "Is there a problem?"

Brynn looked directly at Salena. "Nothing *she* can't handle."

"Salena isn't on tonight, Brynn. Speak with Sergio."

"I'll take care of it, Mama." Chloe scooted her chair away from the table.

"What the hell!" Brynn's tone and words had everyone at the table muffling their conversation.

"Brynn!" Mari's tone was a warning.

"Why do you protect her? Why do you put so much trust in her?" Brynn pointed in Salena's direction.

Salena pushed away from the table and stood.

Brynn stepped farther into the room.

"I do hope the rich guy she's snagged knows what he's getting."

Salena's feet hesitated.

Luca and Gio were on their feet in a breath. "You're out of line," Gio yelled.

"You're fired!" Luca's words had more punch.

Brynn rolled her eyes. "Like I care."

"It's time for you to leave." Mari pointed toward the door.

"Happy to. But before I go." She took a step closer to Salena. "You guys might want to know a little bit about your little golden child here."

Salena found her feet rooted in place.

"No one is listening to you."

"Did you all know Salena sells pictures of herself on the internet? Videos."

Oh, God.

This was not how this was supposed to come out.

"You need to leave." Only Salena's voice was weak.

Someone touched her arm, but she didn't look to see who.

"You'd like that, wouldn't you."

"Papa?" Franny called to her father.

"She has an OnlyMe page." Brynn was smiling, like a cat with a mouse in its jaw, proud of its kill.

Nausea filled the back of Salena's throat.

Everyone in the room completely stopped talking all at once.

"Salena?" Chloe stood beside her, a question in her voice.

"What's OnlyMe?" Brigida asked.

"Babe?" Ryan's voice . . .

Salena couldn't find words, she simply stared at Brynn, who stood there smiling. "Not so shiny now, are you, Princess?"

"It isn't like she says." Salena's breath started to come in short pants that narrowed her field of vision.

"What is OnlyMe?" This time the question came from Mari.

"It's a porn site," Brynn shot out.

"It's not." Salena knew how pathetic she sounded. She couldn't breathe . . . and everyone was staring at her. Almost like the reoccurring naked dream of her running down a high school hallway. Only this was real, and life was crashing around her.

"You're into porn?"

Salena's eyes shot to Ryan's father, who'd asked the question.

Her head started to pound so hard it was difficult to hear what any individual person was saying. And at this point, many of them were talking at the same time.

"No."

"She strips for the highest bidder. I know, I'm one of her subscribers." Brynn wouldn't shut up.

Salena's jaw dropped.

"Oh, Salena, no," Brigida cried out.

"Babe?"

Her eyes found Ryan's, a mask of confusion sat there.

"It's not like that," she managed to choke out.

"You have an OnlyMe page?" he asked.

"Son. I know you want to marry her, but a *stripper?*"

Salena started shaking her head, her eyes moved around the table.

Franny was tugging on her father's arm. "What's porn?"

By now, several servers and customers outside the entrance of the Grotto had stopped doing what they were doing and stood by to watch.

"She's nothing but a slu—"

"Enough!" Gio's voice stopped everyone's conversation. He moved to the front of the room and pushed his chest against Brynn's arm. "Leave. Now."

Brynn backed out of the room, laughing. Gio flanked her and disappeared from sight.

Salena swallowed. "It isn't . . . it isn't." She couldn't do this. Not this way. Her parents wouldn't look at her. Ryan's mother was hiding behind a hand over her eyes. Ryan's father stared at his son.

And Ryan stared at her.

Her feet started to move.

Next thing she knew, she was blowing past everyone in the room.

Elsa stood at the doorway, tried to stop her.

The rain outside pelted as she ran down the street.

CHAPTER THIRTY-TWO

Ryan's body was several seconds behind his brain in processing everything he'd just heard.

"Who knew about this?" he asked.

"Papa, what's OnlyMe?"

"Yes, please. Can someone explain what this is?" Mari asked.

"Cara?" Luca looked at Brooke, who got the hint and took Franny by the hand as she left the room with the baby.

"Tell me she's selling pictures of her feet," Ryan pleaded. Because the thought of anyone else laying eyes on her naked body made him physically ill.

"Feet?" Mari asked rather loudly.

"OnlyMe is a website that people go on for . . . pictures of feet." Chloe didn't sound convinced.

He needed to talk to Salena.

Ryan stood.

"It isn't what you guys are all thinking." Elsa, the woman Ryan had been introduced to earlier, stood in the doorway. "It's not feet. But it's not porn."

"What is it?" Brigida asked.

"She . . ." Elsa looked around the room. "Takes videos of her . . . working out."

"What?" Mari asked.

"Working out? What, like, at the gym?" Dante asked.

Pole dancing.

The picture Ryan had received for Christmas of Salena leaning against the stripper pole shot to his head.

"Oh!" Chloe sounded relieved. "Of course. That makes sense."

"What makes sense?" Brigida asked.

Ryan ran past Elsa and started toward the stairs to Salena's apartment.

"She didn't go that way," Sergio yelled from the bar.

"Where?"

He pointed out the door.

Outside, the sidewalks were nearly empty of pedestrians as rain filled the streets with small rivers of water.

He ran up one block, then another, calling her name.

Ryan doubled back to the restaurant, then went past it for another two blocks.

The alley behind D'Angelo's proved she hadn't taken her car.

"Dammit."

Dripping, he walked back into the restaurant and found his parents preparing to leave.

Aldo and Brigida were already gone.

"That was very *interesting*, son."

Ryan jerked his hands to get the water off his arms. "Screw you, Dad."

Beth leaned forward, touched Ryan's cheek. "We're leaving. I'll call you tomorrow."

They walked away, leaving his sister, Gio, Chloe, and Dante standing around in a room filled with plates of food . . . and no one eating. Luca and Mari were nowhere in sight.

"Did you find her?" Gio asked.

He shook his head. "No. Did any of you know about this?"

Chloe spoke up. "She said she was doing something to make money but didn't say what. Said her parents wouldn't like it and was worried about how you'd take it. But I didn't know what it was. She didn't want to tell me because I can't keep a secret."

Dante huffed.

Gio nodded. "You suck at that."

"So . . . pole dancing?" Ryan asked.

"That's what Elsa whispered to me once everyone started leaving," Chloe revealed.

"How bad can that be?" Ryan asked.

"It's Salena," Gio said as if that explained everything. "You challenge her to something, she'll do it."

Dante laughed. "She's never been arrested, but I wouldn't put it past her."

Ryan found a grin on his face. "Almost."

"What?"

"On our first date. It's a long story . . ." He looked behind him. "Does anyone have a clue where she might go?" He shook off his clothes once again. "It's raining cats and dogs out there, and she ran out without a coat."

"Oh, damn." Gio grabbed his jacket, and they all headed out the door.

~

Salena realized the stupidity of her fleeing long before her feet stopped running.

The sweater dress felt like she wore a blanket that had just come from the washing machine without the courtesy of a spin cycle.

The boots, the ones she'd bought the week before, were molded to her legs. Their fuzzy leather was completely ruined, and the two-inch heels gave her blisters that were sure to last for weeks.

The bay came into view, she turned right and kept going.

She didn't have a purse, a phone . . . anything.

What she did have was one place where she could hide.

As blocks turned into miles, the faces of everyone staring at her kept her company.

Especially Ryan's. Hurt . . . confused.

So much for good impressions with his parents.

The rain fell in sheets, eased, and then pummeled once more, but she was no longer concerned about the puddles she stepped in.

Airport traffic buzzed on her right as she walked a path to Harbor Island.

Every muscle in her body constricted with the wet and cold, which helped move her faster.

The keycode to the dock helped give her access to Dante and Chloe's boat.

Knowing where they hid the key to get inside gave her the oasis she needed.

As soon as the glass door closed behind her and the noise from outside was shut out, the real self-loathing started.

She stripped her boots at the door and hoped to God Dante didn't have any charters booked for early the next day.

Thankfully, the boat was equipped with a heating system that didn't require turning on a generator. Salena moved throughout the vessel, turning up the heat and pulling off her clothes.

The shower in the stateroom was the smallest Salena had ever been in, but she used it anyway.

The water never got hotter than lukewarm and did nothing to ward off the chill that had set deep in her bones.

Both of her feet were bloody with blisters, proving what she already knew about the boots when she bought them.

They were meant for show, not for hiking.

Now they were good for the garbage.

She wrapped her body in a towel and searched the cabin for something . . . anything to wear.

A small stack of T-shirts with Dante's company logo sat in one of the drawers of the closet. So did a pair of shorts, ones that fit Chloe, and a pullover sweatshirt touting San Diego.

At least in the morning, she would have clothes to wear on the long walk back. She'd look homeless, but dressed.

Or she could wait for Dante to show up for work.

Slightly less embarrassing, but probably better.

At least she wouldn't be naked.

Or wearing a soaked sweater dress.

Wearing one of the T-shirts and panties she'd dried with a bath towel the best she could, Salena crawled into bed and pulled the blankets up to her neck.

She couldn't stop shivering.

Running off felt stupid now, but facing everyone wasn't something she'd had the courage to do at the time.

She was exhausted.

Cold.

And profoundly sad.

If she ever saw Brynn again, Salena was bound to find the inside of that cop car once more. This time with an all-expenses-paid trip to the police station, along with free pictures and a special bed to sleep in.

At least the clothes would cover more of her body.

CHAPTER THIRTY-THREE

Emma stayed at Salena's apartment in case she returned.

Ryan and Gio drove around in Ryan's car, looking in one direction, while Chloe and Dante went in another.

The first place Ryan drove was back to his place. Not that Salena could have gotten there on foot as quickly as they'd driven, but maybe she'd found someone to give her a ride.

Her cell phone was found lying on her bed, her purse, which she nearly never took with her, on her kitchen counter.

The fact that she didn't have any ID or anything on her had all of them on edge.

Chloe called Ryan from the studio where Salena worked out.

He put her on speakerphone.

"She's not here."

He and Gio stood in Ryan's living room. "She's not here either."

"We're going to go by our place in case she went there."

Ryan ran a hand through his hair. "Who else does she hang out with?"

"Lately? You. And you know she wouldn't have gone to her parents'."

He didn't like this.

"I can't even leave her a note to call me if she shows up here and we're out looking for her. I don't have a landline."

Gio pointed toward the front door. "You have a video doorbell. Tell her to trip the sensor and leave you a message."

"Damn. Yeah." Ryan found paper and a pen in his newly acquired junk drawer.

If you're seeing this, we're all out searching the city for you. Ring the doorbell and let us know you're okay.

"Okay, we're headed back out."

"She might have gone to a club. One of the places she's worked in before," Chloe suggested.

"No money and soaked?"

"People know her, so maybe." Chloe didn't sound convinced.

Ryan looked at Gio. "What else do we have to go on?"

Gio walked toward the door leading to the garage. "I know a couple of places."

"I'll start calling around in the neighborhood," Chloe said over the phone.

Ryan disconnected the call and followed Gio.

They hit three clubs, none of which were terribly busy and therefore easy to comb through looking for Salena.

Ryan stood back while Gio spoke with staff and patrons alike that he knew.

Salena wasn't there, and no one had seen her. Dressed as she was, she wouldn't have been missed.

Chloe informed them that she wasn't at her and Dante's house and they were headed back to Little Italy to sift through places there.

It was rounding on three hours since Salena ran off.

The rain sputtered off and on, and the wind picked up.

The four of them arrived back at D'Angelo's and congregated in Salena's apartment. Mari and Brooke joined them, Luca was down in the kitchen, warming up food to bring up. Not that Ryan was interested in eating, but that didn't mean the rest of them weren't hungry after going all evening without food.

"Do we call the police to look for her?" Mari asked.

"She's not a missing person, Mama, she's hiding," Chloe said.

"She's going to be sick if she's outside in this weather."

Ryan's thoughts exactly.

"Salena's smart and resourceful. She isn't hiding under a bridge." Gio leaned against the kitchen sink, his hands wrapped around a cup of coffee.

Footsteps announced Luca's arrival.

Dante and Gio swooped in, both saying something to Luca in Italian.

"What the hell was up with that employee . . . Brynn?" Chloe asked.

"She came on right before Salena. Sergio told me tonight that she's been angry since Salena was hired because Brynn thought she was being considered for a manager." Luca stood back, crossed his arms over his chest.

"That child? No. Never," Mari spat.

"She sure burned her bridge in an epic way," Brooke suggested.

Gio shoveled food into his mouth. "And my niece? Did she get an education on OnlyMe tonight?"

Luca groaned. "I'm not happy about that."

"She's fine," Brooke told him. "She understands the internet. You can't keep kids off it."

"That doesn't mean I want her exposed to the seedy side of it."

Ryan cleared his throat. "Then it makes sense that Salena kept it a secret. Your opinion of her matters."

"Salena doesn't put weight on others' opinions," Luca countered.

"Not true," Ryan defended her. "Not by a long shot. Salena is always considering what she says and does around here. Valuing her position at the restaurant and the consideration of the employees. She didn't want you or Mari thinking less of her when we started dating. Hell, I've made out more in my car as an adult than I ever did as a teenager."

Brooke narrowed her gaze on her husband. "Did you tell her she couldn't have Ryan over?"

"No."

Brooke perched her hands on her hips.

"Maybe in the beginning," Luca relented. "But it wasn't Ryan. It was a blanket request."

She turned and looked at Ryan. "He used the same line on me when I moved in here."

"I have children."

"Give it up, Luca," Chloe scolded. "You're turning into Papa."

"I am a papa. You'll see." Luca turned, pointed at Dante. "Get her pregnant and she'll see."

Mari patted Ryan on the back. "Eat."

He wasn't hungry.

"Where would you go if you didn't want to be found but needed to lick your wounds and collect your thoughts?"

"I'd lock myself in my bedroom," Chloe said.

"Or run off to Bali."

Chloe pointed a fork at her husband. "True. But Salena didn't jump on an airplane. And she's not sleeping in her car."

Dante took a bite, the room grew silent.

Chloe all but dropped her plate on the table in front of her. "Shit."

"What? You thought of something?" Ryan asked.

"The boat. It's always there, it's empty. She knows the code to get on the dock and where we hide the key."

Hope blossomed in Ryan's chest.

He was already reaching for his coat.

"I'll drive."

All the way to the harbor, Ryan glanced at the route Salena would have had to walk in the rain.

Dante sat in the passenger seat, Chloe in the back.

"She has to be there," Chloe kept saying.

Ryan slammed his car into park in a reserved space, and they all ran toward the gate. Once there, they slowed their pace to avoid becoming one with the water on the slippery dock.

"There's a light on," Dante pointed out before they reached the boat.

They jumped on board.

Dante pulled at the door and found it unlocked.

Salena's boots sat in a puddle of water.

Ryan nearly sunk to his knees with relief.

"Salena?" Chloe called out.

"She's probably in the bedroom," Dante suggested.

Ryan pushed around them. "Where is that?"

Dante pointed.

Ryan turned to them, held up a hand. "Let me go talk to her."

Chloe waved her phone in the air. "We'll be out here. I'll call the others."

As quietly as he could, Ryan eased the door opened and looked inside.

Salena lay on the bed, curled in a tight little ball under the covers . . . sound asleep.

He closed the door behind him and stood there watching her breathe.

He couldn't help but envision what she must have looked like as a little girl, sweet and vulnerable. Something she tried hard not to be as an adult.

Ryan shrugged out of his coat and toed off his shoes before easing his weight onto the bed.

Before he could settle beside her, he felt her body damn near convulse with a shiver.

He snuggled up behind her and wrapped his arm around her. She was freezing, even under the covers and with the temperature somewhat warm in the room.

"Oh, baby."

He heard her breathing change and then slowly catch.

Ryan kissed the back of her damp head.

He felt her frigid hand grasp his.

He squeezed her closer.

"You had us worried."

"I know," she whispered. "I'm sorry for that. I needed to get out of there." She shivered.

"Jesus, Trouble, you're freezing."

"I can't get warm."

"Let's get you out of here and go home."

She twisted in the bed and looked at him. "I don't have any clothes." She pulled the sheet back and showed him the T-shirt she had on.

"Okay, hold on."

Ryan rolled out of the bed and left the room.

Chloe and Dante were sitting in the main cabin of the boat, quietly talking.

"She needs something dry to wear," he told them. "And can we bump the heat up, she's freezing."

Dante jumped up. "On it."

"Is she okay?"

Ryan shrugged, not really knowing.

Chloe stood. "We'll swing by our place. Grab something."

Ryan tossed his car keys at Dante before going back to Salena.

By now, she was inched up in the bed, her knees pulled to her chest under the covers.

He smiled at her.

"It's not porn," she said straight off.

"I know."

"I don't send naked pictures."

"We don't have to go into this right now."

"And I'm not a stripper. God, your parents must hate me."

Ryan moved to sit on the edge of the bed beside her. "Hate takes time. They might be a little concerned about what's entering their family, but they don't hate you."

"I was going to tell you—"

Now that he knew she was safe, and it was clear she wanted to get everything in the open, Ryan said what he'd been thinking all along. "It's pole dancing, right? That's what everyone was saying."

"Everyone?"

"Your friend Elsa told Chloe, who explained things to us. You're making pole-dancing videos and selling them on OnlyMe, right?"

She slowly nodded.

"Men ask you to take your clothes off?" He swallowed that thought with a shooting pain in his head.

"All the time, but I don't do it. Ashlynn and I have a motto. *Keep it classy, keep it clean.* We thank the subscriber for their message and tell them we're not filling naked requests at this time."

Ryan's eyes shot to hers.

She shook her head. "We want them to subscribe to our channels for as long as we can keep them. There's money in giving them hope we will get naked. I never will."

He rubbed his face, couldn't get the image of some old dude pulling his chain while watching Salena dance.

"For the first time in my life, I found something that I could do to make money that I have complete control of. I create content that people want to watch and get paid for it."

"You've been doing this the whole time you've known me?"

"I started right after we met. I needed a car, Ryan. It was going to take forever with the money I was making at the restaurant. Ashlynn pulled me aside and told me about what she was doing. When you and I first started dating, I didn't feel the need to tell you. Then when I did, it was complicated."

"Why?"

"I didn't know how you were going to take it."

"Do I come off as someone who was going to lose his shit if you told me?" he asked. "My girlfriend pole dances. That's fucking hot. Am I pissed to know that there are other men out there that have watched you . . . yeah. But why lie to me?"

Her eyes welled with unshed tears. "I don't want to lose you."

Ryan placed a hand over her and rested it on her hip. "You're not going to lose me."

"When we first started dating, it wasn't something you needed to know."

"We're more than 'just dating' now."

"I know."

"You're moving in this week."

Her smile was weak. "Chloe told me about Helen."

Hearing HP's name made him pause. "What about her?"

"You didn't tell me about her."

Ryan leaned back.

Salena held his hand and kept him from moving far. "Why?"

He wasn't sure how to answer that. "A dead ex isn't a soft subject."

"Neither is OnlyMe."

"She died a long time ago."

"Yeah, but she's the reason you always ask if I need your help." Salena pushed in a little closer. "I just found out about her. I was a little hurt that you didn't say anything. Then called myself a hypocrite, considering what I was keeping to myself. I don't need you to save me."

"That's not what I'm doing."

She didn't look convinced. "I need the financial autonomy pole dancing gives me. Ashlynn and I have goals with the money we're making. Do you know how good that feels?"

"To make your own money? Yeah. But coming from someone who didn't always have it . . . no." Ryan swallowed, fought hard against the desire to tell her she didn't need to dance for a camera to make money. "There are a lot of creeps out there."

"I know. We have safeguards in place."

The caveman inside of him, the one created by Helen, wanted to tell her to stop.

She placed a hand over his arm. "I'll show you everything, Ryan. All the photos, videos . . . messages. The picture I gave you for Christmas is the most provocative outfit I've worn, and that one was for you. Sometimes I'm wearing a little more than a bikini, but most of the time, it's more. It's sexy stuff. I'm not going to pretend it isn't."

"And hot?"

"Yes. But you knew that about me when we started dating. I am that girl. I've always owned my sexuality. Once I started this, I felt the need to hide it. Living at the D'Angelos'. Franny asks a ton of questions. I didn't want employees at the restaurant to know. Mari or Luca. I'm sure my parents are imagining the worst right now."

"Yeah, they were."

Salena sighed. "Most of the people that know me wouldn't put it past me to be a stripper."

"Chloe said as much earlier."

"I could have easily gone that route, but I didn't. I could double my subscriptions if I did."

Ryan squeezed her hip. "Please, baby, don't."

"I don't need to get naked to make money."

He leaned forward, rested his forehead on her knees. "Okay," he whispered more to himself than her.

Her hand sat on the back of his head. "I'm sorry I kept this from you. It won't happen again."

He tilted his head to the side, looked her in the eye. "You don't overshare."

"No. But this was a big undershare. Not fair to you."

Ryan placed a hand on the side of her face. "I should have told you about Helen."

"Did you love her?" Salena asked quietly.

"No. I felt guilty for not saving her."

"You don't need to save me. I'm not slipping." She leaned into his palm.

"Promise me you'll tell me if you are." This, he needed to hear.

"That's an easy promise to make."

He watched his thumb as he traced the side of her face.

"I expected this to be harder," she told him.

"What?"

"This. You and I. Someone accepting my choices and still sticking around."

"That's what love is about, isn't it? Sticking around during the hard parts."

"What *what* is about?"

"Salena . . . I love you," he whispered.

For a moment, she simply stared, then stuttered, "W-what?"

"I'm not leaving, because I love you. I need you to make me promises because it would gut me if something happened to you."

"Ryan," she whispered his name.

"Someone told me once that when you find the right girl, you just know. I've felt this way the whole time." And damn, it felt good to say it out loud. "We fit, you and I. That's why things aren't hard. Things are tough when you're trying to push a round peg in a square hole. You challenge me, you accept me . . . you love me, too."

Her eyes narrowed.

"If you didn't, it wouldn't matter to you what I thought about OnlyMe. It wouldn't mean jack shit what my parents thought about you, or your parents thought about me. But it does matter. You love me."

She pointed to her chest. "I would know if I loved somebody."

"Are you telling me you don't?"

She pulled back. "No."

Ryan grinned. "Then you do."

"If I'm going to tell someone that I love them. I get to do it. They . . . *you* don't say it for me."

He couldn't stop smiling. "Okay."

"What, okay?"

"I'm waiting."

"For?"

"For you to say it."

She pulled in a breath, held it . . .

Bit her lip to hold back a smile.

He moved closer, his face inches from hers. "I love you, Salena Barone. And someday really soon, I'm going to ask you to marry me. And you're going to say yes."

She didn't blink.

She didn't breathe.

"It's going to be a little scary and a lot amazing. And one day, we're going to have to explain to our kids why we have a stripper pole in our bedroom, but that's okay."

She started to smile. "In our bedroom?"

"We can always tell them we renovated an old firehouse."

"You're really cocky, Rutledge."

"Confident, Trouble. We're meant for each other, and you know it."

He touched his lips to hers briefly.

She kept staring.

"I'm going to say yes?" she asked.

He kissed her again. "Ah-huh."

"When did you conclude this?"

Their noses practically touched. "Remember when I suggested a date and you suggested friends with benefits?"

A tiny smile lifted on her lips. "Depending on the benefit package."

"Right about then."

"We'd just met."

"When you know, you know." He touched his lips to hers again. "And I knew."

"You couldn't possibly—"

"Babe?"

"Yeah?"

"Stop talking." He used the weight of his kiss to push her down into the mattress and seal all of his confessions with his touch.

Her arms circled his body as she stretched out to give him room.

"Ryan?"

"Shhh." He kissed her jaw and moved to her neck.

"I do love you."

He closed his eyes with the sound of those words and continued his journey. "I know."

The purr of approval he'd grown to crave rattled in her chest as she surrendered.

"Hey, guys?" Chloe's voice rang from outside the door.

"We're busy," Salena yelled at her friend.

Ryan stopped, rested his head on her chest, and silently laughed.

"Great. There're clothes out here."

"Thanks," Salena said.

A few seconds of silence, Ryan kissed Salena's collarbone.

"Dante has a charter at ten in the morning if it stops raining."

Salena slammed a hand on the bed in pure frustration. "Go away!"

"I'm leaving Ryan's keys on the clothes."

"Chloe! I swear to God!"

Chloe's laugh traveled until they didn't hear anything but the rain falling outside.

Salena snuggled back into the bed. "Where were we?"

Ryan caught her smiling eyes. "You were confessing your undying love."

CHAPTER THIRTY-FOUR

Holding Ryan's hand, Salena walked into the D'Angelos' restaurant hours before it opened.

Pulling her shoulders back, she led Ryan up the back stairs to Mari's apartment.

"You ready for this?" Ryan asked.

They'd left the boat sometime around two in the morning and made their way home. To her new home. With very little sleep, she and Ryan showered and dressed and started Salena's walk of shame into the place where she lived and worked.

Salena nodded and rapped her knuckles on Mari's door.

The matriarch of the D'Angelo family yelled in Italian for them to come in.

Salena led the way.

The moment Mari saw her, she offered a relieved smiled. "Thank goodness they found you." She crossed and pulled Salena into her arms. "You had us worried."

"I'm sorry."

"As you should be."

The older woman put the back of her hand to Salena's forehead and then touched her cheek. "No fever."

"I'm fine."

The sound of footsteps from the stairway brought Luca through the door. "I thought I heard voices."

Salena's heart thumped faster, seeing him standing there.

His greeting wasn't nearly as welcoming.

Luca shook Ryan's hand and turned to stare at her. "I'm glad you're well."

Salena attempted a smile. "I'm so sorry."

Mari clicked her tongue. "That Brynn should have been fired a long time ago. One rotten tomato ruins the whole box."

"Elsa, though . . . she picked up the slack once Brynn left last night. We like her," Luca said.

Salena waved a hand in the air. "Not about her. About what happened."

Mari nodded a couple of times. "All that food preparation, and no one ate. Yes. Don't let it happen again."

Why weren't they understanding what she was sorry for? "No. Not the food. I am sorry about that, but my secret. How embarrassing it must have been for you—"

Mari pointed to her chest. "For me? I'm not the one that ran out in the rain. That was you."

Salena turned to Luca. "And Franny. I'm sorry she heard all that."

Luca moved to stand beside his mother. "Yes. I am sorry for that, too. I'm not ready for her to grow up."

"I'm sorry, Luca."

He looked directly at her. "Apology accepted."

"I should have told you both."

Mari shrugged. "Not really my business. I do think you should join me at church this Sunday."

Ryan chuckled, placed his hand on Salena's back.

"It's really not that bad," Salena said.

"It's not that clean either. We watched it all last night. I subscribed to your channel. You owe me twenty dollars," Mari said, pointing her finger in Salena's direction. "If I see anything God meant for you to share only with your husband, I'll fire you."

"Don't worry, Mrs. D'Angelo. I'll spank her first," Ryan said.

"She'll like that," Luca added.

Mari smacked her son's arm. But a smile lingered on her lips.

"Okay . . . good. Now, take today off. Get some rest. I expect you back to work tomorrow."

Salena moved into Mari's arms and accepted her warm hug with a tear in her eye.

Luca was next, where Salena offered another apology.

He patted her back and whispered in Italian, "Ryan's a good man. You should keep him."

"That's my plan," she responded.

Twenty minutes later, they stood in her parents' living room, repeating her apology.

They weren't nearly as gracious.

"Why can't you run for exercise like everyone else? Why dance like a—"

Salena cut her father off. "It's not me, Papa. When have I ever done what others do because it's expected?"

"Not once in your whole life."

She sighed. "I should have told you. Not let you find out the way you did."

Her father pointed at her mother. "You embarrassed your mother."

Brigida kept her eyes cast to the floor.

"I'm sorry, Mama."

"Your parents must be appalled," Brigida said to Ryan.

"We spoke to my mother this morning, Mrs. Barone. She wanted to know if she was too old to take pole-dancing lessons. Which grosses me out, but Salena said there are plenty of older women that take them."

"They're not disgusted?" Aldo asked.

Ryan shrugged. "No. They felt bad for how things went last night but understood why Salena felt she needed to keep this to herself. And based on both of your reactions, I understand more clearly why Salena kept it from all of us." *They* referred mainly to Beth. Robert was simply relieved Salena wasn't a stripper. His advice to Ryan was to buy out the OnlyMe platform and cut her channel, and Salena couldn't help but wonder if that was possible. "You don't have to approve of your daughter's choices, but you might want to reevaluate how vehemently you hate them. That level of disapproval will keep us both from sharing our life with you to its fullest."

"*Our* life?" Aldo asked.

Salena looked up at Ryan, who smiled.

"I love your daughter, Mr. Barone."

Hearing Ryan say that was never going to get old, she mused.

He turned to look back at her dad. "I'd ask for your blessing to marry her, but since it doesn't matter if you give it or not, I won't."

Her mother's sharp inhale had Salena watching Brigida's reaction.

Aldo's mouth fell open.

"Your daughter is a beautiful, loving, resourceful woman who has spent most of her life searching for your approval. She has respected your lifestyle even if it wasn't her own. Now it's time for you to respect hers. Our children will be brought up with love and acceptance of who and what they are. They won't experience hate from their own family. From my parents or the two of you."

Salena's heart warmed at Ryan's conviction.

"Children? You're not—"

"No, Papa. I'm not pregnant. I told you that wouldn't happen to me. I kept that promise."

Her mother blew out a held breath.

"Last night, we were going to tell you that I'm moving in with Ryan. We know you won't approve, but we're doing it anyway."

Aldo looked between the two of them, then to Salena's mother.

Silence stretched around them like a fog. Then Aldo's shoulders slumped slightly. "Maybe you can talk her out of this dancing thing."

Salena found a smile.

"I wouldn't count on it, Mr. Barone."

Her mother moved forward. "We love you, Salena. We'll try harder to understand your choices."

"We will?" Aldo asked.

"Shush!" Brigida chided. "Now . . . have you two eaten?"

EPILOGUE

The lights in the studio were dimmed, a fog machine and mood lighting filled the floor with a pink glow.

Ryan had been given a time to arrive. Told to walk into the main studio and close the door.

Ashlynn was meeting him at the door and would lock it behind her as she left.

The moment Salena knew he was in the single chair she'd put out for him, she cut the lights and turned on the music.

He'd seen the videos, the messages . . . everything. Once it was all in the open, she looked at her platform with a new lens. The athleticism it took for her to move the way she did wasn't something she wanted to hide. The conviction to own her own studio and teach others became her goal. OnlyMe would get her there. Ryan offered to help, but she cut him off. This was all her, and she wanted to keep it that way.

The employees at D'Angelo's were the best.

They gave her shit.

Mounds of it.

They'd walk by a pillar in the restaurant, lean against it, and ask if they were doing it right. Sergio brought a cake with a mini-pole stuck in the center with a Barbie doll hanging off it.

Someone piped in "Let's Get It On" in the break room.

No one meant harm and no one cared.

In fact, two of the waitresses had joined the studio, completely unaware that Ashlynn's place existed so close to their homes.

Only now it was Ryan's turn to see Salena's act live and in person.

His silhouette sat outside the lights shining on the single pole Salena wanted him to watch as she slowly made her way into the room.

The routine she'd worked on was one hundred percent for him.

High heels and valentine red lingerie would catch his eye first, but as she drew closer, she kept his gaze exactly where she wanted it to be by tracing her fingernails over her skin as if it were a map pointing to the treasure.

She circled and dipped and made sure to look directly at Ryan several times as she twisted and hung on the pole. The acrobatics alone should have impressed him, but she could tell by the way he squirmed in his seat, the sexier parts of her routine were what did it.

When it came time to end her dance, and the music started to fade, she dismounted from the pole and slowly made her way to Ryan's side.

She placed one hand on his shoulder and straddled his legs as if she were going to give him a lap dance. "Happy Valentine's Day."

He rubbed a hand over the well-manicured beard he was growing out on his chin. "Fuck."

"Was it worth the wait?" she asked.

He lifted his hips to hers, his excitement evident. "How soon can we get one of those in our house?"

"I don't think it goes with the décor." She laughed.

"We have an extra bedroom. We can add on. A home gym." He kissed her.

She kissed him back.

"I'm the luckiest man in the world."

"Take me home. You'll get luckier."

Ryan rounded his hand over her ass and squeezed before lifting her off him with a moan. "Get some clothes on, Trouble."

Twenty minutes later, they were walking into their house, the one Salena had moved into the day after everything blew up. And even though she still had boxes to unpack, she already felt like she was truly home.

"Go upstairs, I'll be there in a minute."

Salena looked at him over her shoulder. "You already gave me flowers."

A dozen roses, one stem at a time, in different places in the house. It was sweet and thoughtful. And Ryan.

He made a shooing motion with his hand. "Just go."

Halfway up the steps.

"Don't change clothes."

She wore the valentine red outfit under the trench coat and nothing else. The drive home had been very exciting. Especially when they passed a cop car and Salena smiled and waved.

She dropped her purse on the dresser and hung the coat in the closet before sitting on the edge of the bed in anticipation of Ryan joining her.

"Close your eyes," he called from outside the door.

"Already?"

"Are they closed?"

She squeezed them shut. "Yes."

"Put out your hands."

"Are we doing this again?" She put her hands out, palms up. "Do I get handcuffs this time?"

"No."

She heard his footfalls enter the room.

"You promised handcuffs."

"If you want me to chain you to the bed, we need a different bed."

With her eyes closed, she wiggled her eyebrows.

She heard Ryan laugh.

"Hold still."

She steadied herself.

"Man, I wish you could see yourself right now."

Sexy clothes, high heels, sitting on the edge of a bed with her hands out as if she were pleading for something. "I bet."

Something warm, and soft, and moving . . . was placed into her hands.

Her eyes shot open. "Oh, God."

"Meow."

A pure white ball of fur sat in her palms, looked up at her, and squeaked out the cutest noise she'd ever heard.

"A kitten?"

Ryan knelt down. "He's not a predator yet, but I'm told his mother likes to drag in anything she kills and drop it at her owner's feet."

Salena brought the tiny thing closer to look at. "You bought me a kitten."

"He's cute, right?"

"You wanted a dog."

Ryan huffed. "There's still room for a dog."

Salena kissed the fluff on the nose. She saw the collar and looked closer. "Does he have a name?"

She twisted the name tag around and sucked in a breath. Instead of a name, the words "Marry Me" were inscribed on the metal.

Salena turned the collar around and saw a ring dangling.

"Ryan?" Her heart caught in her throat. Her pulse kicked in her chest. Nothing had truly prepared her for this moment. The sheer emotion that swelled in her body at the way Ryan looked at her made it hard to breathe.

"Marry me, Salena."

She dropped her hands to her lap, and the kitten started to roam. "You said soon, but I didn't think—"

He nodded. "I know. But there's no reason to wait for me to prove to you I'm not going anywhere. I want this every day and always. Giving you me is the only way I know how to make that happen." He took her hands in his. "Salena Barone . . . will you marry me?"

The kitten pounced on the bed.

"I never thought I'd say yes to this question." Only looking at Ryan, there was no other answer to give. "Yes."

He squeezed her hands in his, whispered, "I love you," and leaned in.

His tender kiss brought tears to her eyes.

"Salena Rutledge," he whispered. "Wife. God, I love the sound of that."

"This is crazy," she whispered back.

"We're going to have the best life."

She rested her arms on his shoulders. "At least now I know who I can call to bail me out of jail."

Ryan kissed her again, then pulled back and reached for the kitten. "I hope you like this. If you don't, we can get something . . ."

The kitten jumped from Ryan's reach and perched himself as if in a stance that said, *Let's play.*

"Get over here."

Only the kitten had other ideas. Tail wagging, it scurried away and snagged the blanket with its claws before dropping to the floor.

Salena scrambled to see if the kitten was okay, but he was already chasing something out of reach under the bed.

"Get over here, you little pain in the ass. I have a girl waiting for a ring." Ryan dropped to all fours and tried to shove his frame under the bed.

Salena sat back and started to laugh.

"You. Little. Shit."

The kitten backed out and ran to the other side.

On his stomach, Ryan reached for him.

A tiny meow, and the ball of fur sat at Salena's feet, looking up.

She reached down and picked it up.

Ryan hunkered back on his knees, hands at his side.

"Not sure what your problem is. He comes right to me," Salena said.

"I see how this is going to be." Ryan pushed to his feet, took the kitten from her hands, and undid the clever packaging for her ring.

Once the ring was in his grasp, he set the kitten down on the bed and reached for Salena's left hand. "Chloe told me you weren't traditional and that you liked colored stones. This is a canary diamond."

An oval canary diamond, wrapped in white gold. And larger than anything Salena ever thought she'd wear.

Ryan slid it on her finger for a perfect fit.

"It's beautiful."

"Are you sure you like it? You're going to wear it for a really long time, so if you don't, my feelings won't be hurt."

Salena kissed him, his promise twinkling on her finger. "I love you, Ryan. It's perfect. You're perfect."

He kissed her back, hands sliding around her waist.

"Meow."

They both looked down, saw the cat clawing at the decorative pillow on the bed.

"I know where I'm taking you on our honeymoon."

Salena shook her head. The man didn't know the meaning of the phrase *taking things slow*. "Can we plan a wedding first?"

Ryan shrugged as if the wedding was already behind them. "Africa."

She sucked in a breath. "To find his big brothers?"

The kitten looked at them as it started to squat as if it was going to pee . . . right on their bed.

Ryan dove after him.

"I have the perfect name," Salena announced.

"Oh yeah?"

"Pita. *Pain in the ass.*"

ACKNOWLEDGMENTS

A warm thank-you to my editors, Maria Gomez and Holly Ingraham, and everyone at Montlake/Amazon Publishing that continues to let me push the envelope with my work.

Jane Dystel, my friend and agent . . . and staunch supporter of all that I do, thank you.

Many years ago, a friend gave me a pole-dancing lesson as a birthday present. Several friends and I showed up to the studio, not knowing what to expect. A little over a dozen women welcomed us and gave us an introduction to pole dancing. There were ladies of all ages and body types flirting with the pole and sucking in the empowerment that I only sense in a room full of women.

The sheer amount of strength it took to move on that pole was indescribable. I certainly didn't have it. If the studio had been closer to my home, I would have signed up to learn more. Instead, I left that day with a bruise the size of a baseball on my shin and a deep appreciation for those that choose this type of exercise.

Monetizing a hobby or a sport is not new, but somehow, pole dancing is associated with strip clubs and casinos. But it's so much more than that. Kudos to those who take the chance and turn their hobby into their profession.

Please keep pushing those boundaries and expanding the norm. And remember, well-behaved women seldom make it into the history books.

Catherine

ABOUT THE AUTHOR

Photo © 2022 Ellen Steinberg

New York Times, Wall Street Journal, and *USA Today* bestselling author Catherine Bybee has written thirty-eight books that have collectively sold more than ten million copies and have been translated into more than twenty languages. Raised in Washington State, Bybee moved to Southern California in the hope of becoming a movie star. After growing bored with waiting tables, she returned to school and became a registered nurse, spending most of her career in urban emergency rooms. She now writes full time and has penned the Not Quite series, the Weekday Brides series, the Most Likely To series, and the First Wives series.